Maria Goretti

and Me

Paul Corrigan

ISBN: 978-0-473-32392-9

A catalogue record for this book is available from the National Library of New Zealand Te Puna Mātauranga o Aotearoa.

Maria Goretti and Me is published by:

Paul Corrigan
45 William Street
Petone
Lower Hutt 5012
NEW ZEALAND

Maria Goretti and Me is fiction.

Art work: Victoria Jurczenko

Author photo: Yvonne Tunnicliffe – evephotographynz.com

Maria Goretti ...

The body of Saint Maria Goretti is kept in a glass case at an Italian cathedral.

Maria (1890-1902) lived in rural Italy.

Dying from at least 14 stab wounds she forgave her killer and would-be rapist.

The Roman Catholic Church canonised her in 1950.

Prologue – a week ago

She was at the lights across the street waiting among the after-lunch and shopper crowd for the traffic lights to turn red. For the 'green man' to tell us we could troop on to the pedestrian crossing without our getting killed.

The girl in her school uniform; dark-blue-light-blue check skirt to demurely below the knees; white blouse, dark blue tie neat at her throat – the school blazer in what I later learned was called Prussian blue; gold and silver badges on the lapel; the school's ornate Catholic crest in woven gold and silver on the left breast pocket. A hold-all, strap looped over her shoulder, rested against her right hip.

Despite the afternoon warmth she appeared to wear her uniform lightly. As if it was, well, what you do when required and in any circumstance, so no point in grumbling about it. I on the other hand sweated. It dribbled warmly from my armpits and my pores. Rivulets of it coursed down my back. My shirt was clammy and I was starting to itch.

She was alone and early that day, a Wednesday in mid-February 1975, usually the hottest month of the New Zealand summer. The same time as Wednesday the week before: 1.30pm.

She waited at the crossing patiently. She radiated an indefinable sense of being older than she was. At ease with patience, with poise. She squinted against the afternoon sun and took in everything and everyone around her: drivers and passengers in stopped cars and passing vehicles

1

on the busy intersection, one of the city's busiest. She was an observer, and it was subconsciously done and with an economy of movement. She did not draw attention to herself.

Then she noticed me. Her lips stretched fractionally. A brown eyebrow arched, and her light, greenstone-coloured eyes – something changed there. From where I stood amid waiting pedestrians on the crossing opposite, perhaps 20 metres from her, I thought I saw a glinting; an amused recognition.

The traffic slowed and stopped as the lights ascended from green to amber to red.

The buzzers and the 'green man' gave us permission to cross. What was I going to say to her? Did I want to speak to her? *Jesus!* What was I going to do?

She stared ahead, past me, as we approached each other on the road. Her stride was assured and swinging. Then a glance my way and a small smile as we were almost abreast of each other.

'We must stop meeting like this,' I blurted.

'Then what are you going to do about it?' she shot back.

Breath seized away, I stopped on the roadway. Then turned. She had reached the other side, and I could tell by her skip on to the kerb and the slightest wiggling of her head that she knew she'd scored a well-aimed riposte. A bull's-eye right into my heart. The thrill that tingles in you electrically through your toes to your fingertips. I was hooked. My heart beat faster. I was in love, and I didn't even know her name. *Oh, yes ...*

Dazed, I wandered the short distance home to my little flat halfway along a street lined with kowhai trees. I had to do something now. I'd tried to be clever rather than throw a chat-up line. She had deftly rapiered back a challenge.

Or was it?

I climbed the inside stairs up to my little flat, a one-bedroom box atop a block of similar concrete block boxes. The three-storey block of 12 was an architect's vision of 'modern': sharp, boxy angles, cubic blocks painted once-shimmering, but now fading, white. I let myself in and made a cup of coffee.

I talked to myself: 'I'm 23. An adult. I work. I have a good job. What on earth am I doing looking at a schoolgirl?'

What indeed?

HOW DID all this start? Nine months earlier, in a provincial New Zealand city where I'd lived and worked for six years, Felicity and I broke up after eight months. That and a flat drama gave me the excuse to look for a job elsewhere. Coincidentally a friend dropped in front of me an advert for a sub-editor on a metropolitan evening paper in the other island.

That sounded perfect to me: overseas enough just for the moment. I would go up a grade or two, save some more money, and get to work on one of the big papers for a year or two before heading off on my Big OE, the Kiwi 'overseas experience'.

My application was accepted sight unseen, as was often the case those days. So here I was, working from early morning to mid-afternoon, same as on my old paper. The pay was good – especially when I worked on the Saturday and late Saturday Sport editions – and so I could afford to live in my comfortable but sparsely furnished little concrete block cube with the ledge that passed as a small balcony. And no more dramas with flatmates.

Most days after work I'd thread through waves of teenagers on their way home from the many schools that dotted the city. Usually at this crossing were groups of girls from the Catholic college next to their cathedral – the one with odd twin spires at the front. By that I mean it had one, full, pointy spire and another that had been left half-finished, apparently for many years.

One day late last year, end of November or early December, I noticed her waiting at the lights among other young women from that school. She was the composed, observant one, subtly aloof from the group. A clutch of younger girls were being loud and 'notice-me, notice-me', perhaps because some boys from another city school were nearby and engaging in similar ritual plumage-spreading and raucous mating calls.

The girl easily turned to her companions and spoke briefly. I don't know what she said, but they waited until she turned to the front again.

3

They variously pouted and wiggled their heads, wrinkled their noses, pulled faces to her back and poked their tongues out. I couldn't help feeling she knew they were doing it. But they heeded whatever she'd said and quietened down.

At the signal everybody crossed from all sides, and in the roadway she and I were in each other's way. I went to my left. She stepped right. Still in front of each other we smiled awkwardly, and both of us stepped to my right.

'Woops,' I said quietly and retreated sideways to let her pass.

'Thanks,' she said pleasantly and smiled again.

One of the girls giggled, and another said something.

I pretty much forgot the encounter after that.

It might have been the next week I saw her again, at the same crossing, among a crowd of girls from her school. Fleeting smiles and eye-contact both ways, perhaps pretending we weren't engaging in this game.

That was the last I saw of her until two weeks ago. My work hours had changed after New Year, from 7am starts to 5.30am. Great for summer, but I wasn't sure how I'd like it in the winter. I went home earlier now, and it seemed that on Wednesdays she left school earlier, too.

Next day, Thursday, I got out of bed at 4.30am for work. I woke up thinking about her. The term 'cradle-snatcher' was not far from my mind, either.

I left work just after 1pm, and made my way home slowly. I loitered about the crossing. No sign of her. But I hit on an idea. In among the corner shops to the left was a small coffee bar tucked between a second-hand bookseller and a gourmet grocery shop. *Ah. Perfect. Ask her if she'd like to go for a cup of coffee.* That seemed harmless enough. The place was small, intimate, yet still public. What might happen after that I had no idea.

Friday was my day off. Tim, a friend and work colleague, was finishing up and heading off to London. So there were going to be 'drinks' at *The Mafeking*, the pub that was our unofficial branch office across the street. We all got off to a steady start about three in the afternoon.

About six Susan Devonshire, the education reporter, was encouraging me to go with her to a nice Chinese restaurant along the road and around the corner.

Until Wednesday afternoon I think I would have been interested. Sue and I were the same age, and we got on well. My mother would call her deeply brown eyes 'come-hither'.

And now they were trained on me.

I thanked Sue, and said another time. I was already fairly pissed. I said I had to be up at 4.30 tomorrow for a long day that didn't end until about 8pm. It was an excuse. At 23 you have stamina.

She gazed at me speculatively for what seemed a long time. It was as if she saw into my heart; saw not so much a lack of interest in her, but an interest elsewhere. A blink of disappointment, and, 'OK, Martin, I'm off tomorrow, so see you Monday.'

A bright, lipsticked smile, a swish of golden, shoulder-length hair, and she was gone with others.

I resolved over the weekend that I would 'accidentally' meet the girl at the intersection on Monday afternoon. It would be: 'Hi. I'm Martin. Just wondering if you'd like to join me for a cup of coffee?' How it would go after that I'd no idea. If she said yes, great. If she said no, then no harm done and life would carry on.

I've always felt I had to work harder than other guys with a girl. When I was at school there were boys who could look at girls who'd just fall for them, flattered beyond belief at the attention.

Adam Stenberg, who was in the sixth form with me, used to say: 'Treat them like shit. You tell them what to do. They don't tell you. You're the boss. They love it.' It seemed to work for him. Even with an 18 year-old friend of his sister's married to a really good guy of 19.

Trying being the 'boss' never worked for me. Felicity was a manipulative witch. She was my first 'serious' girlfriend after I'd left school. Felicity, I realised from this distance, could make me feel guilty. She could make me feel guilty because I hadn't been sensitive to her mood in the week leading up to her 'time of the month'. I was guilty for not 'picking up my signals' when she wanted to be, in her word, 'amorous'. I couldn't drive a car without her telling me that I was going too fast, or too slow, or that I should have paused longer at the 'Give Way' sign. She was the better driver – she thought. She didn't like my Mini. It was difficult to put into first gear. The steering needed fixing. It wasn't and it didn't. When I thought I should be the 'man' in the relationship she complained that I was being domineering and not thinking of her. 'I'm not your little woman who you think you can just order about. I'm not your little slave.'

It was the mid-70s, after all, and feminism was breaking out around the world. So I tried to be 'democratic' then – e.g., give her a choice of whether she wanted, say, to go to the movies or out to the pub. She would throw the ball back at me. I had to decide. I was usually wrong. If we went to a restaurant, for example, the bank-teller in her would loudly itemise the prices and complain about the cost. Or there was always something wrong with the food. Or the music. Something. Even the shirt I wore.

Sex, when we got around to it, became a time of a lot of bloody trial and damned-all ecstasy. The first time, she said, was painful and that I had hurt her by being clumsy and inconsiderate. Next time she complained that I hadn't 'put enough spunk', in the sense of oomph, into the performance, which had left her unsatisfied. And so on and so on and so on. Always kept off-balance. Never able to please. When you keep someone in that state of constant uncertainty they're easy to control because they don't know how to please, and usually we want to please.

Why did I put up with it? Because, I suppose, she was all I had and her behaviour was all I knew in going with a woman. I had grown up the only child of two elderly parents who seemed loving and comfortable with each other, though without being demonstrative.

No-one explained girls to me when I was growing up. My mother gave me the impression that the life of the human female was a trial, especially when they had 'developed'. They bled every month, although Mum didn't put it anywhere as bluntly as that. Mum wrapped it up in a kind of mystery that I decoded only as I got older. But women still carried on regardless, in the noble self-sacrifice that was Women's Lot, whether they were pregnant or had babies. That's what women did because that was expected of them.

Men Were Good For Nothing. Sex, Mum seemed to say, was a necessary duty that women endured to Keep Men Happy. They did not enjoy it. Women were noble and self-sacrificing.

Dad told me nothing about sex. Indeed, he seemed quite sexless. Yet according to Uncle Syd, his brother whom Mum disliked because he had run away with Auntie Kura – his then-girlfriend *and* she was a *Maori* – while he was still married to Auntie Margaret, Dad had been quite the ladies' man before marrying Mum weeks after the war started and he sailed away with the Army.

'I tell you what, Marty,' Uncle Syd confided to me not long after I left school, 'your father was into every bloody sheila he could jump on in Italy. And,' he smiled slyly, 'he knew how to make 'em happy.' Was he talking about the quiet, diffident Dad I knew, who'd worked as a book-keeping clerk for the electric power board since he was 16, apart from the war?

'Yep. The reason he got posted from a cushy billet in Cairo back to the frontline was because he was caught rooting a colonel's mistress.'

Dad? An unsophisticated Kiwi sergeant? And a colonel's girlfriend?

I came to see after that that Mum and Dad lived together, companionably but emotionally separately for nearly 30 years. I never heard them exchange an endearment. They were June and Ralph to one another. I don't think I saw them give each other a hug or kiss. Not even hold hands.

What did they talk about in the big, comfortable double bed they shared? I never heard them argue, either.

It was all a mystery to me. I tried to talk to them about Felicity. I wanted some kind of insight into the mind of a female. Mum changed the subject.

I asked Dad. He shifted in his armchair, glanced at Mum, and then muttered: 'It's better you get over her, Martin, and find someone else.'

Mum joined in airily, 'Yes, dear, it's like that old saying, "There's plenty of other fish left in the sea".' Then she had levered herself out of her armchair. 'I'll just go and make another pot of tea.'

False start

I finished work on Monday just after one o'clock, and decided to go straight back to my flat. Just before 3pm I'd head back to the intersection, which was two streets over from where I lived. I'd position myself so that it would look as if I was walking home from work, so we could 'accidentally' bump into each other. Simple. I'd pop the offer of a cup of coffee, and we'd go from there.

But as so often happens with plans, they don't always go according to plan.

I positioned myself, and when I saw flocks of girls coming down the street I began sauntering towards the intersection. I saw her, but she was approaching the intersection on the other side of the street – in other words, she'd be cater-corner to me.

I hadn't counted on that, and in the pit of my stomach I could feel the stirrings of 'the plan' unravelling.

She was among a group of girls.

The lights changed, and everyone trooped across. I went to cross to her, but it was clear any meeting wouldn't be 'accidental'. Not only that, but she steadfastly was keeping her face averted from me, sticking with the group as they strode over.

So. I reached the kerb, disappointed and flat. That was that, then. She knew I was there, and she probably knew I had been waiting for her.

One last time I turned and looked down the street towards the girls' retreating backs. She had detached herself from the group. She turned and looked back at me. Even from that distance and in that brief instance there was eye-contact, and her lips pursed. I ventured a half-hearted smile, and she turned away and resumed her path towards the city.

I told myself that Divine Intervention had Intervened Divinely. Meeting her Wasn't Meant To Be.

But sleepless night followed. I couldn't get the girl out of my head. My thoughts always came back to her. Who was she and why was I so keen on her even though I didn't know her?

Crossing over

Wednesday. Today, which went like a dream. I had a composure that I couldn't explain. I had the inescapable feeling that I would meet the girl today.

Just after 1pm the paper's final deadline came and went. I didn't need to make any late changes to my lead cable story. The North Vietnamese were closing on Saigon, the hapless capital of the South. Nothing new there. The war, and the two-year fake peace that had followed the signing of a peace deal in Paris in 1973, was ending. So the way was open for me to go home.

It was as if all paths had been cleared to enable me to go.

My heart thumped harder and my stomach knotted as I sauntered up the street. She was approaching the intersection, on this side of the street – and she was alone. *Can't back out now.*

Something was different. It took a moment to pick it: her hair. She'd freed her ginger-blonde hair from the tight bun at the back of her head so that it brushed back to just on the collar. She made a mature impression, which the uniform did nothing to alter. Again she looked cool and unflustered; my shirt clung to my skin, my pants legs were damp from sweat. I itched.

The lights changed, traffic stopped, and everyone flowed on to the roadway. She stayed on the kerb watching me approach, a small smile ghosting her lips. *It will be all right, Martin.*

I mounted the kerb. 'Hi,' I said shakily, trying to sound casual and convincing. 'I was just going to have a cup of coffee on my way home. Care to join me?'

She made me wait two seconds. 'Sure. Cool.' Her smile had grown, and her eyes – light green, but seemed to change greener – were more assessing, sharper.

I pointed across to the little coffee shop. 'I was going over there.'

She was perhaps half a head taller than me – 5ft-8in, or about 1.7 metres. Her eyes: they were steady eyes, wise eyes for someone so young.

The lights changed again and we crossed the intersection together, wordlessly. In a way, I was struck mute – the brain and mouth weren't meshing.

But I couldn't help feeling that she and I were aware of something important getting under way.

Coffee talk

The café was small, not well lit, and more than half-empty. Perfect.

The office lunch crowd had returned to their work. A group of mothers with babies and toddlers were clustered around tables pushed together near the front. At another table, and going by the severe expressions and their tense whispering, a man and woman in their 30s were engaged in A Serious Talk.

The serving area and cash register was at the end. I ordered coffees from the woman with a European accent and took a $1 note out of my wallet to pay for them. You could buy a cup of filtered brown liquid called coffee for 20-40c then. Baristas, lattes, long blacks, flat whites and other expensive caffeine concoctions were wonders still to come.

The girl proffered her own $1 note to the woman behind the counter: 'Thank you, but I'll pay for mine, thanks.'

I was taken aback, I have to say, and murmured: 'It's perfectly all right. I can do this.'

Her eyes were cool: 'I know you can, and I know it's expected that you pay, being the man and all that.' She laid her hand lightly on my arm: 'If I leave this shop liking you then I'll let you pay next time.'

'OK.' Well, that was different.

At a table I held out a chair for her.

Surprise darted across her face – it was as if no-one had extended the courtesy to her. She sat. 'Thank you.'

I took the chair opposite. She relaxed in hers, her hands neatly in her lap.

Everything about her was neat: her hair, even loosed from the constraints of the bun, was neat. Her tie was neatly fastened at her throat. The collar of her blouse was white and neat. Her blazer with its badges neatly spaced and aligned on the left lapel was neat. There were no loose or stray ends with this young lady. Everything was in its place. She was so unlike Felicity. I couldn't help thinking that. You see, Felicity always fussed. In public she worried about her hair. Or her make-up, which she would check with a small mirror from her purse. Or what she wore. Or even what I wore. Felicity did not sit calmly, waiting like this young woman opposite. Felicity was unsettled. Felicity was insecure.

This girl's gaze was expectant. Then I realised. Introduction time. 'I'm Martin,' I said extending a hand across the table.

She didn't take it. Instead: 'Does Martin have a surname?'

Er ... 'Blake.'

'Maria.' She took my hand briefly. Hers was cool and dry. Not quite like mine. 'Nice to meet you, Martin.'

'Does Maria have a surname?'

Her lips twitched; she liked the dig. 'FitzGarratt.'

The coffees arrived on a silver tray. I took the sugar dish and spooned some raw sugar into my coffee. Maria had milk.

Indicating the gold badge on her lapel, I said: 'What's that top one for?' I was trying not to babble.

'It means I'm the school head girl,' she said matter-of-factly.

I could feel my eyes widen, and I involuntarily almost sat up straight. 'Really? And the silver one below it?'

'I'm the deputy president of the Student Council.'

'If you'd been made president what colour badge would that have been?'

'Gold.'

She neatly took a sip of her coffee, and neatly replaced the cup in its saucer.

'So you must be seventh form? What used to be called the upper-sixth?'

'Yes, seventh form.' A significant pause, eyes holding mine. 'I'm 17. A month ago.'

Seventeen. Is that too great a gap in our ages?

'How did you get to be the head girl?'

She sighed and smiled. A shrug – neatly: 'I don't know. Maybe I'm wonderful. Perhaps because the position runs in the family.'

'Oh, how's that?'

'My mother, an aunt, seven of my sisters, and a sister-in-law have been head girl of this school. One sister wasn't chosen because her twin already was.' A pause: 'They still argue over it 20 years later.'

Her gaze across the table was a mixture of pride, resignation, and … and, I thought, of burden. 'And another sister apparently missed out because someone else could have the turn.' She lifted her cup: 'Apparently she still feels the slight.'

'Er, how many in your family?'

Maria sipped her coffee, then replaced the cup in its saucer. I think she was used to answering the question.

'Fourteen.'

Four-Teen? I did my best to control my surprise. 'How did your parents manage that?'

The same unwavering gaze, but amused: 'They probably managed it the same as every other couple who have sex when the woman is fertile. I'm told it's quite easy to do.'

I felt embarrassed. 'Sorry. I didn't mean to be rude. I've known big families, but never as many as 14 kids.'

The woman having the tense conversation pushed her chair back sharply. The mothers turned as one to look. Maria didn't. 'It's Good-*bye*, Ian,' she said, her voice breaking. She gathered her handbag and fled from the café, her sandals clacking quickly across the floor. The mothers made faces at each other; the man put his head in his hands.

The episode had interrupted the flow of conversation between us, and we were silent as we looked for something to say. I opted to stay with

14

badges – a smaller one just above her breast pocket. 'And what's that one for?'

She looked down. 'Oh, that one's because I'm on the Archbishop's Students' Council. He consults us on matters to do with secondary school students, university, teachers' college, and polytech students.'

'You're a rather important person to know then,' I said drily.

'You could say that,' she said, equally drily. 'He's a great friend of my parents and older brother and sisters.'

'What's it like having a bishop as a family friend?'

A neat shrug. 'I honestly don't know. Same as any other family and friends, I suppose. Two of my father's brothers are priests, overseas, so is my mother's, as are a couple of cousins, and my brother Luke is a priest, too.'

Maria sipped her coffee. 'That runs in the family, too, I suppose.'

She delicately dabbed her lips with a paper napkin, which she neatly refolded, and put it and her cup and saucer on to the tray. She leaned forward, crossed her arms, and rested them on the table, and trained her gaze at me. She could make you feel like a specimen under a microscope.

'But what about you, Martin? Where are you from and what do you do?'

I told her I was 23. I thought it best to get that one out of the way first. 'OK,' she said simply. I'd grown up the only child of an elderly couple in a town of about 3500 people. 'Mum's a housewife and Dad works at the electric power board.'

'What do you do now?'

'I work for the *Evening Herald*. I'm a sub-editor there.'

Something in her gaze snapped. A registering. I sensed that she was according me a new respect. 'Really? I never picked you for being a journalist.'

'What did you pick me for?'

'Oh,' she replied airily, 'a second-hand tennis shoe salesman.' Her eyes glinted mischievously, which gave me a lot more encouragement. I was sensing that her reserve might be dissolving.

15

'I did consider that as a career, you know,' I said, leaning towards her, my own elbows resting on the table. Our faces were close across the table, eyes engaging. We chuckled. We were getting comfortable. I was feeling less like a specimen.

The moment was interrupted by a girl aged about 3 lugging a Pippi Longstocking soft toy by a grubby red pigtail arriving at our table. 'Sophie, come back here. Right now!' one of the mothers called with a forced, tired calmness. She had a baby asleep at her breast. Sophie pointedly ignored her mother. She held up the soft toy for our inspection. 'Thith ith Pippi,' she announced proudly.

I was about to make approving noises, perhaps to show Maria my friendliness to small children.

'She's lovely, Sophie,' Maria said briskly and with what I would later come to know as her Head Girl Wintry Smile – her wide lips stretched at the corners to form a grimace – 'but you and I just heard Mummy ask you to go back to her.'

The child stood confused. She was used to ignoring her mother and being admired – adored, even – for being irresistibly cute. Frowning, she resorted to When In Doubt Suck A Thumb.

Chill obvious in her tone, and in her stare, Maria added quietly: 'Thank you for introducing Pippi to us, but you go back to Mummy, as she asked.' A meaningful pause. 'Now.'

Sophie heard the asperity in Maria's tone and slunk away, bottom lip pouting, surprised that a grown-up had stood up to her. The mothers' smiles at Maria were admiring. She turned back to me.

'I can see why you're head girl,' I murmured.

'She's a brat whose witless mother doesn't smack her bottom often enough.'

Jesus.

The coffee shop woman came to our table to take our tray. 'Vill zere be anysink else? More coffee, perhaps?'

As hints go it was unsubtle. I looked at Maria. She shook her head. No, I wouldn't, either.

'Thanks, but no,' I said.

Maria and I made to leave the café. The mothers were gathering up their things and sorting out their kids as we passed them. Sadness seeped into me. The time with Maria had gone quickly. I felt she and I had started to click, and now the time was over. Would she let me buy her coffee next time? Would there be 'next time'? Outside on the footpath I checked my watch. Just after 2pm.

She looked over towards the intersection where we'd met, as if she was weighing up something, and turned back to me. 'Do you live around here, Martin?'

I pointed along the street to the next intersection. 'Yeah. I have my own flat. It's just down there and around the corner.'

Her eyes were speculative: 'Would you like to show me your flat? Would that be all right?'

Keeping up appearances

Eh? 'Yes, if you like, it's only about five minutes, if that.'
Maria chatted as we walked – or, if you can get the distinction, she chattered. It seemed to me that she had decided I was maybe all right. In her family of 14 she had 10 sisters and three brothers. Her oldest brother was 44, and a barrister. She was the youngest. All her siblings had degrees, some even several.
'My father's a surgeon. My mother teaches languages at university.'
'She was able to do that while having all those kids?'
'She had a lot of help. My grandmother, aunts, then as my sisters got older they were roped in to help, too.'
She sounded reflective: 'Pregnancy seemed to give her energy, apparently. My mother is a great organiser and delegator. She trains, then delegates, and walks away and leaves you to it.'
We were a few steps from the intersection, walking close together. Her blazer brushed against the sleeve of my jacket. 'I saw you at the intersection the other day, Martin, and I knew you were looking at me.'
'I was going to approach you, but you seemed to me to be avoiding me.'
'I know. But if you had, and I'd gone and had a cup of coffee with you I would've been having to explain myself at home that night, and a lot of people would be talking about me tomorrow.'

We reached the intersection. 'How's that?' I said, pushing the 'cross' button.

The traffic stopped, the 'green man' went green, and we crossed to the other side.

'Eight of my nieces are at that school.'

'You're an auntie?'

'Well they wouldn't be my nieces if I wasn't,' she said, eyebrow elevated.

Of course. 'Sorry,' I said sheepishly, 'I'm being a bit slow here this afternoon, aren't I?'

Maria laughed, and I liked the sound of it. It was airy and friendly and sounded kind.

We reached the corner of my street. A chapel of an obscure Brethren church stood in stony silence on the corner, as it had done since 1902.

A few steps on and we crossed over to the block where my flat was. We entered the lobby and I led her up the tight spiral stairs past the landings to the third floor to the door of my flat. Inside, Maria dropped her hold-all on to one of the two armchairs. She looked around, noting everything.

My place wasn't plushly furnished by any means. All my furniture I had picked up for $30 in a couple of church mission shops. The three-in-one stereo was new, and that sat on top of a cabinet by the book case away from the sun. Thirty bucks bought a lot then.

She stood in the middle of my little lounge. 'Don't you like living with other people?'

'Hmmm. I do. But at the last flat things got messy.'

'Oh?'

'Very briefly. Five guys in a flat. We get on all right in our guy way. One moves in his girlfriend, which was fine. She and we got on. But then another flattie moves his in, as well.'

'And the girls didn't get on.'

'No. They had been friends because of their boyfriends. But it soon turned to custard when they came under the same roof. It got very dramatic, and two guys who'd been best friends since primary school became sworn enemies. They tried to drag the rest of us into it. The flat broke up. I came here.'

Maria lingered over what my book shelves held. 'I approve of your *Asterix* collection,' she said, taking out *Asterix the Gaul.*

'I just love them. Very funny, very subtle.'

'Oh, I agree.' She put the book back neatly. She went to the top shelf, a thoughtful 'hmmm' and pulled out one of several Wilbur Smith's works. 'You like a bit of breathless derring-do, sex, strong men, and simpering women, too, do you?'

That particular Smith effort – *Eagle in the Sky* – I said, was one of his best. 'I read it over three days. Couldn't put it down. I had tears at times. Quite a deep story, and the main woman character was no simperer.'

She slipped the book back into the shelf. 'Oh, and *Tintin!* I've always loved *Tintin.*'

'He's a journalist. I used to hope as a kid that I could have adventures like that.'

She gazed at me for so long I felt prompted to ask, just to break the silence, I suppose, if she'd like to have another cup of coffee.

No, but perhaps a glass of water.

'Or I've got apple and orange juice in the fridge if you'd prefer that …'

She did.

I opened the 1.25 litre can of Fresh-Up Pure that apparently had the juice of seven apples and two oranges and poured us a drink.

Maria took off her blazer and laid it carefully over the back of an armchair. She unfastened her tie, and undid the top button of her blouse, at her throat. She laid the tie, folded neatly, on the blazer.

Maria sat at the table in front of my much-loved, much-thrashed Hermes 3000 typewriter. She pushed hair behind her ear and smiled. 'This is a very impressive beast. I've never seen one like this. Very nice.'

'It is. I've had it for six years.' She ran her fingers lightly over the keys, the type-bars springing forward at her touch. 'It's very solid and very reliable.'

'May I try it?'

I indicated a pile of copy paper. 'Sure.'

She deftly fed the paper and a backing sheet into the machine, straightened her back as she flexed her fingers, and then began to type.

The Hermes thudded like a rapid-firing machine-gun: The Quick Brown Fox Jumped Over the Slow and Lazy Doggie.

Mary Had a Little Lamb ... and so on.

She took the paper out of the typewriter with a flourish, and handed it to me. I scanned it. 'Very good. No typos, no spelling mistakes.' She held up her glass as if toasting me. 'You could have a future as a newspaper reporter, if you wanted to.'

'Hmmm, maybe not journalism, but I'd like to be a writer one day. A famous one, too.'

She drank from her glass, enjoying the drink. 'Why did you go into journalism, Martin?'

I leaned back against the window sill. 'Because I felt I couldn't do anything else. I didn't want to do anything else.' I held the glass of chilled juice against my cheek. 'My father wanted me to get a nice, safe, steady job in a bank or with a government department, or at the council. It would be a job for life. It would be secure. The thought of doing something like that for the next 40 years just didn't appeal to me.'

She drank again, watching me over the rim.

'I wanted a job where I could do something different every day. Where I could tell stories to people.'

Maria had turned sideways in the chair to face me. 'Mr Miller, my sixth-form English teacher, encouraged me. His brother was the news editor of a newspaper in Bermuda. He said I wrote well.'

She nodded attentively.

'And there was Mr Walton, editor of the local bi-weekly. He'd give me small stories to do – school sports, reviews.'

I shrugged. 'That kind of thing.'

She said nothing, and I didn't know what to do, except babble on. 'So at the end of my sixth-form year, and hoping I'd passed the UE exam, I wrote away to several newspapers. The editor of the *Tribune* replied and offered me a job.'

'You must have been good, then.'

I laughed briefly. 'Um, well, of the six of us they took on, I was one of only two left by the end of the first year.'

'Goodness. Was it that hard?'

'I survived,' I said, shrugging. Those were the days when some newspapers adopted the practice of throwing a cadet reporter in at the deep end. If you swam you survived. If not, somebody – the editor or chief reporter, or both – would suggest you pursue another occupation.

Maria's gaze was unwavering. I shrugged again, conscious that I was shrugging a lot. 'And here I am.'

'What brought you here?' That question caught me off-guard. *Do I fob her off with more about the flat that became fractious, something about seeing an advert for a better position and a higher grade and applying – or do I tell her about Felicity?*

I didn't want to talk about Felicity, but I didn't want to hide anything, either. I wanted Maria to know that I would be truthful with her. So: 'A girl and I broke up. That gave me the opening to look elsewhere. As well as the flat breaking up.'

'Did you love her?'

Jesus! She's persistent!

'I thought I did.' I paused. 'Sometimes we don't see the reality of something until we get out.'

Maria made a sympathetic 'ummm'.

'She didn't love me, I discovered. Over the last couple of months she was going with a guy behind my back.

'And that's pretty much that,' I said, my tone putting an unmistakeable full stop to that line of conversation.

Maria dropped her gaze to something interesting on her skirt. I'd sounded too starchy there.

To fill the silence, I said: 'What's the story about your many nieces at school?'

Her lips straightened grimly – the Head Girl Look. 'Well, the eldest three of my nieces are 16 going on 17. The eldest – Catharine – is just two months younger than me.'

'I see.'

'She's the chief bitch, and the other two are not far behind. Catharine –
I refuse to call her Cath or Cathy, which she prefers, since that implies I
like her – has always resented me. We were virtually brought up
together. And she has always thought of herself as the queen bee.'

'Why was that?'

'She's the first grandchild, so my parents indulged her. Her parents are
pushy, and so they encouraged Catharine to be pushy.'

'I see,' I murmured, increasingly fascinated by what Maria had revealed
of herself and her family in the hour or so since I stopped her on the
street. There was a whole other story, if you like, behind the neat front
of her life.

'But, we were never equals because when we were born the family
decided that even though she and I were the same age I outrank her
because I am her aunt.' She smiled tightly: 'And in the FitzGarratt clan
aunts and uncles get to tell nieces and nephews what to do, and they do
it.'

'Sounds about right,' I said offhandedly.

She stared at me doubtfully: 'Am I boring you, Martin?'

No, she wasn't. 'It sounds toxic.'

'It is. We've grown up with her constantly trying to stir mischief in my
life.'

I thought I saw where she was headed: 'So seeing you talking to me
would give her a lot of fodder to go on?'

Her smile was grateful. 'Exactly.'

'And where she was short of facts she'd make up the rest?'

Maria laughed. 'Yes.'

She paused, then suddenly said: 'She's really dumb, you know. She's
jealous of me being head prefect – she thinks she should be, or at least a
prefect. And so do her parents and my mother. The nuns know what
she's like.'

She giggled: 'I don't know if I should say this because it's so catty, but
the only thing she's got going for her is that she's always had bigger
boobs than me. Even before I had them. And she's always tried to rub
my face in them.'

Er ...

'I don't know what I could possibly say about that, Maria.' We laughed together. A silence, eyes meeting, holding. The anger had receded from her face. I liked her eyes. If it's true that the eyes are a window into a person's soul then I liked her soul, too.

'What about the other nieces?'

'Rachael and Charlotte. Daughters of my twin sisters Rebecca and Esther. Quite bright, but they're followers. They'll go along with anything Catharine says. They try to stir up the younger ones, too.'

Somebody in a flat below opened their ranch-slider, and their radio was doing an afternoon women's programme.

'Is it annoying being an aunt so young?'

The question appeared to take her by surprise. 'In some ways I hate it. On the one hand my siblings and parents have usually treated me as one of the children. They and I don't really identify as brothers and sisters.'

She grimaced. 'But I'm also supposed to be grown-up, responsible, and in charge of my nieces and nephews when we were all together.'

'Like the little girly and the big girl? Neither one or t'other?'

'*Oui*. It's been that way since I was 7.'

She sighed. 'You know, the next oldest to me is Tessa. She's 24. She married an Irishman just before Christmas.'

We chatted on together until nearly 4 o'clock. It was easy and relaxed. She had another drink of juice, and she wasn't averse to some chocolate biscuits. 'I'd just about sell my soul for Crunchie chocolate,' she said.

'A love of chocolate is at least one thing we have in common, then,' I added, and she laughed again, but with a twinkle in her eye that intrigued me.

She explained how she could leave school early on Wednesdays. 'One of the perks of the job. Of being head girl, I mean.'

'How's that?'

'I'm the only girl out of 900 who doesn't have to explain her comings-and-goings. I can leave on Wednesday afternoons because that's sports period … and I don't do sport any more and I don't have to ask permission.'

'They're treating you as an adult, then?'

She nodded. 'Pretty much. Yes, I have to wear the uniform and all that, be an example to all the other girls and all that since part of my job is being uniform policewoman. But Sister Hélène – who has a PhD, by the way – says the freedom and responsibility is very much what I'd find at university.'

She picked up another biscuit, 'I know that anyway because all my family are or have been at the university since before I was born.' She took a neat bite, munched with obvious pleasure, swallowed. 'She wants to extend the privilege to the rest of the girls in the seventh form next year, depending on how I behave.'

That last was tinged with irony. 'Apparently I'm Beyond Reproach and a Paragon of Virtue.' Her eyes grinned.

We discussed my modest record collection. Maria approved of *Goodbye Yellow Brick Road* and *In Search of the Lost Chord*. 'My parents wouldn't approve of these,' she remarked as she held *Black Sabbath* and *Sabbath Bloody Sabbath*. 'And definitely not that, either!' as she held up Led Zeppelin's *Houses of the Holy*; the cover depicted naked children climbing up blocks and rocks.

'I don't, either,' I said, 'not because of that but because the music's a bloody dog.'

She laughed.

It would be 30 years before I played anything by Led Zeppelin again.

But the time was coming to an end. So: 'Will you let me buy you coffee next time, Maria?'

Smiling, but her eyes serious, she said 'no' softly.

What ...?

She was now so close I could sense the fragrance of her, something other than perfume or deodorant. 'We don't need to go to a coffee shop, Martin.'

She looked around and spread her arms, taking in the room. 'What's wrong with here? There's no-one to be nosy. No Pippi Longstocking friend. I don't have to worry about looking over my shoulder.' The soft intensity of her voice was compelling.

Before I realised it I had reached out and taken her hand. She smiled, and twined her fingers into mine, and squeezed gently.

For a moment or two there was no-one in the world but Maria and me. No sound, no people, no light, in a way. Her eyes and mine. We'd come to this in just over a couple of hours.

I found my voice. 'You know, Miss FitzGarratt,' I whispered, 'that's a bloody good idea.'

She smiled and her eyes gleamed like twin gems. I drew her closer and kissed her softly, briefly, on her left cheek, just near the corner of her mouth.

She broke the moment by releasing my hand and turning towards the chair where she had left her blazer and tie.

I watched as she lifted her collar and did up the top button of her blouse. 'Do you have a mirror, Martin?'

I had two: one in my bedroom, the other in the bathroom-shower-toilet, which was en suite. 'You could go in there, if you like,' I said, indicating my room.

So she did, and I watched as she stood in front of my full-length bedroom mirror on the inside of the wardrobe door and neatly and deftly knotted her tie. After finishing touches with that she picked up her blazer off the end of my bed and slipped it on. She turned this way and that, inspecting the look, running her hands down the sides and front. It was as if the uniform, well-fitting as it was, had swallowed her again. Finally she pulled her hair into the bun.

She turned to me: 'Must keep up appearances.'

I WALKED her to the first corner, the one by the chapel. She didn't want us be seen together in public 'yet'. We talked about when we would meet up again. I suggested that we might meet before next Wednesday, 'or is that being a bit too pushy?'

She smiled. 'No, not at all. I'd like that.' She thought for a moment. 'You work on Saturday, but what about Sunday?'

Sunday was fine for me. So the details we sorted out were that her whole family went to Mass at 9am – 'or Marss, as my father refers to it'.

'We all go. The whole famdamily, especially if my brother Luke is saying it. My mother likes to get a blessing from him, and the family expects one for the kids.'

'Does that make everyone holy then until the next week?'

She pondered that one – 'not sure'.

Anyway, after Mass the whole family gathered at the ancestral manor for what she said was 'family day'. They had a pot-luck lunch, and afterwards talking over a few drinks. Often a barbecue to finish off.

'After that everyone starts drifting off home. My parents spend the rest of the evening either preparing for the next week's work or they might talk to me.'

Her smile seemed resigned. 'Anyway, sometimes I slip away and go and see friends. I don't fit in, really. My siblings usually ask me how school is, and then lose interest after I tell them, or they tell me – again – how it was when they were there. My nieces resent me, so then I'm expected to be play-auntie to the younger ones.'

I suggested we go to a small movie theatre I knew of in an out-of-the-way street of one of the farther-out suburbs. They had matinees on Sundays that I sometimes went to. Some of them were obscure European films.

'That would be nice,' she said. 'I'd like that.' Her hand brushed briefly against mine.

'Anything you won't see?'

She laughed. 'I'll follow you. If it's R18 I'll just make sure I look 20.'

'You look 20 anyway,' I said.

Maria looked at me sideways, eyebrows knotted doubtfully. 'Really?'

'Oh, yes. We wouldn't be having this conversation if I'd had any doubts about that.' She smiled again.

I watched her as she strode down the street to the intersection. Everything about her was purposeful, straight-backed, skirt swishing briskly about her legs.

At the corner she glanced back, and waved.

Lives on file

A really useful thing about newspapers – or any media outfit – is that they kept extensive clippings in indexed folders in shelves. I was curious. Or, if you like, just plain nosy.

Maurice Peirse FitzGarratt, the patriarch, was one of the country's leading surgeons. He was an Officer of the Most Excellent Order of the British Empire, 1958, awarded for his services to medicine. A photo showed him and his family gathered for the investiture. 'Mrs O FitzGarratt' stood with him. She held a baby, 'Maria, aged 6 months, the youngest of Dr and Mrs FitzGarratt's large, lively family'. There was a Papal order for him, too, awarded by an aristocratic cardinal visiting from Rome.

Maria's mother, Órla Dominique Marie-Françoise, was a PhD, a professor. She was an OBE, too, awarded in 1969 for services to education 'and to women and children'. At the end of a row of Dr FitzGarratt's children and in-laws was a small Maria in short frock, cardigan, and long, white frilly-topped socks.

They were a family of mostly doctors and lawyers. Luke was a priest. He was illustrated at his ordination in the Vatican seven years ago, his hands joined in prayer, his priest uncles and a bishop arrayed each side of him smiling, his parents on the edges. Matthew was a partner in a leading city law firm, one of their five Queen's Counsel.

Peirse and Órla's children had been achievers at school. All but one of Maria's sisters had been duxes at the college she attended. Esther had been a proxime accessit to her twin sister, Rebecca. Mark and Luke had been duxes of their Catholic boys' school. Matthew and Luke had been half-decent rugby players. Matthew had been first-five in the college 1st XV, and his name showed up in university club rugby stories for years later. Luke had been a 1st XV hooker and schoolboy provincial rep. A sister, Rosaline, had been a leading club tennis champion. Twenty years or so ago Rebecca FitzGarratt had been a provincial netballer.

There was even a Rhodes Scholar: Annette had gone to study at Oxford, attained a PhD, and stayed in the UK. Achieving and doing well at school and university and earning degrees with apparent ease was expected and taken for granted among the FitzGarratts, going by the tone of some of the stories I read.

I wasn't surprised that Maria was the head girl at her school. A story before Christmas announced she would be head girl this year, 'following seven of her sisters in a tradition established by their mother, Professor Órla FitzGarratt, in 1926'. Her birthday had been on January 19.

'Miss FitzGarratt' had been dux of her primary school, aged 12, and at the college had scooped all the important form prizes each year. Her School Certificate mark had been one off 100 per cent. Crikey. I reviewed my own educational record. School Cert – made it over the 200-mark with 16 to spare. University Entrance – scraped the bar as I went over with 204 marks.

Love and tragedy

I waited beside my car for Maria's bus to roll into the terminal known locally as 'the barn'. It was a big, old, rust-streaked shed with broken and cracked windows. The day had become unseasonably cool, and a chill wind hustled discarded newspapers and fish-and-chip wrappings – old newspapers, of course – across the car park. Seagulls shrieked with glee – then complained when they found their prize was all smell and no fish-and-chips.

The Bedford groaned into the terminal and its brakes screeched as it stopped. Maria sat at the front. She smiled when she saw me. Thanking the driver politely for the ride she climbed down the steps. She wore pants and a close-fitting, knitted cream sweater with polo neck. A handbag with tassels hung from her shoulder. As I watched her step nimbly across to me I realised just how much the school uniform concealed – long legs, lissom, almost boyish figure.

We greeted each other warmly enough. I opened the car door for her. A quick, broad smile and 'thank you, Martin'.

On the drive out to the suburbs I told her we'd be seeing *Elvira Madigan*, a Swedish movie about a Danish circus performer and the Swedish army officer who'd fallen in love with her. We chatted easily and we found we liked foreign cinema. I said I often liked European movies because they were so different from Hollywood. They tell a story differently. Long, apparently deep and meaningful silences of an Ingmar Bergman epic might not be exciting when you're used to Hollywood all-action blockbusters, but that's how the Swedes, in particular, tend to do it.

'But the trouble is they're often hacked to pieces by the censor because they often show things that might offend our sensitivities or corrupt us and lead us to perdition,' Maria said.

We arrived at the movie theatre, so I parked the car.

Maria went to open the door. I rested my hand on her shoulder. She turned: 'What?'

'Look,' I said, 'I'm used to opening doors for women, and letting them go first. I know it's sometimes not appreciated by women these days, but that's too bad.'

Her eyes flitted across mine, and I wondered if she was going to object and argue about how she wasn't helpless, could open doors quite well, thank you, and in the climate of the day, the mid-70s, that I was being a sexist pig. Felicity didn't like being made to feel special, except only when she felt like it.

'Maria. I want to treat you properly and with respect. Always. And it starts with little things. I will always open doors for you, let you go first, and I will always pull out a chair for you. I want to do that for you.'

She smiled. 'OK. Thank you.'

Yes, I know now, it sounded too priggish, so I added: 'And I really do want to buy you a cup of coffee.'

She rested her hand on mine, which was still on her shoulder, and squeezed gently.

The theatre was small with an attached café. It was owned and run by Peter, a middle-aged Dane, and Magdalena, who was Polish. Peter told me after I'd been there a few times that she had once been a leading ballet dancer. What he had been before coming to New Zealand he never quite got round to explaining.

'Martin, my friend, welcome. You and your friend' – and he bestowed on Maria a courtly bow – 'will just about have the show to yourselves.'

Elvira Madigan is a love story set in the 1880s. Elvira was 16, a high-wire performer; he was a married father-of-two who deserted his family and his regiment for her. I can't remember when it happened, but Maria took my hand and rested her head on my shoulder. Perhaps it was the music: Mozart's haunting, dreamy *Piano Concerto 21*, ideal for soft-focus love-making amid soft and gentle colours of green and gold and lazily buzzing bees and fluttering butterflies. She was still as the movie descended into the inevitable decline. Elvira and her Sixten had run out of money and the army and police were hunting him, and then there was the sudden, tragic, and inevitable climax.

I went to kiss her as the lights came up because she had tears in her eyes, but she averted her mouth and so my lips landed lightly on her cheek. She smiled shyly.

Magdalena served coffee afterwards – 'made the European way, Martin' – and she laid out Danish tarts. No-one else was around, and so she and Peter joined us at our table. I introduced Maria to them properly, and we chatted about the movie. 'What did you think of it, Maria?' Magdalena said.

Maria cleared her throat: 'It was beautifully done. The camera work was really good.' She looked from them to me: 'But it was very romanticised, wasn't it? The colours, the music, the story. She was beautiful, and her clothes were beautiful, and her hair was always beautiful.'

'You're not a romantic, then, Maria,' Peter teased.

She blushed. 'I am, it's just that I don't know much about it.' We all laughed.

Then she said, and it was to me: 'But you couldn't help feel moved by the story and what people will do for love, despite society's conventions.'

MARIA INSISTED that I drop her off at the bus terminal despite my offer to take her home. 'Do you want to meet up on Wednesday?' I said as we waited for her bus to show.

She took my hand in hers briefly, squeezed it, smiled a warm smile and simply said: 'Yes, I'd like to very much.'

I really wanted to kiss her, but for some reason I felt she was telegraphing that that wouldn't be welcome yet. For whatever reason. Did it matter anyway?

'I'll come around to your flat in any case. Would that be all right?'

That was a surprise. But it was becoming clear that she was wanting to keep things out of the public eye. OK, I didn't mind that, either. I was never one for flaunting. The bus rattled into the stop, and with the familiar screeching of brakes.

'See you Wednesday,' I said.

'Yes. See you Wednesday.' And she went, a sketch of lithe grace in each springy step.

I drove home, and all I had of her was the lingering fragrance of her, of perfume, of the aroma of apples in her hair, and of the milky smell of a young woman. I wished I could have taken it with me up to my flat.

Uniform break

The next Wednesday I was able to leave work at 1pm. Everything had gone smoothly.

'Where are you off to in such a hurry, Martin?' Susan said as I passed her desk while pulling on my jacket.

'Home,' I replied, and kept going. I didn't want to talk about Maria just yet. My heart thumped, and not just from the exertion of it, as I mounted the stairs to my flat. Was she there?

Yes, she was. Immaculate in her uniform, waiting next to my door, reading what looked like a book written in French.

'Hi,' she said, her greeting bright and her grin wide. No caution, no reserve. On impulse I reached to hug her – and she responded with one of her own, and we held each other tightly. Alas it was all too brief because she stepped back. 'Are you going to open the door, Martin,' she said, smiling, and I thought that smile rather secret.

I slipped the key in the lock, pushed open the door, and stood aside for her to go in. 'Thank you,' she whispered, and shutting the door I followed in the wake of a subtle perfume. She put her hold-all on the same chair as she had last Wednesday, and stepped forward and gently took my hands in her own. 'I wasn't really sure about you kissing me last week,' she whispered.

I swallowed.

'And I know you wanted to kiss me properly on Sunday, but I didn't want our first proper kiss to be in public, even though we were alone in a cinema.'

'OK,' I whispered, not sure where she was heading.

'I want our first proper kiss to be here, just you and me. No-one else. Now.'

'OK,' I said, and went to oblige, but she stopped me by putting a finger to my lips.

'You might not understand what I'm going to say, so,' and she took a deep breath, 'but I'll try to explain it anyway.'

She took my hands and held them against the swell of her breasts. Her eyes were on mine, intent and intense, as in momentous intense: a strong green. 'I want to be in this uniform the first time you kiss me properly, Martin.'

Eh?

She must have seen that 'eh?' 'When you kiss me properly I want it to mean that the uniform doesn't matter. That it's irrelevant. That I am who I am, no matter what I'm wearing. I suppose I'm saying, Martin, that this' – and she glanced down at her uniform – 'doesn't define me.'

I stared up at her, into those electric eyes, which suddenly seemed wise – wiser than me? I don't know. I couldn't think of anything to say. It didn't seem to make sense to me, although I could see what she was driving at. A kind of female logic was going on. In any case, whatever I thought was irrelevant.

'OK,' I whispered, and I eased her in, and our lips grazed, a tentative soft nuzzling, and then persistent and now insistently exploring. Her mouth was sweet and open and in turn yielding and demanding. Soft, tiny sounds. Clinging to one another tightly. *God, is this what falling in love is like?*

I broke the kiss, to get our breaths back as much as anything. I glanced at her blazer and whispered: 'This is getting in the way.' She nodded once, and smiled, and she let me slip it from her shoulders. 'It might disturb and mess up the gold prefect's badge anyway,' I whispered. 'Not to mention the silver badge for being deputy president of the student council.'

'Yes that wouldn't be good at all,' she said slowly, like a wondering child, thinking of the enormity of having the badges messed up. 'What would people say? Gold where silver is, and silver where gold is, and both askew.'

'And there's the archbishop's badge, too,' I whispered in the same vein. 'What would his holiness say?'

She giggled at that. 'He's not his holiness. That's the Pope.'

'What is he, then?'

Maria frowned: 'His grace, I think. Yes. His grace.'

I fingered the badge.

'It has a silly pin,' she whispered, 'it could stab me if it was pressed too hard against ... me.'

'Oh, can't have that,' I said as I laid the blazer neatly on the back of the chair. 'I might have to give you mouth-to-mouth.'

'Oh-h-h-h ... Sounds serious.'

I eased her towards me for another kiss. I realised something else. I took her tie in my hand and muttered: 'I think this can come off, too, otherwise it might throttle you.'

Her eyes gleamed, she giggled, and obligingly lifted her chin. 'Don't you want to give me mouth-to-mouth, Martin, because you seem to be finding reasons not to administer it to me.'

'I'm sure I will still be able to find a reason to administer mouth-to-mouth to you, Maria,' and she smiled.

So I lifted the collar undid the tie and the top button. She asked shakily: 'Do you want to undo my hair, too?' I did, and she turned around so I could remove the stretch hair-tie from behind. I ran my fingers through her hair so that it was properly freed. 'You did that rather well, Martin. Have you had a lot of practice?'

'No,' I said, and hugged her. She was narrow-framed, and you might say bony. I lazily caressed her belly, and she took my hands in hers and held them under her breasts and I rested my head on her shoulder. I wanted to bury my face in her hair, my nostrils to breathe in everything of her. And for the first time, I think, I felt I was holding someone who might really be starting to like me.

Maria lifted my hands and kissed them. I nuzzled her ear, and she turned in my embrace and we kissed long and deeply again. We broke apart again for air, her face a flushed, soft pink.

'Maria,' I whispered, feeling wobbly and not just on my feet, taking her hands and drawing her down on the couch, 'if we're going to keep kissing perhaps we should do it in comfort.'

She smiled and when we stretched out side by side she laid her head on my chest for a long time. We didn't say anything. I stroked her hair and then my hand tracked down the ridge of her spine, and up again, and so on lazily, and just listened to her breathe. She must have liked that because she made a small sound like an 'mmm'. I thought she was about to purr, and so kissed her on the forehead. Soon our lips were searching for one another's.

PARTING WAS hard and reluctant, again. Four o'clock came all too soon and we had to untangle ourselves. Maria picked up her tie and blazer and went into my room to get back into her uniform. I leaned on the door jamb and watched as she tied her hair back into its bun and rebuttoned her blouse at her throat. With a briskness I hadn't seen before she did up her tie, making sure that it was scrupulously right. But she smiled tightly at me as she turned side-on left and right and inspected herself in the mirror and made adjustments to straighten her blouse. Then the blazer, which was crisply slipped on as if it was a businessman's jacket. She turned side-to-side again to inspect.

'Is this where you ask me if your bum looks too big in that?' I said.

She stared at me, surprised, I think. Then she poked out her tongue and crossed her eyes – a kind of childish reaction that had us both laughing. 'I don't have a bum,' she said archly. 'Haven't you being paying attention, Martin?'

'Do you sound like that when you're giving a detention to a naughty third-former?'

'No,' she replied with mock severity. 'Third-formers are nothing. I save it for the I-think-I-know-everything fourths, including some of my nieces.'

I went over and stood behind her, and slipped my arms around her and hugged, and we gazed at our reflection in the mirror. She was right. She didn't have a bum.

'I'm not going to say I don't want you to go because that's stating the obvious,' I murmured. She put my hand against her breast. My heart skipped, but I could feel hers beating hard. I tried to swallow.

Tears watered her eyes. 'I'm not sure I can make Sunday.'

I had half-suspected that. But I wasn't going to make a fuss about it. There was plenty of time when I could get her to talk about some of the FitzGarratt's family dynamics.

'It doesn't matter, sweetie,' I murmured, and she smiled at the endearment, the first time I had used one for her. She gave my hand over her heart a fierce squeeze.

'We can still come here on Wednesday if you're able.'

She sniffled and attempted a brave smile.

'Did anyone ask you where you went on Sunday?'

'My mother did. I told her I went to see some friends. She asked if I had a nice time, and that was it. She went back to discussing a university paper with a couple of my sisters and a sister-in-law.'

'OK.'

'One of my nieces was curious.'

We stared thoughtfully into each other's eyes via the reflection. It was occurring to me that all might not be what it seemed in the FitzGarratt family with its public picture of success and achievement and effortless intelligence.

'Gabrielle's 12 and we've always get on well. I'm kind of her favourite aunt, and she often tries to get me on my own, and so I do nice things with her such as paint her nails or brush her hair in a nice way. It's really long, way down her back. Or we go to a movie. Usually when she stays over she comes and crawls into my bed. Often she just wants to talk.'

'What about?'

'Oh, girl things. Reassuring things. Her mother – one of my sisters-in-law – doesn't talk much to her, I think. She's a twin, and her twin brother is a nasty little bully. He's scared of me, though, and I don't do anything to discourage his scarediness.'

I laughed, and so did Maria softly.

'Gabrielle, I think, feels she doesn't fit in with the others.'

Maria paused thoughtfully. 'A girl should feel she's special.'

She sounded wistful.

Thoughts on Hermes

Our parting was reluctant at the chapel corner. I thought she was crying as she set off down the street. She didn't turn around to wave just before she disappeared from view.

The fragrances and aroma of Maria – that sweet, exotic, mix of hormones, fresh flowers, shampoo, musk – lingered in my flat, and it kind of saddened me that they would dissipate. I wanted to keep something of her here until I went to bed.

I sat at my typewriter and stared out the window for a long time, seeing nothing of the roofs of neighbouring houses or blocks of flats. I suppose the old Hermes 3000 is a kind of comforting friend, rather like Pippi Longstocking or other soft toy is to a child. Several hundred stories, letters, and other stuff had been banged out on it. So I fed some paper on to the roller and – what was I going to say? Perhaps I just needed to recap on a few things and try to make sense, and in no particular order. So two of my fingers began to hammer the keys, according to jumbled commands from my brain. Maria and I had become close in the last week with a speed that I still found surprising. We had gone quickly from a tentative, brief, rather formal introduction and a self-conscious holding of hands a week ago, to today where she quite un-self-consciously had held my hands to her breasts.

In this last week I had learned a fair bit about her and her family. In spite of all the numbers and family togetherness I felt Maria might be lonely. She never said 'Mum' or 'Dad', but 'my mother' and 'my father'. She didn't sound particularly close to her siblings. The relative she had spoken most warmly about was a niece. Yet she was the senior pupil of her school. In some schools, especially the older and established ones, being the head boy or girl carried prestige. It helped get them into universities and plum jobs and the 'right' circles and the 'right' marriages. That wasn't so at my old school, a rural state college built to accommodate the baby boomers of the 1950s. I was never considered prefect material. She must have had something going for her.

I doubted she was made head prefect because her name was Maria FitzGarratt, of the well-known and prolific Clan FitzGarratt. She clearly had character – good morals, a strong sense of what seemed right and wrong in her eyes, which might conflict with her Church's view of what was right and wrong, and a strong sense of responsibility, which she had learned in her family at a young age.

I suspected that she would be brave whatever the cost to her. And I had a funny sensation about that, like a peek into the future. Half an instant, then it was gone.

I paused, looked at the growing pile of copy paper with the neat, straight, typewritten lines of my musings.

Another sheet fed into the Hermes. In or out of a school uniform Maria is a grown-up. As she said, the uniform and the blazer don't define her.

She spoke well, and was direct. She wasn't out of her depth the other day when we talked to Peter and Magdalena after the movie. She was used to being in adult company and talking with adults.

I stopped there, poured myself a large bourbon, and then decided to fry up a steak with eggs in my electric frying pan, and boiled up some frozen vegies. Just as I got that under way I realised I would have something of her to take to my bed that night. My shirt reeked of her – her hair, her fragrance. I carefully took it off and went and tucked it under my blankets. That probably sounded screwy; it made sense then.

I put *Goodbye Yellow Brick Road* on the stereo and alternately ate my tea, washed down with bourbon.

I typed some more. Another thing, and this was important: she appeared to trust me. That really warmed me and gave me so much confidence. More than anything I wanted her to learn to trust me. That she could know I wouldn't try to use her, exploit her, hurt or harm her.

NEXT I found myself typing: Does love come into it? I stared at the line for a long time as the room darkened to evening. It's just that I realised I didn't know what love really was.

Love means different things to different people. Love often gets treated like a commodity.

It's buyable, tradable, and disposable.

It's very rarely seen or treated as permanent, as a commitment.

So to my mind love ain't love unless it's for keeps.

I typed on and on, probably not making a hell of a lot of sense. I crawled into bed, hugged my shirt with her smell on it, and drifted off to sleep breathing it all in.

My favourite uncle

On Friday I woke up thinking of Uncle Sydney, my favourite uncle. A bit of a rogue. He resembled the sharp, shady Private Walker from the early series of the British TV comedy *Dad's Army* – moustache, sharp nose, and the sly tapping of the side of his nose, shifty, watchful eyes, and the grin of a used-car salesman, which he was not. He ran one of the biggest insurance companies in New Zealand.

Uncle Syd was the only human being I let call me 'Marty'. He was fun and a man of the world, and I suspect that he never took life too seriously. He was my Dad's younger brother by about 10 years.

Dad sometimes called him 'Brylcreem Boy', partly because of his flashy, snappy clothes, and partly because whereas Dad had signed up to the Army in 1939 when New Zealand declared war on Germany Uncle Syd had already gone on a short-service commission to Mother Britain to join the Royal Air Force.

As befitting his rakish manner and dress Sydney Blake was a fighter ace – a tally of 21 enemy planes. He had been awarded the DSO – for Distinguished Service Order – and DFC and two bars for having been awarded the Distinguished Flying Cross three times.

He had been a wing commander at 23.

Some of his closest friends were men he'd flown with. Many lived in Britain, Australia, South Africa, Rhodesia, Canada, United States. They were their own exclusive club of shared experiences.

A particular friend was an old Italian adversary from North Africa or Malta. Each had shot down the other. The score was: Uncle Syd, 2; *Maggiore* Achille Donald McRoss-Rossi, 2.

'Seednee, we must stop doing this,' the Italian with the grandmother from Ross-shire had implored. 'One day one of us will be killed.'

Major McRoss-Rossi might have liked Uncle Syd, even after the war come to stay with him in New Zealand from his home in Argentina, where he'd settled with his wife, a Kiwi, but Mum sure as hell didn't. There was so much of him to disapprove of. He 'drinks like a fish'. He liked his gin, but I wouldn't say he gulped it down by the bottle. A few deep breaths of oxygen in the cockpit had always got rid of a hangover. He smoked 'and stinks of tobacco', and he liked to bet on the horses. All were serious sins for Mum to judge him on because 'he should be spending that money on his wife and children'.

But here she ran into another problem. Uncle Syd's most serious sin, according to Mum, was that Sydney Milton Blake had abandoned Auntie Margaret – 'who loyally stood by him all through the darkest, desperate hours of the war' – and ran away with Auntie Kura. A girl who worked in his branch office, and who was, ahem, just 18. He was 29. Worse than that, though, Auntie Kura was a Maori, and Mum used a word for her that I cannot bring myself to write. This all happened before I was born. Mum disapproved of men who deserted their wives, and in a way she was right.

Auntie Margaret – Mum always insisted that I still call her 'auntie' – was English, and frah'fleh brittle. I could see why Uncle Syd went for her in the mad days of 1940, between the *Blitzkrieg* through France and the onset of the Battle of Britain. She was a beauty – long, long classical legs, a voluptuous frontage, and that sort of fresh, soap-and-roses complexion Englishwomen are famed for. Blue eyes that dazzled horny young men.

She'd gone to the finest gels' schools in England and Europe. Her family had Money, which impressed Mum very much. But for all that class and education I thought she was empty-headed and shallow. She was ideally suited for a madcap, whirlwind romance and marriage to a handsome Kiwi fighter pilot – and an officer – whose life might end in flames that afternoon. Because then she could repeat the drama of love with urgency with someone else while being the mourning widow. It had to be Dramatic.

Uncle Syd realised after he brought her to New Zealand after the war that Margaret was not built for the long innings. She couldn't – or wouldn't – settle. She didn't like New Zealand. It was 'backward and stifling'. She didn't try to make friends, although she and Mum always got on probably because English-born Mum ladled out the sympathy when Auntie Margaret got in her sherry-soaked cups.

Auntie Margaret refused to have children. She used to cite various reasons. I heard Dad say once that she might have had an abortion during the war.

That provoked Mum. 'Margaret would never do such a thing.'

I never liked Auntie Margaret, and I hadn't seen her since I was 11 when Mum took me on holiday to stay with her. I suspect that Margaret really looked down on Mum, who wasn't her type at all.

Auntie Kura, on the other hand, was warm and scary both at once. She was tall and slim. Her rounded facial features came from her Maori mother and her sharp blue eyes from her father, an Englishman. She was strong, lively, and open, and when aroused, scary. When she wore her hair up with the two white-tipped huia feathers jutting up from the bun she looked like one of those women who perform in Maori groups; a female warrior.

You could go to Auntie Kura's and Uncle Syd's place any time, day or night, and you'd get a loving, warm welcome, as much food as you could eat, and a bed. Dad sometimes used to say that Auntie Kura had brought out the best in Uncle Syd.

She and Uncle Syd were demonstrative in their love. Auntie Kura was kinder to me than Auntie Margaret ever was. They had four good kids. Hemi and Michael were naval sub-lieutenants. Both had gone to Britain to do a two-year course with the Royal Navy. Mihi was in her third year at university, determined on graduating as a lawyer. Heremia was a sixth-former. All five of us got on well.

Mum could never say a nice thing about them. Yet my cousins were encouraged to Excel and Aim High. My father would have been happy for me to be what he was – an unambitious clerk at the power board or in a bank.

But Uncle Syd was a kind of 'man of the world' who could explain some things to me that Dad didn't. As I said, my parents didn't tell me much about girls and sex and relationships. I think he might have regretted leaving Auntie Margaret for the hurt he caused her because he wasn't a man who casually hurt.

But he saw reality as few do. I took Felicity to meet them once. While Auntie Kura showed Felicity hospitality and kindness he took me out to the shed to 'come and have a look at my new boat, Marty'.

It was his old boat. I'd been out on it many times. He was blunt in his message. 'No-one else will tell you this, Martin, but you know I will. You need to break up with her before you get in any deeper. If you marry her you'll end up going the same way as Margaret and me.'

It was like the scales falling from my eyes. I saw Felicity and me with all our faults and insecurities. I was never going to make her happy, because no-one could make her happy. She could not make me happy because she wouldn't give me what I craved in a woman: her trust, her esteem, her love – and, all without the bloody games.

But still I couldn't do it because I didn't know how. Felicity had no such scruples. She'd been two-timing me for weeks.

SO THIS lovely, no-nonsense man was filling my thoughts when I woke up late on Friday morning. I needed to talk to him. At lunchtime I walked into town to the office, something I often did on days off because mail was sent there. I found an office soundproof phone booth that wasn't being used for interviewing or copy-taking. The paper had an arrangement with the Post Office for special lines to enable toll-free calling to the other main centres, the branch offices, and to Parliament. It was regarded as innovative and advanced then.

The phone was answered on the third ring. 'Blake speaking.'

'Hello, Uncle, this is your favourite nephew.'

'All my nephews are my favourites, Martin.'

It was our ritual.

'What's up, Marty?'

'A girl, Uncle. I've fallen in love.'

'Congratulations, lad. But you haven't phoned your favourite uncle just to tell me that, have you?' He coughed, and I heard him light another cigarette. He cleared his throat. 'Have you gone and got her up the duff?'

'No. She's 17, and the head girl of a toffee-nosed Catholic girls' college here, the youngest of a family of 14.'

He grunted. Then: 'And the problem is?'

'I don't know. I'm just worried about how it could look.'

'To who?'

I floundered. 'Well, to other people, I suppose …'

'Marty – what do *you* see in her? Why are *you* attracted to her?'

'She's just quite mature for her age. She's pretty without being overt.'

I was silent for a few moments, and so was Uncle Sydney. 'She just is quite grown-up, and she seems to like me and trust me. I love her company. My heart jumps when she looks at me. I can't wait until I next see her.'

'O-kay,' he drawled. 'And how would you feel if you didn't have her?'

I floundered again. Then: 'Well, broken … lost, I guess.'

'Then, my friend, that's your answer.' I could hear him settling back into his chair. 'Listen, Marty. Bugger what everyone else might think, and by that I include her mother and father.'

That sounded radical.

'She's not a child. If she were 14 I'd be worried about you and phoning her parents. But 17 year-old girls are often quite capable of making up their own minds.' I heard him draw on the cigarette. 'Christ, they're legally able to marry.' He cleared his throat loudly. It sounded like he was speaking through mud.

'Are you rooting her?'

I found that beyond the pale and indicated so, tersely: 'No, Uncle Sydney.'

'Sorry lad.' I heard him drag on the cigarette.

'Marty, your Auntie Koo and I had the same situation to deal with when we got together. I was 11 years older than her. Married. I'd had experience overseas. I'd fought in a war and killed people. She was a supposedly naïve little Maori wahine fresh out of the pa who didn't know anything. She was the eldest daughter of a family of seven whose father had been killed on Crete. Her mother couldn't cope without Kura's help. She was her mother's right-hand woman. And she still went to school and she still got her School Cert.'

He coughed again. 'What I'm saying, Marty, is that maturity is not arbitrary. It's not fixed by age or status. It's individual. You have it and it's developed by experience. Or you don't. That's why I flew with boys younger than you who were squadron leaders in command of men.' He paused. 'What's her name, mate?'

'Maria. Maria FitzGarratt.'

He grunted. 'Well, if you think she's the one for you – and it might turn out she's not but you won't know if you don't try – then go for it. Worry about the rest as and when it comes along.'

Another pause. It sounded as if he was crushing out his cigarette. 'Did you say FitzGarratt? Matthew? The QC? His daughter?'

What a small world. 'Yes, but not his daughter. His youngest sister. Do you know him?'

'We've met. A while ago. He – or more correctly his firm – has represented us in the past.'

In the silence I thought I heard a muffled exchange at the other end. *Time to go, I think.*

'Thanks, Uncle Syd. Pass on my love to Auntie Koo?'

'Sure to, Marty. I'll tell her your news.'

I sat and thought for a while, and then realised that Sue Devonshire was hovering near by. I left the booth, apologising to Sue because I thought she needed it for a phone interview.

'No, it's not that, Martin,' she said, her face parading frank curiosity. She had a small, stapled piece of paper in her hand, which she held out to me. 'I was along at Our Lady of The Immaculate Conception College this morning for a picture and story on their student council.'

My heart jumped, which I hoped Sue didn't notice, as I took the paper. 'At the end the head girl – Maria,' I nodded – 'asked me if I knew you. I of course said yes.' She smiled. 'She quickly wrote this, and stapled the edges, and asked me to give it to you.'

I thanked Sue, who before she smiled again and went back to her desk still wore an expression that she'd love to know what was going on. 'She's the deputy president of the council, but the one who expressed their ideas most clearly. A very able girl. Outstanding, really.'

Yes, I think so, too.

I didn't unpick the note until I'd left the office.

> Hi, Honey: good news! Could you please pick me up at
> the bus terminal about one on Sunday?
> Maria x

I read this tangible piece of her again. The handwriting was feminine, neat, strong, decisive down strokes and confident loops.

Yes, love, I can pick you up.

THE PHONE. I thought I was dreaming. Yet the clock showed 10.30pm, and the phone was calling me insistently and persistently and loudly in my silent, dark, little flat. So no dream. I threw the duvet aside and stumbled out into the lounge. I was rarely phoned.

Uncle Syd. 'Marty, sorry to phone you so late. But this evening, with the help of my good mate Mr Booth the gin-maker, I remembered something that I thought might be useful to you.'

He paused to have another drink.

'You remember about 10 years ago the company posted me to head office in London?'

I did. I'd been very envious of my cousins for living in London at the onset of the Swingin' Sixties. I'd wished I could have gone, too.

'Well, at a function one evening at New Zealand House I was introduced to a very attractive, and very brainy, I might add, Kiwi barrister called Dr Annette FitzGarratt.'

'Yes. One of Maria's 10 sisters. A Rhodes Scholar, according to our clip-file.'

'Well, Marty, I remember she'd said a very curious thing. That it was just as well she'd been awarded the scholarship then because she'd just found out she was pregnant with a daughter. The father was a much older married man, a friend of her parents, she used to babysit his family – and he'd tried to pressure her into having an abortion, which she wouldn't countenance. She'd had the girl here in London, but the family had mostly cut her off.'

Well, well, well. Another crack in the Clan FitzGarratt façade?

'How long ago was this conversation.'

'Hmmm. Maybe 1968? I asked her if she was ever going to come home. She replied sharply that London was her home now.'

Ducks and boys

'Do you have a lot of friends at school?'

The day was warm, and we'd driven 20 or so miles out of the city to a quiet little town that sat by a river. We lay on the bank, under the shade of a tree, watching the water glide by sedately as it had done for millennia. Ducks scurried about on the water or up the bank to inquire of anyone who might feed them. Maria wore a light, sleeveless summer dress with spots, large red buttons up the front. With her sandalled feet the simplicity reminded me of pictures of bare-legged girls in floaty, swishy summer dresses strolling with their boyfriends by rivers in Europe. She sat up and looked out across the river.

'Some. Mostly girls I started college with in '71. We tend to be the swots and in groups that do churchy things and meet about social justice and setting the world to rights and all that. We all feel good afterwards.'

That last sentence more than hinted at irony.

'Do they have boyfriends?'

Thoughtful pause. 'Not really. Or not that I know of. Oddly enough, boys don't come into our conversations a lot. The last time some of us had boyfriends was two years ago when we were fifth-formers.'

She beat away a curious butterfly with a wave of her arm. 'Some Catholic families, like mine, insist that their daughters associate only with boys from the Catholic colleges.'

Ah.

'The trouble with that is that many of the sons of those upstanding Catholic families, particularly if they go to St Brendan's, the snobbiest school of the lot, can't keep their hands to themselves, we found.'

'Really?'

'If I can put it in an old-fashioned way, my sweet' – and we smiled at her endearment – 'some of them have a problem with, well, keeping their hands under control.'

I had absently been stroking her back. 'I love it when you do that.' And she looked down at me with an intense, yearning expression. 'It relaxes me.' An eyebrow arched coquettishly: 'I could fall asleep in your arms.' Then, softly: 'Would you like that, Martin?'

I tried a joke, or what I thought could be a joke: 'You're very bony, Miss FitzGarratt.'

'I know that and you didn't answer the question, Mr Blake.'

'Yes, sweetie. I'd love you to fall asleep in my arms one day.'

She lay down and rested her head on my chest. 'God only knows how they treat their sisters and mothers, those boys.'

She was lost in pensive silence, then said suddenly: 'A lot of boys – men, too, I think – have problems with girls who are intelligent.'

'Oh?'

'Yes, so they belittle and ridicule, often with smiles on their faces. Where do they learn that, Martin?'

'I don't know, Maria. I saw it at school.' I squeezed her: 'If it helps I know you're far more intelligent than me. I just got School Cert and barely made UE. So I got out at the end of my sixth-form year while I thought I was still ahead.'

She kissed my shirt, right on the nipple, and I shivered – deliciously. It was all I could do not to groan. 'Intelligence isn't everything, Martin. Integrity and decency and maturity are.'

And she kissed me again on the nipple. I thought I was going to burst out of my jeans.

'You're way ahead of the rest.'

A duck waddled up, poked its beak about and looked hopefully for a crumb.

'Sorry, duck,' Maria said. It replied in duck language, waddled away to some companions a few yards away. They formed a circle and quacked quietly. As one they turned their heads accusingly towards us, quacked some more, presumably about what awful humans we were. Without any apparent instruction they fell into line and wobbled away. 'They do everything by consensus, did you know that?' I said.

She shook her head.

'I won't go out with Catholic boys. That puts me on a collision course with my parents.'

We lay in contented, but thoughtful, silence until it was time to go home.

Crossed messages

I lay on my bed staring at the ceiling in the dark of my room. After seven hours I still couldn't make sense of what had happened today.

This Wednesday had started badly. At work the teleprinter link from overseas to the New Zealand Press Association in Wellington had gone down moments after starting for the day.

It affected me in that the PA couldn't file overseas stories to newspapers around the country so I couldn't put together the day's international news page as I would.

You can't not put out a page on a newspaper. So to fill the gaping hole I looked around for stock backgrounders from Reuters and The Associated Press and features from services such as Gemini. Fine for the first edition.

Just before midday the PA's teleprinters started to chatter again and the stories spewed out on long, white tongues of paper that folded into piles on the office floor. I had to work frantically to replace most of the stock items and features with current overseas stories.

I left work after two, mentally wrung out after working quickly and furiously since before dawn. Worse, I'd been given Davies to help me. Davies wasn't helpful. I was doing the job that he used to do. He resented me, and so I had to clean up after him where I could. I knew I was late getting home. I was conscious that Maria might be waiting for me at my flat.

I hurried home, hoping she'd be there. She was, outside my door and reading a book. This one looked like German.

'Hi,' she said simply, curtly, barely offering her cheek when I went to kiss her. It was as if she had erected a chill zone around herself.

'Hi,' I said, feeling I should apologise. 'Sorry I'm late. The teleprinter link broke down at the wrong time.'

Maria made no comment. By the time I was inside the flat I knew something was amiss. She looked pale and strained. She excused herself and went to the toilet. I made coffee for us both in a silence that was yelling something was wrong.

I'm not good at silences, especially tense ones. They're deafening and they always bring out my well-hidden insecurities for a play on my emotional jungle gym.

Once again, I would tell myself, I had earned disapproval because I had Done Something Wrong. The result was such a withdrawal of emotional warmth that I felt physically chilled.

Felicity exploited the weakness well. In a way she could control me because I would have done anything for warmth again, my head to be cradled against her plump bosom, to hear her affection. Even if it was fake.

Maria came back into the lounge and just said simply, 'Don't make any for me.'

OK. I asked if she would like something else. Tea? No. Milo? No. I had Coca-Cola and Ginger Ale in the fridge. Would she like something else cold, then?

No. Not 'no thank you', and a smile, but an offhand, dismissive 'No' through almost-clenched teeth.

I stirred my coffee – two teaspoons of Nescafe and two teaspoons of sugar to sweeten it – thoughtfully. The girl I had fallen in love with was standing in my home a few feet from me: moody, distracted, and barely civil.

Every male, I would wager, might understand my predicament. In our basic way of grasping these unpredictable changes in mood and behaviour we would assume a female was having what my mother used to delicately and in exaggeratedly discreet tone call the 'time of the month'.

During this time, or the week leading up to it, males instinctively opt for self-preservation and -protection. We stage tactical withdrawals tactfully. Suddenly the solid ground under our feet is littered with egg shells that we must somehow tiptoe around. We calculate everything so that we don't ignite anger, trigger outbursts, or provoke verbal battles that we can never win.

Sometimes even that trying to placate – even be sympathetic – becomes an irritation. It's a powerful time for a woman because she knows she's pretty well untouchable. Her menstrual period can excuse a lot.

So, right or wrong, I thought I would try to please and placate. I was desperate for things to be normal. 'While I was walking home,' I said, turning from the bench to face her, 'I thought you might be waiting.'

No reaction.

I blundered on: 'So, if you like, I can give you a spare key and you can let yourself in.'

'OK. Thanks.'

I took a key from the shelf and handed it to her. She slipped it into her blazer pocket without comment.

I don't do a lot expecting to get something back. I remember Mrs Barlow from the Sunday school lessons Mum insisted I go to as a child. Mrs Barlow often would talk about giving without counting the cost. That appealed to me. It seemed noble. But this afternoon I did think that perhaps a smile or acknowledgement wouldn't have been out of order from Maria when I in effect gave her permission to enter my home any time.

In return all I got was this bleak-eyed mask. Her hair was fastened back in its usual bun. Her uniform immaculate. She reminded me of Princess Grace of Monaco, whose picture I'd had to use this morning to go with a feature story.

Bugger this. Felicity used to control me with her silences, and I'm not taking it from this one.

'Is there anything wrong, Maria? Are you OK?'

A snipped no. A clipped: 'I'm fine.'

Whenever a woman said 'fine', as if she was stabbing the word in the heart, it meant nothing was 'fine'. Men with even half-good radar know to sheer away quickly. I waited uncertainly.

'Well,' I said, 'I've got to go to the supermarket' – and I saw a flicker in those green eyes – 'can I drop you off somewhere?'

She knew what was happening. She knew I was signalling that if she wasn't going to talk to me then she was better off going. Perhaps not the most tactful thing I did but I didn't care.

'No. I'll see you.' And she was gone. Out the door. I heard her clatter down the steps.

I was numb. And I'd been numb since. Maria's behaviour had been so unexpected. If it was just her period, that's no big deal. I didn't think it would be a big deal for her, either, given that she – or I had thought she – would, as my mother would say, 'get on with it'. But something else was going on. And that was nagging at me and not letting me go off to sleep.

Wake-up kisses

Maria woke me two mornings later with kisses along my shoulder and neck. I'd never heard her steal into the flat and climb on to the bed.

'Are you awake, Martin?' she whispered. Maria was kneeling on my bed beside me; a wobbly smile. Out of uniform she knew how to be elegant – casual dark pants, checked brownie-maroon pullover, blouse with open collar.

I reached up and drew her down and we kissed for a long time. 'Does that answer your question, darling?' Yes, it did.

She snuggled close to me on my duvet. 'What time is it?' I said groggily.

'Um,' and she glanced over at my alarm clock, 'nearly eight-thirty.' She smiled and kissed me lightly on the nose.

'How long have you been here?'

'About five minutes.' She smiled fondly. 'You looked peaceful asleep. Innocent.'

Me? Innocent?

I groaned: 'I'm never awake this early on my day off.' I usually slept til after 10.

'Would you like me to go, honey?'

'No, but I need to get up and go to the loo.'

Another kiss on my nose and a more relaxed smile. 'I'll go and make a cup of coffee and bring you a cream-filled pancake.'

I got up and went into my tiny bathroom for a pee. That done, I thought my breath might be a bit ragged so I cleaned my teeth, as well.

Maria waited until I was back in my bed before bringing in the steaming mug of coffee and a plate with a big rolled pancake filled with whipped cream. She returned to the kitchen, and came back with a cup of coffee for herself and a knife and flannel and climbed back to kneel beside me again.

I thanked her with a kiss. 'What's the flannel for?'

'To wipe your hands with,' she said simply.

Ah.

'I hate to sound like an old fart, but why aren't you at school?'

She smiled over the rim of her cup. 'Saint's feast day. So the archbishop has given all the schools in his diocese the day off.'

'Who's the saint?'

'John of God. One of his favourites.' She sipped neatly.

'Is a feast day like a birthday?'

'Yes. It's actually tomorrow, but he always gives the schools a day off.' She smiled quickly, tightly. 'I thought I'd give you a surprise.'

I got halfway through the pancake, I fed her a quarter, and we left the rest for later. I did need to wipe my hands on the flannel. I dried them on a sheet, and she tut-tutted and rolled her eyes. 'Boys …'

We drank our coffees in companionable silence. But something had to be got out of the way. I didn't know if she was waiting for me to say something or if she knew how to bring it up – or was content to let it slide.

I drew her down beside me on the bed. 'Sweetie, can we talk about Wednesday, please?'

Her eyes were big. 'Yes. And I'm here to apologise to you for how I was.' Her hand touched my face, and slowly caressed it. She went on: 'You probably know what was happening. My period.'

I nodded.

'It wasn't your fault you were late. I mean, there are no guarantees really about either of us turning up.' She pulled a face. 'I might have something to do at school. Anyway, it's just that it turned up unexpectedly as I was coming here and I needed to get changed, and I couldn't get changed until you got here to let me in.' Her eyes caressed my face. 'I was getting desperate, and that kind of took over.'

OK.

'You didn't have to apologise, Martin, and you were more than gracious to me until I think your patience did start to run out.'

I said it seemed something else was bothering her, and that that had worried me more.

She pulled back and tilted her head, a picture of study.

'Am I right?'

'We were spotted on Sunday after you picked me up. Tom, one of my many brothers-in-law, is a policeman. And he was in a patrol car. He saw us as we passed.'

'Is it all that bad?' Maria's family relationships were intriguing me more and more. Why, I suppose, all the secrecy, the tiptoeing?

'I don't know. He bailed me up on my own in the kitchen on Monday evening. He'd come off duty and so had had a few beers after work and then with my father.'

She pulled herself up to kneeling beside me. 'Tom is married to Stella, the sister I get on with best. The sibling I get on with best.' Absent-mindedly she began to let a finger trace wanderingly across my chest. 'He has a habit of being loose-tongued when he's had a few drinks, and that's what worries me.'

I sat up in bed decisively. 'Your family relationships intrigue me. Can you explain why the secrecy? Why you tiptoe?'

'I said the other day my parents will not accept a non-Catholic in the family. Stella was able to marry Tom only because he converted. I don't think he cared one way or the other. He loved her.'

'That's it?'

She took my hand. 'No. I don't want to have to explain you yet. I don't want to share you yet. I want you to myself for a long time before I introduce you to the family.' She licked her lips. 'Martin, I'm a very private person. I suppose I'm the perfect head girl because all that people see of me is the wonderful Maria Goretti FitzGarratt – she's all I have to project. The image of authority, brains, character, Catholic womanly virtue.'

'Goretti?'

She smiled impatiently. 'I'll explain later.'

'OK'

'If Tom opens his mouth then everyone will want to know what's going on. If Catharine or one of the others find out about you then I become the object of gossip and I have to explain who you are and why I'm seeing you.' Her eyes were grave with what came next: 'I imagine that words will be said because you're a few years older than me and I'm still at school. On top of that you're not a Catholic.'

'Does that worry you?'

'No,' she said simply. 'None of that bothers me at all.'

'You said you and Stella got on.'

She nodded. 'Twelve years older than me. She used to look after me when I was little. I was like Gabrielle is to me. Crawl into bed with her, talk, share secrets. She's a doctor. And they still live with us. It's a big house. Eight bedrooms. Two storeys. It can be rattlingly empty even with just five people.'

We were silent for a while and Maria drew me back down beside her and she laid her head on my chest.

'Would Stella respect this secret if you told her, or Tom told her?'

'I'd like to think so. But I don't know.'

We lay like that in thoughtful silence. I kissed her hair and stroked her back slowly until she excused herself and went off to the loo. I wanted to know more about her family. I made us some more coffee. Both of us back on the bed, I said: 'At work we have a big library of clippings. The FitzGarratt family occupy quite a few folders.'

Her eyebrows arched. 'Checking up on us, were you?'

'Your family are very widely known, sweetie.'

'I know.'

'I think I'm impressed with your mother – having lots of babies while carrying on her career.'

A short, sardonic snort. 'Yes, you'd think she and the feminists would be pleased with each other, wouldn't you?'

'How so?'

'Well, she hasn't let her womb get in the way of her pursuing her life, has she? That's what the feminists want – equality. Not being controlled by their fertility. She doesn't identify with them because she doesn't believe in contraception and abortion. She and my father are leading members in Spuc. They hate her because they say she's a rich Catholic bitch who doesn't want them to have the same opportunities she's had. Being able to have an abortion is absolutely key to what they want.'

'I think it's the first time I've heard you speak approvingly of your mother.'

She frowned. 'I suppose you're right. In some ways I do admire her. But the cost is that I don't think my sisters and I would say our mother was particularly maternal. She's done everything the Church would approve of – having a big Catholic family, so accepting every one of us as God's Gift, and she and my father have had the money to pay for all that.'

She took my hand and rested it on her breast. 'I can't remember the last time I got a hug from my mother. There was a quick kiss after Sister Hélène from school rang home and told my parents I was to be the next head girl. My mother's comments were more to the effect of "well, it's to be expected, isn't it? I would have wondered why you were not appointed".'

'How did your father react?'

'He just said he would have been asking questions of me about why I didn't get it, considering that all my sisters bar Rebecca had been made head girl.'

'Crikey,' I murmured, 'your family seems expected to live by some lofty standards.'

She smiled: 'Yes. Picture perfection to the world.'

We were silent, and I glanced over to my alarm clock – only 9.30. Maria saw the movement: 'Am I keeping you from something, Martin?'

I pulled her closer. 'Not at all. I love you being here. I don't have to go anywhere at all today.'

She wrapped her arms around my neck and kissed me. Her eyes were sleepy.

Goretti

Maria stayed all day. It was as if she wanted to make the most of the luxury of our being here alone without the too-soon pain of departure. I went and had a quick shower. She had brought filled rolls from a bakery.

Feelings for each other were running deep. A couple of times as we lay together on my couch in the lounge I nearly said 'I love you'.

Why didn't I?

I suppose that somewhere in my past I'd learned that love was forever. A few pages ago I said that love often got treated like a commodity. That it was buyable, tradable, and disposable. Rarely seen or treated as permanent. Ask Hollywood. So when I did declare my love for Maria FitzGarratt I wanted to be sure – and more importantly I wanted her to be sure – that I meant it. Although grown-up and knowing her own mind and having a sharp insight into her family she was still young; I had become protective of her. I didn't want to hurt her nor did I want to do anything to her that she might regret later.

I tried distraction. 'You were going to tell me about Goretti.'

'Ah. Yes. I'm named after Maria Goretti. She was an Italian girl, aged about 11, who was set upon by a neighbour trying to rape her. Rather than submit – because she said it would be a mortal sin – she told him she would rather die.'

'What happened?'

'He stabbed her. Fourteen or 15 times. Yet she must have been strong because she died many hours later.'

Jesus! 'Sounds awful. Did she understand what he was trying to do to her?'

Her face and tone were matter-of-fact. 'Apparently so. Before she died she forgave him.'

'And what do you think about being named after her?'

'When I was young, about her age, I suppose, I was impressed, maybe honoured.' Her expression was thoughtfully troubled. 'It meant a lot to me that her virginity meant so much to her that she would die for it.'

'What's wrong with that?'

She sighed. 'Well, I think there was another message there for Catholic girls. That it was better to die – even painfully – than suffer the sin that by not dying they might have consented to it. And so get sent to Hell.'

I was learning a lot about the Catholic Church. But it was also clear that Maria Goretti FitzGarratt was seeing it through emerging eyes, too, and measuring the ideal against the reality of her own family's life.

I WALKED her to the corner about half-past four, and we parted with a brief kiss and a hug.

We would get together on Sunday. Perhaps a movie again. 'I'll leave it to you,' she whispered.

Mass meeting

As I worked through Saturday afternoon I was asked to run my eye over some galley-proofs of classified ads. I can't remember now why I was looking at them because we – that is, sub-editors – didn't check classifieds usually.

Anyway, they were notices of church times.

One stuck out at me. Fr Luke FitzGarratt was preaching at the cathedral at 10am tomorrow, celebrating Mass with the archbishop.

The idea stayed with me until I was walking home. I might put on my better clothes and wander around the corner and up the street to the cathedral for 10am Mass tomorrow. The Clan FitzGarratt was likely to be there in force for their blessing from their son, brother, and uncle, and to receive holy communion from his holy hand.

Apart from weddings and funerals I haven't been to church much. My mother, being English-born, was Church of England, and Dad apparently belonged to the Presbyterians.

I was christened into the Anglican Church. I'm told that the only argument they had was over Uncle Syd and Auntie Kura's being my godparents. Mum, of course, opposed it vehemently.

Dad said – so Auntie Koo told me – that if Sydney and Kura were not his son and heir's godparents then he would insist on me being a

Presbyterian. And he would refuse to attend the Anglican christening, too.

The embarrassment *that* would entail compelled my mother to clamp her mouth shut, give way with as much grace as she could muster in the circumstances, and smile stiffly and fakely at her sinful brother-in-law and *that* woman.

My mother used to take me to St John's Church when I was a little boy, and as I got older I was shoo'd off to Sunday school and Mrs Barlow, an elderly and kindly widow of the First World War.

By the time I was in the third form, aged 13, Mum had stopped regular Sunday attendance for about a year. On one Saturday not long after I started college I mentioned to my parents that I wanted to go swimming at a local watering-hole with some kids from my class the next day – Sunday. I was keen to join in and be part of the group. 'We're going in the morning,' I said.

Dad was at the kitchen table reading the morning's paper, tea cup in his hand. He barely looked up: 'Then go.'

I remember looking at Mum, because often it was what she said that mattered. I thought she was going to say something. But she carried on making scones, which she did every Saturday morning.

That's when I stopped going to church, pretty much.

So I got up next morning, showered, shaved, and dressed more neatly than I would for a Sunday.

I timed my arrival to be late. I did not want Maria to know I was there. The cathedral was one of those long, vaulted, echoing places smelling of candles and incense and fresh flowers.

It was packed, but half-way up the main, centre aisle I managed to find a pew to slip into, sliding awkwardly past people who did not like moving from their spots.

I had a clear view of the FitzGarratts, towards the front and across the aisle. They occupied two pews. I guessed that Peirse was the tall, spare man, hunched wide shoulders, and with the wild cap of woolly black-grey hair. Next to him was a small, slim woman with birdlike features, accentuated by grey hair pulled back in a bun. Side-on, I could tell she was Maria's mother.

I would have to guess about the others. Maria and her sisters looked alike. Tall, narrow faces, some with hair tied back. A tall brother – or brother-in-law? One shortish, with a fleshy body, cheeks coloured by exhaustion, purple-white puffy bags under his eyes. Matthew? The QC? Maria was at the far end of the pew next to a younger girl almost as tall as her. Gabrielle?

The Mass began with a hymn accompanied by a full-throttle organ, which did little to disguise something Mum said – 'Catholics aren't singers.'

The singing this morning was meagre and desultory. The bellowing of the berobed, thickset man with mitre atop his head and the lusty reinforcement of a squat, pink-faced priest who I took to be Luke as they strolled past me in a procession didn't disguise it, either.

A lot of ceremony went on up the front, on the altar – incense-swinging, billowing of smoke that was, by the time it reached me, rather fragrant; genuflecting, altar-kissing, ringing incantations.

The archbishop read from an ornate book, which was held in front of him by an altar boy. Luke was off to the side, his hands joined in prayer. In between the archbishop's reading the people in the pews chanted back.

A woman from the FitzGarratt pews rose out of her seat and went to the lectern and read, I presumed, from the Bible. She finished, turned to the archbishop, bowed, and returned to her seat.

Eventually everybody sat, and the archbishop went to a throne to the side. He looked like a king in his ornate robes, surveying everyone and everything from his higher position.

Luke strolled over and knelt before him, head bowed. The archbishop said something and performed a crisp, almost hand-waving blessing above his head.

Luke proceeded to the lectern, his hands together. This must be the sermon. I don't recall a lot of what he said. New Zealand was gripped by an abortion debate in the mid-70s.

Luke mentioned the General Election later in the year. 'It is not proper for me or the archbishop or any Catholic newspaper editor to tell you how to vote,' he intoned, his voice magnified by the microphone fixed in front of him. But it seemed to me that his role there that morning was to deliver the archbishop's message, which was: think carefully about whom you vote for. The lives of the most vulnerable could depend on it. Luke finished, and joined the archbishop at the altar and they said prayers together.

A few minutes later the congregation were told to turn to each other and give what Luke said was the 'sign of peace'. I couldn't avoid it. A man in front of me shook his wife's hand – a lot of husbands and wives were shaking each other's hands. But, having given his wife's hand a perfunctory shake, he turned, smiling, and thrust his hand out, muttered 'peace be with you', and I took it; it felt like a limp fish, and he never once looked me in the eye. Other hands, other shakes.

Then a warm breath by my left ear, and: 'Peace be with you, Martin. Fancy seeing you here.'

Susan Devonshire. *Christ!* How the fuck had I missed seeing her? I composed a smile and turned: 'Cheers, Sue. Fancy meeting you here, too. Where's the rest of the office?'

Sue – red-lipsticked, blushcred, eye-shadowed, tumbly blonde Sue, in light two-piece suit, gloves and pillbox hat – chuckled and we shook hands with genuine warmth. She winked.

The sign of peace was a precursor to holy communion. People formed queues in the centre aisle and shuffled forward slowly towards the archbishop and Luke at the front of the altar.

I watched as the FitzGarratts – first Peirse and Órla and then an older woman for whom he stood aside so she could go first – rose from their places and joined the queue that was shuffling towards Luke.

Maria and the young girl were the last, and I thought Maria was almost reluctant to get up. Just as she neared the end of the pew she suddenly glanced back up the cathedral. Our eyes met, and she showed the barest reaction, but her cheeks coloured and she smiled.

Getting it wrong

Maria skipped from the bus and we embraced eagerly. 'Hello, sweetie,' she breathed softly against my ear. We kissed hard and uncaringly, drawing understanding smiles from a passing couple.

In the car I told her I didn't really have any idea what to do. 'A movie just didn't appeal to me today.'

'Well, why can't we just go back to your flat, and sit and talk?'

'I hope just not talk, Maria,' I said with mock sleaziness.

'I'll think about it,' she said mock-primly.

Well, the day was threatening grumpiness – grey skies, a few spots of wind-driven rain, and a breeze that tended to be icy. So, why not?

'AND WHAT were you doing at Mass this morning?' she said, settling on my lap on the couch in my flat.

'Um. Meeting your family. Well, putting names to faces.'

'What did you think?'

'Who was the tall girl with you?'

'Gabrielle.'

'And the little boy with curly hair and the pouty, cupid lips and sulky eyes was her twin?'

'He's Joseph. Nasty little boy.'

'Oh, Auntie,' I mocked.

'In the last year or so she's grown so tall, he hasn't, and he hates her for it. On top of her being far and away brighter than him.'

I remembered the boy hadn't come up to his sister's shoulder.

'She'll be dux of her convent school this year.' She rested her head on my chest. Maria was black and white in her likes and dislikes. She didn't shy from showing where she stood. I kissed the top of her head, and she turned and nuzzled against my top. Then: 'Did you notice Grannie Annie Fitz?'

Trying to remember. 'The little old lady with the hat and gloves your father stood aside for when everyone went to communion?'

'Yes.'

'She's his mother. She pretty much ran our house while my mother was having babies and pursuing her career and my father his. She did the cooking, the cleaning, nappy-changing. Energetic. Never stopped. Still hasn't stopped. Now she's just about bringing up the great-grandchildren.'

'She looked to have a spring in her step. What age is she?'

Maria sat up. 'Eighty-five, I think. She was married at 17 and had my father exactly nine months later.'

I thought of my mother, for some silly reason. She had me at 42.

'Grannie Annie Fitz had four children by her 21st birthday, and another three by her 25th, and she was a widow at 29 – and pregnant.'

'What happened?'

'My grandfather was one of those Irishmen who had Done Well once he'd got away from Ireland. He owned several businesses and had made lots of money, apparently. He was in his late 30s and looking for a wife when a friend of his introduced him to my grandmother, who was about 16, and she was their maid or something like that.'

Maria crossed her legs. I felt I had to shift to make myself comfortable. She *was* bony ...

'Anyway, he was smitten with her, she was a little Irish girl from County Mayo who was impressed with him and his money, and couldn't believe she'd found such a man.'

'So what happened to your grandfather?'

'Have you heard of the flu epidemic, I think about the end of the First World War?'

I had. I'd even known a proof-reader who'd lived through it. 'OK. Well, he got sick, had a stroke, then a heart attack, and was dead in less than a week. Grannie had seven kids and another on the way. Then the businesses went bad and all she was left with was a huge house, which she turned into a boarding house.'

Maria put her hand on mine, and squeezed. 'That's how they survived. Then she began to buy property to rent out. Houses and shops. She was able to put my father through university, and his sisters and brothers. Even in the Depression she insisted that they still go through their Catholic schools and go on to university.'

'A tough old bird,' I said.

'Oh, yes. She never had an education. She was a simple country girl of 14 when she came out here on her own to be someone else's scullery maid.'

I don't know why I asked this but I did: 'What do you think of her now?'

She glanced at me sharply, and I thought her face seemed troubled. 'I have a lot to admire her for,' Maria said slowly, as if feeling her way. 'She's tough, which I guess she needed to be to survive and bring up eight kids on her own in tough times. She's extraordinarily generous, to those she favours.

'But I think she's a bigot. Deep down – and not too deep down, either – she's an intolerant old biddy and the source of some very mean attitudes in my family. Despite her three rosaries a day and going to Mass every day she's caused a lot of hurt. But because she is Grannie Annie Fitz – and my father in particular won't hear a word said against "My Dear Mother" – and because she has made herself helpful to so many she's able to get away with it.'

Maria lapsed into a long and thoughtful silence. Then, sighing, she got up off my lap and sat astride me. Her face was only inches from mine, and her eyes had taken on a different, serious hue. Her hands were on my shoulders. For an instant I felt my stomach clench, as if I was about to hear something I didn't want to hear. I rested my hands on her hips and waited.

A deep breath: 'What do you think about sex before marriage, Martin?'

I considered for half a second waffling. But I knew enough of Maria that she didn't waffle. She could see through it and she didn't like it. It wasn't taking her seriously. She demanded to be taken seriously, and giving her the gold badge of head prefect and treating her as a not-quite adult wasn't enough for her any more. Indeed, I had a feeling that anger was kettling up inside her.

'It's a bit late for me to answer that I think, Maria.'

'You mean you've already done it.'

'Yes.'

She thought about that.

'With many girls?'

She's not going to hold this against me ...?

'No. Just one.'

'Did you love her? I mean, did you do it for love? Did you seduce her?'

That one was hard to answer, I think, and I was torn between whether to lie and minimise or be truthful. I opted for being truthful, whatever happened.

Felicity and I kind of fell into it because she – well, she signalled it. We'd been going together for about three months, and we'd been out to a party, and she said to come inside her flat for another drink. One thing led to another, as it was going to, and soon we were into it in her bed. She was my first; I wasn't hers. She never said as much, but these things become apparent. She complained afterwards that I'd been clumsy and had hurt her. That she had expected more from me. So I got out of bed, got dressed, and went back to my flat.

Maria's gaze had not wavered, and I was aware that her thumbs were slowly and softly caressing my neck. 'No, Maria, it wasn't love. But I thought it meant something. To both of us.'

'And did it?'

'To me, at the time. Yes. I don't think it meant the same to her.'

The thing was, I didn't know where her line of questioning was leading, and why. 'I suppose I was disappointed afterwards. I suppose I wanted warmth and affection, as much as she did, an expression of appreciation from her for what we had just shared together. It's the most intimate moment between two people. All I got were her complaints.'

Almost as an after-thought I added: 'No, I didn't seduce her, nor would I.'

I realised that last bit sounded bitter. Suddenly it was a bitter memory because for about a year I'd tried to put it in the basket over there in the corner nearly out of sight and mind called Experience.

I allowed myself a grim smile: 'There were a lot of complaints. I could never get it right for her. I didn't get a lot of pleasure or affection out of it.'

'Did you lose respect for her because you had sex with her?'

'No.'

Silence.

Well, my turn to ask some questions.

'Does it bother you?'

She kissed my forehead: 'No,' she whispered.

'But as a well-bred young Catholic woman [I nearly said 'girl'], raised in the tenets of your faith, aren't you taught that sex outside of marriage is sinful and that those who do it are sinners?'

I had intended it as a bit of humour. Before the words had escaped my lips I knew I'd said the wrong thing. I didn't know why, but I saw the colour of her eyes turn a cold, sharp green, pink colour her cheeks, and she roughly pushed herself back from me and stood up.

'Please understand, Martin,' and her voice had that soft, cold chill I'd been waiting for nearly a month to hear, 'that no-one tells me who I may share my body with, or when. And no-one tells me whether I commit a sin by doing so.'

I sat there, stunned, in my male way thinking: *What did I say?*

But then Maria had picked up her jacket and tasselled bag and was heading out the door.

Cold war

I didn't expect Maria to be at my flat the next Wednesday, and she wasn't. I had replayed the conversation in my mind many times. Her reaction … I hadn't expected that. What had triggered it? All I thought I had asked – well, what had I asked?

I had kind of assumed that she was a virgin, was intending to stay a virgin, in keeping with the teachings of her Church, and presumably because of how she'd been brought up. That was OK by me. I was never going to try to force her or manipulate her into it.

I nearly was going to Mass at the cathedral the next Sunday, in the hope that I might get close to a word with her. But I went off that because I thought, bugger it, I wasn't going to be controlled – as I saw it – by her moods and temper.

'If you've got something to say,' in my imagination I said to her, 'then say it. But don't bloody run away from me.'

As well, I wondered if I had blown it and whether I should try to find some way to apologise. It might have been my pride getting in the way, but I decided not to.

When Felicity and I argued and fell out I was always the one who found a reason to go and make up, blaming myself for things I knew I didn't have to blame myself for. I tried always to be reasonable, but it seemed in hindsight as if she saw it as me being weak. I didn't know. But I wasn't going to put up with it again. I didn't bother going to 'the barn' because I knew she wouldn't be there.

On the 10th day of silence I left work about my usual time. I briefly considered going to have a drink with Sue Devonshire. She'd been keen to find out why the unreligious Martin Blake had turned up in the local Catholic cathedral. 'Didn't see you last Sunday, Martin …'

I nearly was going to bring up Maria with her because I thought I needed a female mind to help me figure this out.

But Johnson, the industrial reporter, and so much more assured than me when it came to women, invited himself along and verbally shouldered me aside.

So I walked unhappily up the street to my flat. Maria wasn't at 'our' intersection. Nor was she in the café, but the mothers and Sophie and Pippi Longstocking were.

I climbed the stairs to my flat.

As I turned the key in my door I sensed a fragrance of lingering perfume on the landing.

My heart lurched.

Uniform liberation

Maria stood in the middle of my flat facing the door – a schoolgirl. Hair as usual tied back in a bun, neat, not a strand reckless enough to be loose or out of place; blouse collar was as it should be – no wrinkles there; tie, perfectly knotted; blazer immaculate, the badges of head prefect, student council, and the archbishop's council precisely as and where they should be; feet together, toes of her well-polished black shoes pointing outwards, like a ballerina. Her hands were at her sides.

She was still as a statue. Her gaze – those green eyes that I've described before as electric – was unwavering. Her chin had that determined tilt again.

What the hell's going on? Is this to tell me goodbye?

I was terse. 'Hi.'

'Hello, Martin,' and her voice was timid.

'May I ask what you're doing here?'

'I came to apologise, Martin.'

I couldn't be angry with her. 'Well, I'll apologise first, Maria, for upsetting you.' *Why did I say that?*

Her eyelashes flickered twice.

'I don't know how or why I upset you. It wasn't deliberate.'

'I know.'

Then what the? – anyway: 'But don't you ever walk out on me again. If I say something you don't like or I offend you then you stay and we talk about it.'

She bit her bottom lip and swallowed. 'OK, Martin.'

'Children,' and I knew I was starting to sound lecturing and priggish, 'children, they run away. Adults don't.'

Too harsh.

I tried to sound softer. 'Sweetie. If you walk out on me again, just keep going and don't come back. OK?'

She tried a tentative smile. 'So, you're not going to break off with me then?'

Eh?

'No, Maria. I love you, I really do.'

I spread my arms to her and she threw herself into me and we clung tightly.

She burst into tears, and babbled. 'I'm so sorry darling for walking out and staying away from you and hurting you I've missed you too and I got angry and I don't know why I did because I know you wouldn't deliberately hurt me you're not like that and I was just indulging my stupid pride …', and so on. She shook with her sobs and her muffled words and she sniffled into my neck.

I kissed away the warm, salty tears streaming down her cheek. 'Come on sweetie,' I whispered, 'it's OK. I hate it when girls cry.'

I'd never said that to a girl before, and I didn't know where it came from. But it kind of triggered something in me. I wanted to make it better; to make the tears go away.

She giggled, and the shuddering subsided. 'I love you, Martin,' she whispered direct into my ear, and she kissed it.

'You, too, love,' I replied, and we kissed long and hard and hungrily. I could feel myself sorely tempted. So I thought I would try distraction to cool things.

'Your hair's a bit mussed,' I said mock-gruffly, 'and your tie's a bit off-centre.' I looked at the badges on the blazer. 'And the badges are a bit disarranged. What would his holiness say?'

'His grace. Remember? He might make me do a penance.'

'Yes. Five hundred Hail Marys, you bad, bad Head Gel, you.'

'I s'pose I'd be well-penanced after that.'

But something was going on behind those green eyes.

'Take my blazer off me, Martin, and that will solve the problem of the badges.'

I slipped it over her shoulders and helped her out of it, and laid it neatly over the back of the armchair.

'Now undo my hair, Martin, and that will solve the hair problem.'

Her eyes glittered with the tears still, but they had a decisive edge to them.

I reached behind her head and took the stretch hair tie out, and a couple of pins, and her hair tumbled out above her collar. I smoothed out her hair. It felt silky.

'Now undo my tie, Martin. That will fix that, and the collar, too.'

I did that, and it was beginning to dawn on me, slow laconic, moronic Kiwi bloke that I am: something was going on I hadn't caught up with. This did not feel like the last time we played this game.

She took a deep breath, squared her shoulders. 'Now, Martin,' she whispered, 'unbutton my blouse.'

'What?'

Her gaze didn't waver. 'I want you to undress me. Liberate me from my uniform.'

I swallowed – hard, and my heart raced – hard. 'All of it?'

'All of it.' That was pretty clear.

'I want you to make love to me, Martin.' She paused. 'Make a woman of me.'

Her eyes were round, and large. 'Is that clear enough for you?'

It might have sounded melodramatic, but yes, it was abundantly clear. Yet I had difficulty grasping that this was indeed happening. It didn't usually happen this way, did it?

My hands trembled as I fumbled the buttons undone and pushed her blouse apart. Her bra was cleanly fresh and white, and the cups were small and soft; lacy edges along the top. I brushed one lightly with the back of my hand.

'I wear bras for decorum,' she murmured. 'There's not much to hold up.'

I kissed her, then undid the cuff buttons and she held her arms out so I could tug the blouse out of her skirt. The blouse slipped easily off her shoulders, and the unzipped skirt fell softly to her ankles. She gripped my shoulders for balance as she stepped daintily out of it, one foot, then the other.

She laid the skirt neatly on top of the blazer, the tie, and the blouse. The panties were white, too; a tiny bow was attached to the waistband, just under her neat, oval navel.

'I think,' I murmured, 'that it's important I should take your shoes and socks off.'

'I think so, too.'

I unlaced them, one after the other, trying to stop my hands from trembling. She stepped carefully out of them, and the socks, holding my head for balance.

I got back to my feet. 'Perhaps I'd better join you,' I said shakily, and started on the buttons of my shirt. My fingers were like rubber. I was not being the smooth Casanova of books or the movies. No, I was as nervous as a schoolboy.

She stopped me. 'Here. I'll do it. Arms up.' Maria had a tone that you obeyed. You could see why third-formers, small children, nieces and nephews – and her soon-to-be lover – obeyed.

She lifted my shirt over my head and carefully placed it on the other armchair. I kicked my shoes off, and took off my socks. 'I hope my feet don't stink.' *Stop babbling, Martin!*

She giggled with a snort. 'Now your belt,' and she tugged that undone and pulled my pants down in a way that suggested she had done this many times, but to small children.

I swallowed hard. 'Come on,' I whispered huskily, and led her by the hand into my bedroom. 'We need to find somewhere more comfortable.' That was when I noticed the slats of the venetian blinds had been tilted so they softened and shaded my bedroom. The bed had been made. I never made my bed. Maria smiled pretend innocently.

I unclipped her bra, and helped her shrug it off. Her knickers slid over her hips and fell to her feet. The musky scent of her was giddying, knee-weakening. She took my Jockeys and briskly tugged them down in a way that no-one had since I was a very small boy.

Now we stepped back and saw each other for the first time. My mouth was dry again. The moment of anxiety about *what will he/she think?* passed. Her gaze dropped to a penis that was showing its own interest in proceedings. Her eyes returned to mine. She smiled uncertainly.

'Does it worry you? Looks a bit belligerent ...' *Babbling again ...*

She frowned. 'Hmm. I think I'll manage.'

I felt embarrassed. 'You'd think it could wait until we got into bed,' I muttered.

She giggled briefly. Maria was neither embarrassed nor concerned as she returned, hand on hip, my gaze. Shoulders wide, ribs, curves. Breasts petite and rounded and pale, peaked with neat, pink nipples in pink circles. Slim, boyish flanks, long legs; discreet, sparse, coppery hair; a tantalising glimpse of what the French might call *rose de dessous*.

Maria stretched to tiptoes and executed a slow turn like a dancer so gracefully that she must have done ballet when she was younger.

I swallowed hard, and croaked: 'You're right, you know, you don't have a bum.'

She snorted. 'Remind me to smack yours later.'

I reached out and touched her breast, and she smiled at that. My fingertip gently circled the nipple, and it unfolded pinkly. I touched the other, and her breath caught, and the bud hardened and jutted, too.

'They like that, you touching them,' she whispered.

'Do they like being kissed?'

'I don't know.' That slowly wondrous-tone whisper, like a child. 'They've never been kissed before.' She batted eyelashes extravagantly.

'But I'm sure they wouldn't mind if you kissed them.'

I followed her on to the bed. 'Is this going to be all right for you?'

She nodded.

'I mean, will it be safe for you? You won't get ... um ... well, preg–'

'It's fine, quite safe.' She sounded crisp and sure. *Well, she's the one who should know.* Doctor's daughter, two sisters who were practising doctors. No-one discussed much the notion of unprotected sex then.

We drew each other together and kissed, stroked, touched. *Ohh ...* unhurried, exploring and yielding in our intimate quiet. Her nipples had coloured to a bright rosy pink and I kissed them, and they were springy soft, yet firm.

'Oh, *yes!* We *love* that, Martin. *Oh-h*, you bad, bad man.'

And so we went on unhurriedly, tingling, hearts thudding faster, breathing quickening, until poised over her I said: 'Are you still OK with this, Maria?'

She nodded, her eyes wide and steady. The exquisite plunge that means all and changes everything. Her sharp intake of breath; a drawn-out '*ohh-h*, Martin, *swee-tie*' ...

A restraining touch. 'Just wait a minute if you can, darling. I want to remember this moment forever,' she whispered huskily. So we lay together like that, still, even holding our breathing. Smiling coyly Maria wound her legs about me. 'Now you are in *mein* clutches so you cannot get avay,' she muttered Germanically.

'Who says I want to get away?' I said, and she squeezed my sides hard with her knees.

Maria's eyes gleamed with love and I knew it would be all right. We moved again, carefully, like learning dance steps, finding our rhythm. In time Maria half-whispered 'oh', like she'd had a pleasant surprise. Her eyes opened wide and her mouth formed a round 'O'; she trembled, cried out, and we clung to each other. I'd known nothing like it.

AFTERWARDS, SIDE-BY-SIDE, we lay breathless, waiting for our hearts' thudding to ebb. 'Whew,' Maria whispered.

I turned to kiss her, but she rolled away on to her side and drew her knees to her breasts. Alarmed, I reached out to draw her back to me. 'Are you all right, love?' Was she already regretting what'd we just shared? How did girls feel about giving up their virginity?

'I'm fine, Martin. It's OK. Just hold me, please.' She took my hand and squeezed it hard, and clasped it to her breast. 'And don't talk, darling,' she added. 'Mmmm, that's nice,' she murmured dreamily.

Bells in the distance

We must have slept like that because the light coming through my windows had changed – the sun was heading down towards evening.

'Love?' I whispered, and kissed her shoulder.

'Mmm-?'

'It's getting late. Don't you have to get home?'

Maria barely stirred. 'No. Didn't I tell you?'

'What?'

'My parents have gone away to a doctors' conference in Adelaide. My father's getting an honour. Not back til Monday. Stella and Tom are working their shifts until probably after midnight.'

She turned over now, with big little-girl eyes, and soft little-girl voice: 'So, darling, I'd be home all alone.'

'So you don't have to rush away?'

'Not unless you want me to,' she whispered.

No, I didn't. I was hungry and thirsty now, and I imagined she would be, too. I went out to my kitchenette and poured glasses of fruit juice for us, found a packet of chocolate biscuits, a Crunchie bar that I broke in two, and some mandarins while she went in to the loo. I was peeling the mandarins when she joined me. She had wrapped a towel around her waist. It was like a sarong. Maria put her arms around me and kissed the back of my neck. Her breasts grazed softly across my back.

'I was going to cover myself up with it,' she said, indicating the towel, 'but then I thought it was a bit late being modest now.'

I turned about and we kissed. 'Anyway,' she whispered, 'I don't want to be modest with you.'

We took the drinks and the food back to bed, and we sat cross-legged and drank and ate. She had an appetite, and when she had finished she wiped her hands briskly on the towel.

Her eyes signalled that she had something to say. 'I've been thinking, darling.'

'That sounds ominous.'

She mock-scowled. 'It's time you met the family, Martin.'

A foreboding – like an instant, faint veil of mist – appeared and disappeared in my mind's eye. 'You reckon?'

'Yesss,' and she drew out the 'yesss' in a long, thoughtful hiss. 'I've had enough of creeping around, looking over my shoulder, telling lies and evasions, wondering who is going to find out.' She paused and reached for my hand, and gripped it. 'And of not being able to talk about you.' She smiled tremulously, as if trying to reassure herself. All I could hear inside me was the distant chorus of alarm bells up ahead.

'I love you, Martin,' she said shakily.

'I love you, too, Maria Goretti FitzGarratt.'

Love. Buyable, tradable, disposable, whichever's convenient and whenever.

I remembered what Mrs Barlow at Sunday school used to say about love, because God was love. 'Remember, my dears,' she told us 8 year-olds seated cross-legged in front of her on the mat, her lined, soft face wreathed in a gentle smile, 'love is not just words, but actions, too.'

She shifted on her chair. 'For example, would you be loving your mummy and daddy if you didn't make your beds in the morning or help with the dishes?' That was a simple example. 'Remember, dears, that you can't say you love someone and then do the opposite that isn't loving.'

'Can I rely on you, Martin?' The question was like a stabbing thrust into my belly, and I turned to her. Her eyes were grave, and her chin that determined jut again.

She was just 17, but no kid. She *knew* what was up ahead. What Maria wanted to know was whether I was with her.

I swallowed. 'Yes, my love, you can.'

ABOUT SIX I got out the electric frying pan and a pot to cook us tea. I had some mince in the fridge and I thought I'd combine that with some tomatoes, onions, and whatever else I'd throw in.

My mother had taught me to cook basic things for when I went flatting. Mince then was cheap – 50c a pound, as it was then. She said onions, tomatoes, stock, Worcester sauce 'and a few other odds and ends' could make a decent meal. And so it had proved. I'd serve that with brown rice.

Back then rice wasn't yet as popular as it is now. Back then you had to wash it and dry it, or something, before cooking it. I couldn't be bothered with that. I just ignored it and got on with it.

Maria said she had a history essay to write. Could she use my typewriter? Most certainly, I said, and I remember thinking *how neat*.

It was almost a domestic occasion. She sat at the table, towel still knotted around her waist, grabbed a pile of A4 typing paper, fed a couple of sheets on to the roller. Then she took a pad of notes from her bag, consulted them for a few minutes. And began to type, her expression a picture of concentration. Her long, tapered fingers danced and stabbed deftly at the keys, the type-heads snapping forward like snakes' tongues, cracking at the paper. Page efficiently replaced by another. I bent down and kissed her bare shoulder, and she let me do that, but didn't encourage any more.

Thirty minutes and it was done. Two thousand or so words on five pages. I picked up the sheets, and quickly read her essay. She watched me expectantly as I read. 'This is very good, sweetie. As a sub-editor I would have a very hard time finding anything wrong.'

She liked that and squeezed my bum.

Maria quickly typed some other homework, perhaps about 15 minutes worth, in French, and said, 'I'll do the German later.'

I served up the meal, and we ate it at the table. 'I think sex might have given me an appetite,' she said as she aimed another forkful of food at her mouth.

Afterwards she washed the dishes. I made up the excuse that I'd leave them to dry so I could stand behind her and just hold her. Maria pretended to ignore me and concentrated on washing the dishes. I think she was trying to see how long she could go before her body betrayed her. She was doing well even after I started kissing her along her neck and shoulders and loosened the towel and it fell to the floor.

But the flesh capitulated: 'Oh-h …,' she whispered, 'you evil, evil little man.'

When her breath caught with another soft 'oh!' I took her hand and we went back to bed.

'I DON'T want a shower,' Maria said. 'I want to go to sleep tonight with your smell on me.'

I had tactfully suggested – well, I thought I had tactfully suggested – that she have a shower. 'It's not fair, Martin,' she said, lifting her leg over my hips and perching astride me, 'you can sleep here with the smell of us.'

'There will come a time, my love,' I said, 'when I think you won't have to worry. But in the meantime,' I went on because I thought she was going to grow tears, 'we have to make small sacrifices.'

Maria smiled, bent down, kissed me hungrily, dragging down to my nipple. Her lips and tongue teasing me there was like a jolt of electricity.

'Hmmm. Still a bit sensitive there.' Her eyes had that Head Girl Look: observant, detached, memorising.

'When do you want me to meet your family?'

'Easter. Easter Day. There's usually a big lunch after morning Mass. A lot of people come around. Maybe no-one will notice too much.'

We lay in silence, and Maria rested her head on my chest. Easter was the weekend after this. She went and had a shower then donned her uniform again. Although she appeared to despise it, that didn't stop her observing the school dress code. Everything perfect. Neat. Just so. Irreproachable. She took to the typewriter again so that she could translate a passage of English into German.

'How many languages do you know?'

'Four. English, French, German, Latin. I was going to do Greek, but I rather like history, so I kept going with that.' The typewriter thudded again as she effortlessly rendered The Queen's English into *Deutsche*.

When work needed to be done Maria would do it, and do it properly and until it was finished.

I could understand the mind-set. Anyone who has been a journalist would, I think. You didn't relax until the story was written. If you had to go all day, all night for the story, and then be up until 3am writing it, then that's what you did.

She would be coming here to live with me, I just felt that. And I could picture her here, doing her homework, studying, and probably I would have to find something else to do while she did it. Perhaps I should think about doing that piece of fiction about the princess and the Kiwi farmer. The story would be based on a real princess from a European royal house who fell in love with a Kiwi soldier during World War One. She forsook everything – renounced her titles, gave up any rights to her children being princes and princesses, forwent a life of privilege and wealth, so she could come to New Zealand with the man she had fallen in love with – an outwardly rough man who'd left school at 10 to run the 160-acre family dairy farm after his father was killed by a tree falling on him.

I'd written her obituary. Her husband and older daughter told me all about her. I'd always felt it would make a great novel. Until now I'd never felt really confident about tackling a novel.

Maria finished her homework about 10pm, and I drove her out to the suburb to her house. It was one of the mansion villas typical in the older, wealthier suburbs. What was called 'leafy'. The house was in darkness. 'Thank God for that. I don't have to explain anything to anybody.'

I wanted to go to the door with her, but she replied that that was unnecessary. 'It's quite safe here.'

She hesitated at the gate: 'Darling, do you mind if I come to your place tomorrow.' I hope I concealed it behind nonchalance, but my heart did a joyful somersault. 'Sure. You have a key. Just let yourself in.'

She pecked me on the cheek. 'Thanks. It seems silly to come out here and being on my own.'

I quite agreed.

I went back to my flat. I put washing in the basket for Friday. Yes, she had had enough time to change my sheets today before I got home. I picked up the towels she had used to dry herself after the shower. Yes, a girl; she had used two. They carried the distinctive masculine smell of my coal tar soap. For an odd reason, and I was starting to feel weary, I remember thinking that I hoped no-one at Maria's house would get close enough to notice.

Work ethic

I heard my typewriter thudding rapidly as I walked up the path to the block of flats. Maria had the ranch-slider open, and the windows. She was making herself quite at home. I'd been delayed leaving work – the end was well and truly in sight in Vietnam. I wouldn't be working the next day so I was given two pages to run as a mainly photo feature: American helicopters lifting out of the desperate, clutching reach of hundreds of Vietnamese terrified of what was to come; crewmen of a US navy aircraft carrier tipping Hueys and Chinooks and gunships into the sea because the ship had no room for them; North Vietnamese soldiers riding on tanks waved their AK47s in triumph. Over the border a group of Cambodians belonging to a shadowy group with the strange name of *Khmer Rouge* were beginning to impose their silent, chilling terror. I found a slot for that story.

But this time I felt content arriving back at my flat late; it was like coming home to somebody.

Maria was seated at my typewriter when I walked in. Open books and pages of scribbled notes were all over my table. She turned and held out her arms to me and I bent down and kissed her and was enveloped in an invisible cloud of shampoo and freshness of young woman. She was in uniform, minus blazer, sleeves rolled neatly above her elbow. Tie neat at her throat. 'Hello, my love,' she whispered, and her eyes shone.

'Did you sleep well, darling?'

She frowned. 'No. My mind kept replaying what you did to me yesterday.' She lowered her eyes demurely. 'My body wanted to join in. It felt left out.' Her eyes found mine again. 'In the end I felt left out. My mind and my body were enjoying themselves and I wasn't and I found sleep very difficult.'

'We could rectify that, if you like,' I offered.

'That's thoughtful of you, Martin, but I have homework to do.' She took both my hands in hers. 'Please don't mind. But it's just ingrained in me that you get your work done first. Then you can play.'

I kissed her lightly on the nose. 'It's all right, love. If I had a story to write I'd be telling you the same thing.'

I left her there and went around to the local Four Square superette and got a large can of fruit juice and some biscuits. They had nice rotisserie'd chickens and I bought a big one of those. We could have it cold. At the greengrocer's – an ancient, two-toothed uncle of the superette owner who probably had the freshest and best quality fruit and vegies in the city – I got tomatoes, cucumber, lettuce, and some apples and mandarins. Maria loved mandarins, it seemed to me yesterday.

I poured her apple juice and put the biscuits on the table near the typewriter. She smiled quickly and buried her face in my shirt and kissed my belly. Then she was back to work.

I sat on the couch and watched. Ostensibly I was reading the afternoon paper. But I couldn't ignore her presence. Maria was absorbed in what she was doing. She sat straight-backed at the typewriter, head erect. Most of us in newspaper offices hunched over our typewriters, peering at what we'd written and most likely had rewritten, fretting, chain-smoking, drinking endless cups of coffee, gnawing on nails, glancing furtively at the clock. Some would sip from hip flasks, and it wasn't fizzy drink, either.

But Maria, my Maria, could crack out an A4 page without a break, reaching the end of each rapid-fire line with a 'bing' of the little bell, a discreet – neat – swing of the return handle, and the barrage started again. In an hour she stopped and asked me one question, about the phrasing of a sentence. I thought about it, gave an answer. She said thank you and carried on.

By 5.30 she had finished. I broke up the cold chicken and sliced the tomatoes and cucumber, and washed and broke up the lettuce, and arranged it all on dishes, and served it up.

We ate companionably together, and did the dishes afterwards. We curled up on the couch. Sometimes it's nice just to talk, and I think Maria wanted to talk.

'I liked you from the moment I saw, you, darling,' she whispered,' head resting against my shoulder.

Oh? 'When was that? At the crossing when we got in each other's way?'

She shook her head. 'No. Long before that.'

I had to squint. 'Really?'

'Mmm. One day last year you were at the crossing. I hadn't seen you before. You looked lost. You stood out because you were gazing around like a kid in the big city.'

'I probably was. I hadn't been here very long.'

'Yes. Anyway.' And she glanced at me. Maria knew how to convey Authority with a glance. 'You were standing there, looking lost, and you crossed at the lights, and everybody crossed at the lights. And there was a mother next to you pushing a pram and she had a toddler holding on.'

I was trying to remember.

'No-one tried to get out of her way and make it easier for her to get across, and the toddler was trying to break away and the mum was getting distracted. You spoke to her and took the pram so she could concentrate on the brat, and she was surprised that someone – especially a man – would do that. And you pushed the pram across and manoeuvred it very gently up on to the kerb. You made sure to do it carefully.'

I think I vaguely remembered. But anyway.

'And when she thanked you, you just seemed to smile, gave an embarrassed little wave of the hand and walked away, as if it was nothing. That whole episode impressed me, Martin.'

'Why? Isn't it what anyone would do?'

'No!' She took my face between both her hands. 'Sweetheart. My brothers have never pushed a pram or pushchair in their lives.' Her tone was intense, and her eyes gleamed indignantly. 'None has even bottle-fed their children or changed a nappy. It's beneath them. Two years ago my brother-in-law Nigel wanted to be more involved in bringing up his and Gemma's twin girls. My grandmother took him aside and told him that nappy-changing and bottle-feeding wasn't man's work.'

I didn't know what to say. So many contradictions, I thought. Women who had university degrees who held good and prestigious jobs, but who still expected, or were expected, to do all the baby-caring and child-minding and pram-pushing without help from their husbands. So why all the university degrees?

'And you liked me because of that?'

She sighed exasperatedly: 'Martin Blake. You have no idea how long and how hard it was waiting for you to notice me trying to get your attention.'

She sat astride me on my lap and kissed me. We surfaced for air from that one. 'The school holidays nearly killed me. I thought a lot about you. After we broke up last year, and before school started again when I was in town I used to look around for you, or where you worked or lived.' She took my hands and clutched them to her breasts, and little tears grew in the corners of her eyes. 'I even prayed that you were still around, and I despaired that you might have found someone else or gone away.'

She leaned forward and kissed me softly, lingeringly. 'And then we went and had coffee together. And I was really taken with you because you didn't look as if you were trying hard to impress me. You were as I had imagined you to be – kind and thoughtful and respectful.'

Now, I hadn't expected that. It was almost like I had been a spectator in our story when I thought I had been the instigator.

'Didn't you think it odd that I asked if you could show me your flat?'

'I thought you might have taken a liking to me.'

'I had, darling. When you pulled out the chair for me as a matter of course in the coffee shop it was pretty well sealed for me.' She kissed me again. 'And then you made me wait until you opened the door of the car. No-one's treated me like that.'

I held her face between my hands: 'Sweetie, no girl has let me do that.'

I TOOK Maria home about 10. The house was in darkness again. 'That's good,' she murmured, relieved. 'I wonder if anyone would notice if I didn't come home,' she said in the dark as I made to get out to open the car door for her.

'Do you want to try, it, darling?' I said as she went to kiss me a last time.

We kissed. 'I'm tempted, *liebchen*.'

I drove back to the flat, which suddenly now seemed so empty, and I realised I was becoming to hate that. For months I'd been content here. This was My Place and My Space. This was where I ate what I wanted when I wanted, drank what I wanted and when I wanted. I played the music I wanted when I wanted. I went to bed when I wanted and got up – if it wasn't for work – when I wanted. And now I was missing Maria when she wasn't here.

I didn't have to work tomorrow. But I would get up early because she said they'd be having the school Mass tomorrow morning. She would be doing a Gospel reading, she said. I knew by the expression in her eyes that she would love me to be there. So I would.

Mass devotion

I stood outside the cathedral while nearly 1000 uniformed young women from the adjacent college filed in mostly lady-like manner up its stone steps and into its august portals.

Awaiting their turn were adults – parents, grandparents, family members. I managed to blend in. Matthew FitzGarratt, QC, and a woman I took to be his wife eased past me on the steps; both were talking to a man I recognised as a magistrate and a woman with him.

Another woman who I think I recognised as one of Maria's sisters strode up the steps with Maria's grandmother.

Straight-backed, head erect like her granddaughter Maria, the hawk-eyed and firmly striding Anne FitzGarratt looked a remarkably spry octogenarian for one who had borne eight children and brought them up through adversity. Perhaps that had been her secret to a long life.

I couldn't see any others who might have been FitzGarratts. Nor did I see Maria. Many of the parents and families looked as if they came from backgrounds with money and station. They filled the pews immediately behind the girls, who occupied two-thirds of the cathedral. The lesser classes squeezed into the back, and I sat among them. On my right was a mountain of a wheezing, ham-fisted and barrel-chested man in a suit that didn't suit him.

He was talkative. He introduced himself as Tony and he was a wharfie. 'I don't believe in any of this shit, mate,' he'd wheezed. 'But the Missus does, and so do the lassies.' His 'Missus' shushed him, and he shushed but with a wink to me. His handshake and pat on my shoulder for the sign of peace were warm and genuine.

A dark, tiny woman with sharp, black eyes, her head covered with a black lace shawl, was on my left. Apart from standing, sitting, and kneeling when everyone else did, she took no part in the Mass. She recited her rosary at least four times in a language that might have been Italian.

It was the archbishop again. I overheard a comment that this school's was the only Mass he 'did'.

We didn't sing back at our row, or in the pews where the congregants were older. But that was more than made up by the well-drilled, well-rehearsed teenage girls who praised God and the Virgin Mary with *Hail Queen of Heaven* and '*Immaculate Mary, your praises we sing, You reign now in splendour with Jesus our King. Ah-Vay, Ah-Vay, Ah-Vay Ma-Ree-Ah*'.

The time came for a reading. Maria appeared from the side of the altar. A neat curtsey to the archbishop, who bestowed on her a prelatic smile.

Maria ascended to the lectern, and announced that she was to read a passage from the *Gospel of St John*. That was lost on me.

Anyway, she began to read: it was the story of the woman who'd been caught in the act of adultery. The men who had caught her had dragged her along the road and dumped her in a heap before Jesus.

They had told him what she had done, and that according to the Law, which apparently God himself had given to Moses, the penalty for a woman committing adultery was death by stoning.

In 11 concise verses, I realised many lifetimes later, John had sketched one of the most important stories of the New Testament about the meaning of love and compassion and not judging.

Jesus uttered the famous words: 'He who is without sin among you, let him be the first to throw a stone at her.'

Maria read clearly, steadily, unhurriedly, her amplified voice compelling to listen to. This was something new about her. If she had the jitters about reading in front of a thousand or more people she didn't show it. Her tones, her enunciations floated high through the rafters, reached to the very back, to the heavy wooden doors.

I realised I was proud of her, and a lump formed in my throat and I swallowed hard.

As we all know, the woman's accusers dropped their stones and ran away. Jesus told the woman he didn't condemn her, either, and he instructed her to go away and sin no more. No-one knows whether she did.

I wondered what the message was for these girls. Why that particular passage of the Bible?

I didn't know much about religion except for what Mrs Barlow used to teach us. But it seemed that churches judged and Jesus loved. Mrs Barlow once read to us how Jesus had outraged the Pharisees by drinking and feasting with prostitutes (and you can imagine how I discovered what they were when I consulted Mum and Dad's old Oxford dictionary) and thieves, and the tax-gatherers, whom she said society viewed as the worst of the worst. Why did women who were prostitutes or who had sex outside marriage – as a few young women were eager to, it seemed, then – feel judged and condemned by churches and shun them?

The archbishop didn't say much in his 10 minutes at the lectern. I thought he was going through the motions and was ponderous and patronising.

Mass ended, and girls and their families crowded on to the footpath laughing and talking.

The mountainous wharfie Tony, cigarette between his lips, had his arms around the shoulders of his daughters, three, it seemed. 'See ya, mate,' he said as I passed. Maria seemed to be having a serious conversation with some girls who resembled her and each other. She glanced at me and turned back to the group, which was joined by Matthew and the woman I believed was his wife. Grannie Annie Fitz had waylaid the archbishop. He said something, roared with a bellowing laugh, and she screeched and cackled with unrestrained mirth, secure in his holy favour.

IT WAS midday – there had been a lot of singing and the archbishop had strode up and down the aisles throwing water at the rest of us in the pews, and holy communion took a while, even with priests drafted in to help – and I wasn't sure what to do for the rest of my day off. Anyway, I drove out to have a cup of coffee and some cake at Peter and Magdalena's movie theatre.

'Martin, where have you been?' Magdalena said as I walked in. The café had customers – not a lot, but most seemed to be of the city's theatre and literary set – and so she sat down to 'quiz you about your love life'. She winked and lit a *Gauloise*, the French cigarettes she chain-smoked in every waking hour. 'And that lovely friend Maria? How goes it with her?'

I liked how she remembered Maria's name. I replied that it went well, that Maria and I were going well. I added that she was head girl at Our Lady of The Immaculate Conception College, that she was the youngest in a big, well-known, and academically talented family.

Magdalena listened and smoked and nodded and smiled, with her eyes as well as her mouth. I liked Magdalena. She was warm, and I suspect passionate, and I felt she would be unshakably loyal to those she considered her friends. She lit another cigarette with a dainty flick of a match. A cloud of pungent smoke obscured her face. 'I did not know that she was a school girl, *cheri*.'

'You don't approve?'

Magdalena flicked ash into a heavy Cinzano ashtray. 'What I think doesn't matter, Martin. Age is just a number.'

She drew forcefully on her *Gauloise*. 'I thought she was much older – about your age. But you make a nice couple together.'

The phone rang, and she sighed and got up. 'Come back and see us some time, darling. We have some nice Polish movies. Romantic movies.'

Intimate disclosures

I drove back to my flat about three o'clock and parked the car in the garage. I realised as I sat there that I didn't want to go into the city for work drinks at *The Mafeking*. Usually we drank a lot before staggering off to look for somewhere to eat. And then I still had to get up early next day for a long day. So I thought I would go up to my flat. Maria might turn up. I reached my landing, and the fragrance of her still hung there.

Maria was in my bed, obviously asleep, on her side, her back to me. She breathed slowly, regular and shallow, with a sibilant 'hem … hem …'

I stood in the doorway watching her for perhaps a minute before quietly but quickly getting out of my clothes, tossing them on to the couch next to her neatly placed uniform. She'd fallen asleep reading a book with a French title. I slipped into the bed and kissed her neck, her shoulder. That woke her.

'Oh, Martin,' she purred, and stretched. 'You have a beautiful way of waking up a girl.' She reached for me and we kissed with quick urgency, ragged breathing, and did not waste time. Slowly and gently could come later with the things lovers say afterwards. At the end Maria arched, panted *'I love you!'* and sank her teeth into me.

AS OUR breathing and pulses slowed and the sweat dried on our bodies I turned to her and said: 'Would you like to tell me what all that was about, Maria?'

For the first time I noticed the shadowing under her eyes.

'I had a disagreeable conversation with my sister Stella at breakfast.'

I had an idea what might be coming.

'It seems my sister might have been spying on me.'

Ah.

'About five minutes after I got home last night Tom turned up from work. And he asked me, casually, if I'd been home all evening.'

'And you said yes?'

Maria nodded. 'I was just feeling happy, having been here with you, and so I should have seen the trap.' She changed position so she could see my face better. 'And he said, that's funny, because I rang about 6 o'clock and no-one answered the phone. So I said that perhaps I was in the loo. And he said that Stella had rung about 8 o'clock, and there was no answer.'

'What did you say to that?'

'Nothing. I could see that he – and her – had laid a trap and I had walked right into it.' Hence the worry – the sharp edge of it – in her eyes right then. 'I didn't sleep last night, Martin, and I knew I had the Mass thing today and I wanted that to go well, but I knew my conversation with Tom wasn't the last of it.'

I stroked her back slowly, from her neck down her spine to the cleft of her backside, and back again. 'That's nice when you do that, sweetie. You have a nice touch,' she whispered.

'Breakfast was pretty strained, with her and Tom there. Stella 'accidentally' came into the bathroom just as I was stepping out of the shower.' Maria touched a small bruise on the upper slope of her breast. 'She noticed this – she pointedly stared at it. Anyway, at breakfast she started to question me about where had I been the last two nights. I told her that it was none of her business. She wasn't my mother and father. And she said that because she was the oldest there at home she was like *loco parentis* – you know what that means, Martin?' I did.

'I said I was 17, head prefect at my school, so wasn't a child and that I didn't care about *loco parentis*, thank you very much, and that I was able to look after myself – as I'd had to do for several years now.'

'What did she have to say to that?'

Maria fidgeted, and silently breathed a kind of 'hem' and 'hem'. 'Tom had already told her about you. She said she'd done the washing and had found – and this sounds really disgusting, Martin – *evidence* that I, quote, "you have been up to something".'

Oh, Christ, you poor kid.

'I asked her what she meant. She said that she had detected – and I'm too embarrassed to say it, Martin –'

I kissed her on the forehead. 'It's all right, Maria, I know what she means.'

'Thank you, sweetie. She'd checked it with Tom – can you believe that? (*Yes, sweetie, I can*) – and he apparently confirmed it. And he added he'd detected the smell of coal tar soap on my blouse and bra, too. We don't have coal tar soap in the house. It's *usually 'twa-LETT soap'*, or something common like Lux or Palmolive, which my father and Tom can also use.'

I held her tightly because she had started to cry. 'And she wanted to know how and why I'd got this bruise.' The little purple-maroon mark was incriminating.

Anger boiled in my belly. It was sick, and it seemed the brother-in-law had got some enjoyment out of playing Nose Detective in his sister-in-law's clothing.

'It was humiliating and degrading, Martin.' Her eyes pleaded with mine. 'I've done nothing to be ashamed of.' And she began to sob. 'They've tried to make something beautiful between you and me into something ugly and dirty.'

Her tears dripped on to my chest, and they ran in warm rivulets down my armpit to the sheet.

'I supposed I should have explained some things to you, love, but it never occurred to me,' I said. And I probably wouldn't have known how to broach it.

'It's not your fault, Martin. How were you to know?'

100

We lay in thoughtful silence, and she stopped crying. She hiccupped softly. 'Would you like me to pat your back?' I said. She briefly considered a Head Girl Stare, but laughed softly instead.

'Isn't Stella the sister you've always got on with?'

Maria sniffled; rather, she wiped her nose on my chest before answering. 'Be my guest,' I said.

She started to apologise and wipe her tears away from my chest. I stopped her. 'I was joking.'

She smiled wanly. 'Always. Since I was little she used to take me out with her. Our mother delegated her to get me fitted for my first bra. She got me ready for my periods. Stella was the first person I told when they started. She took me out and bought me new shoes and clothes.' A sniffle. 'I've never encountered her like this. She was quite ugly. It was like we were strangers.'

'And the brother-in-law?'

She scowled. 'Well, I have to say I've always felt uneasy about Tom. I never liked to say it because he was my sister's husband, and because he's a policeman, and his father and grandfather were policemen. But sometimes lately he's seemed to me to be a bit too keen to try to barge into the bathroom when I was there.' Another thoughtful pause: 'But he gets on with my father.'

Her tone turned contemptuous: 'He's ingratiating. He told Stella about seeing you and me. And apparently he's seen us together another time and we didn't know it.'

I wondered when that was. 'What happens now, love? This might not go away.' I was sure it was not going to go away.

'What happens now? You make love to me again, that's what happens now.' She kissed a bruise where my neck joined my shoulder. Her eyes had gone sleepy: 'I promise not to bite so hard this time.'

Butterflies

I offered to drive Maria home early. But she said no-one would be home again. Friday was always busy at the hospital where Stella worked in Emergency. Tom would similarly be busy. 'I don't care if they make phone calls, darling,' Maria said, defiance in her tone and in the tilt of her jaw and the fearless glint in her eyes. *Christ, she's got more courage than I think I would have in her place.*
We had slept in a tangle of each other into the evening and it was well dark.
She headed for the shower. 'See?' she said with a savage triumph as she brandished a soap case taken from her hold-all. 'Lux, as famously used by the women of the Clan FitzGarratt. Lux is supposed to make us women dainty.'
I cooked fish in lemon juice and served it up with rice. The fish was because she observed her Church's rule that Catholics not eat meat on Fridays. 'I do love how you cook such basic food, but do nice things with it, Martin,' she said. I, of course, lapped up the compliment. Mum would probably be proud, too.
Afterwards she began to put on her uniform. Knickers first, then bra. As I hooked the ends together in the centre of her back for her she glanced at the bruise on her breast. 'I hid it like treasure, darling. I thought that if I can't go to sleep with the smell of you on me then I'll go with this.'

On the way out to her place she asked if it was all right to bring her niece Gabrielle on Sunday. I could hardly say no. If it was important to her then that was fine by me.

'I've neglected Gabrielle in the last few weeks, and I want to make it up to her.'

I suggested a movie. Something at Peter and Magdalena's theatre.

'As long as it's suitable for a 12 year-old, fine,' Maria said, and she squeezed my thigh. I nearly drove through a stop sign. She smirked in the dark.

So during a break at work on Saturday I phoned Magdalena and Peter's theatre. She answered: '*Dzień dobry.*'

I explained that we'd like to come out, but that Maria was bringing her niece who was 12. Did they have anything suitable? 'Ja, Martin. I think we have a nice little story. Quite harmless. Private screening just for you and Maria and her niece.'

I WAITED in a soft breeze at the 'bus barn' next afternoon. Maria's bus pulled into the terminal with the customary wheezing and grunting of a geriatric.

The door opened with a loud hiss, and Maria stepped down on to the pavement. She glanced back at the girl coming down the steps of the bus behind her. Maria said something and nodded towards me, and they crossed to where I waited by the car. Gabrielle was nearly as tall as her aunt, pencil-slim, a cautious oval face framed by long, fine hair, held up by a clip at the back. The hair streamed down her back like a glossy, bronze cape. She had careful, grey eyes.

They could have passed as sisters, dressed in matching calf-length skirts belted at the waist, knitted tops, and ankle boots. They walked alike. That same, straight-backed stride with purpose.

'Hello, darling,' Maria said, and we kissed. 'Gabrielle,' Maria said, taking her by the hand, 'this is my friend Martin.'

'Hello, Gabrielle.' She was taller than me by a hair.

'Hi,' she said, glancing at Maria, who smiled reassuringly.

I held the door open for both of them, and Gabrielle folded herself into the back seat, and Maria was beside me.

At the theatre Magdalena said: 'I've found something. A nice little Polish story about young love.' She glanced at Gabrielle, and then at Maria. 'They're all young. No worries.'

She indicated their smallest theatre, which was more like a lounge in a family home but with a big screen. Magdalena said the movie was all in Polish. 'Sorry, my dears, no subtitles. But you'll be able to follow the story. Afterwards come and have coffee or hot chocolate and cake.'

The movie was *Motyle*, or *Butterflies*. Edek – aged perhaps 12 – had come from the city to stay with his aunt, uncle, and cousins. The movie was set in the countryside of Polish forest, glades, and a lake. Edek was attracted to Monika – she was perhaps 11 at most – a long-haired Polish beauty in the making. The mysterious, wraithlike, cartwheeling and bike-riding Monika with a liking for big straw sunhats seemed to be playing a game all of her own, and was several light years ahead of the boys, just out of their reach. Beguiling smiles, bewitching eyes, hinting at promises that boys were too young to grasp.

Jealousy intruded and the game ended in hurt and tears. Maria sat between Gabrielle and me. In her right hand she held mine. In her left, Gabrielle's, and their heads rested together. They giggled quietly when Edek leafed furtively through a medical book showing the female anatomy. 'Boys,' he heard Gabrielle whisper, and they snorted.

We hadn't paid for the movie because Magdalena and Peter weren't supposed to show it because the Censor hadn't seen and rated it yet. But I made sure they got their money's worth from us when we had coffee for me and a particular kind of Polish hot chocolate for Maria and Gabrielle. There were cakes, which prompted Peter to tease them about putting on weight and getting pimples. Gabrielle flushed and took a close interest in an end of her long hair. Maria smiled reassuringly at her and squeezed her hand.

'I think I might have to learn Polish,' Maria mused.

'Do you know other languages?' Magdalena said.

'French, German, and Latin – as well as English, of course.'

Magdalena lit a cigarette, and in a cloud of smoke launched into a rapid stream of French to Maria. I understood not a word, but I did catch a '*cherie*'.

Without hesitation Maria replied in kind, and it seemed to me without stumbling. They went back and forth for a full minute. It was like watching tennis.

'Very good, darling,' Magdalena beamed. 'I lived in Paris after the war. You'd easily pass. Not as a Parisian, perhaps – maybe someone from the east.'

Maria glanced at me shyly, a small smile.

As we chatted on Gabrielle ventured an opinion in what I was beginning to understand her familiar murmur. 'The other girl in the film – Honorka – she seemed to do a lot of the housework while the boys got to play.'

Magdalena winked, and she and Peter complimented her on her perspicacity, a word she understood.

'I knew I had a bright niece,' Maria said, and hugged her warmly. Gabrielle blushed, and her hair drew across her face like a curtain closing.

We stayed on talking to Magdalena and Peter until they had to get ready for a late-afternoon screening of a couple of horror movies. 'They're simply awful,' Peter said, 'but they're enormously hilarious and enormously popular. Full house. We have to turn people away. Let's us screen little-known movies from elsewhere.'

WE WERE between departures when we got back to the bus terminal. 'I'll just go and wait over by the bus shelter, Maria,' Gabrielle murmured. She turned to me: 'Thank you for the outing, Martin. Nice to have met you. By-ee.'

I put my arm around Maria's shoulders. 'Your niece is lovely.'

'She is.' And she glanced at me. 'Like her favourite aunt.'

I chuckled. Sounded like Uncle Syd and me. But I wanted to know if anything more had been said between Maria and Stella.

'Ah. Yesterday morning she tried a different tack. The Nice Big Sister who is Really Concerned for her Little Sister.'

'And?'

'She didn't mean to confront me so aggressively, she said. She was tired and had not slept much. Difficult shift at work. Tom had had to go and tell a mother and father that their son had died in a crash. Then there was a murder. And apparently under all that stress and drama they had also argued at home.'

Maria said all this in a flat, bleak voice.

She hugged herself and moved more into the shelter of my arm. 'I didn't like the look in her eyes, Martin. I couldn't see the sister I thought I knew. They were opaque. Evasive. So were her words, which I thought were weasly.'

I kissed her hair. Gabrielle was seated in the shelter with a book. Maria, I realised, hadn't taken her eyes off her.

'Stella said she just wanted me to tell her the truth. That I could trust her, as I always had. We were sisters, after all. She said she wouldn't tell our mother. She'd let me do that.'

'And what did you say?'

'That I'd met someone, we'd become good friends, and I'd be introducing him to the family soon. But it was as if she was trying to blackmail me – you know, "tell me or I'll tell on you".'

A boy of about 15 sauntered past Gabrielle's shelter. She concentrated on her book as he frankly appraised her. Maria stilled and watched him intently. He passed, and I felt her relax. 'She was still angling to find out what I had been doing with you. I refused to discuss it. I told her it was my business.'

The breeze fluttered at her skirts, the folds flapping across her boots. 'She went on to lecture me about the necessity of a woman saving herself for her husband, how her virginity is a gift to him, and how a woman loses something and becomes cheap in the eyes of a man if she gives it away too easily. He loses respect for her.'

She glanced at me: 'Have I become cheap in your eyes, Martin? Have you lost respect for me? Am I a slut?'

I wasn't going to say no. '… even before I met you, you conveyed a dignity and maturity that stood out from 25 yards and in a crowd.'

Maria put a hand up to mine on her shoulder, and squeezed it. 'You're very sweet, Martin, you know that?'

I tried a self-deprecating reply.

'No, Martin, don't. You put yourself down too much. You undersell yourself.'

Did I? I often used to refer to myself as a typical, laconic, moronic Kiwi bloke – not flashy.

Gabrielle got up and went to look at the timetable. She consulted it, looked into the distance along the street, shrugged at us, and returned to her seat and her book.

'It'll be soon, sweetheart,' Maria called across the 25 yards or so to the shelter.

'In a minute I'll go and sit with her. But I just wanted to say that Stella then tried to scare me by asking if I'd thought what would happen if I got pregnant.'

The thought had occurred to me, and I was about to say so when Maria added: 'She knows bloody well that's not going to happen because she knows bloody well that I can't get pregnant.'

As Manuel, the waiter in *Fawlty Towers*, would say: 'Que?' And she had said 'bloody' twice in one sentence. Maria was not a girl whose lips uttered what is known as swearing. Even the harmless 'bloody' was a stretch.

We heard the bus coming, and Gabrielle put her book into her shoulder bag. Maria turned to kiss me goodbye. 'Another long story, darling. For another time.'

Gathering clouds

Maria came to my flat on Tuesday afternoon. We kissed when she walked in the door, and I could tell she was subdued.

'I told my mother last night that I had a friend, a guy, who was coming to meet the family on Sunday.'

'How did that go?'

Maria frowned. 'I think it went well. She asked if it was anyone from a family she and my father would know. I said you worked for the *Evening Herald*, and that you'd been in the city only a few months. That prompted her to ask how old you were. I said 23.'

'What did she say?'

'Not much. And I don't know whether to be worried by that. Just that she'd look forward to meeting you. Then she said she had to catch up on a backlog of work.'

We stood in the middle of my little lounge for a long time, in our embrace, wordless.

ON WEDNESDAY afternoon when I got home Maria was already at my typewriter doing an essay on the French Revolution. A book review was next. An essay in French after that. Then there was a Latin translation.

We kissed, cuddled, and I left her to it. I'd let Sue Devonshire in on my little secret when she came into the clip-file library and found me poring over old stories about the end of World War 2. The 30th anniversary of VE Day, when the war in Europe ended in May 1945, was weeks away.

'I watched you at that Mass the other week. You seemed to be looking a lot at the FitzGarratts. Then the note from Maria. What's going on?'

Hell. Was I that obvious? I told her I was going with the youngest FitzGarratt.

'Maria. The head prefect at Our Lady of The Immaculate Conception.'

'Si.'

'A very well-known and established family in the city, and very well connected. You don't want to cross them, especially the parents and Matthew, the QC.' Sue laid a delicate, friendly hand on my shoulder. 'Despite their Christian smiles they can fight nasty, especially over any slight to their reputation.'

'Apart from Maria, are any of them nice?'

'I was at school with Tessa. She got married last year and I was invited to her wedding.' She paused in thought. 'I can't say we were great mates. The FitzGarratts and their friends seem to exist on a plane higher than most of us. So I was a bit surprised, yet she made a big enough fuss of me at the reception.'

'What do you know about Our Lady of The Immaculate Conception College?'

Sue smiled. 'I went there for four years. My father's a plumber and my mother worked in an accountant's office to pay for me and my three sisters to go there. It ain't cheap.'

Sue sat in the chair next to mine. 'Girls get a bloody good education there, Martin. The nuns there belong to an order started by French and Belgian noblewomen in the time of Napoleon. They still have access to money from those days. And because they had to prove to the authorities they were at least equal to their state school systems, such as they had then, they made sure their nuns were damned well-educated.'

Sue was warming to her subject, and with obvious pride. 'Our Lady of The Immaculate Conception is probably not the only school in New Zealand whose principal has a PhD. But I doubt if there are many schools in Australia and New Zealand where a doctorate is mandatory for department heads. For the rest, a master's with honours is the absolute minimum.'

The order ran schools in Europe, North and South America, India; Our Lady of The Immaculate Conception was their only one in New Zealand.

'They're top-notch and do a top-notch job.' Sue adopted a self-mocking smile as she preened. 'I mean. Look at me.' And she laughed. 'Sister Lucille wasn't surprised I went into journalism. She always said it would give me great material for the novels she expected me to write.'

Sue switched to being serious again. 'I've met Maria a few times, Martin. I'm not in the least surprised she's head girl. And it's not because it runs in the family. I've heard people say she's one of her family's very brightest. And she'll be dux at the end of the year, too. From what I've heard no-one comes close to a bull's roar to her. Or a cow's.'

Jesus! Dux! Maria didn't talk herself up. She was always matter-of-fact about herself. And she had chipped at me the other day about underselling myself. And yet just watching her work … well that spoke volumes, I guess. I didn't know many reporters who could knock out 500 words – let alone 2000, let alone in another language – almost without pausing frequently. Whatever her family was like, she had absorbed some habits about working and studying.

Sue's gaze had been what I would call shrewd. Large, brown eyes squinting a little, lips puckered expectantly. She slipped a Topaz cigarette – 'freedom is … being yourself when others aren't' – between her lips and lit it with a red Bic disposable lighter.

'How deeply are you in with Maria, Martin?' She spoke softly, almost intimately, like a reporter would to get someone to spill. Her eyes were deeply interested in me, and in my answer.

How does one define 'in'?

I wasn't going to tell her we were sleeping together. 'Deeply enough.'

Sue gazed at me for a long time. I think she wanted to say something, but then decided the better of it. She crushed out her cigarette on an ashtray and got up to leave. 'If you two need a friend, just say. OK, Martin?' She patted my hand.

Yes, Sue, OK.

I came out of my daydream and realised Maria had stopped working, and had spoken to me. She was watching me. A small smile played with her lips.

'Where did you go, my love?' she said, standing, stretching her arms and crossing the room to me. She sat astride me and wrapped her arms around my head and hugged me. *Oh-h-h-h* ... My hands slid slowly along her thighs, idly caressing.

'Hmmm,' she breathed, her eyes clouding. 'That's very nice. Keep doing that.' So I did, and her muscles flexed under my touch.

'But where did you go? You were gazing into space for what seemed ages.' Her face was very close to mine, and her eyes were shifting side-to-side to mine, and her breath was warm and soft. We were in a cloud of her aromas.

I couldn't tell her that I'd been discussing Maria FitzGarratt and family with a friend at work. So I went for a side-step. 'I was thinking. What does a head girl do?'

She drew back, frowning, like, I imagined, a fourth-former had made a barely plausible excuse for some transgression. 'Really? What an odd thing to be wondering about.' Her eyes were twin beams of scepticism. They were unnerving.

I tried distraction again. I shrugged, and eased her back to me and kissed her.

'Well?'

'Well,' she said, smiling, 'I'm a kind of chief policewoman. And I do ceremonial stuff, representing the student body and all that. For some of that I have to smile politely, curtsey, and look respectful and keep my mouth shut unless I have to say the Right Thing.'

She smiled briefly. 'That, my love, is probably what you and people in your trade would call the short story.' She pressed her loins at mine and allowed herself a contented sigh. 'Anyway, the correct wearing of the uniform among the girls is my responsibility. Fourth- and fifth -formers in particular hate it and hate me and the other prefects. There are 12 of us. I tell them they should have pride in their appearance as women. That's mainly what it's about.'

She was stroking my hair absently. 'But some girls don't want to have pride in their appearance. It's not cool these days. And they kick against the rules all the time.'

She sniffed. 'It's a waste of time because I won't budge, and I have the backing of Sister Hélène anyway.'

'You do look the part,' I said.

'Only out there, my love,' she said softly. 'I don't have to here with you.' She kissed me lingeringly. She sighed at a pleasant distraction. 'And keep doing what your hands are doing,' she murmured, a slight husk in her voice. They were caressing her rump. 'I can give detentions – only the head girl can do that. All of us prefects can punish by assigning extra duties to naughty girls, or getting them to write things out.'

'"I must not be a naughty girl" 500 times.'

'Yes.'

Then she looked at me seriously, head tilted: 'Were you a naughty boy at school, Martin?'

'Not very. I was always afraid of getting the cane. And my parents were the type that if you got into trouble at school then you were in a shit heap of trouble at home.' I paused. 'Fear of punishment does that to people, I think. Makes them good rule-keepers but little else.'

By now she was responding unambiguously to what my hands were doing. 'We should continue this next door, love.'

She touched me. 'Hmm. Yes. He's looking for a door to go into.'

IN THE drowsy aftermath we lapsed into a companionable silence after whispering words of love and appreciation. Distant traffic murmured and honked occasionally; birds in the trees outside twittered.

'There's another thing I – and my deputy and a couple of other prefects – do, and it's sort of counselling.'

'Oh? You do seem to have a lot of responsibility put on you.'

'Well,' and she propped herself up on her elbow and rested her head in the palm of her hand, 'that's what a lot of the job is. Training in responsibility and learning to do it without being a bitch about it.'

Her fingers crawled slowly through the hairs on my chest. 'A lot of girls arrive at school not knowing how to take care of themselves. No-one's explained anything to them about their bodies and what's going on with them. Or they've been given very screwy ideas. So we talk to them, and sometimes show them what to do. The nuns are happy for us to do that in most cases because girls can feel embarrassed talking to an adult. Especially a stranger. And especially someone in a habit that no-one would believe would know what a period was.'

'And they do?'

The Head Girl Look: 'I think so, Martin. Under all their habits and veils and rosary bead piety they are women just like the rest of us. I don't think God has excused them from the Curse. Sister Colette is noticeably regular.' She eyed me for some reaction to that.

'Does it embarrass you or make you feel awkward when I talk like that, darling?'

I said it didn't. I've known men who didn't want to know. That seemed silly to me. I was mulling, though, whether to ask her about her comment the other day about her not getting pregnant.

We relapsed into silence. She put her head on my chest and we held hands. It was getting on for 4.30pm. I didn't want her to go, and I don't think she did, either. Partings were getting harder and harder now.

So I attempted delay. 'Have you always been accustomed to responsibility? I can't imagine you not being given responsibility and exercising it.'

Maria thought about that. 'Yes. It runs through the family.' She shrugged. 'Look at my parents. Leaders in their fields and in the groups they're involved with. Then look at all my brothers and sisters. They're all naturally the ones people look to to take the lead.'

She sat up now, and I knew that was prelude to the next step – heading off to the shower, and then disappearing back into the uniform, item by item, in which she looked so immaculate.

'It's an atmosphere you're born into and grow up in. You absorb it without realising it. When you're shown how to change a nappy at age 7, or make up a bottle of milk and heat it, or run a bath for a little one, and it's all shown to you as a matter of course, you think this is normal for everybody. It was the same for all my sisters. We all learned to cook and wash and clean. And to study and get a good education. Education is everything.'

'It sounds very brisk and efficient, in a female sort of way.'

'Well, there's nothing wrong in learning to organise yourself and be responsible for yourself. We pack our own bags because no-one else should be expected to pack them for you. You shouldn't be late. No-one should be expected to hold your hand and do for you what you can do for yourself.'

She took my hand, kissed it tenderly, and rested it gently against her breast. 'I was about 9 before it dawned on me that not everyone came from families of a dozen or more kids.' She leaned over and kissed me on the nipple, the one she'd found – and so had I – was particularly sensitive. She looked up and her eyes were sad. 'But now, my love, I must go and shower the smell of you off me and turn myself into an advertisement for Lux soap.'

I watched as she walked un-self-consciously into my tiny bathroom. She had put her own soap and conditioner and shampoo on the holder in the shower. She had bought a toothbrush and toothpaste, as well.

ALL TOO soon Maria was back being Head Girl, Immaculate Keeper of the Clothing Rules. We said little as I drove her to the bus stop not far from her place. Because of Easter weekend we were unlikely to see each other before Sunday. She gave me instructions on when to turn up. We clung together desperately before I went and opened the car door for her. A grey police Holden with two constables in the front seat cruised past as she stepped on to the footpath. She turned to me, her expression bleak. 'That was Tom driving.'

Meeting the family

Just before midday I drove out to Maria's place on Easter Day for the big lunch of FitzGarratt friends and family. I must have been the first to arrive because apart from Ford and Holden station-wagons, a Leyland P76, and a Jag – even a Fiat *Bambina* – in the drive there didn't seem to be a lot of people about.

The house – vast, two storeys, wood and brick, at least two balconies on the upper level – was set in the middle of grounds dotted with trees already in the middle of the fall. I stepped over shoals of damp leaves cluttering the curving gravel path to the front door.

I mounted wooden steps to the wide, wrap-around veranda at the front of the FitzGarratt house, and pushed a button under an arty-crafty sign that said: 'Press This.' So I did.

Maria answered the door, and smiled nervously as we kissed. 'Come in, darling,' she murmured, and led me by the hand into the dark caverns of a house that some would call rambling.

It was 'lived in' – in other words, not spartanly tidy, but not unkempt, either. Someone had been baking, probably cakes and scones going by the warm aromas. It was like inhaling sugar and cinnamon. Despite my nervousness my mouth watered.

Her parents waited in a small living room that seemed to double as an office or study. Maria adopted a formality I'd never heard before.

'Martin, I'd like you to meet my parents, Peirse and Órla FitzGarratt.'
She turned to them, smiling: 'This is my friend Martin Blake.'

Hands were shaken briefly, formally, along with the 'How do you do?'
I called him 'Doctor', although as a specialist, according to medical
protocol, I supposed he was a 'Mister'.

Peirse was tall, bony-thin, broad across the shoulders, long arms with
big hands that were soft, grey eyes in deep-sunk hollows, and with a
careless tumble of grey-and-black hair about a large head. He reminded
me of a caricature of an absent-minded professor. He was polite.

Órla was small and birdlike, and I wondered how she could have
carried at least 14 babies in her small frame. I could see where Maria
got her strong jaw and determined tilt to her chin from. Her greying hair
was fastened into a loose bun on the back of her head with a large clip.

But what got your attention were her eyes. Brown almost to the point of
black, sharp, not piercing, but certainly the shrewd eyes that could look
into your soul and uncover your secrets, your lies, your inadequacies –
the sort of eyes that would find you out. She, too, was polite.

'Martin is a sub-editor at the *Evening Herald*,' Maria said diffidently.

'Oh, really,' Peirse, said, and he had a light baritonal voice. 'And how
long have you been there?'

I replied about nine months. He went on to tell me that he'd known
O'Neill, the leader writer, since they were at school, and Brady, one of
the feature writers – he'd known his father 'since we were in the
bassinets at the maternity hospital together'. I had no doubt he would
check up on me.

All the time Órla said nothing, letting him and me do the talking while
she watched, lips stretched in her smile. Maria stood to the side hoping,
I think, that her choice of boyfriend would win their approval.

The door opened and we all turned. 'Is this a private meeting or can
anyone join?' The short, fleshy man I'd seen at the Masses I'd guessed
was Matthew, the QC.

'Come in, Matthew,' Peirse called over my head. 'Maria was just
introducing us to Michael.'

'Martin,' Maria murmured as I turned, extending my hand to Matthew,
who strode towards me, his own thrust forward. Maria introduced

Matthew and me with the same formality she had shown moments earlier. His apparent friendliness and informality were striking.

'So you're Maria's catch of the day, then, Martin?' He made a joke about 'the press being full of make-up artists' that I'd heard a dozen or so times before. But I didn't feel a sting about it.

A woman in her mid-40s joined us, an ash blonde who perhaps before marriage and babies had probably been strikingly pretty. The shadows around her eyes connoted worry and lack of sleep, and perhaps of having too much to do.

'This is Kay, my wife, Martin.' I shook a pallidly offered hand, noted her formal smile, and she turned and kissed cheeks with her parents-in-law. The sisters-in-law, Maria and Kay, smiled formally.

The talk followed the usual phatic path – the weather, who was likely to turn up this afternoon, some family gossip such as Matthew and Kay's young son had picked up nits at his new school. Oh, the shuddering horror. Outraged complaints to the school.

'That used to be known only in poor households,' Peirse said.

'But even straitened circumstances among the poor was often no excuse,' Órla added. 'Even in the 30s most mothers were very house-proud.'

Kay had washed and ironed or aired all his bedding. The boy's four sisters' hair had been gone through with a fine-tooth comb. Perhaps that's why she looked so worn. Maria and I had become spectators, standing closely together, seemingly forgotten. Which I was happy about.

Heads turned expectantly to the door at the approaching sound of a rasping, old-woman's voice with an Irish accent elsewhere in the house and the lighter tones of children. She was talking to children, but you could hear the steps of her brogues clumping towards the room we were in.

Anne FitzGarratt burst into the room with a wheezy gust of noise, blue-rinsed bustle, and solid shoes that squeaked as she walked.

'Hello t'ere how're' ye' all Peirse meboy ye bin keepin' well Órla ye're lookin splendid as youse-sual and Matt love how is me favourite oldest grandson hello Kay.'

117

Small, bright blue eyes in a face rutted and aged by years and determined struggle rested on me, rather like a hawk on a carcass in a paddock, before shifting to Maria, and then to Peirse. 'An' who's t'is?'

Maria spoke, and with the same grave formality she'd used for the other introductions: 'Gran, I'd like to introduce my friend Martin.' She turned to me as I extended my hand: 'Martin, this is my grandmother, Mrs FitzGarratt.'

Grannie didn't take the proffered hand. Instead her eyes swept up and down me and she barked: 'Are'ye a *Cahth*-lic?'

'No, Mrs FitzGarratt, I'm not.' And I was acutely aware of several pairs of eyes on me.

'Well, t'en, y' and hor are westin' each other's toim keepin' company, an't ye?' she said in dismissal, and turned away.

Awkward silence, because at first I had to remind myself: *did I just hear that?*

Yes, I had, and so had everyone else. The truth out in the open, unable to be ignored. This old hag had just treated me and Maria – particularly Maria – with a casual, sweeping, and callous contempt. I sneaked a glance at her; her face was impassive. Peirse and Órla looked grave in their politeness, but there was a telling glance between the two.

Maria was In Trouble.

Surprisingly, Matthew tried to rescue matters. 'Martin,' he said with a friendly smile and a hand on my shoulder, 'Come with me. I think I can find you a beer? Ria? Want to come, and we'll find a glass of wine for you.'

She smiled tensely, murmured 'excuse me' to her parents, pointedly ignored her grandmother, took my hand and squeezed it painfully as we went to follow Matthew and Kay from the room.

'Just a moment,' Peirse called. He gestured: 'Close the door, Matthew.' His son cocked an eyebrow, but shut the door.

Peirse turned to Maria and me. 'We need not spend any more time on this,' he said crisply, probably in best detached bedside manner. 'Maria. No. This is not acceptable. You know why. Michael, I must ask you not to see Maria any more. It's simply inappropriate. We are Catholics. You are not. You're not welcome here. Please, just go.' I heard Maria gasp, and he glanced sharply down his nose at her. 'This association with Maria is over.'

Maria was clinging to my hand. 'No,' she said shakily, 'No, you can't do this. I love him! And his name is *Martin!* You are not going to tell me –'

'Maria, go to your room,' her mother said. A measured gap: 'We will discuss this later.'

Maria didn't move. A storm roared in my head.

'Dad …' I heard Matthew start to say.

'No, that's enough. Everybody. This is not open to discussion.' He turned to Maria: 'Do as your mother said.' She didn't move. Neither parent seemed to know what to do. Perhaps appearances had to be kept up. 'Mi – er, Martin. I must ask you, again. Please leave. Matthew? See him off the property.'

I was just beginning to untangle my hand from Maria's unflinching grip when dear old Grannie Annie Fitz lobbed in her grenade. 'An' she's been sleepin' with 'im, haven' ye, yer dor-tee leet-tle trollop,' she sneered in that ugly manner of the accuser.

Fuck! What?

'An' ye t'art nor one wid found out, didn' ye?' she jeered up at her granddaughter's face.

'Slut!' – she spat with relish, and it rhymed with 'foot'.

Even at 85 Grannie Annie Fitz knew how to shock and awe.

Órla's smooth, pencil-black eyebrows concertina'd: 'Maria. Is that true?'

Maria remained mute.

'O' course it's true. She brought hor filt' home an' t'art she could just wash her sin away in t' washin' machine, didn't ye?'

'Gran, I think that's enough,' Matthew began.

She didn't waste time with him, either, even if he was 44 and a Queen's Counsel. 'An' ye can shut yer face, too,' she snarled, her eyes bluer in their viciousness.

His mouth clamped shut.

She turned back to Maria: 'Stroompet! Ye're no better 'n a whore from the streets.'

'Oh, I'm a stroompet and a whore, as well as a trollop and a sloot,' Maria said softly, mockingly. 'My, you have expanded your vocabulary, haven't you?'

I heard Órla and Kay gasp. The old woman raised her hand to slap her. Maria didn't flinch. And, I don't know if it was instinct or what, but my free arm shot out and barred the blow. It hurt. I heard myself say: 'Don't you *dare* hit her.'

Maria's hand squeezed mine harder.

Once again, Matthew intervened. 'I think this has gone far enough, Gran, don't you?'

'Mammie,' Peirse attempted ineffectually, perhaps conscious of appearances, 'please. This is not helpful.'

She spun around to confront him: "Not helpful',' she mimicked nastily. Her forefinger jabbed. 'What ye shuld be doin' is foindin' Luke and makin' t'is little madam go down on hor knees an' confess hor *for-ni-ca-shun.*'

Oh, she loved saying that word, trundling it out slowly and deliciously, syllable by syllable, turning it over like a chocolate in her mouth.

'I've done nothing wrong,' Maria said loudly.

'Have you, er …' and Órla was clearly swallowing her distaste as she asked, 'Maria, what have you been doing?'

'I don't have to explain anything,' and she glanced dismissively at her grandmother.

Peirse cleared his throat. 'That's not a denial, Maria.'

'And while you're still a minor, living under our roof, going to a school we pay to educate you, you're our responsibility,' Órla said decisively. 'And so you will tell us what you've been up to. Sex outside marriage is sinful. Not to mention that you're too young for *that.*'

Maria said nothing; the silence in the small room was tense, and for the first time I heard the heavy, slow *tock-tock-tock* of a wall clock above the fireplace.

She had not let go my hand.

Peirse and Órla stood off to the side, Matthew and Kay to the other; I couldn't tell what they thought of it all. Kay looked troubled.

But Grannie Annie … she couldn't keep quiet. 'Oi'll tell ye wha' she's bin doin',' she rasped. Her forefinger jabbed towards me. 'She's bin spreadin' hor legs for him.'

'Yes, you've said that, Grandmother, but what proof do you have?' Matthew said.

Oh, how QC.

Her old, lined face beamed gleefully. 'I'm pleased y'asked, laddie. Go 'n ask Stella and Tom wha' they found on hor clothes – hor knickers! – when they went to wash them.'

'I think I'm going to be sick,' Maria said dully.

'Yer should be, yer shameless little whore, but not fer wha' yer t'ink.' The full beam of her china blue eyes switched to me: 'They had his *sap* on them,' she jeered. 'T'ey gave me a sniff!'

As if that was a triumph. *Christ …*

'Oh!' Kay gasped, and she burst into tears and fled the room.

Peirse swallowed, and Órla's hand had darted to her open mouth.

I couldn't tell which horrified them most: Grannie's brutally-given revelations, her obvious glee, or the dawning on them that their well-bred, well brought-up, Catholic school head girl daughter had been cavorting in bed with me.

And she turned to me: 'An' he'd been chewin' on her leettle tit-tie …'

Ye Gods …

A small knock at the door.

'Yes!' Peirse shouted.

The door was pushed open timidly. A girl of maybe 11, green eyes in an elfin face framed by long red hair, stood uncertainly. 'I'm sorry, Grandpa. Please excuse me,' she said hesitantly, her eyes skittering across us. 'But his grace the archbishop, Uncle Luke, and Monsignor Great Uncle Brian are here.'

Peirse frowned. *Bloody inconvenient.*

'All right, Antonia,' Órla said in what I took to be a soothing, grandmotherly tone accompanied by a smile. 'Thanks, dear.'

Antonia stood aside as the archbishop strode past her into the room. 'Peirse! Órla!' he boomed, 'wonderful to see you again. Happy Easter!'

Peirse, Órla and Grannie Annie quickly put their smiles on.

'Hello, Ray, you, too.' First-name terms with the archbishop? I thought that quite unusual. I didn't recognise him at first, without his robes and mitre. Here he was dressed in simple black, the usual white collar. He hugged Órla. Luke was a big lad, running to fat, today in jeans, casual shirt and jacket. The third priest, Great Uncle Brian, was Órla's brother.

The archbishop turned to greet Grannie: 'Annie!' And, for God's sake, she creaked into a shallow, shaky curtsey. 'Good afternoon, Yer Grace. Lovely t'at you could spare the toim to be here wit' us.'

She was bestowed a fond kiss on the forehead and another blessing. She glowed brighter.

Matthew was greeted next, and his father suggested he might like to get 'Archbishop Ray and Uncle Brian a whisky'.

The archbishop beamed, and clapped his hands jovially.

Then it was Maria and me. He grinned broadly: 'Ave, Maria,' and he chuckled at his own little joke. She smiled politely.

His attention turned to me: shrewd brown eyes, thick, iron-grey hair combed across his scalp, lined face. An invisible wreath of Hollandia pipe tobacco. 'We've met?'

Ah. An old trick employed by MPs, VIPs, and would-bes-if-they-could-bes. It puts the other person on a kind of defensive. Usually we're polite and we'd answer by introducing ourselves.

Maria beat me to it: 'Your Grace, I would like to introduce my friend Martin Blake. Martin, Archbishop Boyce.' We shook hands cordially enough, and there was a brief attempt at small-talk – the weather, last night's midnight Mass, which the Clan FitzGarratt had attended – before Matthew interposed with a large glass of whisky and we were forgotten.

More arrivals streamed in: a justice of the local Bench of the Supreme Court, a leading Catholic member of Parliament; doctors and lawyers whose names featured in the media, people from the university; wives, families. The house was filling up, voices were loud, and so was the laughter.

I wasn't introduced to Luke; he seemed to avoid Maria. But she did introduce me to her Uncle Brian, the monsignor. He was a towering 6ft-7in. He had a gentle face, a kind glint in his eye, a gentle voice, and a gentle manner. I warmed to him instinctively. Maria stretched up on tiptoe to plant a fond kiss on his cheek. He had one of those voices that came from deep in his chest so that it carried but also sounded as soft as a wave lapping a beach.

Matthew tugged at my sleeve. 'Come on, you, two, while the going's good,' he said. 'I think it's time we got you that drink.'

Family niceties

Following Matthew, Maria and I quickly escaped into the noisy people packing into the house. 'Ria? I didn't know you were called Ria.'
'It surprised me,' she said. 'I haven't been called Ria since I was about 12, and I don't remember ever by Matt, either.'
Matthew led us into a large lounge where the drinks were. Glasses and bottles of beer and spirits and wine waited on a large, cloth-covered trestle table. He threaded a path to it as he greeted friends and relatives and kissed and shook hands. He poured me a beer and a large white wine – McWilliams – for Maria, which he handed to her with a friendly smile and wink. Going by the expression on her face I got the impression she wasn't used to this treatment from her oldest brother and that she was wondering what the catch was.
He selected and poured himself a generous single malt scotch, to which he added a small measure of water. He held his glass up. 'Cheers,' he said.
We cheered quietly and sipped. We manoeuvred into a quiet corner. Maria touched his arm: 'Thanks for your help back in there, Matt. That was awful.'
He grinned and gave his sister a gentle hug. 'No worries, Ria. I won't say this loudly but that old witch can be a bit much.'
'What do we do now?' I said.

He stared into his whisky while he thought. Then: 'Enjoy the party. Nothing's going to happen while all this' – and he indicated the noise and growing crowd around him – 'is happening.'

'But it's not going to go away, is it?' she said.

His grey-blue eyes didn't seem as cold and as impersonal as I'd first thought from a distance, and now they were warmly compassionate. 'No. But you can count on me.'

I glanced at Maria. Her mouth was open, speechless, and her eyes searched his face. She found her words: 'Thank you, Matt. That's most unexpected of you.' Her lips curled and twisted as she thought about what to say next. Her eyes didn't flinch from meeting his: 'You probably know – you must know – that what our grandmother said was true.'

He showed no reaction.

'We – Martin and I – are in love with each other. And … and, well, we haven't waited for the big wedding.'

He smiled, and I was beginning to like this guy more. The less he looked like a respectable Silk and Pillar of the Law the more human he seemed to become.

'I'm sure there's a way around it,' he said. 'Now, if you'll excuse me, I'd better go and find Kay and play nicely with our guests.' He disappeared into the talking and laughing press of family and visitors.

Maria introduced me to more members of her family. Her older twin sisters Rebecca and Esther, both 41, and Bridget, 38, a doctor, and their husbands. They were polite, but Bridget asked Maria, and with a fixed smile and malicious eyes, who had given her the glass of wine.

'Is that a serious question, Bridge?'

Put on the defensive, Bridget tried the wide-eyed, innocent 'what's the problem I was just joking Maria darling calm down ha-ha'. I took an instant dislike to Bridget, and her toadying husband, Mark.

I slid my hand over to Maria's, took it, squeezed it and held on to it as the three sisters and their husbands poured themselves drinks and moved on.

Tessa, youngest before Maria was born, taller by half a head than Maria, slim, flirty eyes and large, batting eyelashes, professionally charming, and her husband, Joe, an Irishman. He was built like a rugby prop, rugged, obviously muscular, thick, wild, brown hair and mutton-chops, and you could tell that was part of the charm for her. They, too, were lawyers.

Maria carefully introduced us with solemn formality. I felt for her, really, because I could sense the deep tension she was under. She had barely touched her wine; for that matter, I was making sure I went very slowly on my beer.

Tessa bestowed a kiss on her little sister's politely proffered cheek and a toothpaste ad's smile on me and a strong, muscular hand. 'You work for the *Evening Herald*, then?' I replied yes, as I wondered how she knew that. 'Sue Devonshire is a big friend of mine,' she went on, and then without stopping. 'We were best friends at school. We did everything together.' I remembered that Sue's version of the friendship had been different. I smiled as warmly as I could, and said that Sue and I were good friends, too. 'Oh? Really? We must all get together some time soon. Have coffee.'

Her brother Mark – yes, another Mark – a lawyer, 36, and less likeable than Matt, I instinctively felt, was next. His wife was Margaret, sharp-eyed, who at a glance took in what every other female in the room was wearing. Gabrielle, their daughter, latched on to Maria with a hug and a secret smile and a barely audible 'Hi, Martin'.

Gabrielle was the door-opening Antonia's older sister. Mark and Margaret moved on. Gabrielle reluctantly, too, after a brisk 'come along, Gabrielle', from her mother.

Gemma, Rosemary, Elizabeth who was Luke's twin, and their husbands. It was a struggle keeping up. I was, I think, a curiosity – not very interesting, but still a curiosity; they had their own young children. But more, I was taking note how they spoke to Maria. I can't say there was a lot of warmth, but … well, with families who can tell? I didn't have brothers and sisters to compare with.

Maria's older nieces came by, as well. They were curious, of course, in a way that only teenage girls can be. 'You are a dark horse, where have you been hiding him, Auntie Maria?' the smirking Catharine simpered. I could feel Maria cringe.

Departure

The FitzGarratt women – Órla, her daughters and daughters-in-law, and older granddaughters – combined to serve up an enormous banquet of food to go with the barbecue'd meat that Peirse, Tom, and the archbishop were presiding over, tongs in one hand, drinks in the other. Maria kept her distance from her mother, and did her bit amid the flock of women as they laid the trestle tables. It was like watching a well-practised machine in action.

The archbishop was called on to bless the feast, which he did, and he led grace, as well. Most of the assembled blessed themselves at the end. I tried to be invisible, but Monsignor Brian struck up a conversation with me. He loved rugby, and he was keenly anticipating the start of the club season. He was chaplain of a Marist team, and coach of another, much younger team of boys he was trying to keep out of borstal or jail or away from the attentions of the law. That sounded like an interesting story to me, but a member of Parliament eased in effortlessly and took over. As I retreated I saw Brian wink resignedly to me over the fat little MP's head.

Later on I was standing within earshot of two politicians. One was a Cabinet minister; the other his political opposite. Neither liked the prime minister, nor the man who would become PM at the election in a few months. The Cabinet minister would lose his job at the General Election later in the year; it would go to the man he was talking to.

JUST AS proceedings were growing raucous under the combined weight of food and drink and joy in Christ's Resurrection Maria took my hand. 'Come with me, darling.'

'Where are we going?'

'Don't you remember? I was told to go to my room.'

'But —'

'I always do as I'm told.'

She couldn't be serious.

She wasn't, and she smiled wanly. 'Come on. We need to talk.'

We mounted a narrow set of stairs and trod quietly down a long hallway of faded-pattern carpet showing the occasional worn spot, around a corner, into a tight alcove. She opened a door and we stepped into a large corner bedroom.

'Crikey', I whispered, awed, as she shut and locked the door behind her. The room, I reckoned, would have been as big as my flat.

It was a girl's room. Fragrant and perfumy, cream and discreet pastel colours, wood panelling. Single bed, impeccably made, between two nightstands – bedside lamp and small radio on one, books in a neat pile beside a white statue with blue edging of the Virgin Mary on the other. A frilly burgundy valance. Neat, tidy, uncluttered, everything in its place – in drawers, the wardrobe, cupboards, bookshelves.

A big, old, government department-issue desk squatted at the window, attended by an old wooden chair with armrests. It was like the ones in our reporters' room. Papers and books were carefully arranged about the table; the big typewriter neatly on a small side table with castors.

She smiled and wrapped her arms around me and rested her head against mine. I stroked her back slowly, and then down to her backside. 'Hmmm,' she purred. 'I'm almost tempted to drag you to my bed and have my way with you, right under their noses.' Then she giggled. 'Or right above their noses.'

'Better not, sweetie,' I murmured into her ear. 'Your grandmother's already had her thrill. Sniffing more of my 'sap' might make her heart race so fast she'll have a heart attack.'

Maria giggled again, and her lips tracked from my cheek to my lips. It was a long kiss.

'That was gruesome. I knew my grandmother could be awful but didn't realise she could be so diabolical. When the target is you then you really see her and her venom for what they are.'

Her hand brushed across my hair. 'I'm sorry you had to hear that, Martin.'

I tried to be reassuring. 'You don't have to apologise, sweetie. You were the one she was calling all the names.'

She smiled, and I kissed her gently. We sat on her bed, side-by-side, holding hands.

'What are we going to do? Your parents have put the stop on us, and I'm supposed to be not here.'

She planted my hand on her breast and held it there with her own. 'I love you, Martin. They're not going to tell me otherwise, and they're not going to tell me we can't see each other.'

'It's going to become very rough for you, love. They're still your parents, and they can cause you a lot of trouble.' She looked down at her lap.

'On top of my not being a Catholic, and we've slept together, and they'll be angry and disappointed about that, and your age, and my age, they're going to think that you're making a big mistake, that you're being emotional –'

'– and yes hormonal. I know, and I'm not mature enough to be making such big decisions, and in a few weeks it'll all have blown over and I'm left shop-soiled and in need of absolution from my holy brother the father to make me pure again …'

We were lost in thought. Outside, and down below, people were leaving, calling farewells, a car was started up, doors banged shut. It was just before four o'clock.

'If it becomes intolerable,' I said finally, 'you can always come to my place.'

She smiled, surprised.

'It's a bit small. This room is much bigger. There's only one bed, but it's big enough for both of us. The bathroom's tiny. We'll have to share.' I shrugged. 'But school will be just around the corner.'

The idea had been lurking at the back of my mind all afternoon.

I knew she'd be in for it with her parents later, and probably Grannie Annie Fitz ringleading it.

I didn't want her to face that alone. I didn't want us to be split apart.

But coming with me also meant … what? What was the future for us? Just bare weeks ago we were falling in love with each other, without care and without worries, and if truth be told we weren't much in adult territory. Now we –

'Can we do it now?'

'You mean – now?' I said, startled.

The Head Girl Stare. 'You, Martin Blake, sub-editor, should know that Now means … Now.'

I felt silly. Things were moving quickly. I don't know if she realised quite how big a step she was taking. But then again, going by the determination in her eyes and the set of her face, the jut of her chin, the firm line of her lips … well, she might do.

I took a deep breath. Let it out. 'All right. What do we do?'

She squeezed my hand, pecked me on the cheek, and stood. 'We pack.'

So from out of her wardrobe and a cupboard she produced a large suitcase and a smaller bag. 'Clean out those drawers and put them in that suitcase,' she ordered. She was good at giving orders, I was thinking. But she was organised. As she'd once said, she, like the rest of her family, had been trained to organise and be organised. So briefs, bras, pantyhose, socks, petticoats, slips, blouses, tops, and pyjamas went into the suitcase. And the statue of Mary, carefully wrapped.

The suitcase still looked half-empty. Other clothing and shoes and boots – wrapped in plastic – filled it up. The school uniform hung from a hanger in a zip-up plastic bag. Maria took the smaller bag to the bathroom to collect what she needed from there. It apparently was her overnight and bathroom bag. All the schoolwork went into the hold-all. She looked at the typewriter. 'Will it be all right if I use yours, darling?'

'My pleasure,' I replied, and kissed her.

In about 15 minutes it was all done. I zipped the suitcase closed and buckled up its twin leather straps. I hefted it: would be a lift, but I could manage it. 'What happens now?'

Maria frowned. 'I don't know, I suppose.'

I sat on the bed. She went over to the door and opened it wide and came back and joined me. 'I'm supposed to leave the door open if I have a boy in here with me,' she said. 'Apart from my brothers, a cousin or two, or a nephew I've never had a boy in here.' She leaned to kiss me on the cheek. 'You're the first man I've ever had in my bedroom, darling,' she whispered against my ear.

I took her hand again, and as we sat I couldn't help thinking: she obeys the rules laid down by authority; at school she polices those rules. But when it comes to what she thinks is her personal sovereignty she stands on it and fights back. We were in for an interesting time.

Footsteps, padding and hesitant along the hallway, the boards creaking. We exchanged glances, and I could feel her tense up.

Gabrielle stood in the doorway. 'Hi,' she murmured. Her eyes slid from Maria, to me, to the bags in the centre of the room. And back to Maria

Maria stretched out her arms: 'Come in, honey,' she said, and the girl came over and sat between us. Maria embraced her and kissed her hair. 'Are you going away, Maria?'

A glance at me over Gabrielle's head. 'Yes, honey. I'm going to stay with Martin.' A reassuring smile for the niece.

'Golly!' She swung from Maria to me, eyes wide. 'That's going to cause a stir.'

Maria stroked her hair slowly, softly. 'Yes, honey, it will.'

'And no-one knows yet? When were you going to tell them?' A troubled pause. 'Will I get into trouble because I know and didn't tell on you?'

Anger flitted across Maria's expression. Then the grown-up, reassuring smile. 'No, darling, you won't get into trouble. And I'm not going to swear you to secrecy, either.'

'Why?'

'Well, it wouldn't be fair on you, would it?'

'OK.'

The smiled at each other.

'Will I still be able to see you?' Gabrielle said.

Maria hugged her briefly, fiercely. 'I don't see why not.' I thought her voice was about to catch with what she said next. 'I'd die if you and I couldn't spend time together.'

'Me, too,' Gabrielle whispered.

They clung together, and Maria kissed her hair, softly fussed with it.

I felt we needed to leave. Although there had been the sounds of guests leaving, other noises in the house and out the back indicated the party was continuing unabated. We could be waiting here for ages before someone decided to come up to Maria's room – if at all. I didn't want a confrontation with the family today. And I wondered if they were willing to risk other people witnessing 'scandalous behaviour'.

I faced Maria over Gabrielle's head. She read my thoughts. It was time to go.

'Gabe,' she whispered, 'We're going in a few minutes. I just want to write a note to Grandpa and Grandmama, and I'll leave it on my typewriter.'

Gabrielle began to cry, and Maria handed her a handkerchief to snuffle into. 'You have that, and stop crying, and I'll just write the note.'

She sat at the typewriter, fed in paper, and her fingers danced across the keys. It didn't take long, and she handed me the sheet to read.

Dear Mum and Dad,

I've left home to stay with Martin.

I know this will be a shock to you; you will be angry with me for this and feel disappointed because you will see it as throwing my upbringing back in your faces.

I can't help that. I've fallen in love with him. I don't see why a religious difference should matter. I'm not prepared to argue with you over it, nor listen to my grandmother's abominations.

Martin has not forced me or coerced me into anything. We love each other. I will be alright.

I love you and the rest of the family. Please be assured of that.

Maria signed it and folded the letter and left it on the roller of the typewriter. She gave Gabrielle a heartfelt hug, and I thought both were going to break down.

'Go on, honey,' Maria instructed her niece and kissed her. Gabrielle left the room reluctantly.

I picked up the suitcase and the overnight bag. Maria gathered up the rest of her things, and we walked back along the hall, down the stairs – and out the front door.

No-one saw us. Grannie Annie was heard loudly bawling something funny in the lounge, and there were answering gusts of laughter. Conversation and laughter rumbled fitfully in pockets throughout the house. We walked along the front path to the gate.

I kept waiting for someone to challenge us, to call us to stop.

No-one did.

Moving in

We dumped Maria's things on my bed. I made us coffee while she deftly unbuckled the straps of her suitcase and unclipped the locks. I went back and leaned against the doorway and watched her move her life into mine.

I didn't have a lot in my chest of drawers – another cheap but solid buy from a church mission shop – so there was plenty of space as armload after armload of her things were distributed through them. She knew where she should put her things.

'I hope we won't mistake each other's bras,' I said.

She glanced at me and laughed gently. The school uniform came out of its hanger bag and my one suit, two other pairs of pants and few shirts on the rack in the wardrobe were pushed aside; everything in its place.

Almost done, but not quite. She was holding the statue of Mary. 'May I put it there?' she said, indicating the top of my chest of drawers. It was fine with me, and she did it reverently, touching its head to her lips as she carefully positioned it by her combs and hairbrush.

Mary had full view of the room, her arms outstretched like a mother's, and Maria looped part of her rosary beads over them. She lapsed into silence, and I realised she was praying before it. I put her empty bags under the bed. Then I embraced her from behind.

'What did you say to her?' I said, nodding to the statue.

Maria glanced over her shoulder at me. 'I just asked her to understand what I'm doing, and to forgive, if necessary.' She took my hands in hers. 'I asked her to help my family to understand. I asked her to help me understand.'

She squeezed my hands. 'In the last few weeks, sweetheart,' she whispered, 'I've realised a lot how much of the Catholic Church is bound up in rules and laws and obeying them if we're to die in a state of grace – sin-free, in other words.'

She half-turned to face me: 'I'm not sure that's what Jesus intended when he founded the Church.'

I didn't know, either. We kissed, and I began to undress her.

'You're becoming quite good at this,' she whispered as I unhooked her bra deftly.

'Regular practice makes perfect.'

She undressed me, also deftly, with neat and economic movements of her hands and fingers. Maria was like that. She kissed me softly, openly. I loved holding her like this. The naked sexual friction of skin and skin. The scent of her. In bed we held each other close like that. She lay back and sighed. 'Thank you, darling, for doing this. Letting me come into your bachelor pad.'

'It's OK,' I said, bending to kiss her belly, which we'd found she liked me to do just below the rim of her navel. 'I'm pleased to have you here.'

Maria sighed again.

'AND I don't have to go home,' she whispered afterwards. 'And I don't have to shower the smell of you off me, either.'

'That's right. We can both suffocate from that.'

She giggled, sighed, and settled her lips on the excitable nipple and began to get a reaction from it by working at it with her teeth and tongue.

'You're being a very greedy woman, you know,' I said raggedly.

'Stop complaining or I *will* go home to mother,' she muttered, bending to her task with focused energy.

MARIA HAD slipped into what I guessed was a contented sleep beside me, my arm around her shoulders, her head on my chest. At some stage soon my arm was going to go numb. I should have been asleep, too. My body ached in that exquisite weariness after sex. Here was a big part of my contentment. Maria wasn't going home afterwards. She would be there when we woke in the morning. We loved each other. That was beyond doubt. I'd joked to Maria as she drowsily drifted off to sleep that the novelty of sleeping with me might wear off. 'I'm sure I fart.'

'I'm sure you do, too. You're a man.'

'And women don't?'

Her eyes widened in mock horror. 'Well,' she said, her expression changing to coy, 'maybe *pets-de-nonne.*'

'Er, which means?'

She hesitated. 'Um, nun farts,' and we laughed softly at that.

So with that unlikely and unromantic thought hanging between us she kissed my chest, snuggled closer, and settled for sleep. Her soft, slow breathing ruffled the hairs on my chest.

I couldn't help feeling apprehensive now. Her family were not going to accept this situation. Could they drag her away? My knowledge of the law was hazy. She was over 16, the legal age for leaving home without parental permission. But she attended a school that they paid to educate her.

And what about the school? They would line up with the family, of course they would. They would be scandalised by their head prefect, their top pupil and behavioural standard-bearer shacking up with her boyfriend.

Oh, yes, the scandal. They'll all tear her to pieces.

Pickering, a photographer at my last newspaper. His niece – the first member of her family to get not only school certificate but also university entrance – got pregnant in the upper-sixth form. Her state school banished her straight away because she might have been a moral hazard to the rest of the school as much as to spare her being a topic of gossip in the town.

Our Lady of The Immaculate Conception was unlikely to be any more understanding.

More thoughts wandered through my brain: here, there, gone before I could catch hold of them.

Maria slept on, 'hem … hem …' She must have been dreaming. She shifted and turned over, snuffled softly. I spooned in behind her and cupped her breast in my hand. That was better. Her heart ticked over, untroubled and steady. A fresh, powerful wave of love, of protectiveness, surged through me; I kissed her lightly on the shoulder and floated off to a kind of sleep.

Holy visit

The knock on the door was sharp and hard-knuckled loud at 9am. I was making toast and coffee for breakfast. Maria was in the shower. The visitor was her brother Luke, the priest.

'Is my sister here? I want to talk to her.' He was in his priestly black with roman collar, and by the set of his face and the imposing way he stood before me he was all business. 'All bull, beef and bustle,' Mum would say.

If he'd said pleasantly, 'Good morning, you must be Martin, we haven't had an opportunity to meet properly, but I'm Luke. May I talk to Maria and you together?' I would have reacted differently.

Instead I replied: 'I'll check.' And shut the door in his face. In the bedroom Maria was vigorously towelling herself dry. 'Your brother Luke is here. Do you want to talk to him?'

She picked up a second towel and energetically rubbed it through her hair while she took her time to think about it. 'No, I don't.'

'Will it do any harm to listen to what he has to say?'

She shrugged. Frowned. 'OK. I'll be out in a minute.'

Luke was still there outside the door, peeved at being made to wait. 'Come in, Father. Maria is getting dressed and will join us shortly.'

He didn't even say thank you. I stood aside as he marched into the flat, his blue eyes recording everything.

I offered him tea or coffee. 'No, thank you,' he said primly. He took up station in front of the bookcase. I sat at the table with my back to the typewriter, we in tense, awkward silence. I couldn't face the toast but I cupped my coffee mug in my hands.

Maria opened my bedroom door. I've never forgotten this. She wore one of my shirts loosely, revealing her knickers. She sat on the couch, cross-legged, giving her brother a full view of her polka-dotted underwear – a confection of red, blue, green, yellow, orange dots. Her breasts were partly exposed because she had not done up more than a couple of buttons. She had left her bra off, too. She was provoking him. 'Hello, Luke.'

The provocation scored a result. He shouted: 'Have you no shame? Go and get some decent clothes on!'

'If you don't like how I'm dressed, Luke,' and she nodded to the door, 'you know the way out.'

He chewed on that. 'Very well, if you're going to behave like a trollop –'

'Father,' I cut in, 'you've turned up here unannounced and uninvited. If you're going to talk to her like that then you can bugger off.'

His face coloured from red to purple, and his eyes blazed a livid blue. They were like his grandmother's.

'Now, what did you come here for?'

He concentrated on her. 'I've come to take you home from this. I've been told that I'm not to leave without you. And I won't. So go and get properly dressed and pack your bags.'

She didn't move, but her top lip curled with scorn. 'Or what? Are you going to drag me out of here by my hair screaming and kicking? A spectacle for the neighbours?'

He went to speak, but she beat him to it. 'Isn't it typical, dear brother, of our family that they send an emissary, and with instructions, too. Our parents don't come here themselves. Why not? Instead they delegate, and to the priest in the family. That's how they deal with difficulties in the family, isn't it? They get someone else to do it. They don't get their hands dirty.'

'Maria, I –'

'You know, Luke, I'm surprised they didn't send our grandmother along with you.' Her cheeks were crimson, and her eyes had gone an eerie shade of green.

He tried placation. He lifted his hands as if in surrender. 'Maria,' he tried in a different tone. 'I don't think you understand the seriousness of your position.' He glanced at me, then turned back to her. 'Can't we talk privately about this? Brother and sister.'

'No, we can't. You haven't come here as a brother. I would get on with it if I were you, Luke, because we haven't had breakfast yet and I'm hungry – you might know that the hungrier I get the more I annoyed I can get.'

His reaction – a blank blink of his eyes – intrigued me. I don't think he did know that.

'Very well. Do you understand the moral – mortal – danger you are in by living here with this man in a state of de facto marriage?'

Maria laughed, a bitter, scornful peal snorted to a sudden stop and an artificially straight face. 'What danger? I'm safely here with the man I love. How is that sinful? Whose business is it?'

His mouth turned meanly down at the corners. 'Very well. The family will not tolerate a scandal. Nor will Our Lady of The Immaculate Conception.'

'Is that a threat, Father?'

He turned to me. 'Just a statement of the position, that's all. Everything has consequences.'

He went for the door. As he opened it he turned, for dramatic, last-word effect: 'You'll be given time to come to your senses, Maria. But just be aware that that time is not unlimited. I really do suggest you kneel at Our Lady's feet and examine your conscience. Pray to the little saint whose name you honour and bear. She will help you. If you feel the need for confession and absolution I'll be only too happy to help you, too.'

And with that the Rev Luke FitzGarratt, PhD, DD, and another doctorate from somewhere, disappeared, closing the door carefully after him.

'Well, that told him where to get off.'

She blew out her lips in disgust. 'He's a fool. That was the first time in ages he's made an effort to have a serious conversation with me.'

I walked over and joined her on the couch, and put an arm around her. She put her head on my shoulder and took my hand in hers. We sat like that in a kind of deflated silence. But …

'Come on, sweetie,' I said, giving her a squeeze and pulling her to her feet. 'You need to eat. I don't want you grumpier than this.'

She crossed her eyes and poked her tongue out.

Friends and enemies

She warmed up after a couple of slices of toast topped with honey, and a cup of coffee. Still, there was a moody undercurrent lurking beneath the surface. Luke's visit had been a warning, to me as much as to her. I didn't know much about her family then. Who they knew, what sort of pressure they could apply. It might sound far-fetched now, but could they threaten my job?

As well, I was learning that Maria when she was worried and preoccupied got busy. She took over the washing machine. Our clothes and towels disappeared into it, and she set it in motion. 'When did you last do the washing, Martin?'

I assured her I did it every week. Going by the raised eyebrow I don't think she believed me. She was right.

She made the bed, and in a way that I'd never made it. Neatly, with hospital corners. Even my mother hadn't been that good. 'I was going to change the sheets, but I think I like the smell of us in them.' She pecked me on the top of my head. She wiped down the window sills. She found the vacuum-cleaner, 'Mikimoto', in the broom cupboard. 'Been a while, has it, Martin?'

I know I should have been charmed by it. But I was nettled, and that irritated me, too. I loved having her there. But this was still my place, and she'd not only moved in – yes, I know, I'd suggested it – but she was taking over the housekeeping, too, with all the assurance and confidence of a female. I was being childish, I knew, and she'd probably feel baffled that I felt that way.

Anyway, I did my bit and washed and dried two days of dishes and cleaned up the piles of papers on the typewriter table. I checked to see if the oven needed cleaning. I decided it was marginal.

I wiped out the sink and hand-basin in the bathroom, and ran a cloth over the shelf, which had become crowded. Her toothbrush, red and medium, lay next to mine, green and hard; her toothpaste was Macleans and mine was Colgate. She'd screwed the cap back on mine. A new Nymph razor and a brush were next to my Gillette. Her Wella shampoo and conditioner and my coal tar soap now co-existed in the shower rack. A fragrant lavender hand soap rested in a holder by the basin. A packet of Tampax and another of Stayfree Napkins had gone into the previously unused bottom drawer of the tiny vanity unit, along with a bottle of pain-killers. The toilet was clean – I'd always made sure of that – but I sprinkled some Ajax in the bowl just to make sure. I put the toilet seat down.

The washing was done and we took it in one overloaded basket down to the communal clotheslines. A 40-something woman from the first floor I knew only as Alice was there. She noted Maria's presence with a raised eyebrow and a knowing smile. They chatted briefly.

I suggested we go and have lunch at Peter and Magdalena's. Maria said she'd like that. The café was busy. Neither Magdalena nor Peter could stop to talk long. But Sue Devonshire was there, and she came over to our table. They already knew each other, and it seemed that Sue had been stood up by Johnson. 'Perhaps he's hung over or stoned, or something,' I said.

'Probably the latter,' Sue replied archly. The way she said it I reckoned Johnson was going to get his balls ripped off and stuffed down his throat. Susan did not take kindly to being treated offhandedly.

Anyway, she helped herself to a chair, lit a cigarette, and put on her professional charming reporter's face and not-too-subtly began milking for information. She was raised eyebrows, immaculately plucked, dancing eyelashes, and irresistible brown eyes: 'Just out for lunch, are you?'

Yes, Sue.

'Have you had a lovely Easter?'

It had been memorable, I said, intending irony.

'Oh, what did you do to make it memorable?'

Oh, very good. I read Sue's expression, the impassive face. Her eyes were knowing. I knew they were. I wondered how she knew, and how much. I didn't think Maria had cottoned on.

Catching her eye, then turning to face Sue, I said: 'If you're not doing anything later, Sue, why not come around and have tea with Maria and me.'

I had just confirmed whatever she knew. 'Sure,' she said, her red lips forming a genuine, white-teethed grin. I thought it a trustworthy smile. We agreed on six. She'd bring a bottle of wine and dessert.

I told her to leave Johnson out of it. A pout of disgust. 'Oh, him …'

She glanced at both of us, and laid a hand on my arm: 'I have to get on,' she said, winked at Maria, 'nice to meet you again, Maria,' and strode away, swinging stylishly between tables for the door.

'Why did you do that?' Maria said, as she nibbled around the edges of a large Danish tart.

'Because she knows.'

'And …?'

'It might be useful to know how she knows, as well as how much.'

'Oh.' She put the tart back on her plate. She stared at it unhappily, her fingers twisting in her lap.

'Sue's a friend. We might need a friend or two.'

'This is going to get ugly, isn't it?' Tears pooled in her eyes. 'I've just realised today how awful it's going to get.' She wiped at her nose. 'I've been fooling myself by being romantic about it all.'

I reached over and took her hand, and her fingers clung to mine like she was drowning.

'Do you want to go back home to your family?'

Her chin jutted firmly, and she blinked away her tears: 'No. I'm never going back.'

'Well, my sweet, there's your answer. And I'm here beside you.'
She smiled wanly.

WE WORKED at the bench of my kitchenette together, like any domestic couple, I suppose. She had perked up since we were at the café. I was organising the herbs and the garlic and the oil for the unfrozen chicken I'd picked up from the superette. Maria was preparing the vegetables, and we were doing very well at it, too, not getting in each other's way.

But I felt I needed to ask her a personal question. And I didn't know how she would take it. The items in the bottom drawer of the vanity unit kept playing on my mind. I felt I had a right to ask, so I did it as casually as I could as I stuffed the chicken cavity with parsley and crushed garlic. 'You know when you said a couple of weeks ago that you couldn't get pregnant … what did you mean?'

She was chopping up parsnips. 'I don't ovulate. Everything else works, but I don't seem to ovulate.' She glanced at me. 'You know what I mean, don't you? I don't produce an egg that could be fertilised.'

She began to peel carrots and I rinsed my hands before glazing the chicken. Which gave me time to think about the next question, feeling very much out of my depth. 'But you have, um, periods, don't you?'

She didn't take offence. I could never have had this conversation with Felicity. Perhaps few guys could have such a talk with their wife or girlfriend. 'Kind of,' she said and she expertly peeled and sliced up the carrots. 'There is a bleed, but not every month. I can go for months without one. Then I can suddenly get caught, as we found a month or so ago.'

And that was it, really. 'Did you mind my asking?'

By now she was starting on the potatoes that would be roasted. The chicken stood ready to go into the oven at four.

'No.' She gouged rot out of a potato. 'It affects you, too.' She leaned over and kissed me hotly and wetly on the ear.

'Steadeh, lass,' I muttered, 'I'm rubbing stuff on a chicken's breast.'

'You're a deviant.' And she firmly swatted my backside with a tea towel.

I cried out in supposed pain.

'Stop that, or I'll give you another one.'

I moaned, 'Oh, yesss …'

'You *are* a deviant.'

WHEN I put the chicken and the potatoes in the oven Maria decided to do some ironing. 'You *do* have an iron.'

'Um. Somewhere. Mum gave me one for Christmas once. Haven't seen it lately. Might be in the broom cupboard.'

I heard her fossicking in the cupboard, and a triumphant 'A-*Hah!*' She brandished it like a trophy.

'Why do you want to do ironing?'

The Head Girl Look, the side-to side wiggling of her head, the theatrical sigh: 'Because I'm a female, Martin, trained to make best use of time and not to waste time. While you baste the chicken every 20 minutes I can be doing something useful – such as ironing. And being a woman I can still carry on a conversation with you while I do it.' And so she picked up the clothes basket and headed out the door.

I realised she had been gone about 15 minutes only when she returned, white, shaking, and frightened.

I pulled her to me. 'What happened?'

Her eyes weren't connecting with mine.

'Maria! What happened?!' *Try to keep the alarm out of your voice ...*

'Tom,' she whispered. The policeman brother-in-law. She trembled hard in my arms, and I held her close.

Oh, Christ.

'He said he was just dropping by to see how I was.'

'And?'

Her wide, frightened eyes. 'He was awful, Martin. Disgusting, really.' She gulped hard.

'He started to take our things off the line and throw them in the basket. Said he would give me a hand.'

She closed her eyes briefly and swallowed. I thought she was going to be sick. 'I didn't know how to stop him. Martin, he – he –'

'What?!'

A deep, calming breath. 'Right. He touched – fingered and fondled, actually – my clothes, my bras, he … he sniffed my knickers and said: "Well, they smell clean this time." And he leered at me.'

Jee-zuss!

'He came to stand right in front of me, over me, and he asked me …' and she swallowed, her eyes sliding away to the side. 'I don't want to say this.'

But she steeled herself. 'And he asked me how I liked you to, to …' and she swallowed again and burst into tears. 'He asked me, Martin, how, well, how did I like you to …. Had I tried doggy-style yet? I've no idea what he's talking about –. And what about – no, that's just too disgusting to even think about.'

Oh, you bastard! I saw red, and held her as she cried on my shoulder.

She was speaking again: … 'when the lady we saw there this morning –'

'Alice.'

She nodded. 'Yes. Alice. Well, she came right over and asked me: "Do you need a hand with getting your laundry in, dear?"'

'And, Martin, she pushed between him and me and told him that he could go. And she knew he was a policeman because he was in uniform and his police car was parked in front of your garage.'

Thank God for Alice. I made a note to thank her tomorrow.

'He didn't like that, but he put on a smirk, tipped his hat, winked at me, and left.'

Maria clung to me. She snuffled against my neck, and while I stroked her back and shoulders and made shushing noises her trembling subsided.

'Have you drunk brandy before?'

She frowned. 'No. I don't usually touch alcohol, other than the seldom glass of wine.'

I believed that. She might have had two sips of wine at her parents' place yesterday. I reached up to the cupboard where I had kept my top shelf. I had a bottle of Napoleon Brandy. 'I'm going to pour you a small one. I'll put in ginger ale, so don't worry.'

I indicated the typewriter. 'I want you to sit down and type it all out. Where you were, what you were doing. The time. Everything you can remember. Witnesses. Or witness. The police car number plate. Was he alone? I'll talk to Alice tomorrow.'

She nodded, and smiled bravely.

I prepared the drink. She eyed it dubiously. 'Maria. Don't be frightened. He's trying to frighten us.'

She sipped the drink; smiled appreciatively. 'That's rather nice, Martin. Thank you.' She kissed me hard on the lips. 'I love you,' she whispered.

I went back to basting the chicken and she, her usual briskness returning, typed out everything. I had no idea how I was going to use the information. But I knew it would be useful to have.

SUE GUSHED into the flat, non-stop prattling gaiety, belling laughter, blonde hair locked away under a red floppy beret, an overcoat with big collar and a knotted belt, calf-length boots. She brandished a bottle of white wine 'to go with the chicken' and she carried an enclosed dish containing a Pavlova – the popular New Zealand dessert Australians try to claim as theirs. She had topped it with whipped cream and slices of kiwifruit. *Oh-h ...*

Conversation was lively but inconsequential fun. Sue paid special attention to Maria and did a very good job of disarming her. She treated Maria as an adult. Maria, with 13 older siblings, would have tolerated nothing less.

Only when dessert was eaten and the coffee had perked and poured did we get down to the important stuff.

'When did you know Maria had moved in with me, Sue?'

'Oh, this morning.' She glanced at Maria. 'Your sister Tessa rang me. Said you'd just walked out, leaving a note. That you were coming here.'

Oh? Now this was interesting.

'Why do you think Tessa phoned you to tell you that?'

Sue, I think, for the first time since I'd known her, seemed uncomfortable. 'She said the family had talked about you until after midnight. She said that if you were to just go home all would be forgiven. They would tolerate your relationship with Martin. As long as it was discreet and did not expose the family to scandal and public ridicule.'

Maria and I exchanged glances.

'That sounds to me like you've been asked to pass on a message, Sue,' Maria said quietly.

Sue glanced at me. I was beginning to feel uneasy about her. 'Your sister asked me to talk to Martin. When I next saw him. That's all.'

'Oh, why?' Maria said. Her tone was dangerously soft.

'She wanted me to get you to see sense – well, that's how she put it, anyway. That you could still carry on with Martin. But as I said a moment ago – discreetly, no scandal, and probably a commitment to marriage. Encourage Martin to become a Catholic.'

I felt betrayed, shafted by someone I had come to regard as a trusted friend. 'When were you going to have that talk with me, Sue?'

Now Sue saw what Maria and I saw. She didn't answer. Her red fingernails had become the focus of intense interest.

'What had you been offered in return, Sue?' I pressed.

We waited, and she looked miserable. 'Introductions, access to people who could help me with my career …' she trailed away. 'That sort of thing,' she added, almost inaudibly.

Maria had gone white, but the points of her cheeks burned, and the intense green had returned to her eyes. But she managed to say, an ominous murmur: 'That's not a lot, Sue.'

Sue breathed in sharply; exhaled. She turned abruptly on Maria and let rip: 'Do you know what it's like being someone not like you and your family? The bloody FitzGarratts and people like them lord it over everyone. The archbishop doesn't even go into ordinary people's houses, yet *you people!* are on first names with him. Because you've got money and position and access and influence.'

Sue's finger jabbed at Maria. 'Do you know what it was like being at Our Lady of The Immaculate Conception with Tessa and her rich-bitch friends? You lot were like royalty. Everyone – including me, I'm sorry to say – sucked up to you. Because you and them were self-selecting Popular.'

I glanced at Maria. Her face was impassive. Green eyes livid.

'Your parents were the great doctor and the wonderful professor and your vast family with all their degrees and important positions and their money. My dad's a plumber and Mum worked in an office to be able to send me and my sisters there. They and I worked damned hard for what I got. For you and your sisters it's all been so easy. For once one of them shows me real, real interest. And all I had to do was just pass on a message to Martin.'

Sue's face was bright red, like her bright red lipstick, and she was breathing hard.

I sighed. A friendship had been revealed as a mirage. 'It's getting late, Sue.'

She left, trying to justify herself as she went out the door and down the stairs.

'SUE'S HURT you, hasn't she, sweetie?' Maria whispered in the dark from her pillow. Her hands cupped my cheeks, a soft, feathery caress; her feet idly stroked my backside.

'I thought she was a friend, someone to trust.'

'I'm sorry, honey, I really am. She seemed such a nice lady.'

Maria drew my lips down to hers. 'If I could kiss it all away, my sweet, I would.' Her whisper was softer than night. She eased her loins gently at mine.

If only it could be that simple. 'It's not your fault, darling,' I murmured and kissed her breast. 'This was just the situation that found her out.'

Maria sighed contentedly and pressed her knees against my flanks. 'Giddy-up,' she ordered.

Brotherly overture

The alarm clock woke me out of a deep, contented sleep at 4.10am. Maria woke with a start, too. 'Is this when you get up?' she said drowsily. It was, and she muttered something inaudible. I headed for the bathroom reluctantly.

I got out of the shower, shaved, and stepped into my room to dry and get dressed. The bed was empty. Maria was moving about in the kitchenette.

'What are you doing?'

'Making breakfast. Go and get dressed.' The toaster popped, and she buttered the slices and added honey. The flat smelled of brewing coffee. I was not used to this. No-one had made me breakfast in the last 10 years.

'You should still be in bed, asleep, Maria. It's the middle of the night.'

'I'm a woman, Martin, trained to be my man's handmaid and to meet his every need.'

'Every need?'

She smiled, and guided me by the arm to the plate of toast and the coffee on the table. 'I want to do this because I love you,' she said. 'Doing things for each other shows we love each other.' She added sternly: 'Now eat.'

Just before she closed the door behind me as I left at 5am Maria said. 'Don't worry, darling. I can get another couple of hours sleep before I go to school.'

ABOUT 10AM my desk phone went, during what was supposed to be morning smoko, and that was the worst time of the day to have a break because all the early deadlines were on us.

'Martin, this is Matt FitzGarratt.'

I just about sat up straight. *Eh?*

'Would you be able to make some time this afternoon to drop into my office?'

'Why?' It sounded sharp, and he picked up on it.

'Look … Martin,' and he was sounding placatory, 'Please do me a favour and relax. I am a friend. I thought I'd made that plain on Sunday.'

We agreed on one-thirty.

THE CHAMBERS of his law firm occupied an old stone building in a street of old, grey masonry and red-brick buildings that were home to the city's lawyers, accountants, stockbrokers, doctors, dentists, insurance companies. The street was a very picture of black leather shoe probity and pinstripe-suit respectability.

Matthew's offices were on the fifth floor. An ancient office lady peered through her bifocals down her long nose as she looked up. I told her I was Matthew's one-thirty appointment, and she shuffled off, her walking-stick a stump-stump-stump punctuation, to announce me.

He welcomed me at his door with a handshake that was friendly rather than formal, and guided me to a chair in front of his desk.

'I'll just go and ask Mrs O'Daly if she could get one of the girls to make us a pot of coffee.'

While he did that I glanced around his office. His desk bore a lofty file that threatened the telephone from beside and above. Other files were heaped in teetering towers on another table, above filing cabinets, and on the floor. I wondered what his little sister – a tyrant of order and tidiness, I was learning – would make of it all. He returned, rubbed his hands briskly together, grinned, 'good, it'll be here in a minute'.

He sat in his chair, then straight to the point: 'How is Maria?'

'She's good. Happy. She's frightened the hell out of the vacuum-cleaner and the iron. I feel I have to wash the dishes more often. I'm learning to put the toilet seat down.'

A non-committal 'hmm'.

Then: what I would call the Queen's Counsel Stare – blue-grey eyes like slates, intimidatingly direct, and I had to resist the urge to squirm. It was alarmingly similar to his sister's. 'She's a bit younger than you. Are you leading her on?'

'No.'

'Do you love her?'

'Yes, I do. Very much so.'

I could feel myself beginning to sweat and my guts knotted. I added: 'But then I would say all that, wouldn't I?'

A pert office junior, bright red hair bouncing softly on her shoulders, brought in the coffee on a silver tray. 'Thanks, Aoife [he pronounced it 'E-fa'],' he said. She smiled and disappeared, closing the door behind her.

Our eyes met again.

'So why am I here, Matthew?'

He leaned forward, elbows on the desk. 'As I said on the phone to you, I'm a friend.'

'OK.'

'And I believe you, by the way. That you love her.'

That relieved me. The knot in my gut loosened.

'It's difficult to know how to be a big brother to a sibling who's the same age as my own daughter. I've never known, really, how to talk to her or treat her as a sister.'

He took a sip of his coffee. His doing that was just like her – neat.

'I was just starting out in law, had just got married. When Kay and I announced to everyone that she was pregnant with Catharine Mum confirmed that she was, too.'

He sat back. 'A story, Martin, which might help. For the last 25 years I've been living a lie. I've really been in love with someone else.'

Her name was Ariel. They were at university together and had fallen in love. 'It became passionate,' which I understood was code for they were sleeping together.

There was no question of their living together, not in early 1950s New Zealand. Social attitudes would not have tolerated it. But they got pretty close to it during a summer of fruit-picking. She was not a Catholic, and that was intolerable to his family.

'She was rather irreligious, which was part of the attraction, I suppose.' So they kept the relationship secret until it could be no longer. He thought his educated parents might be open to a non-Catholic daughter-in-law.

The story was sounding familiar. Only Maria and I hadn't been thinking of anything like marriage yet – it's just that the train of events had got compressed. He and Ariel had had to break off. Grannie Annie had had her say, forcefully, and Peirse was not willing to stand up to her. 'My father simply caved in to her. He always does. I got no support from my parents at all.'

He later met Kay, an office girl working for his uncle, another lawyer. She fell in love with him. She saw his ambition and talent, and a life with money; Kay was the daughter of a returned soldier who'd been gassed in World War One. She was never going to be a challenge to him. She would always be loyal, be at his side, keep his house, bear their children willingly as a good Catholic wife should.

'I do love Kay. I've never betrayed her. Never will. But in a way I have because I've never loved her as I loved Ariel. Not with that same passion, anyway.'

He paused. 'It's been more a dutiful love.' He picked up his coffee and sipped it, returned the cup to the saucer. The mannerism was just like Maria's. 'I hope that goes some way to explaining why you and I are having this conversation.'

'OK. But whose idea was it to send Luke around yesterday morning, try to bring Susan Devonshire into it, and send Tom to sniff her clothing while she was getting in the washing off the line?'

'He *what!*'

'You didn't know Tom had been around?'

'No!'

He stared out the window for a few moments. 'Luke phoned me yesterday morning. Said he'd been to see Maria and you.'

'And?'

He smiled briefly. 'Least said the better.' He shook his head slowly. 'My brother might have three doctorates signifying he knows something about God, but none has given him any of the characteristics of him. Pity. A waste, really. He wasn't always such a judgmental prick.'

'Maria sent him away with a flea in his ear. If he'd turned up with a different attitude he might have got a better hearing.'

'I can imagine.'

'But Tom. He sneaked up on her yesterday afternoon while she was gathering in the washing. He sniffed her clothes, made untoward remarks, and asked her if she'd done doggy-style before a neighbour came out and shoo'd him off.'

Matt frowned in distaste. 'Christ. Tom's a thug. Not very bright. Hasn't progressed much from dragging his knuckles along the ground.'

I had to laugh.

'Stella married him only because of what hung between his legs.'

Matthew picked up a lined legal pad. 'When did this happen?'

I produced from my jacket a photocopy I'd taken of what Maria had typed. 'I got her to type this up straight after it happened. It helped to steady her nerves.'

He frowned as he quickly scanned the paper, then grinned. 'Good man. Good thinking, too. Record every visit, every conversation involving Tom, and pass it on to me. I know his district commander very well. He won't like this at all.'

We gazed at each other in a long silence. I felt I had to take him on trust. He'd extricated us from his parents and grandmother on Sunday.

He knew what I was thinking, I think, because he then produced his ace card. He picked up an envelope and extended it to me. 'In there is a bank book. It's proceeds from a trust fund in her name set up at her birth. It gives her money. A document in there signed by me as trustee and the bank gives her control of that account.'

I took the envelope.

'Martin. I have to go in a minute. But that envelope is why I asked you to see me. I hope it proves what I say. I am a friend. Legally, there's little our parents can do to force Maria back into the fold. She's over 16. So my guess is there'll be pressure from other areas, such as school. They'll try to keep it discreet, too.'

He stood. 'Thanks for coming. I know you'll look after her. Any problems or legal questions, ring me.' He produced a business card. 'I'll instruct the switchboard and ask Mrs O'Daly to take any call or any message from you.'

I thanked him and we shook hands as I went to leave. 'You know, Matthew, you're lucky Maria doesn't work in your office.' I indicated the piles of files. 'She wouldn't tolerate it.'

He grinned sheepishly. 'Terrifying, isn't it? But then Mrs O'Daly – doddery as she is – knows the location of every scrap of paper.'

New friend

I called in on Alice when I got home. It turned out she worked at the Post Office telephone exchange, a night supervisor in the international calls section. My ostensible reason for calling on her was to thank her for going to Maria's aid the day before.

'Pleased to help,' she said, her voice husky from cigarettes. She was single, in her 40s and spoke with a gravelly Southland accent. Maroon lipstick and teal eye shadow suggested attempts to ward off age. 'What he was saying to her and doing was disgusting, Martin.' She drew furiously on a Benson & Hedges. 'No girl – no woman – should be spoken to like that. And him a policeman, too.'

'Would you mind if I could take notes of what you heard?'

That sly smile. 'I heard it all, dearie.' She got off her couch and opened a drawer of a writing desk. She picked out some sheets of paper, and brought them over to me. 'There's my shorthand – Pitman's – timed and dated, and my typewritten transcription.'

I read the typescript. She had everything. Every word, Tom's actions – the number plate of the police car, and a description of the policeman who remained in the car. It was gold. Maybe Matt's office could verify the shorthand. My shorthand was Teeline.

I looked up. 'May I get a copy of this?'

'Keep it, love.' She lit another cigarette. 'He's been here before. I've seen and heard him going up the stairs.'

'Really? When?'

She exhaled a cloud of rolling, twisting, grey smoke. Probably one afternoon a week ago. I think he was expecting to find Maria here.'

That was sinister and now I was doubly worrying.

'She's a lovely girl, Martin. She's always said hello to me if our paths crossed, and made time to talk. She's not stuck-up like some of those little madams at that school.'

Alice pulled on the cigarette, and exhaled slowly. 'Very mature for her age. But in some things just still a little young.'

School friends

Maria got home from school. Everything seemed to have been normal. 'Except that Catharine came and sat next to me in history this morning and asked me how I was. Very odd.'

'Why?'

'It was her whole approach. There were no false smiles, no malicious eyes, no creepy simpering. Just a straight-forward question, I think. An attempt at empathy, maybe.'

We were standing in front of the wardrobe mirror. She was changing out of uniform. I was behind her because she had asked me to take out the stretch tie and hair clips. I did, smoothing out her hair as well, playing with it, enjoying its softness. She smiled. She took my hands and guided them to the buttons of her blouse. In the mirror we watched my hands doing that.

I was trying to keep my mind on the important things: 'What did you tell her?'

'That I was fine, and very happy,' and she leaned back against me, 'and very much in love with the man I love.'

That sounded good. Perhaps Matthew had leaned on his oldest daughter to mind her manners. I slipped her blouse off. She indicated the skirt next.

'Then my nieces Rachael and Charlotte – and they're cousins, of each other, too – they came to me at morning interval and asked if I was all right. They said they wanted bygones to be bygones. I was doing something quite brave, they said.'

A thoughtful scowl. 'It all got a bit girlie in the end – big hugs, a few tears.' The skirt dropped in folds to the floor. 'So we'll see.' Maria frowned. She seemed to be inspecting herself critically in the mirror. I slipped my arms through hers and around her waist, and nuzzled her shoulders. She took my hands in hers and held them against her belly.

'You've got something to tell me, haven't you?' she said to us in the mirror. 'You have a look about you, like you're bursting to tell something important. Like a little boy.'

I couldn't see the 'look', but yes I did have big news. 'Get dressed and I'll go and make us a cup of coffee and I'll tell you all about it.'

I'd decided I wasn't going to worry her about what Alice had told me about Tom's coming up the stairs. She was waiting cross-legged on the bed. I joined her. 'I went to see Matthew today.'

Her eyebrows arched and her eyes widened. 'Why?'

I told her about the phone call, and the discussion with him. She listened intently, asking a question here and there. 'I get the feeling that not all your family are as opposed to us as we might have thought.'

'Well, Matt has been a surprise.' She sipped her coffee. 'Perhaps that explains Catharine's change of heart – if it's a change of heart.'

'Now,' I said, 'look under your pillow.'

'Why?'

'There's a present for you.'

She regarded me suspiciously as she reached back and dug a hand under the pillow. She opened the envelope and shook out the contents on to the bed.

'Hmmm,' she frowned, glancing at me as she picked up the bank book and opened it. 'Oh!' she squealed. 'Oh! My Lord! Martin!' – and she thrust the book at me, mouth wide open. 'Look, sweetie, look!'

She had just over $5300 in the account. Which was a hell of a lot of money then. In some places that would have bought you a house.

'My God! Where did this come from?!' She clutched the book to her chest.

I heard myself say that Matthew had given it to me, that there was a trust, and that the bank book showed the amount from that trust that had been building up over the years.

She leaned over and hugged me. Clung to me. She was talking, babbling excitedly, non-stop. She was telling me she'd never known she had the money, had never heard of it before.

'And darling, I can help towards the rent and the food.'

I told her that was unnecessary. 'No, Martin, I'm not going to live off you. I can help.'

WITH SUPREME effort afterwards she concentrated on her homework. As I cooked tea I happened to look over her shoulder as she typed. Type-overs and cross-outs littered a book review written in German. The typewriter was missing her customary thudding cadence. 'Not having trouble concentrating, are you, *Fraulein* FitzGarratt, hm?'

She glared: 'Silence, *Kleiner Mensch*. Uzzavise you vill suffer teddibly.'

'Oh,' I said hopefully. 'Will I enjoy it?'

She reached over and slapped my backside. 'You might not, but I will.'

'I wouldn't do that, if I were you. It makes me want to strip you naked and have you then and there.'

A sigh. 'Men … only one thing on their grubby minds.' Her fingers began to dance again over the keys.

IN BED later that night she still fizzed about the money. 'I simply don't know what to do with it.'

I offered my thoughts: 'I wouldn't touch it – I mean, don't spend it all at once. Hang on to it until you really need it.'

I WOKE. Footsteps, out on the landing. Heavy, deliberate tread. Official steps. I glanced at Maria in the dark; her breathing continued, slow and shallow.

Good.

I didn't know what to make of them. Four flats were on this level, all at compass points around the building's central core. I'd come across the tenants at various times. The flat across from mine had recently changed tenants – two women and a small, school-age boy. We'd said 'hi' a couple of times. They sounded European; Maria thought Spanish or Italian. To my right, a married couple a bit older than me; they went to work after me and came home late. I knew his name as Will; she was Melanie. Both English. We'd never quite got around to talking much. To my left was a man in his 60s. He kept to himself. We'd nodded to each other and exchanged greetings a handful of times.

I checked the bedside clock. Just after midnight. It was unusual for people to be moving around on this level. I thought I heard a quiet knock on the door, and that bloody scared me. No-one needed to call on me at this time of night.

I left the bed, again checking that Maria was sleeping, and she serenely was, and padded softly out into the lounge. Four steps – heavy shoes or boots – one way, four on return, in front of my door. I took a deep breath, sucked in an extra dollop of courage, and reached for the door handle.

I heard another door open – one of the other flats – and Will: ''ey, mate wha's up?'

'Good evening, sir. Nothing to worry about. Just following up a report about a possible intruder in the building.' That was Tom.

''aven't 'eard or seen anyfing up 'ere, constable. Usually pretty quiet.'

I felt chilled, and began to shiver as I listened through the door.

The guy from the flat next door to the left joined the conversation. 'What's going on?' Sharp. Like a school teacher.

I heard Tom begin a retreat. 'Well, obviously a false report. Sorry to disturb you, gents. I'll be getting on my way back to the station and making my report.' The sounds of his footsteps disappeared down the stairs.

I opened my door. 'Who was that?'

'Oh some policeman, mate,' Will whispered dismissively. 'Some cock-and-bull story about investigatin' a report of an intruder up 'ere. Bullshit.' He scratched his chest. 'G'night.' He shut his door.

I turned to the guy to my left. 'Very odd indeed,' he muttered.

I crawled back into bed and put my arms around Maria. She exuded snug warmth; muttered something sleepily. I snuggled her close to me. It had been a long day.

Policeman's knock

Since Friday was my day off I slept in to 7am. Maria promptly left the bed when her alarm went off and disappeared into the bathroom.

I got up and made her breakfast. I thought she might like that since she had unfailingly got up with me for the last three mornings. She kissed me, her breath a sweet mix of coffee, toast, and jam and crumbs. Somehow I loved it. Then she went and got dressed. I offered to walk with her to the corner. She thanked me but said she was a big girl now.

Just after nine o'clock I dropped off at Matthew FitzGarratt's office the photocopied notes of Tom's latest activities. Mrs O'Daly, who was warming to me – she smiled grandmotherly – assured me she would 'put them on the very centre of Mr Matthew's desk'. I asked if he could meet Maria and me soon.

I was back at my flat before midday, and not long after that there was a heavy knock on the door. Constable Tom Kearns in the doorway. His expression was of a man very pleased with himself. He reminded me of a teacher, Mr Birdling, who wore the same delighted expression when he knew he'd caught you out. He was even more delighted when he slashed your arse with the cane.

'Wrong time of the day for you to be visiting, isn't it?' I said. 'I thought you preferred creeping around in the night.'

His eyes told me he didn't like that, and that he would gain a great deal of satisfaction from making me regret them. He tried the old policeman tactic of standing up close, chest-to-chest, so you had to step back, and he would keep advancing. I didn't step back.

'I'm here, sir, on a reasonable belief that there are illegal drugs on these premises.' He was trying to look and sound official. It was a moment when I wished I knew my law. Did he need a warrant? Did I have to give consent? And he was fully blocking my doorway. A brawny policeman with the build of a rugby prop.

Another door had opened, and it was the recluse on my left, holding a Siamese cat that yowled balefully at Tom. 'What's going on here?' he demanded. The tone insistent, that of someone used to getting a respectful answer. The same tone as the other morning. 'Just why do you keep coming here, constable?'

Tom took a step back, flummoxed by this interruption on his right flank – *you again* – and I quickly fumbled the door chain into its slot. 'Just a moment, constable,' I said. 'I want to check with my lawyer.'

'You have a lawyer?' A hint of derision there.

'Yeah,' I said as I slammed the door shut. 'He's your Queen's Counsel brother-in-law.'

In the half-moment before the door clicked shut I watched Tom's face go pale. I picked up the phone and began dialling Matt FitzGarratt's. The neighbour fired questions sharply at Tom. What was he doing up here? What was his name? His police number? His 'commanding officer'?

Tom lost his policemanly composure, and I heard the wire-glass fire door open and then his heavy footsteps rapidly thumping down the stairs.

I hung up the phone just as it was answered, and went back out to the landing. The recluse was still in his doorway; the Siamese had scurried back into their flat, still yowling crossly. 'Thanks for that,' I said.

'No problem,' he said airily. He was a slight man, a narrow face, the back goatee beard making him look piratical. He retreated into his flat, thought again, cleared his throat and said: 'Are you in some kind of bother?'

'Depends what you mean by bother. My girlfriend is his sister-in-law. Her family apparently aren't happy with her new living arrangements here with me. I don't know what he's playing at, but he's been spending a lot of police time around here.'

'Ahhhh …' and he winked knowingly. 'I know what that can be like.'

'I don't know if I need to add,' I said, 'but there are no drugs here. I don't use them.'

'Oh,' and a smile. He bade me good day, and we shut our doors.

I phoned Matt's office.

'Got your notes this morning, Martin. Just been scanning through them quickly. Well done.'

I told him about Tom's last visit.

'That is disturbing. Creepy really.'

I asked him if he could see Maria and me later today.

He consulted his diary. 'Well, I'm supposed to be over at the Supreme Court at four-thirty. Justice Tyler is retiring, so we're having drinks.'

I heard a 'hmmm'.

'Oh, bugger it. Come in at half-past four, Martin. I'd love to see Maria and you. Tyler's a pompous arsehole so it won't be a hardship to not be there.'

MARIA SAT quietly on the end of the bed still in her uniform as I told her that we were going to see Matthew. I recounted Tom's visit earlier, and about his after-midnighter on Tuesday morning. And about what Alice had told me about Tom's coming up the stairs one day when she might have been here and I wasn't.

Just as quietly she asked me why I hadn't told her all that until now, particularly the visit the other night.

I was so full of telling her the news that my antenna wasn't working as well as it should have been. 'I didn't want to frighten you, love.'

Her tone in reply was mildly Head Girl Frosty, her eyes warning: 'I'd appreciate it, Martin, if you didn't keep secrets from me about us. I'm not a shrinking violet.'

I didn't know how to take this rebuke. Did I try to justify myself, say I was thinking only of her?

She reached a hand out to me, and her strong fingers encircled mine. 'I'm sorry, my darling' she whispered, 'that sounded bitchy. We *are* in this together, aren't we?'

I nodded.

'I wouldn't be here if it wasn't for you. But we share everything, OK? The bad, as well as the good.' And she kissed me softly and squeezed my hand. 'I won't let you be my rock on your own.'

She stood up and started to strip off her uniform. 'I suppose if I'm going to grace my brother's hallowed chambers I'd better make myself presentable.'

Family stories

I drove us into town. Maria said she wanted to shop for some clothes after we'd seen Matt. In most of New Zealand then Friday night was shopping night, when the shops stayed open to up to nine o'clock. No Saturday and Sunday shopping. No malls to trawl through. I had a feeling there might be shopping bags.

I parked in my paper's carpark and we walked around to Matthew's law firm.

In his office Matthew greeted Maria warmly with a hug and a kiss on the cheek. They were brother and sister. Yet there wasn't the closeness of two siblings. He called her 'Sis', she 'Matt'. He observed that she was looking well and she politely returned a smiled 'thank you'. So he was trying, I think, to bridge as best he could the gulfs: the 27-year age difference; their respective positions as oldest and youngest siblings; of outlook and maturity. I hoped she would try in return.

'Tom's behaviour is disturbing,' he said. 'Very soon questions will be going to his bosses about why he has been at or about your address so often. Especially at night. Witnesses, times, dates will be important because we'll be wanting to know what his job book says, and under whose authority has he been going around to your place.'

'How would you get that?' Maria said.

He grinned easily. 'Oh. Simple. Demand it. If we don't get it then we threaten to apply to the courts. His bosses won't like that, Ria.'

He glanced at the papers. 'But I don't like this latest development. Ol' Ploddy is not above 'finding' evidence, particularly in drugs cases, that helps them get a conviction. And they stick together. If one lies they all lie.'

His eyes met mine. 'Just be careful how you go, Martin. All right?'

I nodded.

Right.

Maria reached over and took my hand.

'Why do you think he's doing this?' I said. 'He appears to be taking all this very personally.'

Matt shook his head. 'Who knows?' He grinned. 'But I can say there is a thickening file on Constable Thomas Eric Kearns – he's known to be violent and has a reputation for not going by the book.'

He glanced meaningfully at Maria: 'I know that in his past he has assaulted at least one woman. He was seen to be very, er, vigorous at a Vietnam war protest. But all his fellow coppers around him swore blind that he hadn't done what he'd been accused of doing. '

Maria gasped. 'My God! Stella, does she know –'

'I very much doubt it.' He sighed. 'A man of many faces, our brother-in-law.'

And that was a nice touch from Matt, I thought: 'our brother-in-law'. He was treating his youngest sister as an equal.

'You should know – and I'm sure you do – that the family is unhappy about your actions, Ria. There have been discussions most nights. I'm not privy to a lot of it because I've refused to take part. Dad is disappointed that I have sided with you.'

'Why have you sided with me then, Matthew?' That sounded a bit sharp to me. If he noticed, he didn't show it.

His expression was thoughtful: eyes a mix of regret and determination, cheeks sucked in, lips pursed. 'It's a long story. Well, several stories, really. One is similar to yours, well before you were born, I might add. Another concerns our sister Annette.

'I don't even know her,' Maria said. 'It's like she doesn't exist.'

'That's what it's been like. The dominating influence in our family – for as long as I can remember – has been our grandmother, and what appears to be a hold on Dad.'

'Yes, I know. He's always buckled to her, that's been obvious.'

The conversation continued between the two. As the meeting was winding up and we stood to leave Maria said: 'Catharine and I have talked more this week than we have in the past.' He nodded. 'And she's coming around tomorrow so we can have some time together. Are you happy with that?'

He grinned, and it was the kind of grin that made him seem boyish. 'Certainly I am.' He came around from behind his desk and touched a hand to her shoulder. 'I know you two haven't always got on, but she is firmly in your court.'

Then a sense of regret: 'I can't say the same about Kay. I think she thinks you'll be a bad influence on Cath. But you're the same age, you both leave school at the end of the year so you'll have to learn to start making your own decisions. As parents we have to get used to it.'

'What about Rachael and Charlotte?'

'Don't know about them, I'm afraid. Their parents are not in your camp.'

Maria sounded shaky: 'And Mark and Margaret?' Meaning Gabrielle's parents.

Matthew tried to sound sympathetic. 'I'm afraid most definitely not. Brother Mark is now our parents' main source of in-house legal advice. He gets one up on me. Margaret, I think, will be quite happy to see you out of the way. She's always resented your closeness to Gabrielle.' He saw the effect of those words on Maria. 'Well, that's what Kay and Catharine say.'

He was escorting us out of the building. At the door he said: 'You should expect a visitation from Mater and Pater. Good luck.'

MARIA HEADED for a fashionable, expensive shop to buy underwear. I had never been on such an expedition. I offered to go to a nearby bookshop instead.

'*Nooo,* darling,' and she tugged on my arm, steering me towards the shop. 'You'll be the best person to tell me what you think.'

So I passed verdicts on knickers, frilly and otherwise, whites, colours – she liked pinks, blues, two-tones of pinks, white with flowers and roses; bras, plain and lacy, especially a daring little number in dark pink with matching briefs; slips, camis, tights, and pantyhose. She knew what she liked. 'Only you'll see me wearing these, Martin,' she whispered.

A woman in the shop complimented me on being, as she put it, 'brave enough to come into a shop and do this for his fiancée'.

I smiled blandly. *Fiancée.* I supposed it sounded better than boyfriend. 'Partner' was not in vogue then.

She turned to Maria and said: 'He shows very good taste, by the way.' Maria smiled obliquely as her items were wrapped.

We went to another fashionable, expensive shop, where she bought pants 'for the winter' and the kind of figure-hugging knitted rollneck sweaters that she preferred. A jacket, and a trench coat with fur collar – it made her look taller, older – went into a bag.

I was her bag-carrier. I didn't mind. She was happy.

Next was a chemist shop. Maria didn't use a lot of make-up, but she liked it subdued – 'subtle'. I did quietly go and buy her a bottle of Charlie perfume, which I'd heard was highly prized among women. It seemed so with Maria, because she clapped her hands to her mouth, and said in wide-eyed wonder: '*Oh, Martin!* Oh, my Lord …'

Afterwards she wanted to go to a Chinese restaurant, and she said she was paying. 'It's a little thank you from me, darling.'

During the meal – she had fish, since it was Friday, and she still observed the Catholic Church's laws – she chattered away and laughed. She was so happy. Astonishingly, this was the first time she'd bought clothes and things of her choosing on her own.

Child(ish) play

We fought on Saturday night. I was being childish and puerile, and I knew I was. Like a lot of lovers' verbal brawls this one started over a seemingly trivial thing. It wasn't the toilet seat or the cap on the toothpaste tube, although deep down there might have been a bit of that.

It was over the kitchen cupboards. I got home about 9.30pm, as was usual for my Saturday work day. I was tired. I had helped put out two newspapers since half-past five that morning. It had been a long week, too.

I walked into my flat, and stopped: Maria had changed the furniture around. The table – now cleared of its various piles of paper and the typewriter – occupied the centre of the lounge, covered by a doily, on which sat a vase with flowers.

The couch and the armchairs had been shifted so they formed a snug corner. The bookcase wasn't where it had been.

How the hell had she done it to create such a space in a small room?

Maria unwound from the couch, where she'd been reading a book and listening to the radio, and came over and kissed me. 'Hi, darling. What do you think?' Her arm took in the changes in a sweep.

Well, what did I think? *She could have asked me before she started rearranging my flat.*

My second thought: *she'll be hurt if I criticise what she's done.*

My third thought, which I voiced, was: 'Well, sweetie, it's different.'

I think she sensed my lack of enthusiasm. 'We – Catharine and me – thought it just might look a bit homely. We can have people around for meals.'

'OK,' I said.

Maria had kept a meal for me, which she had cooked earlier with Catharine, and I thanked her and kissed her for that. Crikey, that was something domestic I'd not known since I'd lived at home. I had usually got fish and chips from the little Hungarian shop next to work. Or else made toast. I reached to get a plate from a cupboard above the bench.

Let me explain: I had arranged my pots, pans, plates, cutlery – my kitchenette, in other words – so that everything I used most was close at hand. I thought it was a logical arrangement. My beloved had a different logic. The plates were somewhere else. I checked through the cupboards. Everything was somewhere else.

I erupted. 'What the hell have you done here?!'

A confused frown: 'I just thought –'

'Well you bloody thought wrong, didn't you,' I said, and far, far too loudly and too petulantly.

'Martin, I –'

'It would be really good if you'd just bloody ask what I think before you start trying to reorganise me and my bloody flat.'

Her eyes had distilled to that sharp green; the points of her cheeks flamed.

Ignoring those danger signs, I ranted on.

I don't remember the words now – I didn't after I had shouted them. Maria stood there in front of me, up straight, head held erect, chin unflinching, shoulders back, eyes unblinkingly locked on mine, taking everything I flung at her. She was no coward.

The episode had been less than 30 seconds.

'I'm sorry, Martin,' she said quietly. 'I realise I've made a mistake. I'll put everything back to how it was tomorrow. Now I'm going to bed.'

She gathered up her book off the couch and shut the door of the bedroom quietly behind her. So she wasn't a door-slammer then.

I ate the meal she had prepared, and it felt as if I was chewing sawdust mixed with leather, and it was hard to swallow. Guilt screwed through me as I sat at the table for a long time.

I did a lot of rationalising and justifying, but more than that: why had I erupted?

It shouldn't have been. The girl I loved – and who loved me – was here, under my roof, sharing my bed, didn't have to go home any more. She was here, and had walked out on her family to be here.

We were defying convention and social attitudes. 'Nice' girls didn't have sex, unless it was with their husbands.

'Nice' girls did not shack up with their boyfriends. The Church she had been baptised into was particularly hard on young women who were 'living immoral lives'.

'Erupted' is an apt word. It means that what lurks underneath the surface bursts out, often spectacularly, often violently. It can be the molten lava out of the depths of the earth. It can be the pus from a boil.

So in my introspection I began to dig into what was really at the bottom of my outburst.

The answer I found was not pretty: I was not fully prepared for the sharing of my life with another. I felt a resentment that my life – my quiet, uneventful life with its great job and great prospects, my life in this concrete cocoon with its books, radio, and music, three storeys above the street – had been disrupted.

In about a month Maria and I had gone from admiring each other on opposite street corners, not knowing one another's names, quickly to sharing a bed, and now she was here, my 'constant companion' as the women's mags described the shacked-up, and that had set us up on a collision course with her family.

I hadn't expected events to move so quickly.

In all my 23 years I'd never had a policeman stalk me. Christ, I hadn't had a joint in four years – since it was handed to me by an undercover cop at a party. That had scared the living Bejesus out of me when a friend told me who he was. Back then you went to jail for merely smoking cannabis. Your name was in the papers. Shame and scandal on the family.

And now it seemed as if Maria – in doing something as normal and logical to her as rearranging the furniture and the pots and pans, to make this place her home, too – had unwittingly pressed a hot-button that I didn't know I had.

I washed my plate and knife and fork, dried them, and put them away in their new places, then sat at the table, head in my hands, for a long time. I've always been hard on myself. Uncle Syd and Auntie Koo have often said that. I've never liked hurting people, and I've felt deep guilt long afterwards when I had.

I'd hurt Maria. It wasn't so much the words I'd flung at her, it was that by shouting at her and over such a seemingly trivial matter I'd broken many, if not all, of the threads that were binding us together.

I realised, too, that I'd shown myself to be a pig. A side I thought I never had. Always 'Mr Nice Guy', as Felicity scornfully said as she gave me the flick. Maria might not love me now. I was anxious to repair the damage.

I dreaded turning out the light, opening the door, and going into my – our – bedroom. There was nowhere to hide from what I had done. I was going to have to lie down next to the person I loved and whom I'd hurt. And somehow try to make amends.

The signature line from the weeper *Love Story* – 'Love means never having to say you're sorry', and parroted by lovers and romantics all around the world since – was nonsense.

Love meant the capacity to hurt was greater because when we loved we made ourselves vulnerable to another.

So love did mean saying sorry, humbly, and usually abjectly. I was abject then, wanting nothing more than to remove the hurt and to have us loving each other again.

I crawled into bed.

She had left me plenty of space for my punishment. Maria was on her side of the bed – on the very edge. In her pyjamas, her back to me, knees drawn up, and she had dragged the sheet and blankets over so they were tightly around her; her arms were tight in against her breasts.

She didn't speak. I knew she wasn't asleep because her breathing wasn't slow and shallow, accompanied by the occasional, soft 'hem' … hem' …

'Sweetie?' I tried.

No response.

I reached out to touch her shoulder: it was like stone.

'Don't. *Touch!* Me.'

Glacially icy, grated out through clenched teeth.

So we lay there, in our double bed, until now a place of love and warmth, of secrets and whispers and confidences, where two people could be themselves without fear and shame – and it was colder than an ice floe.

I shivered. Maria, an arm's length from me, could have been 1000 miles away. Catholics might understand my predicament: I did penance, hoping that God – or the Virgin Mary, the lone observer of all this from her place on top of the drawers – might look kindly on me and help Maria to soften her heart and forgive me.

I ventured timidly to make contact with her. I knew she still wasn't sleeping. I snuggled in behind her, and rested my hand on her shoulder – and waited for her response. There was none.

'Ria, look I –'

'Don't. Call. Me. *Ria!'*

I retreated to the cold expanse of the bed and shivered some more. The cold night wore on until out in the trees and under roofs birds tweeted and chipped and fluttered and fussed.

I decided to try again, and more determinedly. 'Maria,' I said, just above a whisper. No response.

'I won't try to touch you. But would you please turn around and face me and at least listen to me.'

No response, but I knew she'd held her breath.

'I'm freezing here. And I'm not just talking about the bed.'

A movement. Her head, inclining towards me. And she slowly turned over until she faced me.

'I'm sorry I shouted at you like that. I'm not apologising for it again. I hate it when you won't talk to me.'

She didn't speak. But she shared the sheet and the blankets towards me, and I spread them over me gratefully. She remained a no-go zone, though, well over on the edge, knees drawn up and her arms wrapped around a pillow against her belly.

I told her about discovering the hot-button. The resentment I felt I had discovered.

'Are you saying you don't love me, Martin, or that you find me an inconvenient presence?'

'No. I do love you. I *do* love you.' I shook my head. 'I know it might not make sense, what I'm saying. In an odd way, I saw something about me I hadn't seen before. It made me realise I do love you.'

She lay there, inscrutable in the grey of dawn, her eyes fixed on mine. The silence dragged.

'I'm not doing this very well, am I?' She didn't answer. 'A few weeks ago you asked me if you could count on me. And I said yes.' Her eyelids flickered.

'When I was a kid I used to go to Sunday school. Mrs Barlow was the teacher. And she said that love wasn't love unless actions went with the words.'

I thought I saw a thawing in those eyes. Less Head Girl. 'I'm trying to match words with actions. I can't say I love you and not show you I do – like having you here, standing by you over your parents, and probably your school.'

I tried my last shot. 'Love is love, and it's meant to be permanent. It's not buyable, disposable, or tradable.'

I sighed miserably, perhaps because I felt I was losing her, and now I was very tired after being awake for 24 hours, the last few in self-inflicted torment. 'Well, that's how I feel about it anyway.'

Maria drew in a deep breath, got rid of the pillow from against her belly, and slid over to me. 'You're cold,' she whispered as her arms slipped around me. 'Come on, sweetie, let me help warm you up.' She was warm, in that bed-fug-sleep way.

Whispers … whispers of love, whispers of apology – 'I won't shift stuff around, sweetie, without asking you first' – for making the other feeling the need to apologise. Loving caresses, reassuring touches, giggles and muffled laughter. Kisses, kisses of love, kisses of reconciliation and forgiveness. The eruption forgotten. Buttons undone, her breasts warm, welcoming my kisses. Then silence and stillness, that moment when … and she shifted her hips as I slid her pyjamas off; her smile and her eyes as welcoming as the warm depths of her body.

Peirse and Órla

The phone woke us. I glanced at my bedside clock as my feet hit the floor: 7.30am. *Fuck, no-one rings at this hour unless it's an emergency.*
'Good morning, Michael.'
'It's Martin,' I heard another voice in the background say.
'Er, yes, *Martin*,' Peirse FitzGarratt added awkwardly.
'Good morning, Doctor. What can I do for you?'
'Maria's mother and I will call to see you about nine-thirty, just after we've been to eight o'clock Mass. Good bye.' *Click.*
I stood nakedly, holding the receiver. There had been no discussion. Just 9.30am. If I'd wanted to be difficult I could've rung back and said that it wasn't convenient to visit.
'That was your father. They're coming around here at nine-thirty.'
She frowned. 'Hmm. I suppose it had to happen some time.' She flung the blankets back and eased herself out of the bed. 'I suppose we'd better get cleaned up and dressed, then.'

THEY RAPPED on the door at 9.30am on the dot.
I glanced at Maria. She had dressed carefully, as a daughter. New slacks, new knitted top and a woven loose cardigan with forearm-length sleeves over that. Her hair was tied back in her severe Head Girl Bun. She had taken great care with her appearance.

She stood by the table, her hands clasped before her, chin up. She took a deep breath, nodded curtly, and I opened the front door, invited her parents in, and stood back while they did.

'Hi,' Maria offered, a tense smile. Neither parent said anything. Her mother glanced meaningfully at the closed bedroom door.

Maria indicated the table, with its doily and epergne with flowers. 'Would you like to sit down? Dad, could I make you both a cup of tea? Mum …'

Her mother ran her eyes up and down her daughter's body, clearly disapproving of what she saw. 'No.' Then: 'We haven't come to talk to you or have a cup of tea with you. Get your things, Maria, you're coming home with us.'

Maria glanced at me. She shook her head decisively. 'No. I'm not getting my things and I'm not going home with you.'

Órla wasn't used to defiance, I don't think, especially from her children, grown up or otherwise. She looked up at Peirse. He was a big man who filled a room with his presence.

He went forward a step, and I thought he was going to hit her. 'Girl, do you understand the position you're in?'

Her eye contact with him was fearless: 'I understand perfectly my position. I'm here, living with the man I love and who loves me. Everybody else seems to have a problem with that.'

'Love,' Órla snarled. 'Love! What do you know about love? Lust, more like it.'

Órla was losing her professorial cool. 'Look at you, you little trollop. Living here like a filthy tart!'

Maria was unflinchingly still, not making any effort to answer her mother or defend herself.

That appeared to goad Órla. 'You were brought up with the best of everything! You were brought up with standards and morals! You weren't dragged up like those loose little wretches who open their legs to every drooling male who comes along with his tongue hanging out!'

Órla, flushed, was now breathing hard. She was not a pretty sight. I had expected that, given the parents' obvious intellect, they might have come at this with a more cerebral approach. Less judgmental, less abusing, less … crude, I suppose.

And something else: they seemed impersonal, in a way, not parents talking to a daughter. It was as if she was at arm's-length, someone they knew not very well. Maria called them 'Mum' and 'Dad', and it didn't fit.

Peirse joined in: 'You're living here in sin with this man,' he said too loudly, a dismissive wave towards me. 'It's *mortal sin*, Maria, your very soul – your eternal life, girl – is in danger. You know the Church's teaching – sex outside of marriage is *a sin*.'

He tried pleading. 'We're *frantic with worry* about you, girl!'

Órla added: 'We're worried that you're making a big mistake. That you think this,' and she indicated the flat and me, 'is love and it's wonderful and there's nothing else like it and it's never happened to anyone else.'

'And one day you find out it's not what you thought it was,' Peirse added, 'and you're left disillusioned, feeling used, abused, and what *decent* man will have you then …'

He petered into an awkward silence, which lengthened. As if the parents had run out of things to say.

So Maria filled the gap. 'I'm not going home with you,' she said crisply. 'I'm never going back home to live.'

Peirse tried to interrupt. 'Excuse me, please. I've listened to you both.'

My God, I was proud of her. She was not getting down to their level.

She turned back to her mother. 'You said you worried that I might be making a big mistake by being here with Martin.'

Órla made to reply, but Maria kept going, coolly, respectfully. 'It might be a mistake. But mistakes aren't always the preserve of the young and silly. We all know that. And if it is a mistake then I'll have to wear that. Just like everyone else has to.'

'What about if you get …' and here Peirse was horrified by the thought, '… pregnant? You'll expect to come running home then and have everyone run after you and your child, prop you up, and clean up after you.'

He vaguely indicated me with a wave of his thumb: 'And you'll sure find that Michael here won't be anywhere around.'

Maria beat me to it. She looked puzzled. 'You of all people know how unlikely that is. I have an anovulatory cycle, remember? The pair of you and Bridget and Stella subjected me to enough tests and examinations by all your doctor friends to establish that,' and that was the first bitterness I heard from her during this visit.

'But,' she said, glancing meaningfully at me, 'I'm sure that *Martin* – and *Martin* is his name – and I will work something out if I did get pregnant.' She smiled tautly. 'After all, I've had plenty of practice from looking after my siblings' and cousins' babies.'

Órla turned suddenly to me: 'Are you a believer in abortion or not?'

As I said a few weeks ago, New Zealand in the mid-70s was gripped by a debate over making abortion more legal, more available. Peirse and Órla were leading lights against that.

I hadn't known until a week or so ago about Maria's difficulties with her cycle. Young men didn't think much beyond the end of their foreskins then. It might be said it has always been so. A common male attitude when I was young was of finding somewhere pleasurable to put it, 'fuck the arse off her', shoot the wad, roll off with a perfunctory kiss and tell her she was great, tell a few more lies to make her feel better, and bugger off. Many males saw pregnancy – and how to avoid it – as 'her' problem. Contraception was not readily available. For many women and girls sex was a form of Russian Roulette, anxious counting of days until the relief of their period's beginning. Many males did not like using condoms, for example. 'It's like rooting in a gumboot' some said triumphantly at the pub or in the footie changing shed. As well, you could get them only from the chemist. In a smallish town the chemist knew you and your parents. Attitudes were different then.

So back to Órla's question. It surprised me. It didn't fit with what appeared to be the purpose of the visit – to shame or force Maria to return to the Ancestral Manor. But I had been thinking about what would happen if I got Maria pregnant. I knew she wouldn't consider an abortion – which then were not easy to get, in any case.

'If Maria became pregnant to me I would do everything in my power to support her. I could not let her face the situation on her own.' Slowly, for her father's benefit, I added: 'I wouldn't abandon her or our child.'

Maria smiled, as if she just knew I wouldn't say anything else.

My reply seemed to lessen the heat in this confrontation. It was as if Órla had accepted the situation: her daughter wasn't going home with her and Peirse and she wanted to know what I would do if I made her daughter pregnant. But her sudden change of tack still hadn't made sense.

Peirse now became belligerent, as if returning to the point of the visit: 'Well, young lady, you need to understand that your wilfulness will have consequences.'

His face was hard. Flint would have been softer.

'First, we'll be notifying the school that you've left home and that you're living here, and with him.'

She never batted an eyelash. I was thinking: *Him. Not Martin. Him.*

'So we'll be withdrawing our financial support – we won't be paying any more for you to be there.' He gestured towards me: 'Michael here can pay for you – that is, if they let you stay on, which I can't imagine their doing because your immoral life here is the very antithesis of how a Catholic girl should be living.'

She didn't flinch.

'There's a trust fund for you started by your grandmother that was to pay for your university tuition, different from the one Matthew administered.'

Peirse sounded like he was enjoying this, being the big man, in effect saying 'this is how it's going to be from now on'. 'Each of you children had one. Yours will be closed and the funds shared around your nieces and nephews.'

She showed no reaction, so in the silence he continued. 'You've rejected your family and all our values. You've rejected a central teaching of the Church. You've hurt your mother and me very deeply. You've disappointed your grandmother. You've caused a scandal – because when it all comes out there will be a scandal and that will be embarrassing to us. We tried to bring you up better than most. Gave you opportunities and advantages that most don't have. You've thrown them like dirty rags back in our faces.'

He gave her time to think about that, and she showed no expression. 'So, until you come to your senses, see the folly of your ways, then come home in a spirit of humble repentance – Luke says he will be available to you whenever you want – stay here and wallow in your filth. You're cut off. Not welcome. No-one will see you, and ...' he paused because he meant this to be the telling blow, 'and Mark and Margaret will ensure you have nothing to do with Gabrielle. You'll not be corrupting her with your sordid life.'

Maria held her composure admirably. She wasn't going to give him the satisfaction of seeing how hard that punch had been. It hurt.

So he tried again: 'We're not having you pollute her with your sewage.' He glanced at Órla, and I might have been wrong, but I sensed she didn't like that. She had come in the door aggressively and name-callingly. But after I had replied about not abandoning Maria if she became pregnant she had shut up.

'Come on, Mother,' he said, 'we'll leave her to wallow in this bordello until she sees the error of her ways.'

He offered me barely a nod and opened the door himself, and strode out on to the landing. The fire door opened, and I heard his steps thudding down the stairs.

Órla, now Órla ... she reached out a hand to her daughter's, squeezed it briefly, there was eye-contact between the two, a glance then at me as she passed, and she followed him.

I shut the door behind them. Maria had turned very pale, and her body shook as tears washed down her cheeks and splotted on to her sweater.

We walked into each other's outstretched arms and clung to one another tightly. I let her cry, just caressing her back, her hair, kissing her lightly.

'I don't care about any of it,' she whispered as her sobs subsided, 'as long as I've got you. But he stabbed me in the heart when he brought Gabrielle into it.'

We clung to each other for a long time.

Searching for an egg

'Come on, Miss FitzGarratt,' I said briskly, pulling her up off the bed where she had gone to cry and brood a couple of hours earlier. 'I think we should have a change of scenery. Can't have you moping about in here all day.'

She consulted the window, scowling. 'It's raining,' she muttered, and sat back on the bed.

I also consulted the window, and the cold, dismal grey, and the bleak breeze stirring the trees down below. 'Showers,' I replied with a fake heartiness. 'You're not made of sugar, my dear. You won't melt under a drop of water or two.'

She eyed me sullenly. 'I might. And it's cold out there, too.'

I needed to distract her, especially from Peirse's brutal remarks about Gabrielle. I opened the wardrobe and selected her new, woollen trench coat, and took it off its hanger. 'This one?'

She nodded dutifully. *Good.* I threw it on the end of the bed. Her new boots were neatly together – all her footwear was neatly in pairs, as were my two pairs now – by the door. I picked them up, plonked them by her feet. She pulled them on, also dutifully.

'Come on, sweetie, up-up,' I ordered, hauled her to her feet. I held her coat for her and she slipped it on. She turned and hugged me tightly. 'Thank you, Martin,' she whispered in a snuffled kind of way.

THE WATERFRONT, and its mixture of gelid, salt-laden breeze off the water, sluggish low cloud eager to shed rain, seagulls that wheeled and soared in the air or strutted along the wharves in search of edible scraps; cargo and passenger ships alongside, flags from Liberia, Panama, Holland, Sweden, Australia, New Zealand and half-a-dozen other countries whipping from main-masts and sterns. The cranes idle because it was a Sunday. We strolled contentedly, arm-in-arm, her hair whipping in the breeze, and Maria pushed away her woe.

'What is an, er …' I struggled for the right word '… what you said to your father. About your, you know, um, cycle?'

She looked at me blankly. Then it registered. 'Oh. Anovulatory.'

'Yes. That one.'

'Ah. Well, that's just the fancy scientific word for what I described a week or so back. That I don't lay eggs.'

'OK.'

She grasped what I was driving at. 'OK, sweetie. Another quick girl-biology lesson. My periods started when I was 12.'

She waited as we passed a couple of visiting Royal Australian Navy destroyers; they were open to the public and people were queuing to go aboard them.

'Anyway. They were regular. Exactly. And for a couple of years I bled like every other girl when I was supposed to. Then I noticed they were not turning up on time, and even not at all – months went by. I mentioned it to Stella. We went over all my dates, which I'd kept in a notebook.

'She talked to Mum, and they talked to Bridget, another doctor in the family. They all talked to each other. Even my grandmother managed to involve herself in it. She insinuated that I'd "been up to something" and was pregnant.'

I fully turned to stare at her. Who would say that? Oh, yes, and now having met the woman I could see she would say that.

'For God's sake! I was 14!'

By asking a simple question about the meaning of a word I didn't understand – and didn't know how to say or spell even – I had pressed a button. Out reeled a story of hurt and dammed-up anger about how she'd been treated.

'Then Mum, Stella and Bridge – and my grandmother tagged along, too – took me to see Dr O'Leary, an old friend of my father's from when they were at school. He's the family GP. Because doctors aren't allowed to treat family members. They all talked some more to each other as if I was something on a specimen tray.'

We walked on, and another young couple strolling arm-in-arm smiled at us and said 'hi' as if we were kindred spirits. We smiled back and said 'hi', too.

'I had to take my pants off so that Dr O'Leary could peer up me. I remember lying there, my legs apart in the stirrups. The couch was cold and hard against my bottom. And his hand was very cold and hard as he stuck his finger into me.'

Jesus ...

'I didn't know what he was looking for. Even I knew he wouldn't find an egg. I started to cry, and my grandmother and Bridget were not very nice. They told me to stop it. Stella held my hand.'

She half-turned to me. 'I'm used to doctors in the family, Martin. I'm the daughter of one and the sister of two and the sister-in-law of another. I'm used to being in the company of family friends who are doctors, and there are a lot of them. I've been used to hearing medical things being discussed in conversations since before I could talk.'

She glanced out over the water. 'But I'm healthy. I've rarely been to a doctor for a medical matter. I've never had a broken bone. I've rarely been sick apart from the pox and the measles. I menstruated normally and with little bother until they decided to stop.'

A seagull begged for food.

'And so it shocked me to lie there, naked from the waist down, and little Dr O'Leary and his thick, framed glasses and his bulgie eyes had his finger prodding around in my vagina. And my grandmother leaning over his shoulder to see what she could see. It hurt. No-one since has been able to tell me why he was allowed to do that. What was he feeling for?'

We walked on in silence for several moments, and her arm in mine stiff with her anger. Christ, there was a lot I didn't know.

'Dr O'Leary couldn't find anything, so I was sent to a gynaecologist, another of my father's friends from medical school. If you don't know, gynaecologists are specialists concerned with the baby-making works – ovaries, fallopian tubes, womb. All that.'

I was trying to keep up.

'And he and my parents and grandmother and Bridget and Stella all talked about me as if I wasn't there. Instead of humiliating me by thrusting his finger up me he ordered that I be X-rayed. And when that didn't show up anything then I had to undergo a scan, like they use for pregnant women. That didn't reveal anything.'

A ship's horn boomed across the harbour, signalling departure.

'And Bridget had a bright idea – this time a woman gynie who was a friend of hers for another opinion. And there were some tests. They consulted literature. I had to answer personal questions about myself in front of my sisters and mother and father, and grandmother. I know they discussed me with other members of the family.'

She let out a long, deep breath. The rage was blowing away, borne like a breeze. 'In the end, Martin, they decided I wasn't laying eggs any more, and probably never would. They didn't know why. It agitated my grandmother that a granddaughter of hers might have to miss out on the joys of pregnancy and childbirth. She prayed rosaries to Our Lady to intervene.'

We strolled on in companionable silence. As her hip bumped against mine I couldn't help thinking – again – how she willingly discussed this matter-of-factly with me, without embarrassment.

She stepped in front of me, a sly grin, and leaned against me almost wearily. 'And since I've been having sex with you, my love, for the last month, it would confirm that I haven't laid a single egg. Otherwise I'd be suffering morning sickness right now.'

WE DROVE to Peter and Magdalena's café and movie theatre for an afternoon coffee and something to eat. No-one was in their theatres. The café was nearly empty and so they had time to sit and talk to us.

We told them Maria and I were living together in my flat. Magdalena turned to Maria and suggested she might find something in their flat interesting. Maria glanced at me, eyebrows raised; I shrugged. It was clear Magdalena was taking Maria off for some girl-talk. Which Peter confirmed when we were alone.

'That's a big step, Martin,' he added. 'How are Maria's family taking it?'

'Mostly not very well. Her parents came around this morning and they tried to order her home. She's in breach of Church teaching about sex only between husband and wife.'

He nodded, slipping a *Gauloise* between his lips and lighting it with a paper match.

'Her oldest brother – he's a Queen's Counsel – has been a surprise, though. He's on her side.'

He nodded and blew a stream of smoke over my head.

'She feels betrayed by the older sister she's always been close to.'

Peter released twin stream of grey smoke from his nostrils. 'Do you love her, Martin?'

'Yes.'

Peter dragged on his cigarette. I felt he was wanting to say something. 'Good, because love is what will hold you together.' He crushed out the cigarette. 'It was the same with Maggie and me, you know. I met her in Paris after the war. In 1951, actually. She was 16, and learning the ballet.' He paused while he took another cigarette out of its packet. 'I was 31.'

That made me sit up straight. 'What did she make of that?'

He lit the cigarette. 'It didn't worry her at all. It was as much her as me. Oddly enough, relationships between young women and older men were not uncommon in Europe then.' He blew more smoke in a pungent stream from his lips.

'I'd rescued her from a mugging and, probably, rape, on the street. But her Polish once-wealthy, aristocratic Catholic family – she's a countess, by the way – didn't like it. They sent her off to Italy where there were relatives.'

He grinned. 'There was a secret rendezvous, middle of the night, and we went on the run. They were nasty people.'

He contemplated smoke curling off the end of his cigarette. 'We were chased all across France, Belgium; Germany even.'

He chuckled. 'Actually, Germany was probably the safest place because the country was still a mess. Easy to be a displaced father and his daughter.' His eyes twinkled. 'Besides, I'd Done My Bit in Europe to help win the war, so I had contacts who were able to provide papers and money for my … daughter and me.'

I laughed at that.

'So, to make a long story short, my young Kiwi friend, after many adventures we came here.' He sat back, grinning, his arms taking in the café and theatre. 'And here we are. We live quietly and safely, maybe not profitably.'

As I said a few weeks ago, Peter was a mysterious man in some ways. He never quite said what he'd done during the war, but he must have had access to money.

Peter was speaking from behind the curtain of smoke '… if you both need a place – a sanctuary, say – you will find it here.'

I offered thanks, and he waved it away with the cigarette smoke, which caught up my nose. 'Mate, Magdalena will be saying the same thing to your girl. She will first want to know if she's all right. But she will be offering you shelter.'

He stubbed out the cigarette. His eyes narrowed, but he grinned. 'We both like you, mate. And we both like Maria. She's got guts and character.'

IN BED that night Maria had draped herself over me, head to toe. 'Magdalena offered to be a kind of big sister.'

'That was very kind of her.'

'It's turned out to be not such a bad day after all,' she whispered, our lips just touching. 'Thank you, darling.'

I squeezed her rump gently. 'I love you.'

'Mmmm. I love you, too.'

Maria kissed me softly then laid her head on my chest. Her hair had the fragrance of apples, fresh and light; I caressed her back, up and down, feathery fingertips, idly and sleepily and she squeezed me with her knees.

'That's nice, darling,' she whispered drowsily. Soon her breathing was that slow 'hem' … 'hem' …

She could go to sleep anywhere.

Friendly cousin

I got home from work about four o'clock on Monday. There'd been a meeting of the chapel – i.e., the office branch of the Journalists' Union to discuss the latest push for a pay rise and a review of allowances. The usual people had had their say. Most of the rest of us nodded our heads and voted 'yes' when required. Journalists used to do that so we could get to the drinks sooner.

Maria was home, and she and her niece Catharine were seated at the table doing homework while they chatted and laughed. Catharine seemed to be a much nicer young woman than I'd first believed. Perhaps I'd taken on the dislike Maria had had. She spoke and behaved to her aunt pleasantly and easily. It was clear she had inherited the FitzGarratt brains. She asked me what it was like working as a journalist.

'I love it. It doesn't seem like work. I never want to do anything else,' I replied. 'And it pays well, too.' Which it did, then.

We talked some more in that vein. After Maria had excused herself to go to the loo Catharine said quietly: 'I really admire her for doing what she's done. Standing up to Grandpa and Gran, and my great-grandmother.'

'What do your cousins think?'

She frowned. 'Hard to say. I think they're waiting and watching to see how it will go. Gabe has been reported as becoming moody and disobedient. Auntie Margaret yanked her out of the bath and dished out a thorough hiding to her the other night. That's what Antonia told my sister Karen. Pretty ugly, apparently.'

I felt sick. Gabrielle, shy, sensitive, murmuring Gabrielle …

'We'll say nothing about that to Maria. She'll only get upset and feel it's her fault.'

The toilet flushed. 'How do you think it will go, Catharine?'

'It'll get uglier before it gets better. The FitzGarratts don't like being made a laughing-stock. And that's how my grandparents and – Dad excepted – and aunts and uncles feel about it.'

IN BED, later, cuddled together: 'What did you and Catharine talk about when I was in the loo?'

'She told me that I was wasted on you, and that I was such a god she should have me instead.'

'Liar,' she said sternly, but she kissed me lasciviously.

Big Wednesday

Maria came into the office just as I was finishing up. Her face was white and her eyes tense. She was attracting a great deal of curious attention and whispered comment from other staff as she stood next to me at my desk.

'Hmm, young Blake, you're in trouble,' rasped Barker, the late 50-something, plum-nosed racing sub, father of seven daughters. 'You haven't been up to no good, have you?' His watery eyes gleamed maliciously as he drew on another of the Pall Malls he chain-smoked.

'That'll do, Wilson,' said Ogle, the chief sub. He nodded permission for me to leave.

Outside on the street Maria urgently took my hand, her grip tight. 'I'm sorry to turn up like this, but Sister Hélène has summoned me to her office.'

'When?'

'It was to be now. She said there were 'certain things' she wished to discuss with me.'

Her eyes were wide, serious, and she sounded breathless. 'I asked if you could be there with me, and she agreed.' A deep breath. 'So two-thirty. I think this is it, my love.'

She had brought the car. I decided I had time to make myself presentable. A quick shower and then donning the suit, with tie.

'My God,' Maria said admiringly. 'You scrub up extremely well. Very handsome.' She pecked me on the cheek and ran a hand around my suit-trousered behind.

'I hope you realise the sacrifice I'm making by doing this,' I grumped. She laughed.

WE SAT on a padded bench in a waiting area outside the principal's office. A comfortable, smiling woman Maria knew as Mrs MacClatchie sat at a reception desk answering the phone, doing some sort of paperwork, typing. Her glasses hung from a cord looped around her neck.

A buzzer at her desk sounded. She pressed a button, and a disembodied voice instructed her to tell Maria and her 'friend' to enter her office.

Maria smiled a thank you at Mrs MacClatchie as we passed her desk. I opened the door, stood back, and ushered Maria inside.

Sister Hélène's office was spacious, tidy, smelled of polish and a sweet scent. Sister Hélène – a petite woman with scholarly grey eyes – stood beside a large, solid, wooden desk. She wore the Cambridge blue habit of her order, the veil white-edged. A huge rosary hung from a leather girdle about her middle. She looked to be in her early 40s, but I've learned since that with Catholic nuns you could never be quite sure.

I shut the door and turned as Maria took the pleats of her skirt between her thumbs and forefingers, spread them like a fan, and launched into a curtsey, bowing her head as she did.

Sister Hélène smiled, but regret was in her unlined face.

'Good afternoon, Sister,' Maria said formally. She gestured towards me. 'This is my friend Martin.'

I nodded, the nun smiled politely, her eyes assessing. She invited Maria and me to sit.

Sister Hélène spent some moments studying Maria, who returned her stare frankly across the large desk. A statue of the Virgin Mary, rosary in joined hands, eyes cast heavenwards, stood on a pedestal to the side.

'Maria, I've asked you here because I have received some news that I must say I find deeply saddening, if true.' She had an accent – middle European and English.

'Yes, Sister.'

'I received a telephone call this morning from a parent who demanded to know why the head prefect of the school – the most senior, most responsible, most *trusted* girl – was allowed to be,' and here she cleared her throat with a discreet cough, 'was allowed to be so while she was living in sin with her boyfriend.'

She looked to Maria, to me, before continuing. 'I had no idea. I telephoned your mother, and she told me that you had left home at Easter and that you were staying with Mr Blake.'

I think she found this all regretful.

'They were going to come to see me on Friday to discuss your future here if you had not returned home.'

She paused, eyebrow arched in query. 'Maria: is this true?'

'Yes, Sister,' Maria said quietly. 'I've never lied to you, and I won't now.'

Hélène's face fell. I think she had been hoping against hope this was untrue.

'Martin and I are in love. I live with him at his flat. That is my home now.'

Hélène fascinated me. I had expected denunciations and condemnation, restatement of Church teaching, but her face, her eyes, were sorrowful.

'I moved in with him after my parents told me we had to break up because Martin's not a Catholic.' She glanced down at her hands, clasped in her lap. 'I wasn't prepared to do that, Sister. Martin's treated me a lot more respectfully than any Catholic boys have – a lot of girls here would say that. I mean, about being treated with respect by Catholic boys. We often aren't.'

Hélène shifted her gaze to me. 'My dear,' she said, returning to Maria, 'in 20 or so years of teaching, here and in Europe, I've never met a more outstanding young woman than you.'

I thought I heard the beginning of something a judge says when delivering a sentence. 'You are far and away among the brightest I have known.' She smiled sadly. 'You have impeccable character. Very adult and responsible. You have mixed kindness and understanding and leadership with a maturity well beyond your years. You have always stood out. You have been an irreproachable example,' and I noticed the past tense, 'to all the girls here, and one for Catholic girls generally.'

'Thank you, Sister,' Maria said softly. Had she noticed the 'have been'? She probably had. Maria knew her tenses.

Anyway, clearly distressed, Sister Hélène delivered her sentence: 'I have to tell you, my dear, that you cannot remain at Our Lady of The Immaculate Conception College while you are living with Martin. The Church does not permit such relationships.'

'I see,' Maria said quietly. The entwining of fingers in her lap was the only sign of the strain she must have felt.

I reached over and took her hand. She smiled quickly, and squeezed. Sister Hélène saw the gesture, permitted herself a tight smile.

She glanced at a paper before her, then continued. 'You could not continue to be head girl, in any case. Parents would not stand for it. They would be scandalised. Girls would talk, and see you as not having the necessary moral authority for upholding the rules … for being an example. You would be the target of gossip. You know how girls can be.'

'Are you expelling me, Sister?'

I thought Hélène was going to burst into tears. 'No, my dear. But I would like you to go away and prayerfully consider your position.' She indicated the statue of Mary. 'Pray to her. Ask your Heavenly Mother for wisdom. Search your heart.'

She was expelling her, but couldn't bring herself to say so. Instead Hélène was offering Maria the chance of going of her own accord. Sparing her as much humiliation and shame as she could. For that alone I warmed to the nun.

'May I speak?' I heard myself saying.

Maria turned to me in surprise, and Sister Hélène nodded graciously.

'Maria is paying a terrible price for being in love, it seems to me.'

Hélène smiled sadly, and perhaps there was a shrug.

'A few weeks ago I came to a Mass at the cathedral. Because Maria was going to give a reading.'

Sister Hélène dropped her gaze, and Maria gave my hand a gentle squeeze. 'Which she did. It was the story Mrs Barlow, my Sunday school teacher, once told –'

'I know the story, Martin,' Sister Hélène interrupted gently. 'I have no wish to judge or condemn Maria, either. But I have 900 other girls to think about, and how they and their families will think about her in the light of the Church's teachings about sex outside marriage.' A pause. 'What the Church teaches about chastity. It puts it at a premium.'

She glanced at Maria sadly. 'And I have to think about you, too, my dear. People can be very awful. I don't want that for you.'

Maria nodded.

'Come back and see me on Friday morning, my dear. Take tomorrow off.'

We left Sister Hélène's office. Maria formally curtseyed again, and the nun reached up and tenderly laid her hand on her cheek.

'Thank you, Sister,' Maria murmured.

I couldn't help thinking that Sister Hélène had treated Maria with more compassion while in a difficult position than her own parents had.

MARIA WANTED to go into the cathedral, so I went with her. She dipped her fingers in the fount at the door and crossed herself, leaving a watery mark on her forehead. She led me by the hand down the long aisle, our footsteps echoing into the rafters. She genuflected reverently at an alcove containing a statue of the Virgin Mary and knelt at a pew before it. I followed and sat while she took out a pair of rosary beads, kissed the crucifix, and proceeded silently to pray.

The statue was bigger than the one she had in our bedroom and the one in Sister Hélène's office.

Here the setting represented the grotto at Lourdes, the town in southern France where a 14 year-old, Bernadette Soubirous, said a woman dressed in white had appeared to her several times and spoken to her. This plaster Mary wore white with a blue sash. A smattering of mainly older people were around us, their heads bent in silent, earnest prayer. Others came forward and lit candles on a stand in front of the grotto.

Bead by bead, Maria whispered her *Hail Marys, Our Fathers, Glory Bes, Hail Holy Queens, O Remember O Most Loving Virgin Mary …*

I wondered what she was praying for. What did she want Mary to do? What if Mary said, 'Leave Martin, Maria. Repent of your fornication, and return to your family and beg their forgiveness. Go and confess all to Luke and he will absolve you.'

That last thought made me feel kind of sick. She was praying to the woman her Church idealised as the most perfect of all women because she had borne Jesus and had been assumed – Church teaching – into Heaven at the end of her life, and still a virgin.

In her Church's eyes Maria was a fornicator.

I looked around at the rest of the cathedral. Jesus was there above the ornate altar, hanging from his cross, as he had for hundreds of years in Catholic churches around the world. *You poor bugger. You came down from the cross, was buried, and rose again – all for the sins of mankind. And you went back to Heaven, so why do they keep you hanging there?*

That train of thought brought me up with a round turn. Where had that come from?

Dear old Mrs Barlow. Jesus had risen from the dead and ascended back to Heaven. 'Remember, my dears,' she had told her wide-eyed, impressionable charges gathered in a semi-circle in front of her chair, 'Jesus never stops loving you.'

She went on and told the story of the Prodigal Son. 'The father is a picture of what God is like,' she said.

So all that left me with a lot more to think about. I was very much in uncharted waters. I slid forward off the pew and knelt beside Maria, and put my arm around her.

'YOU DID a lot of curtseying today.' We were in bed whispering in the dark.

'It's a form of respect, Martin. Like standing for a teacher or older person, or a man for a woman.'

'When will you start curtseying to me?'

She pressed herself against me. 'I already show you more than enough respect, little man. I wouldn't be here if I didn't.'

198

'It looked very classy, your curtsey.'

'Well, in the old days, when my mother was there, it was different. The girls had to go down on both knees and bow their heads when any nun or priest or bishop went past. When my oldest sisters were there that was dropped, but they had to curtsey at the start of each class. When Sister Hélène came she stopped all that, but kept it for her and her office only.'

We lay in one another's arms, in snug, contented silence, drowsy breaths fanning our faces. I wanted to ask if Mary had given her an answer yet. That might have to wait for another day, as would a discussion about the cost she was paying for being with me.

Maria was giving up a position as head girl she obviously relished having; she was not going to join her sisters who'd been duxes of her school. She still had two terms to go to the end of the year.

Maria hadn't backed away from any of it.

Visitors – welcome, unwelcome

Thursday, 7.30am, my desk phone at work clamoured for my attention. 'Robert Tungwell-Urquhart here, Martin,' my neighbour said coolly. I had never known his name, but I recognised the voice – elegant, erudite, a commanding officer type of voice, Uncle Syd would say.

'What can I do for you, Robert?' I asked with less patience than I should have given him. I could hear what sounded like Maria's voice in the background, and his Siamese was yowling agitatedly. *What ...?*

'Your young lady, Maria, is here in my flat in her pyjamas. Three large policemen – one of whom I understand is her brother-in-law – are ransacking your flat for what they say are drugs. They arrived a few minutes ago.'

Jesus Christ!

'She's quite safe in here with me, Martin. She's more worried about Dante – my cat.'

'Could you put her on the phone, please?'

She came on. 'Darling?' And I had never heard so much fright in one word. I knew then they weren't interested in drugs. The bastard had turned up when he knew Maria would be alone.

'Listen, sweetie,' I said, trying to sound calm. 'Listen. I can't leave here just now. But I want you to phone Matt. Tell him what's going on.'

'All right.'

'Phone me back here after you've talked to him.'

I worked on. The phone call had attracted the curiosity of some of my fellow subs.

She phoned back 10 minutes later. 'I got Matt, and he's on his way here now. Tom is banging on Robert's door and making a very loud noise out there. The little boy in the next flat is crying, and so is one of the women.'

The commotion carried down the line. Ogle, the chief sub, Turnbull, sports, and Linwood, the news editor, as well as Barker, and Davies next to me … all had their curious eyes trained on me.

'I'm sorry, sweetie, but I have to go now.'

'I know. I'm all right as long as they can't get in the door and Robert is here.'

I hung up.

'Everything all right, Martin?' Ogle, sharp eyes behind square glasses.

I breathed out in a flutter of pursed lips. 'The police – or rather my girlfriend's brother-in-law who is a cop – are just turning over my flat looking for drugs.'

'An' will they find any?' Barker butted in.

I barely bothered with him. 'He's trying to terrify Maria.'

Ogle studied me for several moments. 'You're all right to keep working?'

'Yeah. Her brother's a lawyer and he's on his way around.'

He nodded, he and Linwood glanced at each other, and we put our heads down to produce a newspaper.

The phone went again just before nine. 'Matthew's just left,' she said, her cool – mostly – restored. 'He came with one of his office girls and she's helping me clean up. He's told her to stay with me until you get home. Robert's here, too.' She giggled. 'I think Dante is having a nervous breakdown, poor boy.'

I was grateful to Dante; he was helping her take her mind off things.

RUTH, THE editor's secretary, stopped by my desk at lunchtime, just as we were wrapping up for the second edition. 'Clyde wants you in his office at one-fifteen,' she said into my ear.

Christ. I'm in trouble now.

Clyde Barnfield sat behind his big, paper-cluttered editor's desk. A permanent pall of stale and fresh Port Royal tobacco smoke hung above it. Paper was scattered over his desk. A Brother typewriter stood on its end to the side. Strips of galley proofs from the day's paper lay like dormant snakes on the frayed carpet.

He was in his mid-40s, the first editor of the paper not to have been a war veteran. His hair flopped over his ears and down to his collar. He had a master's degree in law. His tie was loose at his neck and his sleeves were rolled up, so completing a sketch of a working newspaper editor.

We were joined by Malcolm Ogle, Gavin Linwood, and Clifton, the police reporter. Barnfield finished off rolling a Port Royal, and lit it. Ogle lit his pipe, and it puffed like a train; Hollandia tobacco. Linwood a Rothmans and Clifton a Pall Mall. I was beginning to feel left out.

From behind the plumes of smoke Barnfield squinted. 'Had a bit of trouble at home this morning, Martin?'

'Yes.'

'You doing drugs?'

'No.'

'Why were the police barging into your flat, then?'

Deep breath. 'I'm going with a girl. She lives with me in my flat now. Since Easter. Her family – or most of them, anyway – are against the relationship. Her brother-in-law is a cop and he's been sniffing around and making a nuisance of himself at odd times.'

Ogle was jotting notes.

'I don't take drugs,' I repeated. The joint I had smoked three or so years earlier didn't count now.

Barnfield resumed: 'Who is the girl's family?' Going by the tone of his voice and the look in his eyes I think he knew the answer. Anyway …

'She's a FitzGarratt. Maria, the youngest.'

Linwood whistled. 'You sure have picked the wrong crowd to get into a fight with,' he said.

'So I'm finding out. It might have been different if I was a Catholic.'

Linwood crushed out the cigarette in an ashtray he held on his lap.

'If it helps, Matthew, the QC, is on our side. He went straight around to my flat this morning.'

Barnfield grunted to himself. 'But there are no drugs whatsoever involved in this, Martin?'

'Clyde: if you want me to swear on a Bible I will do so that I am not taking drugs.'

His eyes bored into me, and I wondered what he was thinking, and why he was repeatedly asking me.

He turned to Trevor Clifton, the paper's long-serving police roundsman, renowned in newspaper circles all over the country the last 40 years for his ability to sniff out stories, his professionalism, all the while only partly sober. He stank of stale tobacco and deodorant, mint breath and bad teeth, and unwashed shirts. His tie was always loose, and it was stained. He was widowed when his wife died giving birth to their daughter.

'Trev, would you like to tell Martin here what you told me this morning?'

'Sure. Martin, I have excellent contacts in the police. Always have. Constable Tom Kearns – your young lady's brother-in-law – caught up with me in *The Mafeking* the other morning. I was chatting with a few of the boys in blue and he joined in. He whispered into my shell pink that a member of this newspaper's staff was not only smoking marijuana, but also dealing in it.'

I had trouble believing what I was hearing, and I must have looked like a startled rabbit as I glanced at the others in turn. Certainly I could feel my jaw dropping.

'And he said me?'

Clifton smiled carefully. 'No, not quite. But as I said, he hinted at it. Said his wife's little sister had lost her senses and gone off to shack up with the guy. The family are devastated.'

He paused to light another cigarette. 'She was in the office yesterday afternoon, Martin. Sue said she was a FitzGarratt. She certainly looked one. I put two-and-two together. Then I heard about your troubles this morning.'

I felt sick. 'Well, Maria said they didn't find anything incriminating, no drugs, but there was evidence that Tom, once again, likes sniffing her underwear.'

'Jesus,' I heard Ogle mutter.

Barnfield finished rolling another cigarette. 'Martin, let me be clear with you. If you've had anything to do with drugs since you came to my newspaper then you're gone. I won't have it.'

I went to speak, but he held up a hand. 'It's all right, mate. I believe you. But I have to make my position clear, not just to you, but to everyone on my staff.'

He lit his cigarette, Ogle followed with his pipe, and Linwood scowled at his empty cigarette packet. 'But I find it deeply concerning that a policeman – who, by the way, is known for his unorthodox ways – should be loose in the community and targeting a member of my staff.'

'He's a dirty cunt,' Clifton said. 'My daughter was at school with Stella. She always said she was a cock-tease. Tom Kearns would be giving her what she wanted. He's not her husband because of his brains.'

Ogle jotted more notes.

'If you're looking for a story out of this, I don't know if I can be much help. I won't let Maria become a front-page story.' I glanced around the others. 'She's only 17.'

Some frowning. I knew what they were thinking. They all had daughters.

'You said Matt is on your side?'

'Yes.'

'You don't know how lucky you are,' Linwood said.

MARIA WAS chatting with Aoife, the redhead from Matt's office, in the lounge when I got home. We kissed and held each other for several long moments. 'You OK?' I whispered.

'Yes. Fine now. Just scary at the time. I was about to go into the shower.'

Aoife made to excuse herself. I thanked her for coming and for staying with Maria. 'Oh, t'is not'ing,' and she waved it away. I'd thought she was an office girl, but she was a junior lawyer. 'I've made notes of everyt'ing, we've typed them up already,' she said, and held up a Polaroid. 'And I've taken time-stamped photos, as well.'

She beamed triumphantly. She picked up a print. 'T'is one is of Tom and his friends leavin' the buildin'. We couldn't have arrived a minute sooner.'

She'd talked to Robert; they shared an affection for Siamese cats; Dante was stand-offish. Aoife liked that in a cat.

Aoife stayed a few more minutes, and left after phoning for a taxi. I went next door and offered my thanks to Robert. He waved it off with a tired grin. 'Pleased to be of help, lad. I loathe and detest people like him. Not much different from Nazi bullies.'

I felt he didn't want to say much more so I headed for the door. He stopped me. 'Maria is a very courageous young woman. He kept her in the bedroom, then he got distracted, and she dashed for it and hammered on my door. She was amazingly calm. She was thinking about you, Dante, the women and boy next door ...' He smiled.

Dante stalked past, vivid blue eyes unblinkingly dismissive, tail stiff like a question-mark. 'He likes her.'

'HE JUST barged in with this ugly grin on his face, two big goons behind him,' she said, settled onto my lap, and I held her close to me. 'He did most of it. He went for the drawers first, particularly where my things were, and dragged them all out.'

'What did the others do?'

Maria frowned thoughtfully. 'I don't think they were as interested as he was. One looked in the fridge, and then closed the door again. The other lifted a cushion on the couch here.'

'How were you able to dash for it?'

'Oh, that was easy. The two out here started talking about nothing in particular – I think they'd given up – and Tom was turning over the mattress of the bed, and sniffing at it.' She grinned. 'So I just skipped out, closing the door quietly after me. They hadn't noticed until they heard me knocking at Robert's door.'

I held her in silence, nuzzling her hair. She seemed calm now. I wasn't so sure I felt calm at all. I was worried about how easy it could be to be framed.

In the town I grew up in the local constables sometimes dished out their own form of punishment. When I was a reporter I remember talking to a grizzled senior sergeant – who'd known Dad during the war – about how policemen sometimes took the law into their own hands.

'We do it, Martin, for their bloody good. A kick up the arse or a clout around the lugs just might be enough to make them think. We never want to see them in court. It's a tragedy when they do because once they start they keep on that road.'

Tom Kearns was taking this very personally. And why? Was Stella pulling the strings? Peirse and Órla? Grannie Annie? I hoped Matt could make some sense of this.

'The women in the flat opposite us are from Chile,' Maria said. 'Sisters-in-law, and Hugo – he's the little boy – is their nephew.' I tried to figure out such a family arrangement. '… and policemen hammering on doors at dawn and shouting terrify them.'

Maria turned towards me, and her eyes were very green. 'That more than anything else – making that little boy cry because he was afraid – makes me the angriest.'

MORE KNOCKS on the door. I tensed, but girls' voices were on the other side of the door rather than loud, police bullies.

Maria let them in: Catharine, and her twin sisters, Jacqueline and Anne, 14, all in school uniform.

'Hi, Auntie,' the twins murmured, apparently sincerely. Maria hugged them both in turn, which I thought surprised the girls. As if they hadn't hugged much before.

They took in the flat, their eyes lingering at the open door to the bedroom beyond and the fastidiously made bed; as a den of iniquity and sin it would seem ordinary and tidy. Their aunt, dressed in sensible pants, blouse, sleeveless pullover, groomed, modest, would have looked a very unlikely Jezebel wallowing in her debauchery.

I made coffee and Milo and opened the biscuit tins while Maria and her nieces chatted. She didn't mention Tom's visit this morning.

But there was gossip. It had been Joseph, Gabrielle's twin brother. He had opened his spiteful, mischievous mouth to his mates after football last Saturday morning.

The mother of one of the boys had heard it. She quizzed him, consulted her daughters who were at the college. They hadn't known a thing (so most of the FitzGarratt grandchildren had kept their mouths shut). She mentioned it to her husband. He was one of the wealthiest businessmen in the city, owned a fair bit of prime property, was on first-name terms with the archbishop and chaired his business advisory board, was the prelate's personal representative on Our Lady of The Immaculate Conception's board, knew Peirse and Órla and family well. Confirmation hadn't been hard. A FitzGarratt had been only too happy to provide the ammunition.

Maria was like a cancer who had to be excised from the school body lest she infected the rest.

The girls had some things to say about Joseph, who, for a boy of 12, had amassed more than his fair share of cousinly loathing. 'Little boy, little you-know-what …,' a smirky giggle, especially when Jacqueline or Anne held up her thumb and forefinger a little apart.

Maria told them she would be going back to school in the morning to leave, and Catharine took her hand and squeezed it. They smiled comfortingly at one another. Anne – Maria told me later they could be told apart because Anne's ears were a little smaller than Jacqueline's – said, 'Does that mean you're not going to tell me off about my loose tie any more then, Maria?'

The question, I thought, had caught Maria by surprise. But she recovered, smiled quickly, and said, 'No. I don't care any more.'

BUT SHE let herself go hours later in the dark. We were drowsily whispering about the day, the next day, and then Anne's comment came up, and Maria crumpled in mid-sentence. She sobbed hard, tried apologising, and turned over, facing away from me.

I reached for her to turn back. She tried to shake me off.

'Come on, Maria. Don't turn away from me.' I kept an insistent grip on her pyjama top. She reluctantly rolled back and I gathered her in close and held her head into my shoulder. Her tears were hot, and there were plenty of them, and they mixed into the hair of my chest as her body shook and convulsed. I never knew someone could weep so hard for so long. Her sobs subsided, and clutching me, she slipped off to sleep like a child.

Leaving Friday

The phone clamoured at 7am, waking us. 'God, this is getting tough,' I grumped as I left the bed to answer it, 'I wanted to sleep in with the girl I love.'

Maria laughed briefly, merrily, and that made me feel a lot better.

'Matt here, Martin. We're going to see Chief Superintendent Angus Shannon at midday with a dossier on Tom. You, Maria, me. Can you be at my chambers by half-past eleven.' It was a politely worded order, not a request.

'If you have a suit, I suggest you wear it. Maria as formal as she can.'

Just after nine o'clock she checked herself in her uniform for the last time in the wardrobe mirror. She gathered up her school textbooks and fed them carefully into the hold-all. 'All right,' she said briefly. 'Let's get it over with.'

Mrs MacClatchie was frosty and disapproving. 'You can leave the books there,' she said primly, offhandedly nodding towards a table, and resumed her typing.

Inside her office Sister Hélène smiled benevolently as Maria curtseyed, head bowed. *They're pretty much throwing her out of here, yet she scrupulously shows respect to them.*

Another nun was off to the side, her back to the window, holding a large envelope in front of her. She stepped forward. Maria introduced us with her usual grave formality. Dr Sister Margarethe had taught Maria her languages for the last five years. She reminded me of the aristocratic mother abbess from *The Sound of Music*. The skin around her eyes was puffy, and she didn't look as if she was about to launch into *Climb Every Moun-tain*.

One by one, her expression impassive, Maria removed her badges and laid them carefully on Sister Hélène's desk: the archbishop's council, the silver deputy president of the school council, and last the gold badge of the head girl.

'No, my dear,' Sister Hélène said. 'I want you to keep that.'

That flummoxed Maria. 'No, Sister, I couldn't possibly. I –'

Margarethe said something, pleading, and it sounded German.

I intervened. 'Keep it, darling. Please.' Our eyes met, and then she dropped her gaze. 'Thank you, Sister,' she said quietly.

Hélène reached out to Margarethe, who handed over the envelope. She held it towards Maria as if it was a gift. 'All your records, Maria, and from Sister here and me references attesting to your good character.' She glanced at me. 'Your present living arrangements do not change that.'

Maria swallowed, and in a small voiced thanked them. She handed the envelope to me – it was bulky – signed some forms, and it was time to leave.

She curtseyed to Hélène, who reached up and took her face between her hands, and drew Maria's head down and kissed her fondly on the cheek. Margarethe reached out, clasped Maria's hand in her own, whispered something in German, and tears tumbled down her cheeks.

'Thank you, Sister,' Maria said quietly – and curtseyed.

Both smiled, and I reached for the door because I thought I was going to cry, too. 'Thank you, both of you, for treating her with some dignity and kindness in the circumstances.'

Mrs MacClatchie pointedly ignored Maria as we left her reception space, but the dozen or so prefects and senior girls waiting near the front door didn't. Hugs, kisses, tears, farewells.

'GOOD TO see you both,' Matthew said breezily, and he hugged his sister. He glanced approvingly at his Rolex watch. 'You're early.' He handed me a large envelope. 'That's your copy. Everything that Shannon will see is in there.'

'What's the guts of it?' I said.

'The guts, my friend, is that I could quote you chapter and verse of several acts of Parliament and police regulations that Tom breached. He's in very deep shtook. That's the short story.'

Aoife joined us, and she and Maria exchanged smiles. Mrs O'Daly ordered a taxi, which took us around to the Central Police Station.

Chief Superintendent Shannon was a giant of a man, perhaps 6ft-5in, in his 50s, trim and muscular in his dark tunic, steel-grey eyes that had seen too much of what they wished they hadn't, and deep, hard grooves carved around his mouth. He spoke in a hard voice.

He bade us to sit in front of his desk after Matthew made the introductions – they were on first-name terms. His eyes bore into me – *have we got anything on you?* – and he appeared to pay scant attention to Maria and Aoife.

Matthew passed over the file, and explained what it was about. Shannon read quickly. Pages turned over, aided by a lick of a large fingertip. Lips occasionally pursed, a scowl, a soft grunt or two. He turned his attention to Maria. 'This is all true?'

'Yes, Chief Superintendent,' she said gravely.

He turned to Matthew: 'I'm going to have to interview Constable Kearns, and others who I would have expected to know what would be his duties and when.' He laid his eyes on me – they were unsettling – before returning his attention to Matt. 'But going by what I see here I'm not much impressed.'

He turned back to Maria. 'Young lady,' and his tone was unexpectedly gentle, 'please accept my apologies on behalf of the P'lice for how Constable Kearns has behaved towards you. You should not have been subjected to that.'

'Thank you,' she replied.

WE WERE going to walk back to the flat. As we passed the paper office I decided to show to the editor our copy of the files Matt had given us. Yes, he had told me yesterday he believed me. But he was a lawyer, as well as a newspaper man, so proof – paperwork – well, he would like that. I said as much to Maria.

'OK,' she said.

Barnfield looked up from marking a galley proof as I knocked on his door. 'Come in, Martin.' Maria followed me in, and he stood for her, which I thought was a nice touch.

I introduced them and he wiped his hands hurriedly on a sheet of copy paper before offering one to Maria. 'You don't want printer's ink on your hand,' he said, coming from behind his desk. She took it lightly anyway.

I indicated the envelope I carried, that it was the file Matt had compiled. 'I thought you should have a look at it, particularly since you asked me several times yesterday whether I was involved in drugs.'

He took the packet, but did not open it.

'That's our copy of the file Maria's brother Matthew compiled for the police. We've just come from seeing Shannon, the district commander.' I nodded to the files. 'I think it backs my story.'

We sat in silence as Barnfield opened the envelope carefully and digested the file. He scanned quickly, expertly, pretty much as Shannon had. 'Jesus Christ,' he muttered as he wrapped it up. He glanced at Maria, still in her Catholic school uniform. 'Excuse me,' he apologised.

She smiled politely. I didn't take what is called the Lord's name in vain in her hearing. She'd never said anything, but the first time I did I caught an expression that conveyed her discomfort.

He hunched forward, elbows on the desk. 'There's the makings of a bloody good story in here.'

I knew what he was saying. Rogue cop behaving beyond badly. He's married into a leading family of lawyers, doctors, and academics, local Catholic aristocracy. The youngest of the family forced in the nicest possible way to leave her toffee-nosed Catholic girls' school where she was head girl because of her shacking up with a staff member from this newspaper, and forgoing the certainty of being awarded dux.

Maria grasped it, too. 'I hope you're not thinking of making me and my family a front page spectacle.'

'No, sweetie, we're not. I said yesterday I wouldn't allow that. He's just saying there's information in that envelope that would make a bloody good story.'

'Well, please keep me out of it.'

A LETTER was in my mailbox addressed to Maria. The envelope didn't have a stamp or postmark so someone must have delivered it by hand.

'Oh,' she said after she'd unfolded the note. 'It's from Uncle Brian.' The tall monsignor.

'He says that if I want somewhere to go for Sunday Mass then I'd be welcome at his church.' She kissed the note. 'How sweet of him to do that.' It was a tonic to Maria. 'Mass is 9.30am.'

'I'll go with you.'

Delight lit up her face. 'Will you?' Then a frown. 'But you don't have to.'

'It'll be fine.'

Maria threw her arms around me and kissed me repeatedly.

MUCH LATER, in the dark, Maria slept, her head on my chest, a leg thrown over mine. I'd told her that she clearly did love sex.

'I know,' she'd replied. 'I was worried at first because I half-felt I shouldn't because I'm a female.' Moments later she whispered: 'But only with you, Martin. I'm not a slut, am I? I'm not promiscuous.'

I'd assured her she wasn't.

Anyway, I couldn't sleep. I was trying to figure out things that were riddles to me.

Despite rejecting her Church's teaching about sex and marriage, and the rejection of her by most of her family and her school, she still prayed to their statues, threaded the rosary through her fingers, and there was her delight – a girlish joy – that her uncle the monsignor had invited her to attend Mass at his church.

I didn't know how to ask her about it. Perhaps, for the moment, I didn't have to because it wasn't important.

I was also thinking about our future together. What was she going to do now? She had swung between getting a job until the end of the year or finding a school to enrol in to finish the end of the year. She was going to university next year.

Things had moved quickly. Should we get married?

Avuncular

Monsignor Uncle Brian's parish church was new, in a new suburb that was largely the creation of the Ministry of Works and the Housing Corporation, State agencies, to give the baby-boomers and their babies good homes.

His church, wide, roomy, of modern design rather than long and formal, was packed with young families, mortgaged or renting, all facing the same hurdles of trying to get ahead and bring up families. The sense of solidarity was palpable in the church. Everyone seemed to know each other, and there was a ready smile and a quiet greeting for newcomers and visitors.

We found a pew about the middle, between an Island couple in their 20s with a toddler and another baby in the works and a harried-looking husband and wife with three youngsters who would not keep still.

A boy of about 4 poked a finger at Maria's arm. She did not smile understandingly. He withered under the Head Girl Stare. She must have scared the mother, too, because she shifted him away and put him under his father's ineffectual thumb.

His older sister, about 11, understood the Head Girl Stare and behaved.

Maria relaxed because there seemed to be no-one from her school.

In Uncle Brian's church the congregation sang enthusiastically, led by a long-haired and bearded guitarist with large, round glasses and a ring in his ear. He appeared to be dressed in tatty second-hand clothes and wore sandals on his feet.

The vocalist bore her hair in a floppy, untidy bun; her sail-like, shapeless dress looked to be of 'natural' fabrics, a favourite of the hippies then. Peace symbols and a rainbow with yellow clouds had been screen-printed on to it.

The violinist sported an enormous floppy hat, a *Godspell* blouse, jeans, and sandals.

The songs were modern – 'contemporary' – and not hymns at all, even if the red book they came from called itself a 'hymnal'. *'Take my hands and make them as your own ...'*

I liked the one that began *'Love is his word, love is his way feasting with men ...'*

By *'Love is his mark, love is his sign...'* the third verse, I'd got a hang of the tune and sang along to the end.

That pleased Maria. She smiled as she sang and squeezed my hand. 'I love you,' she whispered into my ear.

Uncle Brian's vestments were far less ornate than those worn by the archbishop or Luke at the cathedral. Brian was a benign presence on the altar, it seemed to me. Those who had jobs to do he stood back and let them, all with an easy grace. He performed his duties without fuss, and his sermon was succinct and in plain words.

Brian told them life can be tough, can be unfair, and that people can be treated unjustly.

His advice: trust God. Trust him in everything. Love one another, 'and I know this can be very hard', he said with a grin, 'but love those who do you ill, who kick you, who beat you and cheat you. Love them, because that's what Jesus did. He let them take him, beat him with sticks and whips, spit on him, put a crown of thorns on his head, and nail him to a cross. And you know what, my dear people? First, he asked God to forgive them. Second, he defeated them when he rose from the dead three days later. He's your example.'

I sneaked a sideways look at Maria. She was rapt. It was as if her uncle had said words she so desperately wanted to hear.

We kissed for the sign of peace. Then holy communion. 'Do you want to come up with me?' she hissed.

I looked blankly. 'How can I? I'm not a Catholic.'

She put a hand on mine. 'I don't think that matters.'

OK.

'I don't think Uncle Brian will make a public spectacle of refusing you communion.'

OK. Sounded likely.

'Do what I do.' She showed me how to cup my hands when I got to Uncle Brian. 'When he holds the wafer in front of you and says "Body of Christ", you say 'amen', and he puts it in your hand, you put it in your mouth, make the sign of the cross and you step to the side.' She looked intently into my eyes to make sure I had understood. 'Do what I do.'

Right.

We joined the queue, which shuffled towards the altar. Maria was in front of me, and when she reached Uncle Brian he greeted her with a big grin and the kindest eyes, rested a large hand on her head, murmured a blessing, and made the sign of the cross over her. He offered her the host from a wooden bowl, which she took in her hands.

He recognised me, paused, took a white wafer from the bowl, said "Body of Christ", I mumbled 'amen', it was deposited in my hand, he smiled, and I stepped away as I put the wafer on to my tongue. It was tasteless.

I don't know what I expected to be the result of that. A bright light of revelation from a happy God or a bolt of lightning and thunder from an angry God.

Maria was on her knees back in the pew, her head in her hands. I knelt, as well. I had no idea what to pray for, or whether anyone up there would be listening. She sat up when communion was over.

I wondered if she was sinning against the laws of the Church or against God.

Some of his earthly friends were behaving in a way that I don't think Mrs Barlow would be happy with.

BRIAN WAS at the main door speaking to parishioners as they filed out of the church. They all seemed to like him. There was a genuine warmth, and I liked it that he knew all of them, and their children, by name, resting a hand on their head, ruffling hair. He smiled warmly to Maria as we approached him, and he bent down and kissed her on the cheek.

'You remember Martin, Uncle Brian?'

He had, and his handshake was firm, his greeting friendly. His hands were twice as big as mine. 'Yes I do, of course. How are you, Martin?'

He suggested to Maria that we go over to his presbytery 'and we can catch up over a cup of tea or coffee'. That sounded like another Serious Talk was coming, and it put me on my guard.

I NEEDN'T have worried. The Oxford Dictionary defines 'avuncular' as 'like an uncle in being kind and friendly towards a younger or less experienced person'. It comes from the Latin *avunculus*, meaning 'maternal uncle'. So it was an apt word for Uncle Brian. He was her mother's older brother.

The presbytery, like the church, the school out the back, and the suburb, was new. It was a modest, three-bedroom house. Brian made the tea and coffee himself, not just for us but also for his curate, Jack.

'We don't have a live-in housekeeper, but Mrs Walters comes in a couple of times to vacuum and do the laundry. Otherwise young Jack and I are like bachelors or flatmates.'

'I've had to teach him a lot about that,' said Jack lightly before he left to say Mass elsewhere.

Comfortably settled in his TV-watching armchair Uncle Brian asked Maria if she was all right. She assured him she was.

More directly, he asked me if I was looking after her. She assured him that I was.

'I hope he can speak for himself,' he said pointedly but genially.

She smiled apologetically.

I told him I thought I was. 'But with girls, you know, sometimes you're never sure.'

He guffawed.

'I'll speak to you later, Martin,' Maria said severely, but with a tiny stretching of lips.

'Monsignor,' I said, 'can you tell me what the fuss is about over the religion thing?'

He considered the question. 'Generally, it is not unusual for people to oppose their children marrying those from another religion. It's not just a Catholic thing. I have in my congregation right now a young lady whose Presbyterian family have cut her off because she married a Catholic boy.'

He sipped from his cup. 'Her father refused to give her away, her mother forbade her sister from being bridesmaid. None came to the wedding. All that did was weld them more closely to one another.'

He turned back to me: 'So, in short, you can find it anywhere, and in any religion. And it comes up in another way, too. I have another couple, she's Irish and he's English. Nothing to do with religion. Both are Catholic. It's just that he comes from Birmingham, England, and she's from Ballina, Republic of Catholic Ireland.'

For a few moments he chewed over his thoughts about what to say next. To Maria, he said: 'With the FitzGarratts, the only reason I can see for it is your grandmother's blanket and blind opposition to anything and anyone not Catholic. It's partly, but not wholly, an Irish, thing. Not all Irish are like that. But some of them who came from the more remote country areas, you'd find that. It's the notion of the values of the faith being kept pure so they can be passed to the children.'

'You're not like that, Uncle,' Maria said. 'Auntie Theresa and Auntie Bernadette are nothing like that.' She turned to me: 'Mum's and Uncle Brian's younger sisters.'

'Well, my dear, our family are a little bit different from the FitzGarratts. Our father was Irish, our mother was a mixture of French and Irish. She came from a well-off, educated family in Reims.' It sounded as if he was saying 'we're not like them'.

'And she died.'

'Yes, she did. I was 14, your mother 12, and the other two girls were 10 and 7. Our father was a hard-working, but not all that successful, businessman and accountant. He did not have a lot of time for us. Your mother largely brought up our sisters. She was a girl herself. Yet she had inherited her mother's brains. Money from our mother's family enabled your mother to go to university. And me, although I went on to the seminary.'

He paused there, and I thought that what he said next was deeply interesting. 'Your father was a hard-working, ambitious, and up-and-coming young man. He was going to be a doctor. No doubt about it. Your mother was very pretty, and ferociously intelligent. I'd say she was brighter than your father. They were both attracted to each other, physically and mentally. And he had money – or else his mother's money.'

He put aside his cup and saucer. 'Your mother craved financial security and social respectability, and to use her brains. Your father – or rather your grandmother – expected babies, and lots of them.'

I thought that explained a lot. Anyway, he appeared to steer the conversation away from the FitzGarratts. I glanced around the walls of the lounge. There was a photo of a much younger Brian and other priests with a man who looked as if he was a pope.

I asked about it.

He smiled. 'Yes, Pius XI – in my opinion one of the greatest. He had just ordained me, in 1935.'

'I didn't know you had been ordained by the pope, Uncle.'

He smiled, proudly.' I studied there for four years, was ordained, and served in various parishes in Ireland, France, Italy until World War 2 started. That's where I learned the most, among working people, poor people, struggling people.' He added, with a hint of sharpness: 'I don't have as many doctorates as Luke, but I do have one. Frankly, though, after many years I've concluded that doctorates do nothing to help show people who Jesus is.'

A few minutes later we were heading for the door. He and Maria kissed cheeks again, and he shook hands with me adding a hand to my shoulder. His final words were: 'If you two decide whether you want to make your arrangement permanent then come and see me, and we can talk about getting you married.'

'YOU HAVE had an adventurous week,' Magdalena said while they took a cigarette break. The lunch crowd were slow turning up. 'Having the police thump on your door would have been frightening. I know what that can be like.'

Peter nodded grimly. They shared a glance. 'I know we've already said it, but if you need somewhere to stay – either for a while or a long while – we have room for you.'

'Yes,' Magdalena added. 'It would be nice to have two young lovebirds around the place.' She winked at Peter: 'It might help us rediscover our lustful youth, eh, darling?'

He grinned a 'I'll deal with you later' grin.

We both fell over ourselves to say how nice that was of them. They waved it away in clouds of cigarette smoke. 'It's nothing. Really. And Maria, if you need a job, we could probably find you something here.'

'I might go to Mass with you one day,' Magdalena said. 'It's been a long time.' Maria reached over and took her hand, and they held it for a long time.

'WOULD YOU want me to become a Catholic?' I whispered in the dark that night.

'Not unless it's something you wanted to do. I don't want you to just for my sake.'

'I just hope Jesus and his mother are a lot nicer and kinder and more understanding than some of their friends down here. Apart from your Uncle Brian, Sister Hélène, and your oldest brother, some of them aren't very nice representatives of the Catholic Church.'

She kissed my chest. 'Sometimes you say the truest things.'

Hard schools

Maria had been crying when I got home from work. Before she saw me off to work that morning she said she'd try to enrol at another school to finish out the year.

'What happened?'

'I went to Regina Victoria Girls' College, a State school. The deputy headmistress handles enrolments. Everything was going well. I'd filled out the form. She was reading my reports and other stuff from Our Lady of The Immaculate Conception, noting I'd been head girl, how Sister Hélène's reference was impressive, adding nice things such as how I should fit in well there.'

'And?'

'She picked up the form, and noted that I lived here, care of you, my fiancé. You're my next-of-kin. Along with Matt.'

Uh-oh.

'She demanded to know why I wasn't living with my parents, why weren't they enrolling me, and who were you. I said you were my fiancé. "You are living with a man you say is your fiancé *in a de facto* relationship?"' Maria imitated the woman's quivering, rising tone.

'I said yes. She became very snooty and said she would ring my parents to check whether they would approve of enrolling me. I told her it was nothing to do with my parents.'

'Did you walk out then?'

'Well, she got me to wait while she went and found the principal.' She sighed. 'And she was a starchy old battleaxe spinster. Compared with her Sister Hélène's a pushover. She told me that she "will not entertain at all having you in my school while you are living with a man. Girls with good character and breeding don't do that".'

So that was that.

'I then went to Julius Vogel High School. They're co-ed. Supposedly progressive. They've done away with uniforms. The principal was nicer, I think. But he said he wouldn't enrol me unless I had my parents' permission. It appeared to be a legal thing.'

'Why have you been crying, then?'

She glanced at me as if I had sprung a second head, but then seemed to think it wasn't such a silly question after all. 'I suppose I didn't think anyone would care. I didn't think anyone would judge me as anything other than as someone with good character.'

LATER I asked if she was going to keep trying to find a school to take her, and would she like me to go with her.

'No, thank you, sweetie. When it comes down to it I can do without it. I've already got my UE. Seventh form was for the A Bursary to get me a better place at university and more of the fees paid. If I'd got dux then there would have been scholarships, as well.' She shrugged. 'I'll manage.'

Unexpected help

I'd been home about 10 minutes on Wednesday. A soft knock on the door. We were wary about unexpected knocks on our door, so I waited. On the other side it sounded like Dante the Siamese and a placatory voice trying to calm him.

Robert Tungwell-Urquhart, smiling, a deeply suspicious, round-eyed Dante in his arms. He and Maria saw each other, and he yowled happily because when Maria held out her arms to him he readily leapt across from his manservant's arms.

She carried him over to the couch, sat down and stroked him and kissed his head and told him what a beautiful, lovely boy he was. Oh, yes. He arched and preened over that, his eyes closed in pleasure; a rattle that passed for purring started in his throat and they bunted foreheads.

'He does like you, my dear,' Robert said, also pleased. She was being gooey and cooey, and that was a revelation. I'd never seen or heard her like that.

I made coffee and found some biscuits. Robert settled himself at the table. He started chatting about my Hermes 3000 typewriter. He said he preferred Olivetti's Lettera 32, which he'd had for about 10 years.

Anyway, Dante decided he'd exhausted his ration of love for Maria. He lifted his head off the softness of her breast and abruptly dropped softly to the floor. Nose up and leading the way, he strutted off to inspect the bedroom, tail up like an exclamation mark.

Whereupon Robert came to the point of his visit. He had observed that Maria was no longer going to school. He had guessed, 'given how these things go', that she had been expelled or had left of her own accord.

'Pretty much the same thing, I think,' I said.

'Quite,' and the sadness on his face was deep and genuine. He turned to Maria. 'You said the other day, after that obnoxious bully was here being a nuisance, that you were doing French, German, Latin, and History.'

'Yes,' her eyebrows contracting. 'And English.'

'Quite.' A quick, fox-like smile. 'Will you try to enrol elsewhere?'

'Yes. I've tried.'

'And no luck.'

'No. I'm a rotten apple who will infect the rest with my scandalous life.'

He sat back in the chair, an obviously neat and fastidious little man in corduroy and tweed, sensitive fingers that were now thoughtfully stroking his little goatee. 'Could I help?'

Maria glanced at me before answering. 'How?'

He smiled, and cleared his throat. 'Well, let me explain.'

Robert was a scholar, a near-contemporary of the great New Zealand writer Dan Davin. In the early 30s Robert had studied Classics, English, French, Latin, History, and German at the University of Otago. They were all first-class honours, and I could see that Maria was hugely impressed. But those who awarded Rhodes Scholarships had not been. His application was turned down. 'I think Davin got it, on his second try.'

But Robert's family – descendants of wealthy Scots and Ulster colonists who owned farms and property, not just in New Zealand but throughout the 'empire', had money. So he was able to go to Balliol College, at the University of Oxford.

He had Done Well – more first-class MA honours and he went on to lecture at another Oxford college.

War was declared. He joined the Royal Air Force Volunteer Reserve. Flew fighters throughout the war. Demobbed as a squadron leader. Earned a Ph.D. Went back to his lecturing. Fell in love – 'head over heels in love' – and they went off to Southern Rhodesia, where he had been offered a professorship.

'We had 12 happy years in Salisbury. Then someone was spiteful, and made a complaint under public decency laws against Gerald and me. Everyone had known, but no-one cared because we were discreet.'

Robert's brown eyes met mine. He must have seen the surprise in my face – or at least the surprise I was trying to conceal that he'd just revealed he was a homosexual. In his eyes I now saw deep hurt and perhaps an expected rejection.

I can't say that I was much enlightened then. I'd seen men kissing each other on the lips and trading tongues and groping each other. It had repelled me. Ross Price, a prefect at school, had made a pass at me in the picture theatre when I was 13, and it had left me feeling ashamed because it had suggested that I had telegraphed something to him. Otherwise, why would he have done it? I never told anyone.

Robert smiled tightly, perhaps sadly. 'Yes. In today's vernacular, I'm a poof. A fairy. Queer.'

I glanced at Maria. 'It seems we're in similar boats then, Robert,' she said. 'I'm virtually excommunicated by my family for loving Martin and living here with him. You were ostracised for loving Gerald.'

I was impressed. I hadn't thought of it like that.

'People find reasons to judge others, Martin, as you and Maria have been finding out.'

I nodded and felt ashamed.

'Anyway,' he said briskly, rubbing his hands together, grinning, 'enough of that. As you might have gathered, I was establishing my credentials while coming to a point.'

He turned back to Maria. 'If you think it would help, I could tutor you until the end of the year.'

Her face lit up. 'Really? I'd like that. Thank you!'

He spoke rapidly to her in Latin. With barely a beat she replied. He nodded approvingly.

Next, he let rip a guttural stream of German that sounded like the clanking of *panzer* treads. She replied, sitting up straight now, concentrating like an attentive pupil.

'Hmm,' he said, 'sounds as if you come from St Pauli, one of the more, er, salubrious suburbs of Hamburg.'

'That would be Sister Margarethe. She was from Hamburg. Her mother had worked on the *Reeperbahn*.' *The kindly sister was the daughter of a prostitute?*

'And you have a good grasp of idiom, too, Maria,' Robert added.

Next was French, and the conversation went on for some time. She never faltered. She was enjoying it.

Robert smiled his approval. 'You've been taught very well, Maria.'

'I never knew you were so bright,' I added.

She poked her tongue out, but smiled. The details were worked out. He asked to see her records and reports and assignments, and they pored over them. Sometimes conversing in English, alternating Latin, German, and French. They were animated, gestures with hands, each enjoying the other's company.

I watched them and listened. Maria was bright. I'd seen her crack out assignments with ease and a professional single-mindedness. I knew she was beyond me. She would do well at university. She would do well beyond university.

A thought niggled deep down inside me: *will I be able to hang on to her?* Which led to another thought: *am I a waypoint on her journey to someone and somewhere else?*

I didn't want to think about that, about a life without her or her with someone else.

Robert said he would go and see Sister Hélène tomorrow and ask if she would be willing to let Maria continue to Bursary exams as a de facto pupil and tutored by him. They supply any course curriculum work; they could 'peer review' what he did. 'You won't get any prizes, but you will finish the curriculum, sit Bursary, and that will set you up for university next year.'

She asked me what I thought.

'Do it,' I said. 'You need something to do. You can't sit in here facing the walls. You'll go crazy.'

So they agreed. Mondays and Thursdays, 7am-midday. Both were early-birds. Forty dollars a week, which for some people then was about a week's pay. Robert prepared to take his leave. Maria found Dante asleep on her side of our bed. He objected sourly to being moved, but she clutched him to her bosom and kissed him. He loved that, and his purr clattered lustily.

After that we drove out to Magdalena and Peter's. Maria would work in their café and theatres on Thursday afternoons and Saturdays, which was a good arrangement because she wouldn't be on her own in the flat all day.

LATER IN bed I kissed her breasts lingeringly with reverence, telling each in turn: 'I love you.'

'Why are you doing that?' she said, after a long, pleased sigh.

'Dante. I thought he was liking them too much. I'm just reminding them I love them, too.'

Maria giggled softly and locked her legs more tightly around me. 'You're silly.'

Family matters, right?

On Friday morning Robert dropped in early, but without Dante. Instead he carried a cardboard box of textbooks. He'd had a meeting with Sister Hélène and Sister Margarethe the day before. They would 'in their words, "be only too delighted to provide all and any curriculum materials Maria requires". So that's very good. They regard you highly.'

He'd struck up a good rapport with the nuns, especially Hélène. 'Ancient Hungarian aristocracy. Was kept in Switzerland during the war. Because of the Communists after that she stayed, studied, and then entered a French convent.' So he liked and respected her.

I'd learned a little bit more about Robert Tungwell-Urquhart since Wednesday.

These days if you want to find out something you just type your inquiry into your Google, Bing, or some other browser on your computer. Hit 'enter', and often a flood of information results. Some of it is what you want.

In 1975 I had to resort to the trusty clippings file and a book on fighter aces of the RAF. Yes, there was Pilot Officer Robert Tungwell-Urquhart, May 1940, in a grainy photo of a group of fighter pilots in France. Among them the brilliant Kiwi ace, 'Cobber' Kain, just over a week before he crashed his Hurricane and died.

August 1940 and Flight Lieutenant Tungwell-Urquhart had just been awarded the Distinguished Flying Cross for shooting down five German aircraft and damaging several more during the Battle of Britain.

And so on until July 1945, and Squadron Leader Tungwell-Urquhart was receiving from King George VI at Buckingham Palace a Distinguished Service Order, to go with the DFC and two Bars. He had shot down 19 German and Italian aircraft during the war, shared, damaged and probabled many more, and destroyed trucks and trains and barges and strafed untold numbers of the enemy to oblivion. He had been aggressive and brave, and shown outstanding leadership of various fighter squadrons.

He was one of those New Zealanders who – out of all proportion to their numbers, some British newspapers liked to remark – had contributed outstandingly to the RAF. One of more than 80 New Zealanders known to be fighter aces. He couldn't have been 30. I wondered if Uncle Syd and he had known each other during the war.

MARIA WAS looking at her curriculum work for a couple of hours as a preparation for her first tutorial with Robert. Her attention to the task was clinical. He was taking her up several levels – 'more university than upper-sixth', he said.

So I picked up the phone.

'Blake speaking.'

'Hello, Uncle, this is your favourite nephew.'

'All my nephews are my favourites, Martin.'

I heard him light a cigarette. 'I've been wondering how you were going with Miss FitzGarratt.'

'Maria's here with me now, Uncle. She's been living here with me since Easter.'

Maria looked up from the typewriter.

'Christ, Marty,' he spluttered, 'you don't let the grass grow under your feet, do you?'

I quickly recounted the main points. When I mentioned Tom's behaviour I heard a shocked '*Jee-zus*'.

'But there have been some good points. Her oldest brother Matthew has turned out to be a friend, as well as brother. Her uncle is a monsignor, and he's welcomed her to his church.'

We chatted on. Just as we were about to hang up I asked him if he remembered Robert Tungwell-Urquhart, DSO, DFC and two Bars, from the war.

'Name rings a bell.' He paused. 'Yes. Once in London, at the Palace. We were receiving our gongs from His Maj. A bit limp-wristed, he seemed to me. But then he wasn't by any means the only one.'

I said that he lived next door and had offered to tutor Maria. Uncle Sydney had to go, finished by wishing me – 'and your young lady, she sounds a lot nicer than the other one' – well. 'Stay in touch, lad. Let's get a look at her some time soon.'

'Who was that?' Maria said after I hung up.

'My Uncle Syd – my favourite uncle. Dad's brother. He says I should take you to meet them. You'd probably like them, I think.'

'But what about your own parents?'

'What about them?'

'Have you told them about me – us?'

'No.'

'Why not?'

Which was a very good question, because, I suppose, it was about the relationship my parents and I had.

When I left home and went 400 miles away to work I wrote to them every week, as a dutiful son would. Dad wasn't a writer, and he wasn't one who communicated much.

Mum was what might be called a 'chatty' writer. She could write 10 pages filled with chatty gossip about Mrs Borman, the poor widow along the street whose lawns I used to mow; about Mr and Mrs French over the back, whose garden was a source of such abundance; over in Tyndale St Mrs Cameron had left Mr Cameron again because of his affairs, his drinking and gambling, and his blackening her eyes and splitting her lip. But she always went back for the sake of the children. And so on and so on.

Mum never wrote about herself; 'Dad says hello and hopes you're keeping well'. Dad was always 'keeping well'.

So we now corresponded every few weeks. I went home for a week or so every year. I slept in the same bed I had since I was 2, in the same bedroom, surrounded by all my old books and other things. Even the bedside radio was still there, in exactly the same place and the same angle I'd had it, and on the same station.

To find something to talk about we used to find different ways of bringing up the same old topics.

I was still 'young Martin' to my parents' friends, and I suppose to my parents. Even as I turned into my 20s and became more established in my craft. We would watch the news on TV at tea time, and neither of my parents acknowledged that that's the job their son did.

As well, the visits back home were becoming increasingly lonely. Most of the people I went to school with had gone – to university, teachers' college, the cities for their bright lights and jobs – anywhere and everywhere to get away from the suffocation of what they thought was small-town life.

Those who stayed behind were often content. And that's not to sound askance at them. We all have to make our own choices. They stayed for the security and comfort of the town they'd known all their lives – the jobs in the shops, at the dairy factories, the banks, the Post Office, the Railways, with the plumbers and the builders, the garages, the local farmers. I encountered more and more of them, married at 19 or 20, a baby not far behind or a child already at school; they were buying houses.

The only things we had in common was our growing up there together before we scattered to wherever. They had no interest in what I did. At the pub their conversations were all about what they were all doing. Working on a newspaper wasn't 'a real job'. Not really. I tried to be interested. I didn't belong there any more.

The two people I most felt I could say anything that mattered to were Uncle Syd and Auntie Koo. Uncle Syd got me to see the reality that was Felicity. Uncle Syd and Auntie Kura encouraged me to stick at school past the fifth form, and to get a job on a newspaper. 'You're not a clerk with no ambition and no vision like your father, Marty. You have a definite talent and you should be exercising it.' My cousins had been encouraged to be ambitious.

More concisely, I explained some of all that to Maria.

She grimaced. 'I think it's similar to the relationship I have with my parents. Distant. Nothing much important to talk about. Perhaps by the time they got to me they had exhausted it all. I was perhaps one or two kids too far for them.'

'I noticed that when you called them Mum and Dad it sounded like it was something you didn't do often,' I said.

'Hmm, yes, I know. It sounded awkward. But I couldn't say 'Mother' and 'Father', either. A bit too Victorian.'

So I phoned home. Mum picked up the phone. Dad was home for lunch, and he was finally going to retire this year. 'I'll have to find him plenty of jobs to do,' she said brightly. 'Don't want him getting under my feet every day. Like having you at home when you were small.'

My mother's new fear. The thought of Dad being at home terrified her. They would not be able to hide from each other any more. Their lack of commonality would become too apparent for them to ignore. Could they keep on pretending?

Anyway, after trying to make her son feel guilty for not having been in touch much these last few months – 'your letters must have been lost in the mail and you'll have been busy in your new job, of course, dear' – Mum asked me how I was, and remarked that it must be something special for me to phone. 'But it's gone midday now, so you don't have to pay morning toll rates.'

Yes.

I told her I'd met a girl.

'Oh, yes. That's nice,' she said brightly. My mother expressing polite interest.

Then I gave her as concise a version of the story as I could. Mum did not interrupt. 'Maria's living here now, with me.'

'I see,' Mum said, and in those two words I heard the approaching shrivelling winter of her disapproval.

'A schoolgirl, Martin. What were you thinking? She'll know nothing about the world and what's what.' A pause for breath, sharp and quick: 'Are you sure you haven't led her on? Young girls can be very flighty and impressionable.'

And: 'I don't approve of this modern trend of living together, Martin. I thought you knew that. What will people think?'

Maria's parents: 'They must be worried sick. Fancy. She just walks out. And she'd have had a decent upbringing herself. Goodness gracious! A *doctor's* daughter! If she was my daughter she'd be marched home quick-smart and then a waddy across her bottom. A good *thrashing!* She wouldn't dare do it again. The world is getting *faar* too permissive. I'm surprised at you, Martin.'

Maria's character: 'What sort of morals does she have that she's not only *sleeping* with you, Martin, but she's *living* with you? There are words for describing girls like her.'

'Yes, Mum, and she's been called them by her Irish, church-going grandmother.'

'Well, mark my words, that young lady – although lady is probably too nice a word for the likes of her – will in time come to regret her behaviour. She will.'

And: horrors. 'What if she gets pregnant, Martin? What will she do then? You said she was a Catholic? Probably doesn't use anything, silly girl. Probably relies on the rhythm. Or the moon. Probably against abortion, too. I don't want an illegitimate grandchild. Poor kiddy – other children will be so awful to it.'

'Mum, Parliament removed the word illegitimate from the statute book in September 1968.'

'Oh, did they? Still won't matter. Laws don't necessarily change attitudes, you know, Martin. People know what's right and what's wrong. Laws often don't.'

Maria was following this intently, and left the chair and came over and took my hand and kissed it and held it against her cheek. She said later that my face had gone white with hurt and disappointment. She'd never seen me look like that: 'I thought you were going to cry, darling.'

'I certainly don't approve, Martin,' Mum was saying again. 'Dad and I are very hurt and very disappointed. We always expected you'd find a *nice* girl. One you could bring home and introduce to your parents. *Par-TIC-ularly* to your mother.'

That cut my soul like a lash.

I did the best I could to hold together as I bid Mum goodbye and hung up.

Maria didn't say a word. She led me to the couch, sat down with me, wrapped her arms tightly around me, and cuddled me as I burst into tears and cried for the first time since I was 9. The woman who'd given me a cuddle then was Auntie Koo.

THE PHONE clamoured about 9pm just as we were heading for bed.

'Dad here, Martin.'

I nearly dropped the phone. My father had never phoned me once since I'd left home.

'Mum's gone out to her ladies' evening at Mrs Prestidge's.'

My mother's crocheting circle – Mrs Prestidge, Miss Scott the kindy teacher, Mrs Larkin, Mrs Turner, and Mum. My mother's Friday night fixture from before I was born. Somehow I didn't think Mum would be proudly telling the ladies about her son's new domestic arrangements.

Anyway, Dad. 'I heard your mother on the phone to you today. She told me what you'd said.'

I sighed sadly. What was Dad going to add? 'Yes, Dad.'

'Uncle Syd's just rung me. Told me a bit more. About you and your young lady and your situation.' I could almost hear the words clunking over in Dad's head. He was not a man who was Deep and Meaningful and skilled with words. Dad was an awkward man.

'Son. Your mother's your mother. You know how she is. And she can think what she thinks.'

Maria stood behind me and embraced me, resting her head against my shoulder.

'But, Martin – and no disrespect to your mother now – not at all – I happen to view things differently.'

Suddenly I felt warm.

'Martin – Marty. If you two love each other. And you're being a man and taking care of her. Well. Son. It doesn't matter. Doesn't matter at all. What people think. Well. Doesn't matter a tinker's cuss.'

'Thanks Dad,' I whispered. Something caught in my throat, and I thought I might burst into tears again. I'd never had such a conversation with him. I couldn't remember if he'd ever called me 'Marty' before. Always that had been Uncle Syd's preserve. Now I didn't mind.

'Son. I'm gonna tell you something I've never said to you before. It's this: I'm, I'm proud 'o ya. Yep. You been a good boy all ya life. Mostly. I was surprised you wanted to work on a newspaper. But you've, er, kept ya nose clean. Stuck to it. And you're doing really well. I know y'are. Ah, old Wally Walton – you'll know who I mean, the editor of the local sausage-wrapper – he told me a few weeks ago he'd heard on, on, ya know, the grape vine, some good things about you in your new job.'

He paused while more words and phrases turned over in his mind. For me, Maria could have battered me to the floor with a strand of her hair. I had never heard such words from my father. Ever.

He was speaking again: '… if ya love one another, son, take good care of each other, ya can't go wrong. Ya don't need a piece a paper to prove ya love one another. Plenny o' people have the piece of paper, an' all the photos an' that from the big wedding, but, son, they don' love one another.'

I wondered if he was talking about him and Mum. But he would never say. It would be extreme disloyalty for a man of his age, generation, and values to criticise his wife like that to someone else. Even to his son. So perhaps he was leaving me to infer it from his remarks.

Awkward silence. I had an uncharitable thought. Had Dad been drinking? But, no, my Dad had never been a drinker. Unlike Uncle Syd, who thoroughly loved to have a drink – several drinks, because that's what old fighter pilots had done. Drink up, party, for tomorrow we might die.

'Thanks, Dad. I appreciate your ringing and saying these things.'

Another silence, and I could hear him breathing more heavily. 'Is, is. Ah, your young lady there with you right now?'

What's he up to? 'She's standing right here with her arms around me, Dad, listening to you with a smile on her face.' I had to swallow hard, because the tears were not far off.

'Ah. Ah. Son, you couldn't sort of let me talk to 'er, couldja? To say hello, so to speak?' He pulled rank. 'After all, mate *(mate?)*, I am your Dad.'

I handed the phone to Maria. 'Dad would like to say hello to you.'

Eyebrow arching, she took it: 'Good evening, Mr Blake. Maria here.' Her tone was sweet.

I put my ear close, to listen in as well.

'Well, ah, hello, Maria, I'm Martin's dad. Ralph's the name. I'm pleased to meet you, young lady.'

'And I'm thrilled to meet Martin's dad. I hope one day we can do it face-to-face.'

'Well, m'dear, that's a pleasure both you and I can certainly look forward to.'

You old bugger! And he invited her to call him Ralph.

'Are you making him behave himself?'

'Oh, yes,' she said, grinning widely, eyes glinting mischievously at me, 'he's been easy to live with. You and your wife have trained him well. I hope you're proud of him.'

They were both doing a very good job of starting off on the right foot with one another. I was proud of them both. As they talked I noticed something else: my father was losing his awkwardness. A warmth and an easiness was there I could not remember having heard before.

'I hope he is looking after you, Maria, and being a man and taking care of you.'

'Oh, Mr Blake, you need have no worries. I couldn't have gone through the last few weeks without Martin. He has a lot of hidden strengths.'

'That's good. Any problems, Maria, you let me know. I'll give him an earful or two. And he's still not too big that I can't give him a clip or two over the ear.'

Her laugh was a light, pealing string of musical notes. 'Oh, Ralph, you sound a really lovely man.'

Eh? I bet it's been a long time since a female has said that to him.

They bade each other farewell with new-found fondness, and Dad and I wished each other goodnight after probably our first decent conversation in our lives.

In bed Maria and I agreed that we'd probably be a bit tired tomorrow. 'I'm beginning to wonder if we're having too much sex,' she said as she straddled me and made herself comfortable.

'Don't know,' I replied. 'If you're worried you can get off me if you like.'

In response I got something like the Head Girl Stare, and she bent and bit my sensitive nipple, hard. I yelped. Pleasure and pain.

Farewell, Tom

The next Friday, at the end of what I felt had been a 'normal' week. Maria had settled into her routine with Robert. She was working her hours with Magdalena and Peter. She said she and Magdalena conversed a lot on French.

No-one was looking at me sideways at work. Wilson Barker had stopped baiting me lewdly after I said to him: 'Would your wife and daughters put up with you saying something like that to them?' He couldn't say anything because the gossip was that his sainted, virginal youngest daughter had gone and got herself 'up the duff', ending her first year at university.

The 'enemy' FitzGarratts had gone quiet. Uncle Brian had been as welcoming at last Sunday's Mass as he had been before. Maria's niece Catharine and a younger sister called by after school, with news. Maria had been the target of gossip, some malicious, most not, but dying away. Sister Hélène had been right. Maria could not have continued at the school, let alone as head girl.

So by Friday we were settling in with each other and being a couple. We had disagreements, and I was starting to lose my nervousness about them. We could bicker but we could still love one another, couldn't we? Making up was great. We had tentatively looked at a future together. Maria wanted to do at least three years at university. Perhaps she could go on overseas? How did I feel about that? I was very happy. I was confident I could get work anywhere.

But there was the tradition thing. Should we get married? 'But Martin, dear, you haven't asked me yet.' I wanted everything to settle down for a bit before anything like that.

On Friday morning we got a phone call from Aoife at Matt's chambers. 'Can you be free at 4pm, please? Chief Superintendent Shannon wants to see us.'

TOM HAD been sacked from the police, and far more quickly and with less protracted 'process' and 'procedure' than would be employed these days.

'I investigated the matters you alleged,' Angus Shannon said, more to Maria and me than to Matthew. 'I'm more than satisfied you have told the truth. Kearns resigned from the P'lice at midday today.'

Maria and I offered our thanks, sounding subdued. I had an odd feeling in my guts, and I was uneasy about it.

'No charges laid, Angus, under the Police Act or regulations?' Matthew said.

Shannon grinned, pulling on the lobe of a large ear. 'Not really, Matt. We could have. But like the Law Society and the judiciary we don't like washing our dirty linen in public. Not a good look. Bad for public confidence.'

He made a sucking sound between his teeth. 'It wasn't hard to find out about what Kearns had been up to. He was a well-known bastard –' and here the hardened cop stopped himself, turned to Maria, 'I apologise, young lady for my language – and sometimes for the sake of law and order we tolerate some, er, unorthodox behaviour. Generally we try to confine it to ne'er-do-wells such as thugs and thieves and little buggers setting out on a life of crime. We teach them lessons that their parents should have taught them.'

Matthew, the lawyer, said: 'I didn't hear that, Angus. But his behaviour towards Maria and Martin flies beyond the pale. Disgusting, really.'

Shannon closed a manila folder on his desk. 'Presented with evidence that we had caught him out, that the constables who'd been with him had squealed so they'd save their own necks, well, he had no choice but to offer his resignation immediately, which I accepted immediately – and without regret.'

I was worried, though. I didn't think we'd heard the last from Thomas Kearns.

LATE FRIDAY afternoon, knock-off time from work, and Matthew seemed neither in a hurry to return to his chambers or to go home to his family. He took us to a discreet little bar.

It appeared to be the drinking haunt of lawyers, doctors, accountants, sharebrokers, shipping agents, executives – professionals, in other words, who could afford to pay to drink in surroundings unsullied by smelly, uncouth men in dirty overalls and hob-nailed boots.

He found us a table near a window. The visit threw up a potential problem straight away. At 17 Maria was well and truly under the age of someone allowed on licensed premises. She had brought it up.

'Oh, that's easy,' Matthew said airily. 'You're my sister. Or you can be Martin's fiancée. We're responsible for you in the eyes of the law. It's fine. The police don't come here.'

He and Aoife sat together. It wasn't lost on me that they seemed more friends than Queen's Counsel and a junior solicitor. I recalled what he'd said to me a few weeks ago about him and Kay. He seemed to be saying then that he wouldn't do the dirty on her. But, as I was finding out, sometimes things are not what they seem.

He was a whisky man, and only the very best. Twenty-five year-old Scottish single-malt labels I'd never heard of and prices that seemed like a day's pay. But, he was a QC and I guess he could afford it. He urged me to try one with him, which I did. I'd never tasted so many different flavours at once in one sip.

Aoife liked Black Russians. She told Maria they were a nice drink, so she had one, too. 'I could get to like these,' she said after an exploratory, lip-smacking sip.

'You know, Matt,' she said, 'I'm just starting to get used to the fact that I can call you Matt, rather than Matthew.'

He squinted at her. 'Why's that?'

'I suppose because of the huge distance between us. You're old enough to be my father. Your oldest child is a couple of months younger than me. We never seemed like brother and sister – I mean, we couldn't even have a decent brother-sister fight.'

Aoife found that funny and giggled.

'And you never seemed like my sister, either, Ria.'

He leaned on the table, resting his chin on his knuckles. 'Let's just say that long before you took up the same space in our mother's womb that we all had the novelty for me had worn off.'

'What do you mean?'

'Well, 12 months after I was born another baby had joined me in competing for our mother's attention.'

'Rosaline.'

He nodded.

Maria turned to me: 'Rosaline is a Carmelite sister in Australia.'

'And then in mid-nineteen-thirty-something Mum and Dad boarded a ship and sailed off to Edinburgh so he could do further training; she added to her degree. They left Rosaline and me behind in the tender care of our grandmother and our various aunts.'

Was he angry and bitter about it? Still?

'When they came back they had two new twin faces – Rebecca and Esther, who were very much the centre of Peirse and Órla's affections. Not only that, our mother told us that God had sent them another little angel. By now I knew what that meant.'

He sipped his whisky – his second now. 'I still remember the thrashing I got from our father when I shouted I'd wished that Rebecca and Esther had been thrown into the ocean from the ship and hoped the new angel would die, too. I was 6. Our father was always good at dishing out thrashings to his oldest children when they were young.' He arched an eyebrow: 'I don't think you got many. Either you were a very good girl or he was feeling his age. I suspect it was the latter.'

Maria reached across the table and rested her hand on his – a gesture Aoife noted enviously. Matthew seemed taken aback. But he smiled, squeezed her hand, before continuing.

242

'I'm not going to get maudlin, my dear, sweet little sister, who has had the courage to do something none of us have done – and that is to buck the parents, and in effect say 'fuck you' to our grandmother.'

Aoife's eyes widened at that.

'But you can see what I'm going to say, I think. The Mother Factory was churning out baby after baby. No sooner had we all traipsed off to church for the baptism by whoever was the archbishop than we'd find the Sperm Tank had been emptied again, and the Mother Factory was cooking up another bun in the oven. And all the while she was keeping up her own career and palming off her children to other people.' Another sip, for punctuation effect. 'All God's will.'

He put a hand on his and Maria's: 'Do you know why Rosaline took herself off to the nunnery?'

Maria shook her head. I noticed she had barely touched her drink after her first sip. 'It was nothing to do with a desire to be a bride of Christ. She was fed up with being turned into the 'little mother' and made to look after her younger sisters and brothers. Well before you were born – so don't take it personally – she decided she'd had enough. Despite two master's degrees and half a PhD. So she found an order that emphasised peace and quiet and no speaking, joined it, and pretty much disappeared from our lives.'

He chuckled bitterly. 'But we all got to go to her profession, and our parents could smile proudly with her, and the Catholic newspapers could rabbit on about our family's Commitment to the Faith and our generosity in supplying a nun then a priest.'

He drained his glass. 'For the love of God, what did ordinary, good Catholics do to deserve Luke for a priest?'

'Maybe you and I should talk again, Matt,' Maria said. 'You've told me a lot in the last half-hour.'

His expression was weary. 'I have, haven't I? I'll just finish by saying that by the time you arrived I couldn't have cared less.' He hastened, 'I know that sounds bloody awful. But that's not how I feel now. And I hope I'm making up for it. It's just that, well, I was establishing my own career, Kay and I had bought our house, and Kay was pregnant with Catharine.'

'It's all right, Matt, I think I understand,' and she stood and stretched over the table to give him a hug and kiss, which made Aoife more envious, we agreed later. Yep, the crush was more Aoife's than Matt's.

'I have to apologise to you for something else, Maria. It's good that you and Catharine have started to get on better. Her attitudes towards you all these years have largely been what she's picked up from me.'

She said nothing.

'I always thought you were spoiled and was getting from our parents what we had missed out on because they were too busy being the well-known doctor and the university teacher and Mother Factory and The Leading Voices of Faith and Reason. Childish, I know, and I don't think you got a lot of love and care from our parents, particularly the Mother Factory. Anyway I apologise. It wasn't all Catharine's fault.'

He smiled sadly. 'Oddly enough, Kay always used to stick up for you. She felt sorry for you. But now she really doesn't approve of you and Martin shacking up.' He paused for a discreet burp. 'I think she worries that you will infect the girls – not just mine, but all the nieces.'

Aoife excused herself to go to the loo; I think she wanted Maria to go with her. Maria stayed put.

'Shall I tell you what upsets Kay the most about you, Maria?'

'Am I going to like this?'

He smiled: 'Kay worries that you'll get pregnant and so have to get married, that you won't be able to wear white at your wedding, and most all, that everyone will know and so will talk.'

'That's all?'

'Yep.'

'But everybody knows. Catharine and Jacqueline told me the other day. And everyone is not horrified, either.'

Aoife returned, excused herself and said she was going home.'

'She has a thing going for you,' Maria said as Aoife threaded through the throngs of men.

Matthew looked thoughtful. 'Yes, I know. It's a pity because I don't encourage her. It might sound odd, but I admire her most for her brains than for notions concerning sex.'

The first punch is the hurtest

I never saw the punch coming.

Maria had driven the car to pick me up from Saturday night work because of a rain storm.

I got out and unlocked the garage doors so she could drive in, which she did. I waited by the door as she unfolded herself from the Clubman.

The rain was pissing down, trickling down my neck, and she unaccountably was taking what seemed a long time getting out of the car.

Something … I turned and glimpsed too late the sudden, dark shape, a blurry glimpse of Tom's enraged features. The sharp jab of his big, hard, ex-policeman's fist into my solar plexus. Excruciating pain exploding in my belly. I couldn't breathe. My heart seemed to stop.

'Cunt,' he grunted.

He grabbed hold of me as I sank to the ground, just as his knee came up to crush my nose. It caught my ear instead – and I still remember how much that hurt.

'You little fuck!'

He slammed me back against the garage door or wall and rammed his knee into my balls.

I squealed like a pig – the high-pitched, unnerving shriek when they know they're about to be killed.

'Heh. Like a fucking little bitch, eh?'

He was enjoying himself. I remember going down in a heap in the wet, curling up like a baby.

God, he could hurt. My back, my ribs, hips, thighs, my head. *Thud!* after sickening *Thud!* after sickening, crunching *Thud.*

They say that under extreme stress – such as getting a physical beating – your mind takes you elsewhere, to where it convinces itself and you that this is not happening. That really everything is lovely. Apparently it's a form of protection against the horror.

My mind was telling me each time Tom Kearns' huge, steel-capped boots kicked and stomped me in the head and body that it wasn't happening.

But it was.

And Tom sucking his breath in through his teeth, and grunting with the exertion. Cursing, cursing, *Thud! Thud!* ...

My mind found a new place – a new heaven, a new earth to take me to.

And as it spirited me away I heard screaming – *Maria, oh, God, don't let him touch Maria!*

Another voice shouting – Alice. *Thank God Maria's not alone!*

A male voice. 'You odious bastard!' Robert. *Oh, thank you, Jesus!*

And then, the last sound: a solid, dull thud, like a cricket bat cracking a skull.

Somewhere in Heaven …

My hearing kicked in first. So voices, hushed voices. Dad? Uncle Syd? Auntie Kura? Yes, Auntie Koo: soothing, a sound I remembered from my childhood and I was in her lap. She was cradling my head to her warm, comfortable bosom as she put something on my cut knee. Or was it the bee sting on my foot? Tried to think. Whatever, the pain always went away when Auntie Koo set her mind to making it go away.

It hurt to think about it. All I could see were Technicolor visions of squares and circles swirling and spiralling and leaping and dancing against the inside of my eyelids.

My eyes didn't want to open. I didn't know why. I was removed from everything, just being in suffusing comfort. I had no idea why that was, either. It all seemed very strange.

Dad – yes, it was Dad – he said something. His voice was rough with anger. It had been a long time since I'd heard Dad's voice so angry rough. Somebody was a mongrel. 'You've been very brave, Maria, for such a young lass.'

What was he talking about? Maria. Who's Maria? I should know who Maria is. The mysterious Maria sounded as if she had been crying. 'It's all my fault,' she said shakily. 'I took too long getting out of the car. I thought I'd dropped something out of my purse and –'

Auntie Koo was shushing her. 'No, darling, you're not to blame yourself.'

A hand took mine, and it was held to lips that kissed it. Tears from a face were wiped against it, and there was a sniffle.

What were they all talking about? Who, what, why, when, where, and how? What was this all about? So many questions …

A voice within me said: 'That's enough of that, young man. Come back to Heaven.'

MORE VOICES drifting up to Heaven.

'I'm very grateful that you were on hand to be with Maria when it happened,' Dad was saying.

'Oh, it was the least I could do,' Alice said. 'He's just a jumped-up coward. Should never have been a policeman.'

'And you, too, Mr Tungwell-Urquhart.'

'Oh, please, Ralph. Robert will do perfectly.'

'Maria was very brave, Mr Blake.' A smoker's cough. Alice. 'She leapt on 'is back to try to stop him kicking Martin all over the place.'

My right hand was held tightly by one I vaguely remembered. Occasionally whoever held it lifted it and kissed it. My left hand was held by a strong, rough hand. A man's hand, and it squeezed in time with when Dad was speaking.

I wanted to know who they were talking about. Who was Martin? But Heaven said, from the middle of the cloud of cotton wool I was lying in, 'shhh, not yet, Martin.' Ah. So I must be Martin?

'When I got there,' Alice was saying, 'he was trying to swing Maria off, and that's when she sank her teeth into his ear.'

'She probably saved his life,' another voice said. I didn't recognise that one. Matthew?

'Well she certainly distracted him long enough so I could clout him,' Robert said.

Maria said something.

'He'll be all right, darling,' I heard Auntie Koo saying. Maria burst into tears, and she seemed to be the one holding my right hand, and she wiped her tears with it again.

'Maria: listen to me,' I heard Uncle Syd say softly. 'He's just been given a good hiding. Nothing's broken, so the doctor's say.'

In Heaven's depthless, cotton softness they were all discussing me. I must be Martin, yes. But what had happened? And why were circles and spirals of a myriad colours looping and dancing and coming and going on the inside of my eyelids? A memory streaked like a comet through me: a man's snarling face, a fist being pulled back, a crunch of boot in my back, a girl screaming *'Martin, Oh God Martin, No-o –!'*

Heaven enfolded me in its infinite, loving embrace. 'That's enough of that,' a voice of infinite gentleness whispered.

HEAVEN, WITH soulful, worried eyes, let me take another baby step, knowing I had to. I opened my eyes. I needed to see who all the people talking were. I needed to start making sense of why I was wherever I was, and why they were there. Where was I, even?

Someone took the wrappings away from my eyes. My vision was fuzzy and blurred. It was all like an out-of-focus picture and shapes and figures swam and lurched in front of me. The bright lights over my head made me blink awkwardly.

Maria was to my right. Something clicked over in my brain now, and I knew who she was. She burst into tears, and said: 'His eyes have just opened.'

'Thank Christ for that,' I heard Dad say.

Faces pitched and swayed in front of me.

The voices in a babble expressed their relief and joy at this development. 'I'll ring his mother tonight and let her know. She's been very worried about him.'

'Sweetie,' Maria whispered, her hand clutching mine, 'can you speak?'

My eyes cleared for her. Maria's face was a mess: blotched and pimply, purply, puffy pouches under anxious eyes. She had been crying a lot. A bruise discoloured her right cheek. Her hair was greasy and tied back in her severe Head Girl Bun. She was thin and her breath was stale pepperminty. Auntie Koo loomed tall behind her, her big hands on Maria's shoulders, squeezing them gently.

Dad was in a chair on the other side of the bed. I was understanding now that I was in a hospital bed. Where were the nurses? Ah. One was over by the door; a big-bosomed woman in starchy white, her white cap perched on a pile of chestnut hair. Her sharp eyes watched everything and everybody.

Dad had tears. I'd never known Dad to have tears. His eyes – which had always had the look of the careful about them – exuded a bright, solid love. Crikey. The things you find out in a crisis …

Uncle Syd was leaning over the bed, grinning, his Private Walker moustache impeccable as usual. His breath smelled of stale tobacco.

I went to speak. My throat gave up a croak.

'It's good to see you awake, son,' Dad said, his big, rough hand squeezing mine in his clasp.

Maria leaned over and kissed me tenderly on the lips. 'I love you, darling,' she whispered.

'Carefully now,' the starchy nurse commanded.

Maria sat back contritely.

Heaven reached down and with one powerful movement scooped me up and returned me to its depthless, infinite oblivion.

HEAVEN WAS like a wise mother, I've decided. Heaven shielded me from mental and physical agony. But like a wise mother Heaven knew the time had arrived for me to be led totteringly back into reality, to pain.

They were still there – Maria, Dad, Uncle Syd and Auntie Koo. Robert, too. He and Uncle Syd must have discovered their wartime connection because I was listening to war stories – the jokes, the funny times, the capers – never death and killing – before I realised that I was back in my hospital bed.

I knew who I was now, and who they were, and that I was in a hospital room, but a different one, but I didn't know why. And how long had I been here, I managed to croak.

'Since Saturday night,' Maria said.

'It's Thursday afternoon now – five o'clock,' Dad said.

Minds do funny things – often they prompt the oddest, silliest questions, remarks, observations.

'So why have I been here since Saturday night?'

That perplexed them, and I think they all looked to each other to see who was going to answer the question. Dad nodded to Maria.

'Sweetie, Tom beat you up just after I had parked the car in the garage.'

'Why did he do that?'

Uncle Syd chuckled: 'That's a very good question, my favourite nephew –'

'I thought all your nephews were your favourites, Uncle Sydney.'

That astonished them.

'I'm very pleased to hear you say that, Marty,' he said sincerely.

I didn't understand why an irrelevant comment that interrupted him should please him.

He grinned broadly though. 'But as I was going to say before my nephew rudely interrupted me. Your friend Robert here just about took Tom's head off with a cricket bat.'

'Jesus …' I whispered wonderingly. Maria let that one pass.

'Young Thomas is an exceedingly crook boy. Robert hit 'im for six.' Uncle sounded very satisfied. 'His brains have been so mashed and scrambled that he'll never be the same again. He'll never talk again and will never walk again. He will be spoonfed puree'd mush like a baby til the day he dies. He'll need his nappies changed. He's a vegie.' He grinned. 'One well-aimed hit, Marty. That's all it took. Even Robert was surprised.'

'Stella is demanding the police charge Robert for using excessive force,' Maria said worriedly.

'They're welcome to try,' Robert said lightly.

I looked around them all. 'When did you get here?'

Dad: 'Maria rang home about 1am on Sunday just after you'd been admitted here. I rang Uncle Syd and Auntie Kura straight after that. NAC got us on flights on Sunday morning. Maria and the Polish lady met us at the airport and we were here on Sunday afternoon.'

I was trying to figure out something, but I wasn't sure what. 'When were Robert and Alice both here?'

They glanced around at each other. 'Tuesday afternoon, I think,' Auntie Koo said, and shrugged.

'Tuesday,' Robert said.

'I heard you.'

They nodded.

'And when did I wake up.'

'Oh, that woulda been yesterday, son.' He glanced at the others for confirmation. 'Yeh. Yesterday morning. The docs and the nurses were quite happy with you yesterday.'

A doctor in his 40s came in, followed by Nurse Starchy. He checked my eyes with a penlight, and I had to open my mouth and go 'ahh'.

The doctor spoke in plain English. No bones had been broken, so I had been lucky. They estimated Tom had managed to punch, knee, kick, and stomp on me 'with considerable force' no fewer than 20 times in less than a frenzied, violent minute. I was being kept in my euphoric state by pain-killers. 'Tomorrow we'll start weaning you off them. We don't want you getting too attached to them.'

'When can I go home?'

He glanced at Starchy: 'I'd say Monday morning at the latest.'

I said to Maria that I needed to get back to work.

'Maria rang your editor here on Sunday morning,' Dad said. 'She explained what had happened.' He nodded approvingly at her. 'She's been very good at keeping all the right people in the know.'

She smiled wearily. 'Mr Barnfield was here on Monday morning. He says you needn't hurry back to work. He thinks they'll manage without you.'

Heaven decided that was enough. My eyes shut and the infinite soft ocean swallowed me up.

HEAVEN DECIDED that I could be tipped out of the soft nest. The friendly doctor now said I could go home on Sunday morning. I had recovered well. They had cut back the pain-killers and I was feeling aches deep to the bone. Walking, even moving my head, could be painful. But bearable. The agony in my crotch – I'd never known anything like it, which prompted Uncle Syd to joke: 'It might be grateful for the rest, nephew.' He winked at Maria. She blushed deeply but uncomfortably. Auntie Koo, who had been 'mother' to Maria, glared him a silent 'I will speak to you later.' He looked away sheepishly. She would have his guts for garters, and he knew it.

Uncle Sydney had hired a car, and he and Dad and Maria collected me from the hospital to bring me back to the flat.

I discovered later my coming out of hospital had provoked a family drama. Dad had wanted to take me and Maria home to Mum.

He had phoned Mum. 'Martin is of course welcome, Ralph. But that girl is not welcome in my house. Goodness gracious. What were you thinking? Where would she sleep?'

Mum's reaction had devastated him. Uncle Syd told me that the last time he'd seen Dad cry was way back when they were boys.

Other discoveries:

People had shown unexpected kindnesses. Magdalena and Peter had made their spare flat available to Dad, Uncle Syd, and Auntie Kura.

Uncle Syd and Dad saw that Maria needed an older shoulder to lean on. Maria had objected. Auntie Koo had had a quiet talk to her, woman-to-woman. Maria relented. She had moved into my flat and she and Maria had slept in our bed together for nearly a week. The grown-ups had combined to gently persuade Maria her 24-hour presence at my hospital bed was not necessary. 'Martin's not going to die, Maria, I can tell you that without a doubt,' Dad told her. Dad hid his deep worry that he might be wrong. But he would never show that worry in front of a 17 year-old girl.

Alice had baked. Robert had brought messages of prayers for my recovery from Sister Hélène. Monsignor Uncle Brian was suddenly there. Maria told me he said a quiet prayer over me and blessed me, then he prayed for her and Dad, and for Uncle Syd and Auntie Koo.

Matthew threatened the hospital with injunctions to prevent any of the Doctors FitzGarratt from getting anywhere near Maria and me. Aoife told Maria that he'd conveyed the same message to the family.

He added that Tom would not be charged. 'No point. The poor bastard's done for.'

'What about Robert, though?' Maria said.

'Well, he might have used excessive force. But, you know, it was dark, he was defending a young girl from potential attack, and he was acting to stop Martin having the living shit being kicked out of him.'

He grinned: 'It's not as if Robert repeatedly battered him. He hit him only once.'

That was the blow I'd heard.

'Stella's angry; but something Kay said, and it might be that she's relieved so she can be shot of him.'

His grin was hard: 'Well, she's making arrangements already for his care at a sanatorium far from here for the brain-damaged. He'll be out of sight and out of mind.'

'So much for love,' Maria said.

'It gives her an excuse to play the tragic,' he said.

The *Evening Herald* had run a carefully worded story about the assault on me on page 5. It gave my name and age, said I was a staff member of the newspaper, that the alleged assailant was an ex-policeman who had been injured when a member of the public rushed to my aid. 'Police would not speculate on the reasons for the assault,' Trevor Clifton had written.

Clyde Barnfield and Malcolm Ogle had visited the hospital. They spoke to Dad, Auntie Kura, and Maria. 'We couldn't not have run the story,' my editor told them.

'But we didn't draw undue attention to it,' Malcolm Ogle said. 'We'll try to shield you as best we can from any publicity,' he told Maria, 'but we can't give any guarantees. We know the opposition is sniffing about, and if they start to sniff out the whole story, well ...'

'Martin would understand,' Barnfield added.

They had come bearing gifts. 'Get well' and 'Thinking of you' cards with messages from the staff. A bottle of bourbon 'to help with your recovery'. Susan Devonshire had sent a bunch of flowers for Maria.

Dante's hellish welcome

The climb to the top floor to my flat had exhausted me. Dad and Uncle Syd guided me up the stairs as if I was an infirm geriatric.

By the top I was drenched in sweat, as well. Alice, Robert, and the Chilean sisters-in-law, Catalina and Pilar, had given our flat a good clean, and it smelled spring fresh. They had provided food. Now they crowded into the flat. The Chileans' welcome was brief. They were leaving their flat later that day.

Flopped down on the couch, I mumbled a few words of thanks for everything they had done, particularly their help to Maria.

Dante the Siamese discovered compassion in his stony, feline little heart. He leapt spritely on to my knee, disregarding the pain he caused me as his sharp claws 'kneaded the dough' on my barely pain-killered bruises and his black head forcefully bunted my battered jaw.

Going by the purr crackling out of his throat and the pleased expression on his face he seemed happy. But bugger you, Martin … He made himself more welcome by curling up on my lap while he observed everyone and everything.

Eventually he discarded me without a glance – Dante's love was buyable, tradable, and disposable. He rubbed against Uncle Syd's leg before Maria crossly picked him up.

Maria put me to bed after everyone had gone. Dad had wanted to stay, but Auntie Koo gently took him by the elbow and smoothly guided him towards the door. 'If they need you, Ralph, you're a telephone call away. And you need a good sleep, too.'

Maria undressed me carefully as if I was a frail old man, and I saw in the wardrobe mirror what I looked like. I've never forgotten the image reflected back to me. The saying 'bruised black-and-blue' didn't do it justice. There was purple, black, pink, yellow – and colours I couldn't give names to. Toe prints of Tom's steel-capped boot were studded along my back and shoulders and my arms, my backside, and down the back of my thighs. I was swollen and bruised between my legs. Tom had tried to stomp on and kick my head in. Bruises lopsided my face. Stitches had been put into gashes on the side of my head.

Maria stood beside me, staring in horror at the mirror. She hadn't seen it all before. I took her hand. 'Don't be upset, love. It might turn out to be an improvement.' She laughed, which is what I wanted her to do anyway. I didn't want her to cry any more.

Curling up foetally had saved me from a great deal of worse damage, the doctor said. 'But I have to tell you, mate, I'm astounded no bones are broken.'

'Oh, he's of good solid stock, Doctor, don't you worry about that,' Dad had said proudly.

Maria slipped in beside me. She was bonier than before; more ribs, hollows around her shoulders, hip bones protruding.

'I've got you back to myself,' she whispered, and tucked my head carefully to her warm, familiar breasts like a mother does to her child.

I kissed the small slope of one and snuffled against the nipple. 'I'm happy, too,' I remember saying, and then Heaven laid us down together on a cushion of dreamless oblivion.

SHE HAD barely slept for a week. She had cried for me, worried for me, suffered for me. And with the greatest kindness my father, uncle and aunt had had to prise her away from my side so she could rest.

'You don't have to do it all on your own,' Auntie Kura had told her, 'even though as a woman you think you should.'

Nice touch, that, by my shrewd aunt. She was treating Maria as an adult. But Maria had not rested easily. Auntie Koo had told me that later. In our bed that she and Maria shared she had held and soothed her as she worried herself to restless sleep.

They had let her be the decision-maker for me. She had proved best at talking to the doctors. The doctor's daughter and sister wasn't deferential like Dad and Uncle Syd would be. Maria could decode their language and turn it into plain English for my father, uncle, and aunt.

Visitors

We slept for about 20 hours, which did Maria a lot of good. The strain was still in her face, but the blotches had faded, even in the last day. The bruise was a pale green-yellow, but smaller. She didn't know how she'd got it.

How much good the sleep did me I couldn't say. I'd spent most of the last week asleep. It was a relief to be back in my own bed and to have Maria beside me.

The pain-killers were being gradually cut back, and so I was adjusting to the dull aches all through my body. The agony in my scrotum was becoming more a discomfortable ache. The laconic doctor told me it could be weeks before that particular hurt went away.

He glanced at Maria before adding: 'And I wouldn't be thinking of any sort of strenuous activity over the next six weeks.' Maria's lips twitched fractionally.

Anyway, about 8am a knock on the door. I was still in bed and Maria was making breakfast for us both.

Robert. He was wondering why Maria hadn't shown for their Monday tutorial at their usual time, seven o'clock.

She was not impressed. 'Well, as I'm sure you're aware, Robert, my boyfriend has just come out of hospital a week after he got a kicking from my brother-in-law,' she said with wincingly sharp sarcasm. 'I've got rather a bit on my plate.'

Robert was unruffled. 'The immediate crisis is over,' he said crisply. 'Martin's on the mend, and that will take time. There's nothing much anyone can do about that – even Martin.'

'Well, then, you –'

'Maria.' He was sympathetic and gentle, but his saying her name stopped her in her verbal tracks. He was telling her, in the nicest possible way, to shut up and listen. 'You need to start getting yourself back to normality. You need it for yourself, and you need it for Martin.'

'But –'

'My dear, I repeat: the crisis is over. Normality and routine have to be re-established. You need to get yourself back to normal. By doing that you help Martin get back to normal.'

'But what if he needs me?'

'He's a big boy,' Robert said airily. 'He has a voice, and I'm sure he knows how to use it. He knows how to use the telephone, as well. We're only next door.'

While she pondered that he just added: 'Ten o'clock for today. Just a gentle session. Resetting the compass, so to speak. Don't be late.' That sounded headmasterly.

She sulked afterwards. I told her he was right. That earned me a Head Girl Scowl. 'I hoped you would stand up for me, Martin.'

'You've been under a lot of strain since it happened,' I said. 'You've had worry way beyond your years.'

'So you're saying I'm just a silly, brainless little girl?'

Sick as I was, I recognised a red flag. It was becoming one of those circular discussions males get into with women. The guts of it is that the guy never wins. Or, as Felicity used to say: 'You're not meant to win, you idiot.'

I was exhausted again. My patience was spiralling down the gurgler quickly. 'Maria. Just go and do it. Please.'

She noted the exasperation, frowned as she considered whether to keep at it; she humphed, put herself through the shower for 10 minutes, emerged, dried herself with her customary two towels, and dug into the bottom drawer where the tampons were and pulled one out. She waved it at me and smiled. *'Monatsblutung.'*

SHE WAS a lot happier after she returned from Robert's. While she was next door with him I'd moved to the couch. They gave me Dante to babysit. He ignored me and curled up on Maria's side of the bed. She had even left her pyjamas so he could sleep on them. I tried to talk to him in Maria-speak: 'Are you a wuvvy boo'ful boy?' I cooed. Yes, that's how she talked to him. I told him he was an ingrate.

Anyway, the radio and *Asterix in Britain* were proving good company. *Asterix and the Roman Agent* was next. Maria even had a copy in French. She kissed me on her return, fussed about me, chatted.

'Did you know Robert does a bit of writing?' she said.

No, I hadn't. But Robert – whom I'd thought was a hermetical recluse – hermetical recluse? Tautology? – doesn't matter, was a guy I thought had shut himself away from sight and mind, chain-smokingly enjoyed classical music with Dante on his lap.

But Robert, she said, edited and proofread academic textbooks from all around the world. He peer-reviewed everything from theses to academic papers. He wrote articles for academic journals overseas.

'He starts his work at six in the morning. He'd hear you go off to work. Said you were very regular. He works into the evening. He's very busy.'

WE HAD just finished the lunch she made – Ryvita biscuits topped with cottage cheese and tomato for her, scrambled egg for me so I could eat easily. An assertive knock at the door. It sounded like a FitzGarratt knock. Maria opened it.

Felicity.

Black hair neatly tied back. Earrings too dangly and junky against her doll's made-up face. Slim and cool. Blouse at least one size too small and cut too low, top button straining between breasts. Waistcoat jacket that somehow was out of place. Skirt high up thighs, barely covering her backside. Black tights. Red platform ankle boots. Cloying perfume. Ughh …

I don't think she had expected Maria. But anyway she unleashed a tidal wave of sickening, false charm. 'Hi I'm Felicity I'm an old friend of

Martin's and I've just been transferred to a branch here and I saw a story in the paper last week about how he had been beaten up and I thought How Awful! poor Martin for something like that to happen to such a nice guy …' meanwhile edging into the room and Maria was so taken aback she stood aside to let her pass '… and anyway I didn't know how to contact him so I rang his newspaper and said I was an old dear friend of his and they told me where you lived and here I am!'

Then her eyes, which had been switching between Maria and me, settled on me like a fly on poo. 'Oh, Martin! What did he do to you?' She prepared herself for the harrowing task of doing sympathy sympathetically.

Maria was recovering and flaring like an enraged cat; I expected hissing, snarling, and slashing claws imminently. I couldn't be bothered. I didn't want this woman who'd treated me with contempt back in my life. She had no reason to be in my flat.

'Maria, I'd do it myself, but would you mind showing Felicity back out.'

Felicity put on her Hurt Face, which I remembered well, and that made me angrier because it was so false and manipulative. 'But Martin I only came along to see how you were.' She dug into her handbag and pulled out a small bottle of bourbon. 'Look,' she said through a desperate grin, 'I brought along a little something to help with your recovery I'm sure –'

'Listen, you stupid cow, you're not wanted here.' Maria's voice sliced across the room. Her eyes were that eerie green when she was really, really pissed off, and her cheekbones were rosy points.

Felicity recoiled. 'But, but –'

'The only decent and clever thing you did, lady, was to dump him. Because that means I get to have him instead, and unlike you I love him and appreciate him. He was wasted on you.'

'Now,' she said dangerously, pointing to the door, 'get out and never come back.'

Felicity's lips trembled. Yes, I knew that one, too, and the crying eyes, but she shrivelled as she turned and left.

Maria sat beside me and hugged me gingerly. 'All right, sweetie?'

'Yes,' and I kissed her, not hard, but where the bruise on her cheek was dying. In my mind I was trying to kiss it better.

'You must be missing terrifying third- or fourth -formers, darling, to let rip like that.'

'Not really.' Her eyes had lost their intense green. 'It's just the silly bitch made me so angry. Her gall that she thought she could just waltz in here. And most females if they've got half a brain know never to antagonise another who's being visited by the Curse. We can get quite cross.'

Yes.

MORE KNOCKING on the door woke me. 'This is like a railway station,' I grumbled. I'd been dozing in the late afternoon, and Maria was swotting at the table.

Dad, Uncle Syd, and Auntie Koo. They had come with a big announcement. They felt the time was right to go back home; they would fly out tonight.

'The crisis is over,' Uncle Syd said, and I glanced at Maria, and she permitted herself a small, rueful smile. 'He's going to live. There's nothing more we can do.'

Dad rested a gentle hand on Maria's shoulder. 'My dear, we're leaving him in your capable hands – because we've seen how capable you are.'

Tears watered her eyes, and she blushed deeply.

'You've been a revelation to us this last week,' Uncle Syd said.

'Thank you,' she said in a small voice.

'Any problems with 'im, Maria,' Dad said, trying to mask his feelings under joviality, 'well, young lady, you know my phone number.'

She took his big, rough hands in hers. 'You really are a lovely man, you know, once you drop that old gruff front. I see a lot of you in your son.'

Really? No-one's ever said that about Dad and me before.

He lapped it up, especially when she threw her arms about his neck and hugged him tightly. The old bugger tried to gruff it out, but he kissed her cheek – not the bruised one, though.

A teenage girl had shown him love and shown him that he was loveable. I don't think Dad knew how to cope with that.

Auntie Kura wanted 'a girl talk' with Maria for a few moments, and so they disappeared into the bedroom and closed the door.

'Yep,' Dad said, 'it's time to go home. I can report everything to Mum and reassure her you're all right and in good hands. She's been worried about yer. Make no mistake about that. She might not show it, but she does. She's like every mother. They always worry for their children.'

I glanced at Uncle Syd. Very poker-faced.

They left shortly afterwards. Uncle Syd found Robert and they thanked him again, promised to keep in touch, and said all those other things people say when they go through farewell rituals. And there was the old fighter pilot bond.

They delivered admonitions to me to look after myself and to stay in touch, and to Maria to look after herself and not take any nonsense from me. It must have been unthinkable that I could expect nonsense from her. But that's often the way, isn't it? Men and boys are expected to be sources of nonsense that women will roll their eyes for.

For the first time in my life I had tears in my eyes as Dad and I bade each other farewell with a heartfelt, robust hug. Our first, and it physically hurt me. I didn't care. How was it that I'd got to 23 without really knowing who my Dad was? They all had fond hugs for Maria.Then they were gone.

SUE DEVONSHIRE was next, and next morning. Maria answered the door. She turned back to me: 'Do you want to see her?'

Sue was beyond the door, on the landing. I got up and staggered to the door. Sue waited awkwardly, feet turned in a little, clutching a handbag tightly across her front. Her smile at me was tentative; nervous. Her eyes guarded.

She expected me to say 'bugger off', but I couldn't. I don't do grudges very well. Sue had been pathetic rather than malicious in her betrayal; she had sent flowers to Maria while I was in hospital. Let bygones be bygones. 'Come on in, Sue.'

She smiled gratefully and stepped in diffidently. I indicated a seat, but she said she wanted to stand. 'I haven't come to add to your problems, Martin, or to cause any more hurt, or to upset you.'

Maria stood off to the side, watchful.

'It's not upsetting me you should worry about, Sue,' I said as I sank back to the couch. I nodded at Maria. 'She's got the Curse. The last female who tried to upset me got the stiletto point of her tongue and scurried frightened away. So I'd watch yourself.'

'Thank you for broadcasting that, Martin,' Maria said crossly.

Sue glanced over her shoulder at her. 'Men ...'

'I know,' Maria replied. 'No tact whatsoever. I'll speak severely to him later.'

My attempt at a joke had melted the atmosphere. They had affected a 'girls' solidarity'.

'I'll keep it brief,' Sue said. 'I just want to apologise. I backed the wrong horse. I thought I was trying to help. I was wrong. I apologise.'

Maria and I shared glances. Forgive and forget.

I staggered painfully back to my feet. 'Apology accepted. Thank you for coming. Matter already forgotten.' I held out my arms to her. We hugged. I hoped we would back be friends like we used to be.

She and Maria hugged. 'Thank you for the flowers,' Maria whispered, and they hugged again. I thought there were going to be tears. Sue stayed for a cup of coffee, and then after a decent interval declared that she'd better get off to work.

THE KNOCK on the door mid-afternoon was discreet, barely heard because it was so soft – not a hard knuckle-knocker. Maria was clattering out a history assignment on the typewriter, the radio was tuned to a new private music station, the gas heater was burning, and I was curled up on the couch with the machinations of Tortuous Convolvulus in *Asterix and the Roman Agent*.

Maria opened the door.

'Mum,' she said.

'GOOD AFTERNOON, Maria,' I heard Órla say.

A tense silence, mother and daughter facing each other uneasily across the doorway.

'May I come in, please?'

'Have you come here to call me more names and judge me, Mum, because if you –'

'May I come in? Please?'

'I'll see how Martin is,' Maria said, part-closing the door.

I told her it was fine. 'She's your mother.' Could she be worse than mine? She couldn't do any worse to us than her now brain-dead son-in-law.

Maria opened the door and stood aside. Órla entered carefully, as if she was walking on eggshells in her sensible, dark slip-ons, in her subdued skirt and matching jacket, blue-white striped blouse, maroon bow at the throat, clutching a handbag.

I staggered to my feet for her. 'Mrs FitzGarratt, good afternoon.'

'Hello, Martin,' she said. She acknowledged my gesture with a brief smile. Maria was tense behind her. *Say one word out of place, Mum, and ...*

I slumped back to the couch.

Órla turned back to Maria. 'I do come in peace,' she said quietly.

Maria offered her mother tea. Mother declined politely. Maria offered her mother an armchair. Mother declined that politely, too. 'I'll stand by the heater, if you don't mind, until my legs warm up.'

Well, that was a hint at humour.

'What can we do for you, Mrs FitzGarratt?'

'Órla, please.' Her sharp, dark eyes, I think, were trying to convey warmth.

'I don't want to be rude, Mrs FitzGarratt, but can we pass on that until I know whether your visit is indeed in peace.'

She nodded, a rueful glance. 'How are you?'

'I'm mending, thank you.'

She turned to her 14th child. 'And you, Maria. How are you?'

'Good, thanks, Mum. And very happy in spite of the last week.'

Maria moved over to stand beside me and rested a hand on my shoulder. The silence stretched out and was awkward. Mother and daughter too strained, too distant to be comfortable with one another. Eye-contact between them fleeting. But Maria was calling her 'Mum'. I liked that.

Perhaps if I'd been in better shape I might have tried to make more of an effort, to be forgiving, to reach out, to build bridges and all that. She obviously had come with a purpose. Did she … 'Mrs FitzGarratt, would you prefer to talk to Maria alone?'

That was probably it, and I think she was about to say so when her 11th daughter answered first. 'No, Martin, thank you. Whatever my mother has to say she can say to both of us.' The look she was directing at Órla was giving no quarter. She reached down for my hand.

'I see.' She took a deep breath. 'The family is in some turmoil over Tom's attack on you. Stella has in effect been made a widow. Tom will require full-time care for the rest of his life.'

'Mum,' Maria said sharply, 'he brought it on himself. I don't care about Tom. He was a sleaze.'

Órla put up a placating hand. 'Please … I came to tell you that Stella told me something last evening that I find utterly repugnant.' She did sit now, and so Maria sat next to me.

'On Sunday Stella was going through Tom's things. She found two cheques each of $1000 – signed by your grandmother.'

'What were they for?' Maria said.

'Oh, that's easy, sweetie. She was paying him to stir mischief. Isn't that correct, Mrs FitzGarratt?'

Maria's eyes were wide, as was her mouth. 'But that's … that's –'

'I'm very much afraid so,' Órla said.

This is the story that she told, between long pauses, almost as if she was having difficulty believing it herself: Grannie Annie Fitz had been enraged and outraged that her granddaughter had gone off 'to wallow loike a sow in her pigstoy of sin'.

Peirse and Órla had wrung their hands and agonised. They didn't want a scandal. Mark and the other lawyers in the family had advised them they couldn't force Maria to return to the family bosom and the salvation of Luke's confessional. She was over 16. While some might view her shacking up with Mr Blake as disgraceful, immoral, and even deeply upsetting, they weren't doing anything illegal.

In other words, unless Maria was in a state of danger, which they had to prove, they couldn't do anything about it. Going before a magistrate for

266

a court order forcing Maria to return home could end messily in public. Certain newspapers feasted on those kinds of stories.

Grannie Annie Fitz had berated her son and daughter-in-law for being 'weak as pisswater' and not dragging the girl home from her pit of sin and thrashing sense into her, as she would no doubt have done.

She had pointed the finger at Órla for not keeping a close eye on 'that girl'. Peirse was exempted from criticism.

Grannie Annie had long taken a liking to Tom. She treated him like a favourite grandson. Encouraged by her he had converted to the One True Faith so he would be acceptable to marry Stella. He loved and lusted after Stella.

In turn, Stella needed urgently to marry him because her love and lust was in danger of taking her over and there would be – oh, horror – sex before marriage. It happens sometimes to otherwise intelligent, rational people.

Stella didn't care about his lack of brains – she had more than enough for both of them, was a clever female, and so he could easily be controlled and manipulated. What had mattered to her was the weapon – apparently enormous and skilfully used – between his legs.

They had become favourites of Grannie Annic. So the perfect person to scare us into breaking up and Maria thus returned – shop-soiled but chastened, and after a confession of her squalid immorality to Luke, forgiven – was her thuggish grandson-in-law.

He was easily biddable for $2000, which then was a lot of money. To please his wife's grandmother he terrified his teenage sister-in-law, tried to fit me up on a bogus drugs count, and then put me in hospital for a week.

'What does Stella say about all this?' Maria said.

'She's very upset.'

'Just upset, Mum?' I squeezed Maria's hand. *Please*, I was saying, *not now*.

'Well, obviously,' Órla said defensively.

'How much did she know?'

'She says she didn't. Nor did he tell her he had been dismissed from the police.'

Maria turned to me. I shrugged: you have to take her at her word.

'And Dad? What does he say?'

'He took the cheques and asked his mother what they were about. She said that Tom had been talking how he and Stella were looking for a house, but didn't have enough cash for a deposit. She said it was a loan.'

'And Dad, as usual, believed her.'

Órla's gaze said more than her neutral, one-word answer. 'Yes.'

Another silence ensued. 'Then he and his mother tore up the cheques and burned them.'

She withdrew a small, white handkerchief from her sleeve and dabbed an eye and her nose. Composed, she tucked it back. 'That's what I came to tell you.'

'Will Stella be becoming to see us, Mrs FitzGarratt?'

'That will be up to her. She wasn't responsible for Tom's behaviour. She didn't know about it.'

I was knackered now, I needed a pain-killer and my groin was beginning to throb agonisingly, so perhaps I wasn't in the best shape to say what came next.

'This is what I don't understand: when Maria and I had been going together for a few weeks she told me about how of her 10 sisters Stella was closest to her. Stella, who I suppose was 11 or so when Maria was born, used to look after her.'

Mother and daughter glanced at each other. 'Stella had time for her. Always.'

Maria was nodding. Órla's gaze didn't waver yet I had no idea what she was thinking.

'What might be useful to know,' I said, 'what turned Stella from being Maria's closest sister, friend, confidante into a malicious bitch who took to sniffing her own sister's clothing?'

Órla's features reddened. 'I take exception to your language.'

'Oh, really?' I shifted on the couch, because my balls and I were angry. 'Do you remember what you called your daughter here the last time you were in my flat?'

I didn't wait for answer. 'You called her a trollop. And being expert in English you'll know what means. What mother calls her daughter that?

Worse, you and your husband allowed an Irish peasant to call her a whore and a strumpet.'

Órla, to her credit, retreated. 'I'm sorry, Maria,' she whispered.

That stopped everything. Professor FitzGarratt sat gazing at the handbag solidly on her lap. Her daughter squeezed my hand, and I was nearly passing out.

After a long silence, Órla spoke: 'Stella was concerned for Maria. She's just 17, after all, and that's still very young …' her voice trailed off.

Maria was going to say something but I raised a finger to stop her.

'Professor. In a minute I'm going to have to go back to bed. I'm sore. My body and I are bloody angry, and I'm badly in need of a pain-killer.'

Maria made to get up and get me one, but I motioned her to stay put.

'Mrs FitzGarratt, this has all been so bloody unnecessary. Maria and I took a liking to each other. We fell in love. I was careful of her age. I tried to take care to ensure she wasn't being pushed into something that was beyond her. Certainly I wasn't 20 years older than her, like her late grandfather was with her grandmother. I needn't have worried. Maria is way beyond her 17 years. Haven't you noticed? Because it sounds like you haven't. You and your husband should be proud of her.'

Maria squeezed my hand. 'So yes, we made love with each other – or, if you like it plain and simple, we had sex. Maria was not forced into it. I would never do that.'

'It's true, Mum,' Maria said softly. She glanced slyly at me. 'I had to nudge him along a bit.'

Órla blinked twice.

I continued. 'But back to sex. That's what people do, don't they, when they love each other? Even your Church teaches that, doesn't it? Sex expresses love between two people.

'Ah, but we're not married.'

I had to swallow hard to concentrate. Those goolies … 'My parents have been married for over 30 years. They even have the wedding portrait up on the lounge wall at home. My mother is very proud of her wedding and engagement rings. But I have to tell you the Antarctic seems a warmer place that my parents' union.'

I glanced at Maria; her smile proud.

So I ploughed on. 'I should thank Tom, you know, for putting me in hospital. Because if he hadn't I wouldn't have met my Dad in the last week for the first time in my life.'

I could feel tears now. 'I realised yesterday that in all my 23 years I didn't know Ralph Morgan Blake for who he really was but as the caricature I'd grown up with.'

I was mentally and physically on the ropes. The effort to try to think straight was nearly impossible. 'The point of this diatribe is to say that having the wedding ceremony and the piece of paper doesn't guarantee anything.'

'Yes, I understand the modern, permissive view,' she said, 'but marriage is the very foundation for a family.'

'We haven't got that far yet.'

Maria choked back a giggle.

Her mother's look was sharp. 'I don't approve of your living like this, Maria. I don't imagine many mothers would.'

Maria opened her mouth to reply.

'And so we come to religion,' I said. I paused, gathering thoughts, strength, forcing the pain from my swollen balls. 'Tell me, Professor, what is so great about a religion that stops people loving each other if one doesn't belong to it?

'Why couldn't Matthew marry Ariel?'

'Who?' Maria glanced at me, then at her mother, who held up her hand. She was letting me have my say, whether it made sense of not.

I drove on: 'Why did Tom have to become a Catholic to marry Stella?

'Why did your youngest child willingly come to live here because you, your husband and your mother-in-law – particularly your foul-mouthed mother-in-law – backed her into a corner where she had to choose between me or your stricture that she couldn't go with a non-Catholic?

'What is so great about a Church that demands the head girl of one of its schools has to leave in disgrace because she happens to love me? What was the bloody disgrace?'

She shifted uncomfortably in the chair. 'Well, it's not just us. You find many faiths – Anglican, Methodist, Baptist, Jewish, Muslim …' she shrugged '… Chinese, Indian … many people prefer their children to marry in their own beliefs and culture.'

Which was true. But I wasn't interested in that. I had some things I wanted to say to this woman, and since I was weakening I thought I was coming to an end.

'Mrs FitzGarratt, I went with Maria into the cathedral after she had left the school. She knelt and prayed with her rosary before a statue of Mary. She often prays before a statue here, too, in our bedroom. I have to say – I wonder why she does it. Who would want to continue in a Church that treats her like a leper? I wouldn't want to be one of you for all the much-cliché'd tea in China, thanks.'

Neither spoke when I stopped for breath. I was drenched in sweat, but feeling chilled.

'The only saving grace in this whole sad business has been Matt, Monsignor Uncle Brian, and Sisters Hélène and Margarethe. Your brother invited her to go to Mass and to holy communion at his church.'

Something in her eyes and a glance at Maria …

'Did you know that, Mrs FitzGarratt?'

'No.'

'I go with her. Unlike your hellfire-breathing son Luke with all his doctorates Uncle Brian doesn't treat her like an outcast. She can go to him for holy communion.'

Órla turned back to Maria. She seemed to be longing for something.

'We have a neighbour, Robert. Like you he's a professor – or was. But he's arranged with Sister Hélène for Maria to continue her schoolwork. They peer-review it.'

'It's there on the table,' Maria said, and Órla glanced at the pile of books.

I couldn't do any more. I staggered to my feet, bursting into tears, and they rolled hot, wet and heavy, down my ruined face.

'I'm sorry, Mrs FitzGarratt but I have to go. Stay and talk to Maria if you both want to.'

Maria stood to help me into the bedroom. I turned to her mother, who had also got to her feet, for one last shot. The pain in my balls … I felt on the edge of throwing up. 'What a pity that you couldn't see what my father, uncle and aunt could so easily see last week – that you have a daughter you can be proud of. She coped last week with a strength that would have defeated most older people. And she's your daughter.'

MUCH LATER after Maria had helped me back to bed, the pain-killers had dulled my physical pains, and I was drifting back to bottomless softness, I heard them talking quietly out in the lounge. I think it was about the work Robert had set her. The last thing I heard was their quiet laughter.

I WOKE and it was dark. Maria was spooned in carefully behind me. Her breathing was warm against my neck and shoulders. Somehow I was holding her hand to my chest.
'You awake, sweetie?' I whispered.
'Mmm … yes, just.'
'How did it end up with your mother?'
A thoughtful pause. 'It was good, I think. I showed her my work, and she was really interested in that. She knew of Robert. I was going to take her to meet him but she was a bit reluctant. Perhaps too soon.'
I grunted and drew her hand to my lips and kissed it.
'But you, my love, you were a revelation out there.'
'How so?'
She kissed my neck. 'I've never picked you for an orator, Martin.'
'I wouldn't have, either.'
'You were impressive. And passionate! You stood up for me. And cried, too.'
'I was sore.'
She kissed me again, and hugged me gently. 'She still doesn't approve of my living here. But she said she could learn to live with it.'
'That's good, sweetie.'
'Today's been the first time my mother and I have really talked, and in a way as if she was interested – like a mother would be.'
Perhaps more good will come out of this whole sorry business.
'She'll visit more often, I think. What do you think about that?'
'As long as she comes in peace.'

Back to work

I started back to work after a month. Clyde Barnfield and Malcolm Ogle were very relaxed and made it easy for me.

Originally, the plan entailed that I start three days a week. That quickly passed, and I was back at my desk full-time. In running the cable page Davies had not endeared himself to anyone in my absence. 'The guy's an ass,' said Turnbull, the sports sub, whose desk abutted mine. 'As well as doing my own stuff I was having to clean up after him.' I sympathised.

In the first week Maria went to do her usual shifts for Magdalena and Peter, which I had insisted she do. 'I'm not going to die,' I said.

Her mother visited twice, once when I wasn't there. The other time she brought Catharine and Gabrielle. The meeting was emotional. Aunt and close niece clung tightly to each other and wept. Both told the other they missed her, and Maria and she disappeared into the bedroom and shut the door.

Catharine said Gran had managed to prise Gabrielle from her parents' suspicious grip on a pretext of taking her shopping to buy a birthday gift for another cousin.

Órla smiled. 'That's half true, Catharine. We're still going to buy a gift.'

I was beginning to like her. Something was going on with Órla FitzGarratt. When Maria called her 'Mum' or referred to her as 'Mum' it sounded different. Not as contrived as it had. Their conversation was less formal, less strained; mostly confined, though, to her course work with Robert.

On the other visit Maria introduced her to Robert, and they had a long talk together. Órla had opened her purse and pressed on Robert a cheque for $250. 'That's to help with your tutoring of Maria.'

He had looked to Maria: was this all right? She was taken aback and began to object.

Órla had been firm. 'I haven't been the most maternal of mothers, Maria, particularly to you. But this is a practical way I can help a little. I know who Robert is, and I can only say, my girl, that you are in very capable hands. I'm impressed and relieved.'

'IS THE old fella back in working order?' Wilson Barker had leered across the subbery. I ignored him, but the answer was yes. My body had repaired itself well. My, er, 'old fella' signalled unmistakably one afternoon after work that it found my bending over Maria as she sat at the typewriter arousing. For the first time in weeks. It was the erotic mix of natural young-woman scent, soap, shampoo, her warmth, touch, her skin and … Signal traffic between brain, senses, and what the Italians – reputedly great lovers – crudely call *cacchio*, *cazzo* and even *cazzone* intensified.

She read the look in my eye, blushed, and protested that she had to finish the assignment on Japan's march to war in the 1930s.

'I know,' I whispered and I hoisted her up gently.

'Oh, Martin, put me down, you'll damage yourself!' She protested increasingly feebly.

With great care I laid her out on the bed, and she studied me with half-closed, amused eyes and a smile. She obligingly raised her hips and I tugged her knickers off. I couldn't struggle and fumble out of my pants quickly enough, and the spectacle prompted her to paroxysms of snorting giggling. My stumbling haste was undignified. As I joined her on the bed she became quiet and her eyes went deep, as if ageless and wise. She held up her arms up to me. 'Come here, little man,' she whispered.

'Do you think I've recovered fully now, sweetie?'
She took the now-shrivelled *pene* and toggled it between thumb and forefinger and it flopped about like a limp sausage. 'Hmmm. It's been a long time, Martin,' she said clinically. 'I think you might have to do a rerun. Just to make sure it's OK and in full working order.'

Dad and me

Winter passed chillingly, frostily, and wetly. Spring was just ahead.

Uncle Syd and Auntie Kura shouted Maria and me a short holiday in Hawai'i. They, my younger two cousins Mihi and Heremia, and Dad, came, too. Mum didn't. She wouldn't like the heat. It would make her skin erupt. Everyone sympathised.

We stayed at one of the big, expensive hotels that line Waikiki Beach. You lift your head from the pillow and the endless immensity of the deep blue Pacific stretches away from you.

We swam in the warm waters off the beach and laughed at the friendly little sea turtles that would pop their heads up out of the water just at your shoulder.

We took the tour out to the memorial that straddles the most famous victim of the Japanese air attack on Pearl Harbor, December 7, 1941 – the former USS *Arizona*.

The old battleship's shattered body lies where the Imperial Japanese Navy's bombers caught her alongside on 'Battleship Row' on what everybody who was there agreed had been a beautiful, sunny, Sunday morning. The photo and film footage of her blowing up is the most enduring image of the attack.

The names of over 1100 dead including the ship's captain and a rear admiral have been carved into a marble wall on the memorial.

Just below your feet on the memorial platform they're still there, her ship's company, and will be forever. They can be joined by the ashes of her crewmen who survived the attack that morning.

I couldn't help but have tears in my eyes. Neither could Uncle Syd and Auntie Kura. Tears still didn't come easily to Dad.

On my 24th birthday I slipped from our bed early before Maria awoke. Dad and I walked along the manicured golden beach; he turned and said to me: 'I'd love Maria as my daughter-in-law, son. Nothing would make me happier.'

Oh? 'She virtually is now, Dad.'

He clapped a big hand on my shoulder: 'Virtually is not the same as is, Martin.'

I chewed on that. 'What's the difference then, Dad?'

'It's about commitment. Formalising it. Crossing a line in the sand and saying, "Here I stand".'

'But Dad,' I said carefully, 'I'm not sure that going through a ceremony and getting a certificate proves anything.'

'Look, son. I won't pretend to you that from the outside Mum and I don't look flash as a man and wife.'

I wanted to say something, but a voice inside me firmly said *shut up!* So I did.

His hand was still on my shoulder. 'Son, your mother and I have our ups and downs. We always have had. But I can tell you that when I got off the boat in '46 from the bloody war she was like a balm, a salve, to me.'

She was? 'How, Dad? Because if I may say so Mum has never seemed the salving, maternal, loving type.'

He glanced sideways at me, and for a second I thought I had gone too far.

'Marty, I was a wreck – I'd been shelled, bombed, shot at for nearly five years.' (And, disrespectfully, I couldn't help but think of the colonel's girlfriend.) 'Your mother provided the necessary strength and understanding. She was practical, ordinary, nothing flighty, but she was *loyal.*' As well as emphasising the word in tone, he squeezed my shoulder.

This was entirely at odds with what I had believed and understood of my parents and their life together.

'We love one another, Martin. Not the fancy, Hollywood idea of love. I mean the love that is commitment to each other, through thick and thin.'

'But Dad, she didn't even come and see me when I was in hospital. Her attitude to Maria is a disgrace, if I may say so.'

We trudged to the end of the beach in silence, his big hand still on my shoulder.

'I've never said – and I'll never say – it's perfect, son. And I'll never say there aren't hurts, and on both sides. And her attitude to Maria is one of them. But even your mother knows that she's a minority of one where that particular lass is concerned.'

'It hurts, Dad.'

My father hugged me; a robust, masculine squeeze, and so comforting – why hadn't he when I was a kid? 'I know it does, son, I know it does. But you have to remember that people were pretty hard and unforgiving about women and girls who romped in the sheets with a fella they weren't married to. She's a product of a much harsher era and attitude. She doesn't know anything different.'

So he gave me much to think about, the old bugger.

'Another thing, son, what are you doing about, well, you know, not getting Maria up the duff, so to speak?'

I nearly laughed. Not so much at the question but at Dad's circumspect tone, almost his embarrassment at mentioning the subject.

'She can't, Dad.'

'Can't what?'

'Can't conceive.' He frowned. I spared him the detail; he would be embarrassed. 'A woman thing.'

'Ah. Right you are.'

We walked in companionable silence. 'I'm sorry about the problem Maria has, Martin, not being able to conceive. Grandchildren would have been lovely,' he said wistfully.

We turned around and headed back the way we'd come. The sun was bathing the tops of the high-rises along the beach in a soft pinky-bronze glow. 'I'll hate to have to tell your mother that, Martin. Mum's been terrified that you and Maria'd have a kiddie out of wedlock, which would mean she'd feel ashamed and embarrassed, and what would she say to people.'

'Then, Dad, don't tell her.'

My father looked sideways at me for a long time – father-son conspiracy of silence passed between us. We grinned in a way that I couldn't remember our having done so before.

BACK IN bed I told Maria what Dad had said, about our getting married. 'Let's think about it when I'm a little more older, sweetie. Just now I think I like the salacity of wallowing in libidinous sin with you.'

'That sounded like a mouthful, Maria.'

She fixed me with a Head Girl Stare and took my sensitive nipple between her teeth and tugged on it. I gasped.

'Happy birthday, my love.'

Maternal visits

Órla was visiting weekly, roughly a Tuesday or Wednesday afternoon. She and Maria took to exchanging pecks on their cheeks when she arrived and giving each other a hug as she left.

She and we were relaxing. Mother and daughter had the same love of languages. They would speak fluently in Latin, switching to French, which seemed to be their favourite, and then to German. Órla and Maria would discuss the work she was doing with Robert.

She would engage me in conversation about my work, what I thought was going on in the world. We kept the topics of conversation away from anything that might provoke a clash.

She was able to bring Gabrielle more frequently. Margaret, the girl's mother, was finding her hands full with Joseph, who was getting into trouble at school. He was starting fights with other kids.

'Joey' attacked a nun whose Irish father and 10 brothers had taught her and her sister boxing. That hadn't gone well. The pint-sized Sister Mary Celestine had sat him on his bum, stunned. Gabrielle, though, had become less troublesome to her parents because of her visits to Maria.

'He's frustrated, apparently. Gabrielle's growing much taller, filling out, doing brilliantly at school, losing her gawkiness,' his grandmother said. 'Meanwhile, he's stuck where he is and is a very cross and unpleasant little boy.'

Something else was odd: Órla had begun to turn up at Uncle Brian's church on Sundays, joining us in the pew. At the sign of peace Maria and her mother would kiss respectfully on their cheeks; Órla and I shook hands formally, the smiles less awkward.

Uncle Brian never refused me holy communion. Where were the rest of the FitzGarratts? We didn't feel we could ask. After the Mass she and Brian would disappear off together into his presbytery.

Matthew and Catharine would let slip clues when they visited. Órla and Peirse were living separate lives, though under the same roof. Órla had moved into Maria's old bedroom where she 'slept better'. The bedroom was as far from the marital boudoir as it could get, in the other end of the house. Grannie Annie had taken up residence. Catharine reported the atmosphere in the ancestral manor as being 'strained'. Her great-grandmother was having a lot to say to her oldest son; not very many words for her daughter-in-law.

Peirse went off to give an address at a pro-life conference in Chicago. Órla did not go, when in the past she would have. The family were treading warily around their parents.

Why had Órla and Peirse in effect separated, and separated now?

Faultlines

Matt believed he had the answer. 'I have a theory,' he said one bright, spring Sunday afternoon as talk moved, as it tended to do, on to FitzGarratt matters. 'It's what I call the faultline effect.'

We were seated in a semi-circle to the afternoon sun, the ranch-slider open to the balcony. Matthew the QC was in shorts, polo shirt, jandals, and he had arrived with several bottles of chilled beer. For his sister crisp, cold *Liebfraumilch*.

'I'm not allowed to buy this for my oldest daughter,' he said.

Catharine, who was with him, smiled sourly. 'Mum doesn't want me to get too attached to alcohol,' she said. The sly look on her face suggested she was no stranger to it, either. She and Maria companionably shared the bottle, niece more so than aunt.

Catharine was evidently her father's companion when he came to visit us. She was his driver home. Kay was resigned to it, apparently, while still fearing that her teenage sister-in-law would infect her daughter with her 'morals, or lack of them'.

And Aoife? Where was she? Well, Aoife had left Matt's law firm, armed with an impressive and truthful CV and her fare paid, for a position offered to her in Dublin with a 'pre-eminent' law firm. She was Doing Very Well. 'It was an opportunity that we couldn't offer her here,' Matt had said carefully some weeks ago.

Anyway, sprawled back in the armchair and squinting against the spring sun, he was about to elaborate on the 'faultline effect'. He poured himself another beer.

'All right. Peirse and Órla. They've been married about 45 years. They've weathered Depression and war together. They've a house. Careers. Successful careers. They have influence and standing in the community and in their professional and Church circles. People seek them out for advice and to take a lead, such as in the current debate about abortion, contraception, sterilisation. The pair of them have churned out a sizeable number of little Peirses and Órlas.'

He glanced at Maria. 'All 14 of us have been well-educated. Some might say over-educated. We've been expected to Excel in our studies, at school and at university. And it's been taken for granted that we're leaders. Or will be.'

Maria nodded. 'True.'

'On the surface everything looks good and solid. The married couple are happy together. Inseparable and unbreakable. Things sail along well.'

So ...

'But something comes along, and that something has come out of the blue. It's unexpected.'

'Well, they would be when they come out of the blue,' Maria said.

We all laughed.

'Yes. But it's the one thing that breaks things. It's different from all the others.'

'The straw that breaks the camel's back, to use a cliché,' Maria said.

He put his glass on the carpet beside his chair. His gaze became clear. 'I've been trying to figure it out. Why are our parents, Maria, living separate lives?'

'You're asking me, or is that a rhetorical question?'

'Hmmm. Rhetorical.'

'All right, then. Tell us.'

'I'll go back a bit. From my earliest memories our father has only ever listened to one person.'

'Our grandmother.'

283

'Why?' Catharine said.

'Good question, daughter. Perhaps it's because of a special mother-son bond. Probably.'

He picked up his glass, saw it was empty, poured himself another drink. 'But from my earliest memories our grandmother has been the dominating voice in our family, and what she's said has always been into the ear of our father.'

He held up a finger. 'He has always done what she told him to do. She told him he was going to be a doctor. And so he became a doctor. And he did well – but to please her. She told him he should marry our mother – and he did. She pretty much picked Mum for him because she knew her father. Uncle Brian training to be a priest helped, too. Good, solid Catholic family with good, solid Catholic values.'

He drained half his glass, and gazed at the bottom. 'At university I fall in love with the very pretty and rather Bohemian Ariel. And –'

'Who?' Maria and Catharine chimed.

Matt smiled, and sombrely, too: 'A girl. But she wasn't a Catholic, had no intention of being one, and I was talked into giving her up for the sake of marrying in the Faith and having children in the Faith and passing on the Faith to the children.'

'This was before Mum, obviously,' Catharine said.

'Yes.'

'There's a lot I don't think I know about you, Dad. You sound like you're a bit of a secret rebel.' He smiled lazily.

She was going to quiz him some more but he got in first. 'Anyway, that was Grannie Annie and our father, and Mum went along with it.' He shrugged. 'I suppose she had to. But the further the distance from Ariel and me I would say I was weak.' He muttered inaudibly at his glass; sighed.

'Then there was our sister Annette, who has been living in exile for nearly 20 years.'

'You don't hear about her,' Catharine said.

Added Maria: 'I don't know her at all. Well, I don't remember her, anyway.'

'No', Matt said, filling his glass again. He offered me the bottle. I shook my head and indicated my half-full glass. 'Very odd, you know, Martin. For a newspaperman you have a very small intake. Is that because of my sister?'

It wasn't, I grinned, but Maria directed at him a Head Girl Stare.

'Anyway, Annette. Lovely girl, always. Lots of fun as a girl. Chaste, pious, a bit of a dreamer. Staggeringly bright.'

Now Matthew was sounding regretful. 'She didn't have a bad bone in her body and she would never do harm to anybody. And despite her brilliance and insight there was a certain näiveté about her. She saw the good in everyone. So much so she didn't see the evil in the bastard who got into her one night while his wife was in hospital having another of their children and she was looking after his older kids for him.'

'What?!' Catharine said, sitting up bolt upright.

Maria followed up: 'I've never heard this before, Matt.'

He glanced a smile at me. I'd obviously kept the secret he'd told me, although I couldn't remember if I'd realised it was a secret. Maria had never mentioned it, so I hadn't, either.

'Our father's good friend Dr Victor Joseph Gibson took advantage of Annette, and in doing so he got her pregnant. It couldn't be kept a secret because Annette didn't believe in abortion. Neither do the rest of us – and it would have been incredibly hard to get anyway, because of the law – but Gibson … oh, dear, me … Vic Gibson tried to make her have one anyway. There was a struck-off medical practitioner in Wellington who was well-known for 'rectifying' these matters for 250 pounds a time. A lot of dosh.'

'My God,' Maria breathed, appalled. 'I never knew.'

'Me neither,' Catharine added.

'Well, I did. I was there, in my mid-20s, and Annette was completing her law degree. Then she got the Rhodes Scholarship just as she found she was pregnant. There was an awful to-do. Our grandmother guessed her secret first.' He glanced at his sister and daughter. 'It's not hard to guess the obvious why.'

Catharine coloured: 'Dad ...'

Matt kept going: 'She confronted Annette. Notice I said "she confronted Annette". She didn't go to our parents with her concerns first. No. After extracting a confession from Annette and berating her and slapping her around the head and face for behaving like an alley cat, she –'

'Sounds familiar,' Maria muttered.

'Quite. Well, she dragged Annette to our parents and gleefully proclaimed her fall from grace and that, quote, "she's grawin' a lettle *bah*-stard in hor belleh".'

'I think I want to be sick,' Catharine said.

'Oh, my dear girl, I don't blame you. It gets worse. Annette was blamed for the whole business. Leading him on. Giving him "the doe's eye". Taking advantage of him.'

'Well,' I ventured, 'she must have had some responsibility for what happened. Unless he raped her.'

They all turned as one to face me. I thought I had dropped a clanger.

'You're right, Martin,' Matt said. 'She does bear part of the responsibility. She was 21, so hardly young. But he was a man we'd all known since we were babies. He was 'Uncle Vic' to us and his wife was 'Auntie Grace'. All us older kids knew each other like cousins. Annette trusted him like she would her father or an uncle.'

He paused significantly. 'He had intent. She didn't.'

Matt reached down and refilled his glass, and drank the lot. 'Thirsty work, this,' he said, wiping his lips. 'He made her feel sorry for him. He felt lonely. His wife was in the home. She'd been there for two months because the pregnancy had run into trouble. He was 40, handsome in that Irish way, charming, persuasive.'

'Manipulative,' I said.

'Very.'

'So what happened?'

'Oh, simple, mate. Gibson could see what the fallout was going to be. Shame and scandal and all that. Ruinous, spectacular loss of reputation in the public place. So, as I said before, he tried to get her to have the abortion.'

'I am going to be sick,' Catharine blurted and got up and tearfully raced off to the toilet. 'I better see if she's all right,' Maria said, and followed. Matt and I sat in contemplative silence, listening to Catharine crying in the bedroom, and Maria softly offering comforting words.

'Martin, mate, do you have anything stronger? Like scotch, bourbon?'

I had both, but he took the bottle of Jameson's and poured himself a generous helping. I opted for Jim Beam and ginger ale.

Maria came back and sat down. 'She doesn't want to hear any more so she'll lie down on our bed for a bit.' She picked up her glass of wine and drank. 'She's feeling a bit emotional, you know ...'

'What about you, Ria? Do you want to hear the rest?'

Her jaw was set, and her eyes sharp and green. 'Not really. But Annette is my sister, even if I don't know her. I should hear it all, since I've always been considered too young to know the dreary, ugly, dramatic stuff.'

'OK.' And he drank half the contents of his glass. 'Ohhh, that's better.'

He contemplated the glass. 'Our father remembered that I was a barrister. He rang me one day and told me to negotiate terms with Gibson.'

'I suppose you were the best person to do it,' I said.

'Well, perhaps. But I was so bloody angry with how they were treating her. They wanted their own daughter gone, out of the country, out of sight, out of mind. So everything would look good. Gibson's precious public standing was far too important for him to lose.'

His tone was bitter and he was repeating. 'Scandal for the family and for Victor Gibson had to be avoided. Annette and her "little boondle of shairme" –'

'Our grandmother.'

'Yes. So they had to disappear.'

'So what did you negotiate, Matt?' I said.

His teeth-bared grin was hard. 'Oh, it was easy. Ten thousand pounds – which then was about two years' pay for a man in his position – to Annette straight away, so she could set up in Oxford and have someone look after her baby while she did her scholarship.'

He finished his Jameson's, and then went and poured another. His cheeks were flushed a maroon hue. His eyes glittered.

Seated again: 'He tried to cry poverty. But faced with the reality of what would happen if his wife and other people found out he came up with the money. Sold some property, I think. Dunno. Don' care. And I twisted his arm some more by extracting from him one thousand pounds a year until the child turned 16.'

'The child,' Maria said. '"The child". Does "The child" have a name?'

'Oh. Yes. Sorry, forgot you'd not be privy to any of this. Claudia Niamh. She'd be about the same age as you and Catharine.'

'Do you or anyone in the family stay in touch with her?' I said.

'Rosaline might. Her being in the convent, who would know? A few years ago there were some professional communications between the legal firm she works for and mine; nothing between her and me.'

He paused, staring out the window into the distance.

'The last time I saw Annette was when Rosie and I drove her down to the ship taking her off to England. We helped her settle into her cabin, and that was it. She sailed away to the sounds of the band playing *Auld Lang Syne* ...'

He finished his drink.

'I've been to the UK for work. But I've never been able to meet up with Annette.'

'But for the family,' Maria said softly, 'she'd been tucked away out of sight, out of mind, which was all that mattered.'

She and Matt gazed at each other for long moments. 'Yes,' he whispered.

THE CONVERSATION, though interesting enough, had veered away from why he thought Órla had in effect split from Peirse.

As well, not much had been said in the last few minutes. Matt had excused himself to go for a pee. We heard him talking to Catharine in our room. She sounded tearful. He had poured himself another generous Jameson's, and wolfed down some crackers with dip. Maria got up and prepared some more snacks. He waited for her to return and sit.

I cleared my throat. 'Matt, you've been talking about faultlines, and about Annette, but where does Maria fit into all this?'

He sat up straight, and his eyes seemed to clear. 'I think, that for our mother, the reaction of most of the family to Maria coming to live here with you has been a step too far.'

'I think it is, too,' Catharine said from the bedroom doorway, where she leaned with folded arms against the jamb. 'She gives hints. Like she's been too focused on the dogma and the doctrine and the theory and not on who Maria is and what she is experiencing with Martin.'

Maria nodded. 'She's been trying harder with me lately for the first time than I can remember.'

'Well, it sounds as if they've all made decisions about loyalties – Dad and our grandmother and most of the family on one side, and Mum and me on the other,' Matt added, his words now slurring.

'And me,' Catharine said. 'And, Dad, your other daughters, plus our cousins Rachael and Charlotte, and of course Gabrielle. We all believe Maria has been treated appallingly.'

Matt grunted. His eyes were steely opaque. He was pissed, I think.

'We don't really like your grandmother any more, Dad. She's an embarrassment. And her 'love' always comes with strings.'

'Buyable, tradable, saleable, disposable – a commodity that she always has control of,' I heard my voice saying, perhaps slurringly, too. 'Nothing to do with love at all.'

Aunt and niece turned to me as one. Then glanced at each other before turning back to face me.

'Yes,' they said in unison.

Matt stumbled to his feet, swaying as he dug into his shorts pocket. He fished out his keys and held them out to Catharine. 'I think the time has come, dear daughter, for you to drive your father home and he face your mother's disapproval once again.'

'Oh, Dad,' she said severely. But her eyes glinted dangerously as the keys dropped into her hand. 'We'll take the long way home – so you can compose yourself.'

MARIA'S ANGER that evening was evident in how she brushed her hair. Usually after her shower she'd perch on the end of the bed and face the mirror. A towel like a sarong loosely around her waist, and I'd lie back in bed and watch her – her back straight, the rippling play of muscles in her shoulders and arm, the movement of her neck. And she would watch me in the mirror watching her as she brushed her hair 100 times. I used to say she didn't need to brush hair 100 times.

'You're not a female, Martin.'

She'd let her hair grow down on to her shoulders since she left school. It was often arousing to watch her, and she knew it, too. So she would slowly and carefully brush her hair and smirk knowingly.

And sometimes she would half-turn to me and smile; I would reach out to her and draw her to me and we would end up in that tangle of limbs. She would complain about her hair getting mussed when she'd spent so long brushing it. I, of course, was uncaring and selfish for not caring about her hair getting into a mess.

It was one of our little games.

But tonight she attacked her hair savagely. The strokes were rough and abrupt, and in the mirror's reflection her jaw had that particular jutting set that indicated deep displeasure. Her eyes avoided mine.

I waited until she had joined me under the covers, and she lay stiffly beside me, gazing at the ceiling, arms straight at her sides.

'Would you like to tell me about it?'

No reply.

I took her hand in mind and gave it a gentle squeeze. No reaction. I squeezed her hand again.

She turned to face me. 'You're angry, sweetie. Talk to me.'

She burst into tears and rolled into my arms, and sobbed and sobbed and sobbed, her body rocking against me. I stroked her back comfortingly for a long time.

'How could anyone do that?' I heard her whisper against my shoulder. 'How could they do that to their own daughter? Send her away like that.' Sniffle-sniffle. 'She was pregnant, for God's sake. Who would *do* that?'

Heartless people, that's who. The question was rhetorical anyway.

'Martin?'

'Yes, love.'

She took my hand and tucked it under her pyjama top and rested it on her breast. 'Love me, Martin, nice and slowly and gently. I don't want you to go to sleep tonight with an angry, upset me beside you.'

Family inquiries

Since she'd moved in with me Maria made sure to get up in the morning when I did. She made me breakfast while I was in the shower and getting dressed for work. We talked and bantered, and she would send me off to work with a kiss, then get on with her increasingly demanding workload set by Robert.

But no banter this morning. 'I want to get in touch with Annette,' she said suddenly.

'Oh, why?'

'I'm so ashamed of how the family have treated her. I feel as if I'm complicit.'

'But, Maria, you were a baby. You're not responsible for their actions.'

Irritation ghosted across her face. 'I know that, Martin.' Head Girl Frost chilled the air.

'Sweetie, please, I'm not knocking the idea. It *is* a good idea.'

Her sideways glance at me was suspicious.

'But what I'm wanting to know – because it will help you understand – is *why* do you want to get in touch with her. Forget Catholic guilt about your family's treatment of her. You're not responsible for their behaviour.'

She took my hand. 'Sorry. I want to write to her and introduce myself, tell her about myself, and about you and me, say how great it would be if she could write back because I'd really like to one day meet her and Claudia.'

'Wonderful. Stick to that.'

'But how will I know where to write?'

'Matt will know.'

'No!' she said sharply. 'I don't want him or anyone else to know.'

OK.

'Not yet, anyway.'

'Well, she might be in a British or European *Who's Who*. Would you like me to make some inquiries for you?'

Her face lit up. 'Oh, *liebchen*, yes, that would be great.'

She hugged me and kissed me. 'Thank you, Martin.'

AFTER I finished for the afternoon I scoured the books in the newspaper's reference section. Nothing. Not even in the British and International copies of *Who's Who*. Nothing new in the clip-files. *Hmmm* ... I went into a phone booth and dialled Uncle Syd.

We went through our ritual.

I told him Maria wanted to write to her sister Annette. 'But she doesn't know where to write. Do you know where she works?'

I heard Uncle Syd suck in his breath through his teeth. 'The short answer is no, Marty.'

'Oh.'

'I have extensive contacts in London. Leave it with me.'

That night I told Maria about the call.

'Thank you, sweetie. This means a lot to me.'

'TAKE THIS down, Marty,' Uncle Syd said, and he proceeded to painstakingly pass on Annette FitzGarratt's work address, and phone number – in the West German port city of Hamburg.

'She works for a firm that represents an association of shipping companies. She's quite a senior person there. They're an internationally regarded outfit, boy.'

He'd managed to get it all in 24 hours.

Dear Annette

On Friday morning, my day off, she showed me the letter. She had written it, too, in her own hand – direct, assertive strokes, controlled loops.

'You didn't type it,' I said.

'I shall forbear to make the obvious reply, my sweet …'

'Sorry. Yes. Still early.'

I settled down with the letter, written on foolscap lecture pad paper.

Dear Annette

Hi. I am Maria, your youngest sister. We've never met. I'm 17. I never knew until last Sunday why you went away, and why your name is never mentioned by our parents and siblings. Nor why there are no photos of you anywhere in the family home you and I grew up in.

Now I do.

I think you and I might share a few things in common.

A good start, dear,' I said. She came and sat with me on the couch, and took an intense interest in a hair of Dante's that somehow had stayed on her top.

… I incurred the family's displeasure because of my boyfriend. I was told to give him up because he's not a Catholic. Our grandmother told our parents that I'd been sleeping with him. That what I was doing was sinful and dirty. I was a strumpet and a trollop. I left home and came to live with him.

Deftly, concisely, she sketched everything.

On the last page: It hasn't all been bad. Matthew – whom I barely knew because he was so much older and had a family of his own – has turned out to be a good friend and a revelation. Not such the stiff Queen's Counsel after all.

Their mother: She was always so distant, so detached. I didn't know her. After Tom's attack on Martin she came around to see us ... we get on better now ...

Stella: ... she was the biggest let-down and betrayal because she'd taken me under her wing long ago. We were so close.

Uncle Brian: ... has not judged me at all. We go to Mass at his parish, and he lets Martin have holy communion.

Their oldest nieces: ... they're the same age as Claudia and me. They're appalled at how I have been treated.

Their grandmother: ... nothing's changed there.

About me: I love Martin, and I know that despite my moods and insisting that he not leave the toilet seat up he loves me, too.

'I think you assume too much there, Maria,' I said.

She replied with a Head Girl Stare and a sharp elbow to my ribs. Followed by a peck on my cheek.

Please write back, Annette, she began the last paragraph. I would love to hear from you. Perhaps one day we will meet – you and Claudia, and Martin and me. Perhaps Matthew. Maybe our oldest nieces. I don't want our grandmother's malignance to continue to poison our family. I am ashamed of how you were treated. Martin says I shouldn't be because I wasn't part of what was done to you.

In a way he is right. But we're sisters, you and me, and we come from the same Mother Factory and Sperm Tank (Matthew's expression!). I feel I can't not make contact with you now that I know about you. That's why I have written to you.

Love, Maria

'Crikey,' I said as I handed the sheets back.

'Why 'crikey'?'

'Because, my love, it's a mature and courageous letter. You've done well.'

She took my face in her hands and turned it towards her. Her eyes were very large. 'You mean that?'

'I do. You've extended a hand of love and healing to her. She might accept it. In which case she'll make you very happy.'

'Yes.'

'On the other, if she says 'fuck off', or ignores you, which I think you will find harder, you will feel crushed and disappointed.'

She kissed me hard. Then: 'Sometimes I think, Martin, that you're not as dumb as you pretend to be.'

'Who says I'm pretending?'

'Oh-h,' she muttered, swatted me on the hand, and got up and walked away.

MARIA CAREFULLY typed out her sister's address on a *Par Avion* envelope. She slipped a photo of her and me in with the letter; we were standing at the airport before flying off to meet the family in Hawai'i.

I walked with her into the central post office to see it off. But first I used our office photocopier to do a copy. At the CPO she got an attack of the jitters as her hand with the letter was poised at the International Air Mail slot. 'This is right, isn't it?'

'Yes. And how she replies will be up to her. You've done all you can do.' The letter slid into the slot. 'Now we wait.'

Later, on the walk back to the flat she told me she was going to tackle her mother about what she did when Annette became pregnant.

'Why?'

We were rounding the café corner, where we had gone for that first cup of coffee.

'What do you mean?'

'What's your approach going to be? Are you going to do it to make her justify herself? Or are you really interested in what she has to say?'

She had stopped, and folded her arms defensively across her chest. The warm breeze slapped the hem of her dress against her legs.

'There is a difference.'

'I just want to know, Martin, that's all.'

I went back and took her hand. 'I know you do. All I'm saying is take care with how you do it. She might feel like shit about it now. If so, be a little sympathetic to that. Don't lock her back into something that's about back then.'

Maria gazed at me for several long moments. Behind those eyes I could imagine the cogs spinning. It was one thing to be to be angry and indignant about a sweet young woman wronged before Maria was born; it was another to be magnanimous and understanding.

'After all, it's what you want from them, isn't it? Understanding and compassion from them for you?'

I watched her eyes change. Acceptance.

Maria squeezed my hand, and smiled. 'Promise me you'll never let me become a bitch, darling.'

'Bet on it,' I said, and we walked home.

Fast post

Annette's reply via *Luftpost* was in our letterbox three weeks later.

Dear Maria, her letter crisply typewritten on white bonded note paper began.

I nearly didn't open your letter when I saw 'M FitzGarratt' on the back of the envelope. I'd made up my mind long ago not to let my family intrude into my life again. However, the address – or the street anyway – sounded familiar. Nearly inner-city, if I remember correctly, and certainly not that of our parents' house. My curiosity was piqued.

Thank you for writing. I left New Zealand when our mother was four or five months pregnant with you, so, no, we don't know each other.

Yet in that odd, familial way, we do know each other. Matthew is right about coming from the same Sperm Tank and Mother Factory – I laughed when I read that. It was delightful to see that he still has his old irreverent sense of humour.

You have the FitzGarratt way of expressing yourself – direct, excellent vocabulary, intelligent, well-schooled. You sound so familiar.'

Maria read on aloud.

You sound so mature for your age. Such a rebel! I would never have contemplated at 17 taking the step you did and going to live with my boyfriend. Even sleeping with him would have been out of the question!

I wasn't a rebel. I was caught out because my misguided zeal to be helpful and caring and feel needed by a family ours knew was overtaken in a moment of weakness.

Anyway, it's all turned out for the best. Claudia – or 'Cloudia' as the Germans say it – is, as you've guessed, 17, and she goes to a very good private school here in Hamburg.

She had married. Jürgen was Swiss and ran a Hamburg-based regional bank.

All those jokes and jibes about Swiss bankers being dull gnomes are untrue – well, in my husband's case it is.

He had been widowed with two young daughters, Sabine and Carolin, who were now 13 and 14.

He is one of those men who is a 'girls' Dad. Just naturally good with daughters – Claudi adores him. And he, her. The girls get on well. Sometimes I think they'd all prefer Jürgen as their mother figure too. He is firm with them, but they love that about him. I'm the bad Mama, I'm afraid.

Annette had made some peace with her past. Her present was agreeable and satisfying, and she wasn't going to let the past be her ball and chain. That's why she hadn't bothered with the family back home.

No vitriol was spewed against Gibson – not even mentioned;

Peirse – one brief, passing reference;

Matthew – fond, but in passing;

the Carmelite Rosaline – she stopped writing after Claudia was born;

Uncle Brian – I'm so glad you found him kind. That's my recollection of him also;

Grannie Annie – not even a mention;

Luke – he was a belligerent teenage boy with smelly feet and sweaty armpits but had been sweet to start with;

Their mother – I haven't thought about her role in my situation for many years. I thought she was firmly one of the Troika that wanted me out of sight and out of mind. Having read your comments, I wondered last night if she was as hard line as the others about it. Can't put my finger on it. I don't think she was maternal, which leaves me wondering why she had all us children. We can't all have been God's Will – were we?

She had a revelation. I remember feeling sorry for you before you were born. Our mother greeted her pregnancies with God's will equanimity – except for you. She wept copiously when she found she was pregnant with you. You were not supposed to have happened. She was nearly 50 and supposedly had gone through the change. You must have been the last live egg left in the factory. Anyway, she was very bad-tempered about it and I recall a couple of times her shouting at our father and blaming him.

Maria reacted sourly: 'Wonderful. An unwanted baby.' She put the letter down and turned to me. 'It's a funny thing, Martin. I've always felt I wasn't wanted.'

I put my arm around her. 'It's OK, sweetie. I love you and want you and always will.'

I'd tried to jest about it, but I had the feeling the news had still hurt her more than she cared to admit.

'Anyway …'

Annette had saved Stella for nearly last. Don't be too hard on her. I was her special big sister. Like she was with you. Like you with Gabrielle. Stella was distraught about my situation and being exiled abroad. She was 11. When it became clear that I had fouled my nest, so to speak, I was separated off from the rest of the clan. In case the infection spread, I suppose. I wrote her a letter that Uncle Brian said he would give her. I remember telling her I was sorry I was going away and leaving her, not to worry, and perhaps she might like to be a special big sister to the baby Mum was carrying – which was you. Going by your letter she turned out to be very good – until recently.

Maria put the letter down again. 'Perhaps I should try to talk to Stella.'

Annette finished. I don't know if I've written the kind of letter you expected to get. I am not angry any more. I was for the time it took me to get my doctorate. But I realised that if I was to be a good mother for Claudi then I had to focus on her, get myself a job and make a home, and put the past behind us. I bear no grudges.

She thanked Maria for writing to her. She hoped she would do so again.

She had included two coloured photos: There was no mistaking Annette for Maria's sister. Allowing for 20 years difference, they were alike – tallish, rectangular face, strong cheekbones, alert, shrewd eyes behind round glasses. Big, luminous eyes stared out from Claudia's pixie face; her hair was cut boyishly, lending a touch of the ethereal.

The other photo had been shot on a hot, summer beach somewhere: Annette and Jürgen; him handsome, tall, athletic, early 40s; Claudia and her step-sisters bronzed, slender in bikinis, sun-flecked sea in the background.

MARIA WAS preoccupied and moody for the rest of the day. So she did what she always did when she was bothered: she got busy.

The vacuum-cleaner roared and terrorised dust everywhere and swallowed a spider and its web that somehow had escaped notice. Dante's fur was sucked off the bedclothes. The washing machine flogged sheets and pillow cases. The toilet was cleaned amid much grunting. The shower and hand-basin weren't spared, either. Books on the shelves were snapped to attention. Records and cassettes were slapped into tidy order. I went to help, out of a sense of duty, and hung out the washing.

She was snippish, a signal she wanted me out of the way, so I left her to it and went off to buy groceries. I stayed away for nearly three hours until the middle of the afternoon.

The more I thought about it the more I realised Annette had written an extraordinary letter. She could have had every excuse for being bitter and angry and unforgiving towards her family.

Instead of lobbing angry salvoes from Hamburg she had told her youngest sister not to be angry on her behalf, nor to feel ashamed for how she, Annette, was treated by the rest of the family. She had implied that she was as much responsible for Claudia as Gibson was.

The typewriter was thudding out an assignment when I got back. A queue of other work stretched along the table. As I passed behind her at the table she stopped typing, grabbed my hand, and kissed it. A quick smile. Reddened eyes; she had been crying. Back to work.

IN BED that night: 'If my body changes its mind and lets me have babies I promise I'll never reject any of them or let them grow up feeling unwanted,' she whispered.

But Maria didn't get off to sleep, instead rolling over vigorously one way and then back the other. Loud, frustrated sighs. Bedding was kicked. Pillow beaten and re-beaten into shape. I'd had enough by 1am. I had to be getting up at four o'clock for a long Saturday and hadn't been able to sleep, either.

'Sweetie?'

'Uhnn …'

'Can we talk for a minute?'

'Uhn … sorry, this is not helping you get off to sleep.' She rolled back over to face me, and her hand touched my cheek. 'I'm sorry, darling.'

'It's not that. Why didn't you read out to me the postscript of Annette's letter?'

In the dark I sensed her becoming still. Very Head Girl. 'You read my letter,' she accused.

'Well, yeah. You left it open on the couch earlier tonight.'

'That didn't mean you could just pick it up and read it.'

Eh?

'But, Maria, we've both been open with each other's mail. I didn't do anything we hadn't done before.'

'You should have asked, considering I hadn't read it out.'

She rolled away from me and curled up into the foetal 'don't talk to me, don't come near me' position.

I wasn't having any of that.

In her postscript, which she had written on a separate page, Annette said: I'm not sure I approve of what you've done, going and living with Martin. You're very young still, and moving in with him is a big, drastic step.

You probably didn't want me to write that, but motherhood and accumulated wisdom can change your outlook on things. I would be most unhappy if Claudia or the other girls did such a thing.

Have you thought about what you'd do if you fell pregnant and how having a baby can affect your life?

I nudged her tentatively, but she didn't move. I thought about letting the subject drop until her mood improved. But …

'Why did the postscript upset you so much, Maria?'

She delayed answering, and I nearly asked her again. My hand gripped her shoulder. I wanted her to face me. She wouldn't move.

'Why do you think, Martin? She bloody well as good as told me I was a silly little girl who wasn't old enough to know her own mind about being in love.'

'OK. But why has it got so deep under your skin?'

302

'Because it's not true,' she snapped.

'No, it isn't. If it's not true – and we agree it isn't – then why are you so upset about it?'

In her silence a siren from a police car or an ambulance wailed across the city. I was about to repeat the question, and more demandingly, when she rolled back to face me.

'When I wrote to her I thought I was extending a kind of olive branch – not just from me, but also from the rest of my family. She was treated terribly. I wanted to make a connection. I thought we might have something in common – being punished by our family for something we had done that everyone thought was wrong.'

'And she didn't see it the same way. Because she's made a good life for herself and Claudia on the other side of the world.'

Her unhappy frown, just inches from my face. 'Yes. And then, without being asked her opinion on the matter, she dismissed me and my life with you. She knows nothing about me. Even that I can't get pregnant. I felt trampled on. That's what hurt.'

I gathered her to me. 'Don't worry about her,' I whispered, caressing, trying to sound comforting, 'Just as you don't worry about what anyone else thinks.'

I kissed her forehead. 'Look. I fell in love with you one day on a street corner because you were different from all the other girls and women around you. Despite your uniform, your badges of rank and all that, you had a presence and a poise that made you stand out – you had a maturity that to me looked way beyond your years. I wanted to know you, and if possible be the one to love you.'

My lips found her cheek, which was wet, and then her lips.

'What she thinks doesn't matter.'

Maria returned a kiss. 'Thanks, sweetie.'

'But now, my love,' I whispered sternly, 'I really do have to get some sleep otherwise I'll fall asleep at my desk.'

'Can't have that,' she giggled, and kissed me again.

Surprises

We had not seen Matthew and Catharine for nearly six weeks. Apart from a quick catch-up after a Sunday Mass more than a month ago we hadn't seen Órla, either. Maria had a lot to tell her brother, but she wasn't sure how to broach the subject of Annette with their mother. Anyway, surprises ...

I'd just parked the car after we'd been to Mass. Alice from the first floor was tending a little flower garden she'd made her own. We stopped to chat, about the garden, the flowers, the weather.

Then she dropped a bombshell.

'How do you feel about your Mum moving in next door to you, Maria?'

I wasn't sure I'd heard correctly. Alice was still on her knees, little weeding fork in her rubber-gloved hand, smiling and squinting up against the sun. I heard Maria say, *'Wha-aat?!'*

Alice's eyes darted between Maria and me. She put her hand up to shade her face. 'Oops. Have I just put my foot in it? Didn't you know, dear?' She was aghast at having broken the news.

I glanced at Maria. Her mouth and eyes were wide in disbelief and her cheeks were flushed.

'No, Alice, we didn't,' I said. 'What do you mean next door?'

'Look, I'm sorry, Martin ... Maria, but –'

Maria recovered quickly. She put her hand on Alice's shoulder. 'It's OK, Alice. My mother hasn't said anything to us. But, what and when?'

'Well,' Alice said carefully, 'the flat right next to yours. The one the English couple had for a while.'

Ah. Will and Melanie had left when I was in hospital. Then there'd been a couple with a baby who never stopped crying. They worried that it was disturbing and annoying us. I said it wasn't. They left because it was a big hike getting a pram up three flights of stairs. Then there'd been another couple. But he walked out after a big row. She moved out. The place had been empty for weeks.

Maria turned to me. 'Did you know?'

I shook my head. 'I would have said, love. It looks like she's left your father. Can't hush up that one.'

'Your mother was here on Thursday afternoon, Maria. While you were at work, I suppose. And then she was here again yesterday morning. A van full of stuff, and some young men moved her in.'

She had made sure we wouldn't be around.

Maria glanced up to the top floor of the flats. 'Well, well, well,' she said drily. 'I supposed I'd better go and say hello.'

Alice winked. 'Good luck, dears.'

MARIA KNOCKED on her mother's door. No reply. 'Either she's out or she doesn't want to talk to you,' I said.

She frowned, knocked again without result, I unlocked our door, and Robert appeared from his flat.

'Ah, hello, you, two.' He grinned, and he was holding Dante, whose purr clattered into action and he started to dribble when he saw Maria. She held out her arms to him; he didn't hesitate, leapt over, and she cuddled him. She coo'd to him in French. He closed his eyes and bunted her.

'I see you know about your mother's move,' Robert said.

'Alice has just told us,' I replied. 'When did you know?'

'Oh, Thursday afternoon. She was here with a man from the property company. She thought it – the little flat – would be just perfect for her.'

'And she moved in yesterday while we weren't here,' Maria said. 'Deliberately making sure we weren't around …'

'I heard her go out this morning, after you left to go to church.'

We invited Robert in for a cup of coffee. We had buns, rolls, and cakes from a new hot bread shop that had become popular. In New Zealand those days shops didn't generally open on Sundays unless they were granted an exemption from the council or some government department. Hot bread shops were still getting under way.

Just as Robert was leaving, a reluctant Dante in his arms gazing longingly back at Maria, Matthew arrived with Catharine and her same-age cousins, Rachael and Charlotte.

'Can't stay here long,' he said. 'If the nieces' parents find out we've been here I'll get into some trouble. The official story is the other girls are having driving lessons with me.'

Maria and her nieces launched into hug-fests.

'I take it you have caught up with the news of our mother.'

'Not an hour ago,' I said.

'She's left Grandpa,' Rachael said.

'The family are said to be reeling,' Matt added. I had visions, as I always do when I hear of people, towns, cities, and countries 'reeling', of FitzGarratts, well, 'reeling' – sorry, a journalistic in-joke there.

'No-one can believe it. Nearly 50 years together,' Rachael chipped in.

'And she's moved in right next door to us.'

'How do you feel about that, Maria,' Charlotte asked.

She replied carefully: 'I don't know how I feel about it yet.'

'Grandpa was drinking a lot all day yesterday,' Charlotte said.

'Charley …' her two cousins ssh'd her.

Charlotte was the shortest of the girls, livid blue eyes that denoted stubbornness, and I suspect one who wouldn't be easily shushed. The tumbly ringlets of her red hair rippled as she shook her head. 'Well, it's true. No point hiding it.'

And by then we were all aware that their mother and grandmother was in our doorway.

Family announcement

'Hello, Órla,' I said, 'speak of the Devil and all that.'

'Well, if my youngest son is to be believed, I am the Devil Incarnate.' Her dark eyes were amused, but resigned.

Her granddaughters hugged her in turn, which comforted her. 'Hello, Mum,' Matt said a little too brightly, 'what's new?'

The question was so blatantly absurd we all laughed, if awkwardly.

'Would you like a cup of tea or coffee, Órla?' I offered.

She glanced at Maria, who had neither hugged her mother nor, from what I could see, greeted her. Órla declined. She had aged and lost weight since we'd last seen her. Her children and granddaughters slipped into an awkward silence.

'Órla,' I said, thinking I should take charge, 'please, sit down, take the load off your feet, have a cup of tea and maybe something to eat.'

Charlotte took her grandmother's arm and guided her to the couch. 'Come on, Gran, you look like a really old lady just now.'

Órla said, with mock severity, 'you haven't lost your customary lack of tact, have you, Charlotte?'

Her granddaughter's grin was 'I don't care'.

Anyway, Órla acquiesced, and sank tiredly to the couch. Catharine set about making her grandmother some tea. I glanced at Maria. The signal was: *please, whatever you feel about your mother now living next door to us, please, get her something to eat. The rest can come later.*

She received the signal, for which I was much relieved, and said: 'We've been going to this new hot bread shop after church, Mum. They have more-ish croissants with chicken, apricot, cream cheese, avocado, and cranberry sauce.'

Her mother smiled. 'Thank you, dear, it sounds delicious.'

Conversation was inconsequential while she ate the croissant – more accurately, she wolfed it down, despite the economy and neatness of her mannerisms, traits she shared with her youngest daughter.

Rachael handed her a paper napkin when she finished. She used it to neatly dab her lips and wipe her fingers. She carefully brushed crumbs from her jacket into the palm of her hand.

'Maria does that, too,' I said. 'Exactly like that.'

I was encouraged that mother and daughter exchanged a knowing smile. Catharine took the crumbs and put them in the rubbish.

Matt cleared his throat. 'To repeat my question, Mum, what's new?'

She glanced at her granddaughters arrayed either side of her on the couch, as if she thought that perhaps they might be a little young to hear her discuss the ruin of her marriage.

She shrugged. She and Peirse had become increasingly estranged since Maria had left home. 'Or, perhaps I should say, the estrangement had become more and more open. I think it had been sitting there for a long time. You can go for years – decades even – papering over cracks or pretending they're not there. You concentrate on other things. Find distractions that keep things 'nice', keeps things together.'

Tom's attack on me, Grannie Annie's collusion with him, her mother-in-law's moving into the home – it all became too much.

'I was happy to stay in the house for the sake of appearances. A united front, you understand, as long as I didn't have to have a lot to do with my husband. But as far as I was concerned Dad – Grandpa – and I had reached the end of the road. Much of our lives had become separate anyway. My mother-in-law's moving in was the last straw. She has always had my husband's ear.'

She didn't add any more, and no-one else knew what to say next.

A loud, old-woman's sigh, and she levered herself off the couch, knees creaking. 'If you'll excuse me I must go and have a nap. I've slept very little the past few nights.'

She rested a hand on Maria's shoulder. 'We'll talk again later.' Maria nodded.

To Matthew, she said: 'I'll make an appointment to see you in a few days, Matt. I think there might be a few legal things to sort out.'

Nobody said much after Órla left. She had aged; even her shutting her flat's door sounded weary. Matt and the girls now didn't look to be in any hurry to leave.

'I have something that might interest you, Matt,' Maria said. 'And you others.'

She gave him the photocopy of her letter to Annette, which he sat down and read.

He finished. 'Has she replied?'

She handed him Annette's letter. Catharine asked if they could see Maria's letter to Annette.

Matt looked up when he'd finished. 'Congratulations, Maria. That's quite a coup. I didn't know about Hamburg, nor about the marriage.'

She beamed at the compliment.

'No, seriously. I'm pleased you've been able to get her to reply.'

He borrowed a pen and noted down Annette's address details in a small notebook. 'I think I'll give her a bell,' he said. 'Going by her comments she might not be displeased.'

He hugged Maria. 'This has been a big moment in our family,' he said. 'I hope it's a first step to repairing a serious injustice.'

The girls read Annette's letter, but Maria withheld the contentious postscript. They commented on the photos and how wonderful the beach was. The three cousins decided they would write to Annette, and to Claudia, introducing themselves. They had photos. 'I don't know if I'd look as nice as them in a bikini, though,' Rachael said worriedly. She was on the fleshy side, and had what would be referred to today as 'body image issues'.

'Then don't wear a bikini,' Matthew said, prompting stiletto glares from his sister, daughter, and nieces.

His arched eyebrows sought male help from me. I didn't like the odds ranged against us so I shrugged.

Eventually they left. 'Suppose the driving lessons had better continue.'

'That's right, Uncle Matt, otherwise you'll have been lying and you being a Queen's Counsel that might not look good,' Charlotte said as they left.

ÓRLA JOINED us for tea that evening. I felt we couldn't not invite her now we knew she was our neighbour.

She picked at her food, and conversation was spasmodic and stilted. Maria, I knew, wanted to ask her – demand even – why she chose next door to us to live.

Órla headed it off. 'Before you ask, Maria,' she said, resting a hand on her daughter's arm, 'I didn't move in next door to spite you, nor to spy on you.'

'Why did you then?'

Her mother kept her hand on Maria's arm. Trying to sound conciliatory. 'Simply because it was available. For the first time in over 45 years I've had to find somewhere to live. And on my own. It needed to be enough just for me and for my books.' She squeezed Maria's arm. 'My dear, I don't need eight bedrooms any more. That place was too big, even when you still lived there.'

Maria glanced at me. I wanted to convey to her as best I could: *please, be reasonable, she's your mother.* Which was what I had said during the afternoon.

'I'm retiring at the end of the year. I need to look at my life now and see how I'm going to live out the remainder of it.'

'Well, it's not as if you're an old lady, is it, Mum?' Maria said.

Her mother laughed, and I think that perhaps she sounded relieved. 'We'll see. For the past 45 years I've been someone else's wife, mother, grandmother, as well as having a most fulfilling career in academia. I never thought much about what would happen after that.'

She paused, glancing at her rings, still on her fingers. 'I thought Dad and I would go on forever, until death parted us.'

'But next door can't have been the only empty flat in the whole city, though,' Maria said. She was still suspicious.

Órla sat back straight in her chair. 'No, dear,' she said softly. 'This might be difficult for me to explain – or express.'

She extended her hand again, to Maria's. 'I haven't been the most maternal of mothers, especially with you. I am ashamed to say it, but by the time I got to you I had become well and truly tired of babies and toddlers. I was a grandmother, for heaven's sake, but still one with a functioning brain that I wanted to keep using.'

I thought of Annette's comments. Maria's glance at me indicated she was thinking the same thing.

'A proper, breast-beating *mea culpa* with sackcloth and ashes will happen some time, Maria, but you and I aren't ready for that just yet.' She ventured another smile. 'As I said a few moments ago, I haven't moved in to spy on you or intrude on your life here with Martin. I won't be next door with my ear to the wall.'

I had to stop a grin there. Maria had muttered earlier: 'I don't want her over there listening to us in bed.'

'... you are still my daughter, and I do love you, although it might not have seemed I did. I am interested in you and do care about you.'

'But ...'

'Please ...' Órla was quiet but firm. 'From now on you won't see me at all unless you invite me in.' That stopped everything, a triangle of people looking at each other in turn. 'I won't be a nuisance.'

She picked up her knife and fork and attacked the salad. 'Besides,' she said, her fork pausing halfway to her lips, 'I've got to get used to being single. I haven't been single since I was 20. So there are big changes for me, too.'

Maria leaned over and gave her mother a long, heart-felt hug.

Later, the meal long over, over tea and coffee, I raised her mention of Luke earlier in the day.

'Hmm, yes. I don't think I ever realised just how disagreeable my youngest son is. Why he decided to become a priest is beyond my comprehension.'

He had lectured her and quoted Church teaching. The scriptures. He had wagged his finger. He had told her that what she was doing was sinful and a 'massive breach' of her wedding vows, and that she would not be welcome in circles of the Church where she and Peirse had been a fixture for decades.

He had told her to go away and 'seek Our Lady, the source of all wisdom'.

Father Luke FitzGarratt had told Órla he was ashamed to call her his mother. Many of people she thought were friends must have felt the same. 'I've already had notes and messages from people I thought were my friends telling me they never want to have anything to do with me again.'

I thought: *what a terrible discovery. To get to 65 and you begin to find out who your friends are, and that there aren't many of them about.* What times had been shared? Wedding invitations. How many holidays together? How many kids had grown up playing together? How many confidences whispered and exchanged?

All that trust and friendship supposedly built up – and then an event none had probably foreseen had ripped the veils away revealing the truth. Their lives and friendships had turned out to be an illusion and a delusion.

Maria had taken her mother's hand and held on to it and they gazed silently at one another. At 17 Maria had found out who her friends were when she came to live with me. Some had been unexpected – Matthew, his daughter Catharine, and she and Maria had been virtually lifelong enemies. Her nieces Rachael and Charlotte. Stella had turned her back on her. Luke was a judgmental prick.

Then there was my Dad, already dreaming of when Maria would be his daughter-in-law and the mother of his grandchildren.

'God will give her babies,' said my half-believing father. He'd found a reason to live a bit longer. He was still 'quietly working on' Mum. Uncle Syd and Auntie Kura never failed to include Maria in their letters and always spoke to her in phone calls. Magdalena and Peter had created work for her, probably at cost to their pockets. Robert had taken over teaching her. Dante made her coo and be frivolously protective.

I heard Mrs Barlow saying once, and it might have been to Andrea Chambers, distressed because her 'best' friend had ditched her to be 'best' friend with another 'best' friend: 'Don't worry, dearie, sometimes you have to lose your so-called friends to find your real friends.'

'The archbishop sent a letter with Luke requesting my resignation from all the Church committees and associations I'm on.'

I felt sick. On the other hand, Monsignor Uncle Brian had neither abandoned his sister nor his niece.

On being harmless

Maria waited until the next Sunday before tackling her mother about Annette. 'I've been in contact with Annette, Mum.'

Órla did well to contain her surprise. 'Oh, really, dear. How did that come about?'

Her face had tightened up; wary. Maria told her how Matt had related the story of Annette's getting pregnant and then departure to Oxford.

'It upset me, Mum, that our church-going, Catholic family shunted her off like that, out of sight and out of mind – and she was *pregnant*, for God's sake.'

Her mother gazed at her for long moments. Her fingers had become entwined, and now they were locked tight. 'I see,' she said, barely a whisper.

'So we found out where she lived, and I wrote to her. And she wrote back.'

Maria produced the photocopy of her letter and Annette's reply. Órla read both letters without expression. She gazed for several minutes at the photos of her daughter and granddaughter. It was as if by intensely staring at the photos she was projecting herself into the picture, into where they were. Trying to connect.

'What do you think, Mum?'

Órla looked up, her eyes desolately sad.

'I think I need a few days to take this in, Maria,' she said softly.

Maria persisted. 'Who thought Dr Gibson's reputation was more important than Annette and her baby? And the FitzGarratt name?'

Maria waited for a reply. Her mother stared blankly at the table.

'Why was it decided that Annette should be banished out of the country to save everyone embarrassment?'

Órla remained silent.

Maria added what my mother would have called a 'nyah' into her tone. In other words, she sounded acidic. 'What did you have to say about Annette back then, Mum?'

Órla began to tremble.

'Did you speak up for your daughter, Mother?'

Too sharp!

Órla sobbed once. It was loud and wrenched from the deep. Tears fell down her cheeks, and she fumbled for a small handkerchief wedged under her watch strap. 'Oh, God,' she whispered.

She dabbed her eyes and wiped her nose. Sitting up straight and gathering herself, she said: 'I'm sorry, but I can't discuss this right now.' She pushed her chair back and got up to leave the table.

'But –' Maria started, flushing, and I reached over and put my hand on her wrist. And squeezed hard.

'Wha –?' and she saw the warning in my eye: *leave it.*

In a blur, Órla through more tears asked that she be excused, apologised for leaving, for not having dessert, for 'leaving you with all the dishes', and hurried out. Her keys clinked loudly as she tried her own door.

Maria rounded on me: 'Why did you stop me?'

I don't like seeing anyone suffer. In my life I've tried – not always successfully – to avoid hurting or shitting on anyone. 'You lack the killer instinct,' my first chief reporter had chided me several years ago.

Anyway, Órla was suffering. I tried to take Maria's hands, a conciliatory gesture. She wasn't having any of it and shook them away.

'Look,' I said, 'one of the things you learn in my job is how to talk to people, to interview them. It can be like a game, especially when they might not want to talk to you.'

Her arms folded defensively across her breasts. Her eyes glinted for attack. They were a virid green.

This was going to be hard work.

'You can, if you are careful, get everything you want to know from your mum. But you'll get nothing if you force her to be defensive. She will clam up, run away as she did just now, and avoid you.'

'But I want to know. I think I have a right to know what she did.' Her jaw jutted truculently.

I nearly dropped it and backed off. One didn't get into an argument lightly with Maria, particularly when she was in full, self-righteous flight. She could dominate an argument in ways I'd yet to even learn. She knew how to deflect, to feint, to sidestep, to turn a debate on its head.

I closed towards her. 'Why do you need to know? And your 'right to know' comes from where? Who says you have a right?'

She didn't like that. Her lips were ruler-straight and Head Girl Wintry.

But I bore on – it would be frosty in bed tonight, and maybe tomorrow night, too, but I could live with that. 'I'm just trying to be helpful here. You want to know the story from your mother. Fine. But I'm telling you you'll get more out of her if she knows you're not going to judge and condemn her and nail her to a bloody wall.'

I waited. It dawned on me that despite the 'I am Lady Fortress' manner she was listening. I reached out and took her hands, and this time she didn't resist. The lips wobbled to stay straight.

I was encouraged. 'Sweetie. There are times when I've learned to be harmless. Even thick. Because I've found that if I come across as non-threatening yet interested and sympathetic people drop their guard. And then they'll just about tell you anything.'

I squeezed her hands. I suppose trying to be reassuring. We held one another's gaze; I didn't feel so much like a science specimen under a microscope. 'I suggest that you wait for a few days, then approach your mother again and first ask her if you and she can talk about it some time.'

'OK,' she said. Her eyes were thawing.

'Be at pains to reassure her that you just want to know, as one of the family, because being the youngest and not born you missed out on it all. You'd like to hear it from her than from Matt, or Stella, or Tessa, or somebody else.'

And then, perhaps a bit wearily, I added: 'Apologise for sounding like a Gestapo interrogator with the thumbscrews in your handbag.'

She squeezed my hands. 'Anything else?'

A picture came into my mind: of Órla staring at the photos, almost as if she was willing herself into them. 'You might find that she would like to talk about it. Did you notice how she stared at the photos?'

Maria shrugged. 'Mmm.'

'It was as if she was trying to connect with them.'

Maria was smiling now, in a lip-wobbling way. 'Let your mother talk. Ask questions where you need to. You never know where it might lead to.'

A tear squeezed out the corner of her eye. 'Oh, come here, little man,' and she drew my head to her breast. She held it there, and I heard her heart beating as she kissed the top of my head.

'Remember,' I mumbled against the soft swell of her bosom and caressed her back slowly, 'how you were judged when you came and lived here? Wasn't very pleasant, was it?'

She stepped us into the bedroom. The table wasn't cleared, the dishes not done. Dried washing was still a-tumble in the basket.

Since Maria had taken up living with me everything was done before we went to bed. Especially on a Sunday. She had decreed. Sunday was the start of the week.

'But what about the dishes and so on?' I said, realising how stupid it sounded. She had unbuttoned my shirt and was working on the zip of my jeans.

She stopped what she was doing. I was a specimen under a microscope again. Or a naughty little boy. 'Rules can be broken sometimes. You've just saved me from being a bitchy bitch again.'

She tugged my pants and underpants down and they bunched at my ankles. 'I just want to show you how much I love you, and you worry about the fucking dishes?'

I was shocked. 'You've just said 'fucking'. You never swear.' Even the innocuous 'bloody' was a stretch.

She yanked my shirt off and flung it aside with a flourish. 'Like most women I can be pushed to extremes by a dullard man annoying me.'

She shoved me so I sprawled back on the bed and advanced on me lifting off her top. Even her nipples jutted their own bright, pink annoyance. 'And your preoccupation with the fucking dishes when I'm trying to get your *membrum virile* – ahem – to seed my perfumed garden is pissing me off.'

Talking dirty without even a blush, and in Latin, too ...

LATER, HOURS later, I woke because the familiar 'hem ... hem' of Maria's breathing when she was asleep had stopped.

'You awake?' I whispered.

'Yes. I've been thinking. Poor Mum.'

I heard her slide from the bed, and the *sshursussh* of her getting dressed.

'What are you doing?'

'Shhh. Go back to sleep. I'm going to talk to Mum.'

My bedside clock read 12.35am. I heard her knock softly on the door of her mother's flat. The door opened. A muffled 'Oh, Mum ...'

I heard and felt her get back into bed. I glanced at my clock – 2.10am.

'All right?'

Maria snuggled close: 'Yes. I think she's had to put up with a lot, and just buried it under behind a brave, professorial, and very Catholic wife and mother face.'

Exam curtseys

I got home from work, my nostrils pleasantly assaulted by the agreeable fragrances of the fresh flowers that sat in a vase in the middle of the table.

Maria was agitated. Robert had phoned from the school with a message. He was bringing Sister Hélène around to talk to Maria about the bursary exams, which were now only two weeks away.

'She's coming here, Martin. God, I wish I'd had more notice then I could properly clean and tidy.' She'd had time to whip around the corner to the local florist.

I looked around the living room and attached kitchenette. Nothing was out of place. There wouldn't be. I doubt there was even a speck of dirt on the carpet to sully a holy sole.

A knock on the door. With a glance she indicated that I should open it. Smiling warmly Sister Hélène entered our den of sin, Robert in tow. Probably out of habit and unable to stop herself, Maria curtseyed gravely, bowing her head, as if she was still in uniform and in her former headmistress's office.

Hélène was taken aback: 'Oh, Maria, my dear, please. Thank you, but that is not necessary,' her lilt flowed through the room. 'Especially in your own home.'

I liked that last bit – 'your own home'.

'You've always been very good to me, Sister.'

Hélène embraced Maria, and kissed her on the cheek. I made tea and coffee while they sat around the table and got down to the business of exams.

Maria would take her place in the classroom again among her former classmates. Where she would sit the exams had worried Robert, and he had gone to discuss the matter with Hélène. It had not been a difficulty for the nun. Maria would sit them at the school. There would be no problem.

'And she said it, Martin,' he told me a couple of days later, 'in a rather steely, Germanic manner. I pity any bastard who ever tries to cross her.'

Apparently Luke and some school committee members had tried to tell her Maria should be fully cut off from the school. People were talking. Hélène had told them to mind their own business.

Now she had a surprise for Maria. 'My dear, have you got rid of your uniform?'

Er, no. Why?

'Good.' Hélène was evidently pleased and relieved. 'Because you will need to wear it to the examinations. You have a unique ex officio status because, although you're not at the school and Robert has been teaching you, we've done the bureaucratic side that keeps officials happy.'

She made a dismissive gesture with small hands. 'You're not part of us, yet you are, if that makes sense. So you need to be in uniform, as the other girls will be.'

LATER IN the evening Maria went to the wardrobe and took out the uniform. Matter-of-factly she clad herself in it. Even doing up the tie. I watched. She turned from side to side in critical self-inspection. I was reminded of the first time I'd seen her do that. We hadn't even kissed then.

'Looks good to me,' I said, and it did, if a little strange to see her back in uniform after this time. 'How does it fit?'

She glanced at my reflection in the mirror. 'It's perfect. As if I've never been out of it.'

'Do you mind having to get into uniform again?'

'Not at all. It will be nice to blend in with all the others. It's only for a week.'

I stood behind her and wrapped my arms around her. 'You look the part, sweetie, but in a way you don't. You've outgrown this.' My hands glided down her flanks. 'This isn't you any more.'

And she hadn't been back then in February, I remembered. Maria seemed older than her years. We contemplated our reflections now.

'Would you like me to liberate you from your uniform again?'

'Yes, please,' she whispered huskily.

Last supper

Two Monday mornings later I headed out the door. I kissed Maria and wished her well for the English exam. I did the same on Tuesday (French), Wednesday (Latin), Thursday (German). Her mother slipped a card under our door wishing her well. Órla called in during evenings for 'debriefs'.

History, her last exam, was on Friday afternoon. Exams had always been a trial and terror for me. But all week Maria was calm and matter-of-fact about it. She knew her stuff, had prepared with professional zeal, she knew she would pass, the question was simply by how much. Robert had always said she would easily pass the 300 marks needed for the A bursary.

He came in with Dante, and as he and she fussed over one another, now he casually mentioned that 100 per cent was not impossible with her.

This time I walked with her around to the college, at the gate kissed her goodbye – to the cheers of some younger girls and she blushed – and she was gone.

For want of something better to do I walked into the cathedral, down to the grotto, where the statue of Mary presided. I sat in a pew and ... well, what was I doing here?

I stared at the unseeing eyes of the statue of the woman Catholics venerated as mother of God. I didn't understand the faith, and I didn't get why Maria still believed in it after the treatment of her by some of God's so-called friends down here. Perhaps she didn't believe all of it, but her faith in God and the woman whose statue towered over me was what mattered. The doctrines of the Church didn't.

Some candles were burning in slots in a bar before the grotto, lit by silent, worried, devoted, fervent believers. I got up and went and lit one. 'If you could just keep an eye on her today that would be good,' I whispered, crossed myself, and left.

MARIA BROUGHT the nieces home for an impromptu celebration of the end of the exams: Catharine and her younger twin sisters Anne and Jacqueline, bright young things who'd sat school certificate a year ahead of their contemporaries, and Charlotte and Rachael. 'Rach' had brought along her younger sister Bernadette, who'd never been to my flat.

They trooped in, girl-noisy and happy, relieved and pleased it was all over and ready to let their hair down. They could relax for a few days until they had to go back for school prize-giving. Which Maria would not be able to do. Anyway, sleeves were rolled up, ties were discarded.

I found a bottle of *Asti Spumante* for them, which wasn't enough, especially the older three who in a few weeks saw themselves, 17 and nearly 18, free of parental and school restraint and loving the thought of freedom at university. They could barely wait.

But they needed feeding and so I went and bought fish and chips because it was Friday, bags of junk food and soft drink, and stopped off at a bottle store and picked up more *Asti*. It was going to be quite a night.

I got back, and the girls had been joined by Órla and Robert, and Dante, who shamelessly played off his new admirers against each other. He stuck his nose in the air when Maria scolded him pleadingly. She resorted to French, which always sounded attractive skipping from her lips.

That didn't work.

She tried German, which she managed to sound authoritarian as the words goose-stepped from her lips. He stared scornfully and unblinkingly and schmoozed with Órla instead. She was as standoffish as he was. She would be a challenge. He liked that. Dante understood the game of play-hard-to-get.

But everything went well. The girls ate – carefully, but they ate. They sipped *Asti* under their grandmother's careful but indulgent eye. They sang to LPs and cassettes on the stereo – ABBA and the Bay City Rollers were popular, much to Órla's horror – and they swapped stories and laughed and screamed and joked. Even Órla's 'horror' was good-natured and in fun.

'You know, Gran,' Charlotte said, 'it's neat having you here this evening with us. You're not so uptight.' That prompted an exchange of glances between Órla and Maria.

Anyway, they were family and they were friends and enjoying one of the best times of their lives. Christmas was under a month away, then New Year. There was so much to look forward to.

Twenty-four hours later two of them would be dead.

Not next-of-kin

Maria had rung me in the afternoon at work to tell me she and the girls were going to an end-of-exams party that night. 'I won't be home until late, darling, so don't worry.'

She would get herself home either with a friend or a taxi. I told her that if she was stuck she should ring me. Our last words to one another were: 'I love you.' Well, hers were the German *'Ich liebe dich'*, the French *à bientôt*. Then a whispered kiss.

Instead of going home after work as I normally did on a Saturday night I went with some others from the job to a quiet bar at the back of *The Mafeking*. The 10 o'clock closing law was ignored here – by journalists and off-duty cops especially – as long as everyone was discreet.

By the time I got home just before midnight I'd had a few drinks and was ready for a long, deep sleep. I thought nothing of it that Maria wasn't there. I hoped that it was a good party. I undressed clumsily and tumbled into bed and fell asleep hugging her pillow.

I didn't hear the police come up the stairs and knock about 2am.

Not on my door, but on Órla's. She was Maria's mother. Next-of-kin.

I wasn't.

After they broke the news to her she quickly had dressed and gone down the stairs with them. Alice went to her door because she heard footsteps on the stairs and Órla's sobbing, and a police sergeant trying to comfort her.

I woke just before eight o'clock. Maria wasn't beside me nor was she in the flat. Her side of the bed was cold. Her pyjamas were folded neatly under her pillow. She hadn't come home. I wasn't worried. I'd often slept over at a party. Once in a baby's cot.

The lead item on the local 8am radio news was that two teenage girls had died overnight after a car was driven into them as they crossed the street.

I sat down slowly, chilled. I didn't like the sound of that.

Maria hadn't said where the party would be, and I hadn't asked. 'The police will not release the names of the two dead girls until all next-of-kin have been notified,' the newsreader intoned. He went on to the next item.

I barely heard it. I was deeply afraid now.

The knock on the door – so soft, so tentative – startled me. I strode swiftly to open it, desperately willing that Maria be on the other side, smiling, and throwing her arms around me and kissing away my groundless worries. *But she has her own key ...*

Alice. 'Martin,' she began hesitantly, her eyes searching past me into our flat, looking for Maria. Now urgency in her voice: 'Martin, is Maria here?'

And in that moment we both all but knew. The realisation was there in our eyes. But still the human mind clings to hope. She stepped into my flat, taking my arm and shutting the door. 'Come on, love,' she said gently.

We sat on the couch.

'I heard voices on the stairs about two, Martin. Maria's mother was coming down with two policemen. She was crying, and one was trying to comfort her.'

Oh, my God. Maria. Why hadn't they come to me, too?

Another knock on the door. Robert, in a dressing gown, and Dante, huge eyes unblinking, demanding where Maria was. *I don't know either, mate.*

'Martin, I've just heard on the news about two girls being killed on a street last night. Have you heard from Maria?' He and she had spoken on her way out, about seven o'clock. The party was in the suburb where the girls were killed.

I didn't know what to do. Alice made coffee. She was going to make a lot of tea and coffee that day.

Robert thought the police should know. He tried them on the phone using his best squadron leader-professor voice.

They couldn't or wouldn't tell me anything unless I was 'the deceased's' next-of-kin. 'He might not be strictly, legally, next-of-kin, Sergeant,' Robert said softly, icily, 'but Miss FitzGarratt has been living here with Mr Blake for the last several months. They were practically engaged.'

I didn't hear what the sergeant at the other end said, but Robert's features stiffened in fury. 'Thank you, Sergeant,' and he hung up.

'Christ almighty,' he whispered. He glanced at Alice. 'Sorry.'

She grinned. 'Don't mind me, Rob, I grew up in Ohai. All the men in my family were coalminers.'

I was now thoroughly alarmed. The police watch house sergeant had pretty much confirmed my worst fears. I phoned Matt's house. No answer.

Robert phoned the hospital. They had nothing to say.

'Try the ambulance,' I said.

They gave information only out to the press, they said, and could not give names of those they carried to hospital until the police gave the OK. Robert gently pressed the point. His voice sounded like Authority and he knew how to do it.

He said he was inquiring on behalf of a friend who worked for the *Evening Herald*. 'His fiancée, Miss Maria FitzGarratt, has not returned home this morning from a party she attended last evening in that suburb and he is deeply anxious about her. He believes that one of the victims might be her. He has not been able to find out any information. No-one will tell him anything.'

The ambulance officer 'hemmed', 'hawed', sucked air noisily through his teeth. Robert waited expectantly.

The ambulance officer spoke. After a moment's silence, Robert said: 'Thank you. You've been most kind.' He put the phone back in the cradle slowly, tears welling in his eyes.

'Martin,' he cleared his throat, blinking, 'Martin, it was Maria and Catharine ...' and he began to cry. I got up and hugged him hard. Alice wrapped her arms around both our shoulders and burst into tears, too. Dante, not to be left out, yowled eerily in a way I'd never heard him before. His tail lowered, he walked into the bedroom and jumped up on our bed – and began to knead the dough on Maria's side.

Another knock on the door. Trevor Clifton, the paper's police reporter, looking hungover, which he was, the reek of whisky preceding him invisibly, and Clyde Barnfield, my editor. He let Trevor break the news.

'Martin,' he began gently, 'I've been told something awful by the police this morning that you should know – if you don't already.'

'What have they told you, Trevor? A desk sergeant refused to tell Robert anything on the phone a few minutes ago. Because I'm not next-of-kin.'

'OK. Well, he was just being official and officious and covering his arse.'

I mentioned Robert's call to the ambulance, and what he'd been told.

He nodded. Maria had been one of a group of girls standing in the middle of a quiet, suburban street saying goodnight to one another. A car up the street took off. The driver was showing off and he apparently was drunk. He was 17. He didn't have his lights on. He wasn't even supposed to have the car that night. It was a 351hp Ford Falcon, which he'd not driven unsupervised before that night.

'A couple of girls told the cops that Maria twigged first, and she screamed a warning and pushed the others out of the way – all in a split-second.'

In saving others, she had taken the full brunt of an accelerating, souped-up, wheels- spinning and -screeching Ford Falcon slamming into her.

'They said she didn't have a show of surviving the impact, mate.'

Oh, Jesus God. I tried to imagine it. Then I didn't want to. No. I didn't want to remember Maria like that.

'She wouldn't have felt a thing.'

'What about Catharine?' I could hear the dullness in my voice.

'Mate, she wasn't fast enough. She'd had a few drinks. Maria was trying to save her.'

I sat there, asking questions, discussing. The shock had not hit home yet.

Both expressed their condolence. 'Take the week off, Martin, you're gonna need it,' Barnfield said, his hand on my shoulder. 'Anything you need, just say, all right?'

Alice and Robert assured him they would keep an eye on me. I appreciated his gesture, and Clifton's coming to tell me, and the cops who broke the rules to make sure I knew.

Trevor cleared his throat delicately. 'Martin, would you be willing to let us have a photo of Maria we can use with the story? Do you have a nice one?'

I nearly told him to fuck off, which was unreasonable and churlish. I'd asked relatives and friends for a photo of a dead loved one. I thought the FitzGarratts might provide one that might not be nice. Something formal, or dated. Perhaps in school uniform.

I got up and found a packet of photos from Hawai'i. There was one of her on a beach, a lei around her neck. Her wide, open grin. I gave him that one.

Trevor had one last message: 'Martin, the embargo on Maria and Catharine's name is lifted at noon today. It'll be on the radio.'

He paused: 'Expect a phone call or visit, too, from *The National Journal*.' The opposition.

They left. I thought of Mum and Dad, especially Dad. I didn't want him to hear about Maria over the radio. I picked up the phone, and he answered. I broke the news to him. He sucked in his breath; a long sigh. Then, his voice resolute: 'I'll be there as quick as I can, son.'

Next were Uncle Syd and Auntie Kura. She answered. Syd had gone out to play an early round of golf with Heremia, their youngest. Auntie Koo cried and cried and cried, a wailing the like I'd never heard before – my insides shivered at the sound of it.

Magdalena and Peter: he answered. 'Oh, sweet Jesus, Martin, I am so sorry. She loved you so much, man.'

While I made the phone calls Robert went back to his flat for a shower and to get dressed. Dante steadfastly refused to leave our – now my – bed. I wrapped Maria's pyjamas around him and he settled and started a subdued purr. I showered, shaved, and got dressed. Maria and Catharine's deaths was still the lead item on the radio news. A youth was 'helping police with their inquiries'.

It was time to visit the FitzGarratts.

Closed ranks

Robert insisted on driving me, in my car. I wished I'd driven instead. 'Been a while since you've done this, Robert?' I said as he crashed the gears, after having stalled the car once and backed it over-enthusiastically out of the garage.

'Sorry,' he muttered.

I tried to make him feel better. 'I bet you were more at home in a Spitfire with a Focke-Wulf up your arse.'

He chuckled. 'I preferred to be in a Hurricane or a P40 if anyone was shooting cannon-shells at my arse.'

We parked outside the FitzGarratts' house. Cars filled the driveway and several more were parked out front. One had the name of an undertakers' firm on it. *Oh, God …*

The sky was clear, the day already warm. Birds sang and twittered in the street. A bird teased a cat from the safety of a small kowhai tree. A dog across the street barked – a lapper-yapper.

I opened the front gate; we glanced at each other. 'Ready, lad?'

I nodded, and we approached the front door, which opened as we mounted the steps on to the veranda. Maria's brother Mark stood square in the doorway.

'Hello, Mark,' I said.

'You are …?'

What? He knows bloody well who I am.

'Mark, I'm Martin.'

He was playing superciliously dumb. 'Martin ... Martin. Oh. Yes, of course.' Then: 'What do you want?'

What do you mean, 'What do you want?'?

'Maria's dead. Catharine, too.'

'We're well aware of that, obviously. The undertaker's here now and we're rather busy.'

I was groping, sounding futile and juvenile. 'Well, that's why I'm here ... and to pay my respects to the family ... to help plan the funer –' I didn't like his dismissive expression. It sounded foolish. But I couldn't believe this family were shutting me out. 'She lived with me ...' I blundered on desperately.

'Let me put this plainly to you, Mr Blake. You have no legal standing here. You and Maria were not married. You are not next-of-kin. *We* are. What *you* think you are in this is *irrelevant*.'

'Jesus Christ, man,' Robert remonstrated. 'Show some humanity.'

Mark wasted no time with that. 'Look. We're very busy. We've suffered a great shock and loss. You understand. Now, if you'll excuse me,' and he nodded towards the gate.

My brain had stopped registering. He stepped back inside and the door was shut decisively. I couldn't move. What I'd just heard ... I didn't believe people could be like that.

'Come on, Martin,' Robert whispered, and he turned me around and steered me towards the gate.

'Martin!'

The voice was high, girlish, and distressed. We turned around. Maria's niece Gabrielle had come around the side of the house and was running towards us, her arms out. She was crying. We embraced, and she gabbled tearfully: 'Oh Martin I'm so sorry ...'

We clung to each other, and she trembled. I whispered something comforting.

A voice, sharp, angry: 'Gabrielle! That's enough of that! You get back in here. *Now!*' It might have been her mother, or one of her aunts.

Reluctantly, and with a hurried kiss on my cheek, Gabrielle turned and walked deliberately slowly up to the front door. Just before it closed on her, she turned and gave me a defiant little wave.

Maria would have been proud of her.

Daze

The day blurred. Heaven returned and applied its soothing balm. Magdalena turned up with food and drink. She, Robert, and Alice managed the visitors for me.

There were a lot of them. They trooped up the stairs to my flat, paid their respects, made offers of 'anything I can do, you know you just only need say …' and went away again.

Sue Devonshire brought flowers and cried softly. I comforted her. Senior girls from the school, mostly the prefects, they came in groups. I comforted them, as well, as they wept together.

Members of the paper's staff, even Wilson Barker, awkward. Mrs Barker, Thelma, was kind; she had baked biscuits.

Sister Hélène arrived with Sister Margarethe. I didn't know if you hugged nuns. Hélène solved the problem by gathering me to her robes and she held me for a long time. It was odd: I had the feeling I was in the arms of an angel, and there was that light, airy fragrance about her. Margarethe was tearful, and it was clear she had been weeping for a long time. 'She was one in a million, Martin – a million,' she whispered.

The National Journal phoned. Robert referred them to the police. The next morning I was reported as being 'too distraught to make a statement'. All day it went on. Monsignor Uncle Brian was last. He'd been up all night, he said, and had administered the Church's last rites for the dying – extreme unction, he called it – to Maria and Catharine as they lay on the street.

'She was still alive?'

He shook his head. 'No, Martin, not Maria, no. Catharine lived a little longer, although unconscious. The Church believes that a person's soul doesn't immediately leave the body when they die.'

I didn't understand that, but I found it comforting. He had dedicated his Mass that morning to the girls, he said.

He'd seen Maria in the state she had died. I wanted to ask him something about that. But I couldn't figure out properly *what* to ask. He read my thoughts. 'No, Martin, you don't want to know now.'

Then he had breathed in heavily, as if steeling himself. 'Now I must go and pay my respects to my sister and her family.'

THE FIRST long, dazy day of my de facto widowhood ended. Robert, Alice, and Magdalena withdrew after I'd assured them that, yes, I'd be all right. Magdalena wanted to take me home. I said I needed to be here in case the FitzGarratts phoned or turned up.

Really, I just wanted to be on my own.

Red raw stump of pain

The reality hit me like a punch as I was about to go to bed. A silly – or seemingly silly – little thing did it.

I'd just brushed my teeth.

I screwed the cap back on to the toothpaste, just as she had trained me to do, and put my brush back in the holder next to Maria's.

Next to Maria's – her toothbrush, her toothpaste, her razor, her little aromatic hand soaps she liked to use – all in the bathroom that she would never again use.

Tears erupted. Robert told me some time later that he'd heard my agonised howl from his flat.

It was the first time I'd known the red raw stump of pain, the emotional heart's ache that's so real and intense that it's physical.

Her life had been cut off in one, violent second. I had no-one to love now. I never even said goodbye. That was the worst part. I wished I could have died with her because I didn't want the pain of living without her.

I sobbed in my bed hugging her pillow. All her sweet fragrances and aromas were still there. But Maria wasn't.

I knew then I would never know such love for a long time, if ever. I would have given anything to have her with me again.

Friendly and unfriendly

Dad, Uncle Syd, and Auntie Koo came from the airport early. My outpouring of grief the night before had restored my equilibrium. How does the human psyche make that happen?

Over breakfast I told them what I knew. Apparently the story had been on the TV news the night before, too, as well as in the morning papers. Dad bristled when I told them how Robert and I'd been turned away at the FitzGarratts'.

Auntie Koo thought that couldn't have been deliberate. 'It's probably because they've just suffered a huge tragedy, Marty.' She glanced around the table – still with Maria's schoolwork in neat folders on it – and went on: 'Decent people don't behave like that. They're Catholics. That must count for something.'

Dad and Uncle Syd exchanged sceptical glances.

'Well,' Dad said to Uncle Syd, 'I think you and I should go over there and have a chat to them, brother. Pay our respects. We've all lost someone we loved. Christ …' And I thought he was going to burst into tears again. 'Offer our help. Tell them Martin's grieving.'

Going by the set of his face I don't think Uncle Syd believed anything would come of it. 'But, yeah, good idea. After 24 hours they might have reviewed their attitude.'

Not two hours later, their heavy tread up the stairs told me the FitzGarratts had changed not.

Dad and Uncle Syd's eyes confirmed it. And their terse unwillingness to tell us what had been said left my imagination working busily. The fact was the FitzGarratts were excluding me. They had shut me out of Maria's life in her death.

Noticeable omissions

The death notices for Maria and Catharine in the *Evening Herald* ran for more than two columns.

Maria Goretti FitzGarratt was the Dearly Loved Youngest Daughter of Mr Peirse, OBE, and Professor Órla FitzGarratt, OBE.

She was the Dearly Loved Sister and Sister-in-Law of her brothers and brothers-in-law and of her sisters and sisters-in-law.

Annette was not mentioned.

Maria was the Much-Loved Aunt of her nieces including the late Catharine, and nephews, every one named. Except Claudia.

Maria was merely Granddaughter of Mrs Anne FitzGarratt, Catharine was her Very Much Loved and Treasured Great-Granddaughter. And so on.

'In her 18th year. *Requiescat in Pace.*'

The requiem Mass was set for 1pm on Wednesday.

Her siblings posted their own, separate, family notices for her and for Catharine.

Matthew's notice for Maria was different from the others. As well as being Loved Youngest Sister of Matthew FitzGarratt, QC, and Kay FitzGarratt, Maria was A Loved Aunt of the Late Catharine, and of Jacqueline and Anne, and Francis. Then: 'Loved Close Friend of Martin Blake.' And: 'Loved Sister of Dr Annette FitzGarratt-Kroeger, of

Hamburg, West Germany, and Aunt of Claudia FitzGarratt, Also of Hamburg, West Germany.'

To the rest of the FitzGarratts I was non-existent.

But thanks, Matt.

THE *EVENING Herald* had made Maria and Catharine a front page story, concentrating on the court appearance that morning of the driver. He had been charged with careless use of a motor vehicle causing death, dangerous driving, exceeding the speed limit in a 30mph area, and of being under the influence of alcohol. He was remanded without plea. His lawyer had got his name suppressed.

Two days later his younger sister found him dead in the garage. The police said 'there were no suspicious circumstances', which was code for he hanged himself. He was 17.

Mysteries of the rosary

The rosary was to be recited at the cathedral the night before the funeral. I turned to Magdalena. 'What's the rosary for?'

'Now you ask, I don't know. Tradition, I suppose.' She shrugged.

'You're the resident Catholic among us.'

Her second shrug was of the sort you associate with the French. An expressive 'I don't know'.

'I haven't had a lot to do with the Church for a while, Martin.'

Uncle Syd laughed.

'I have rosary beads somewhere at home,' Magdalena said.

Anyway, we were all going. I took Maria's, which she had left strung on her Mary statue's arms. They'd been made out of amber, the beads linked with a gold chain; a golden Jesus was nailed to an ornate wooden cross.

The FitzGarratts gave us another foretaste of what we could expect from them as we mounted the steps to enter the cathedral.

Three of Maria's sisters – or sisters-in-law – and a male were greeting people with hugs and cheesy, tearful smiles at the door. They found reasons to be distracted as we passed them.

We paused as Sue and Magdalena dipped their fingers into a fount of water, and made the sign of the cross. Because they did, and because

Maria used to do it when she went into a church, I did, too. And all the others behind me followed.

The two coffins – side-by-side, polished and each topped with flowers – had been rolled on their trolleys into position in front of the altar. The sight of them dominated my attention.

As we filed up the aisle, me leading, several FitzGarratt heads turned, and there was whispering and nodding, and I didn't like the sight nor feel of that. FitzGarratt men – Matt was noticeably absent – formed a barrier across the aisle near the front.

It was also clear that they had commandeered the front pews either side of the coffins – a signboard said in chalk: 'Members of the FitzGarratt Family and Relatives only, please.'

Black bows fastened to the side of the first four rows reinforced the point. Our group stopped in front of the FitzGarratts. Mark, and with him Joe, the muscular Irishman built like a prop, married to Tessa. I vaguely knew others. There were eight. Brothers-in-law, cousins, maybe.

'What's going on, Mark?' I said, just above a whisper.

'It's quite clear what's going on, Mr Blake. This is far as you and your party go.'

Joe the muscular Irishman flexed his shoulders, and some of the others did, too. They looked like rugby players, and probably not averse to a bit of physical rough-and-tumble.

'But –'

'Mr Blake, I do appreciate that you *feel* you should be here and that you *feel* you should be part of the proceedings. Well, you're not, and this point was made to these gentlemen,' and he indicated Dad and Uncle Syd, 'when they turned up yesterday unannounced and uninvited at our parents' house.'

I was about to say something … what? I don't remember now, my brain slipped a cog.

Joe the Irishman, with his greasy, toothy smile that never made it to his eyes, took over. 'Look, *Marr*-tin. T'ere are plenty of other seats you and yer friends can go and sit in. We don' mind t'at. We oondistand you had a leetle t'ing goin' with Maria.' Distaste for our 't'ing' crawled across his face. 'O-*Kay*. But we're hor fam'ly – and so was Catharine, let's not forget hor – and it's our *sad responsibil'ty* as their family to farewell them as we see fit. So –'

'We were in love! It was not a thing!' I said, too loudly, and I heard that echoing out into the still largely empty cathedral.

'Is there something I can help with?'

The question came out of nowhere, and everyone turned to its source. If he wasn't in the black cassock with roman collar of a Catholic priest you would have thought he was a genial little garden gnome – or leprechaun. He was smiling carefully.

Well, his lips were, prompting an irreverent thought: *Do these Catholics smile only with their lips?*

Mark turned on charm. 'Oh, hi, Pat. We're just sorting out a little matter here.'

He was verbally showing off who owned some turf here. *I know this priest by his first name, see? We're FitzGarratts and we can do that. We're always able to get our own way because we have money, status, and We Know The Right People. The archbishop is our friend.*

'Oh, yes?'

'Yes. Mr Blake, here, was Maria's, er, boyfriend. And he and his party have expressed their wish to sit in the front pews over there, which have been reserved for our family and special friends and guests. Next to her and Catharine's caskets.'

'I see,' the little priest said blandly – perhaps a little too blandly.

'Yes, my brother-in-law Joe and I have just been explaining to them that that's out of the question.' Then in a practised tone of smiling, apologetic reasonableness, he gestured wide. 'There are plenty of seats elsewhere here available to them. We were just explaining that to them.' *See? We're reasonable people, really.*

The gnome's smile contracted, and he glanced at me. In that glance I saw a shrewd little man. He stepped back, swiftly took in the reserved pews, the coffins, the rest of the church, which was rapidly filling up.

'Mark,' he said, the smile gone now. 'Who gave you permission that you could reserve pews in my church? Who did you ask?'

'Well, my brother Luke said –'

'Luke did. I don't recall your brother Luke coming and asking me if he could do that.'

Mark shuffled uncomfortably, and he glanced uncertainly at Joe, then elsewhere, reluctantly back at the Irish gnome.

'Mons, we just assumed he had. If –'

'You're a lawyer. You're trained never to assume. May I remind you, Mr FitzGarratt, *aaand* your family, particularly your brother, that I am dean of this cathedral. This is my bailiwick.'

'Yes, but –'

'Yes but nutt'n', Sor. Nobody sets asoide seatin' for t'emselves an' to the ex-cloo-sion of others in my cat'edral without my say-so. T'at includes yer brother. An' it includes the archbishop.'

'Jesus, that's sat them down,' Uncle Syd breathed.

In effect dismissing them, the gnome turned to me. 'Are you Martin?' He spoke kindly, and stuck out his hand, which I shook. He had a firm grip. 'Monsignor Greggorie, Martin. My condolences to ye. Follow me, please.'

Without a second look at the FitzGarratts he trotted ahead of us down to the front pews. Maria's coffin was right there, on the left, varnished, fragrant wood, topped by a gleaming, metal crucifix and nameplate, as well as the bunch of flowers.

While Monsignor Greggorie issued instructions about removing the black bows, to the hushed, livid protests of the FitzGarratts, my family, friends and I surrounded the coffin, resting our hands on it.

Magdalena crossed herself. Sue followed.

My well of tears had refilled; I broke into more sobs, and my tears splashed heavily on to the polished surface. To the obvious chagrin of the FitzGarratts nearby I whispered between my sobs how much I loved her, and all the other things a grieving lover says to a beloved who's never coming back.

I kissed her polished nameplate, and Dad and Uncle Syd led me back to the front pew just before the rosary got under way.

Luke and Monsignor Uncle Brian led it, alternating the decades of the 'Glorious Mysteries'. I didn't understand any of that, but I'd been with

Maria long enough to know how to say 'Holy Mary, Mother of God …', and to recite the 'O Remember O Most Loving Virgin Mary …'

The recitations ended and an altar boy handed Luke a censer.

This was a metal container, like a bowl but with slots, suspended on chains. Hot coals were inside. Luke spooned incense on to them. Smoke plumed from it. He strode down to the coffins and swung the bowl backwards and forwards over them. It clanked against its chains, exhaling clouds of acrid but aromatic smoke that began infiltrating to all the corners of the cathedral. Uncle Brian followed and threw droplets of water over the coffins.

The cathedral emptied out. The FitzGarratts and the Blakes went their separate ways, ignoring the other.

'For religious people they are pretty ugly, aren't they?' my schoolboy cousin Heremia said.

That's for sure. How had Maria managed to turn out so differently?

Funeral acts

The archbishop celebrated the requiem Mass.

Luke, Uncle Brian, Monsignor Greggorie and a couple of elderly priests assisted. Maria had once explained to me that having several celebrants on the altar was called a concelebrated Mass. Most of the concelebrating was left to Luke and Uncle Brian except at the Eucharist. That seemed to be the archbishop's job.

Luke did the eulogy. His rotund, ringing declarations expressed his grief 'on behalf of my family' for the fate that had befallen 'my deeply loved, treasured and irreplaceable youngest sister Maria,' and for his 'much admired niece Catharine, my parents' oldest grandchild.'

He extolled their virtues and achievements and all their other good qualities.

Luke was doing a performance. In a week or so a Catholic weekly would report admiringly how 'Father Luke FitzGarratt had steeled himself for the unenviable, heart-breaking task of presiding with dignity over the funeral for his much-loved youngest sister, Maria, and their niece Catharine'.

I thought *bullshit!* when it was shown to me. The last time he'd spoken to Maria he'd called her a trollop and threatened her with hellfire.

LUKE RETURNED to his chair and sat with a theatrical gathering of his robes. The cathedral was silent, but for a cough, a baby's cry, a rustling of paper.

Monsignor Uncle Brian rose from his chair, which was on the left side of the archbishop's throne. He strode heavily without hurry across the width of the altar, genuflecting to the tabernacle as he did so, to the lectern.

Going by the archbishop's glance, Brian's action was unexpected. He was breaking with the order of the service.

Luke had a 'what the –?' expression.

Brian gripped the sides of the lectern and leaned down to the microphone. 'Many of you will no doubt be aware,' he said, relaxed voice gliding over the congregation, 'that my niece Maria had a close friend in her life these past few months.'

Luke's cheeks mottled red with fury and he made to get up. The archbishop lifted a restraining finger: the merest gesture containing the full force of all his ecclesiastical authority.

The atmosphere in the cathedral tensed. Everybody knew Maria had been living with me. But the FitzGarratts had been trying to airbrush that for the sake of appearances.

'Maria's friend is Martin,' Brian's voice ambled on, unconcerned at the ruffling of sensibilities he was unleashing in the FitzGarratts' pews across the aisle from me.

'He is here today, as he would be, since Maria and he loved one another. And I can assure you, my dear people, that they did, for they came to my parish church every Sunday to attend Mass. I gave them both communion every time.'

I could hear whispering behind me, and all around me, a shuffling on varnished pews, and I felt as if a thousand pairs of eyes were trained on me – or on the crosshairs that I imagined were on my back. I glanced at Luke: his eyes bulged hate. His lips were clamped hard trying to contain it.

'My dear people, it is appropriate, I feel,' – and the velvet timbre carried the slightest hint of steel, since he was possibly challenging his boss and he was kicking his family's feelings in the shins – 'that Martin should be given the opportunity to say a few words about Maria … if he wishes.'

He turned to me. 'Martin? Would you like to come up and say a few words?'

Jesus!

'Christ, now he's done it,' Uncle Syd muttered. Over on the other side of the aisle much the same oathy sentiments were being whispered behind hands.

But manners, you see, won out. They were in their church, their holy of holies. They would keep up their churchy faces and manners until later. Then the knives would be out, glinting in the sun, poised for the best time to plunge. They would not forgive him nor the other monsignor, Patric Greggorie.

Brian moved aside from the lectern. He was smiling, beckoning and nodding to me. So was Monsignor Greggorie, from his seat this side of Luke's. The archbishop sat impassively, letting things play.

I felt Dad nudge me to my feet, and my mind was blank – utterly, utterly blank – as I slowly walked past Maria's coffin, and I bent over and kissed its cold, hard surface. My legs felt like stone as I mounted the steps.

Brian took my arm, and he motioned to the lectern. He was smiling reassuringly.

As he guided me into position I knew then what I wanted to do. The Bible was still open on the lectern. Mrs Barlow had once read to us a passage that she said was what Heaven would be like. Thirteen or 14 years later I knew what it was and where it would be.

As I flipped over the pages to get to the passage three things happened almost at once.

Dad joined me on the altar, and he and Monsignor Uncle Brian flanked me, each a hand on my shoulders.

A tall, pencil-slim figure rose from her seat among her relatives, approached the altar, and skipped up the altar steps, her chin set, her red-rimmed eyes ablaze with an 'I don't care' defiance. Gabrielle. Whispers out there in the pews. A wry smile by Matt. She smiled tearfully and bravely, and took my hand in her own bony grip, and squeezed hard. It was just like her aunt would have done.

I found the place and the reading I wanted. And, somehow, the third thing: I felt what I can only describe was a presence. I almost looked around, because I half-expected to see Maria there, amused. A warmth and a strength flowed through me. It was one of those moments that you just know will be right.

Anyway, a quick glance at the hundreds of faces down in the church. Many seemed politely curious.

The FitzGarratts' eyes were like massed daggers. Grannie Annie's glittered a bright, penetrating hate. The 12 year-old Gabrielle would pay dearly for her act of kindness, there was no doubt about that. Her parents' glares and her odious twin's smirk prophesied it. I couldn't see Órla's expression. Her head was down, the brim of her hat hiding her face.

'This reading is from *The Book of Revelation to John*. Chapter 21,' and I heard my amplified words loft through the rafters to the far doors. I read: 'Then I saw a new heaven and a new earth; for the first heaven and the first earth passed away, and there is no longer any sea.

'And I saw the holy city, new Jerusalem, coming down out of heaven from God, made ready as a bride adorned for her husband.

'And I heard a loud voice from the throne, saying, "Behold, the tabernacle of God is among men, and He will dwell among them, and they shall be His people, and God Himself will be among them."'

My voice wobbled and caught, and I had to clear my throat for verse 4:

'and he will wipe away every tear from their eyes; and there will no longer be any death; there will no longer be any mourning, or crying, or pain; the first things have passed away.'

In the silence I heard Uncle Brian say softly: 'Good man.' Dad patted my shoulder. Gabrielle planted a quick kiss on my cheek.

Dazed, I heard myself say next: 'I remembered this passage, which Mrs Barlow read to us once at Sunday school. When I was maybe 9 or 10. She said it was a picture of Paradise.'

What was I to say next? 'I'm not religious, although I was known to say a Hail Mary or two with Maria. But it seems to me that passage there was God saying Maria is in Paradise with him. '

I saw smiles out there in the body of the church, particularly in the ranks of the schoolgirls.

'I hope so.'

Gabrielle turned, and with a sob hugged me.

Auntie Kura rose regally and initiated a *waiata tangi*. Tears washed down her cheeks. Her hands fluttered at her side, an action known as *wiri*, as her streaming, flowing lament ascended effortlessly to the high-beamed roof of the cathedral and hovered above the hundreds of mourners. Mihi stood and added her voice. From elsewhere in the church another woman's voice; and then another and another, until they were a harmonious, spine-shivering chorus gripping hundreds of people in its spell.

IN THIS account I have portrayed Archbishop Raymond Boyce cynically. I could never see what I imagined was the Jesus in him. But I have to give him credit here. As my aunt and cousin led the tributes to Maria and Catharine and bade their spirits farewell he shut up an enraged Luke with a single, icy, manhood-shrivelling stare. He let the *waiata* flow on, which it did for several eerie minutes. Mourners sobbed, among them Maria's mother. Peirse stared fixedly ahead. Not once did he put his arm around his wife's shoulders to offer her comfort. My eyes blurred with more tears, and for her: how could he not do that?

The archbishop waited for nearly a minute after the *waiata* died into the silence before standing decisively. Clearly affected by what he had heard, he simply said, his voice husky: 'Thank you, ladies. I've never heard anything so powerful.' He cleared his throat, 'So poignant …'

The Mass resumed.

AT HOLY communion Uncle Brian showed his independence again. The FitzGarratts were the first to go up. He instead stood apart from the archbishop and Luke, and indicated to me that I could go up, too. I hesitated. Behind me, Magdalena and Sue Devonshire nudged me to my feet and we three filed up and received communion from him.

Maria and Catharine were carried from the cathedral by their male relatives. The cortege wound through the city to the cemetery and to the freshly dug graves that awaited them.

Monsignor Uncle Brian intervened again so that after Peirse and Órla had led mourners in tossing earth on to Maria's coffin I was next.

Uncle Brian was making a lot of enemies among his relatives that day.

In the mingling at the graveside Órla and I found ourselves face-to-face. It was only a moment: in the depths of her eyes I saw not only the inexpressible sadness of a mother who had lost her child, but something else: a resigned, shattering defeat.

I whispered: 'I'm sorry, Órla.' She extended a small, black-gloved hand to my cheek, smiled, and murmured, 'thank you, Martin. I'm sorry for you, too.'

Her son-in-law Joe ignored me as he took her arm, and she meekly let him lead her away. I never saw her again.

Clothes raid

They came at 10 o'clock on the Saturday morning after the funeral. There was the characteristic FitzGarratt commanding knock on my door. Four of them – Tessa, in front, now the youngest, switched on her smile.

'Hi, Martin,' she breezed, 'we've come to discuss with you a rather sensitive matter.'

'I know you, Tessa, but who are they?'

Something like an invisible shutter slotted down over her eyes. But the practised smile remained. 'Oh, yes, of course.' She turned: 'These are my sisters Gemma, Elizabeth, and Rosemary.'

They didn't bother with the hypocrisy of smiles. Gemma was another lawyer, Elizabeth was an economist and Luke's twin – they shared the same icy blue eyes – and Rosemary was a historian.

'Thank you. What can I do for you?'

'Couldn't we perhaps go inside, Martin, and discuss this?' Elizabeth pressed.

'Not until you tell me what you want.'

Tessa smiled sweetly. 'All right,' and she brandished an envelope.

I opened it, and, in this case the cliché is true about blood running cold. Mine did. That's how it felt, anyway. The letter was from the FitzGarratts' lawyers – signed by a QC. It demanded that I return to the

FitzGarratt family 'all personal possessions and property owned by the late Maria Goretti FitzGarratt, lately of your address, at that address'. It cited this law, that law, section this, section that, sub-section (this), and of course (part that) notwithstanding.

'You can't do this,' I said.

Oh, these women knew they could. Doing little to control her cat-like smugness Gemma said: 'The law says we can.'

'And three of us here have law degrees, so we're pretty sure of our ground,' Elizabeth added.

'We could go and get a court order, if you like,' Rosemary said helpfully, her big, round sunglasses perched jauntily on her head.

'The point is, Martin,' Tessa said, 'Maria was a minor. So even though she was old enough to leave home – get married even, but she didn't – the fact is she died intestate.'

'So her property returns to us, as spelt out by law,' Gemma said.

That seemed to be that.

I nearly invited them in when: 'Now, if you don't mind, we'll just go and get her belongings,' Rosemary said smoothly.

I noticed then the suitcases they'd brought. And she made to elbow her way past me.

I stepped back, held my arm out across the doorway. 'Excuse me. This is my home. As I understand the law – and you may correct me if you like – you'd be trespassing if you entered here without my permission, right?'

'Er, yes,' Tessa said. 'Technically.'

'There's no 'technically' about it. I am the occupier. I give the permission. And I haven't yet.'

'But we're here to have our property returned,' Rosemary said crossly. 'You have to co-operate.'

I held up their letter so they could all see it. I pointed to '… return to the FitzGarratt family …'

'That means only that I have to give back to you what was Maria's.'

Now I felt a malicious pleasure, which I did little to conceal. 'It says nothing about that I have to let you into my home and rummage around in it for what you want. 'Return' means that I give it back to you.'

They hadn't expected that. 'But –' Gemma began.

'Be back here at 2 o'clock. I'll have her things packed and ready for you to pick up.'

'That's not convenient nor satisfactory,' Rosemary snapped.

'Too bad.'

I began to shut the door. 'You may leave your suitcases. I'll have them ready for you at 2 o'clock.'

Four pairs of eyes, four pairs of laser-focused hate.

'Your choice,' I said.

'Ok, Martin,' Tessa said as if she was granting me a favour. 'Two o'clock.'

AUNTIE KOO and Mihi arrived perhaps 20 minutes later. They found me tearful in the bedroom surrounded by the suitcases. I hadn't even started. I told them what had happened. Mihi demanded to know why I hadn't talked to a lawyer.

'I did,' I replied. 'There were four of them.'

'I mean an independent one, silly.'

I shrugged. I didn't care any more. As it happened, Maria's clothes would have to go eventually. I somehow knew that. It's just that I wasn't ready for them to go *now*. Mihi and her mother had arrived at the same conclusion, but sooner than me.

On Thursday she and Auntie Koo had tactfully drawn me aside, and with some discreet throat-clearing told me that that day was nearly soon. Pointing to the laundry basket Mihi told me that there were items of Maria's 'that really must be washed'. Her mother nodded, in the way that women do when they understand things males don't. The scents, fragrances, aromas of Maria were everywhere – in our bed, in her clothes in the wardrobe and in the drawers. Her invisible presence was still here. I acquiesced, but had refused to let them wash the bedding. She was still there.

So now they were preparing to put eight months of Maria's life with me into suitcases. They set to it. I watched as drawers were yanked open and Maria's knickers, bras, slips, tights, socks – everything neatly folded, disappeared by the arms-full into her sisters' suitcases. Her dresses and pants and coats and jackets and blouses were taken from the wardrobe, carefully and lovingly folded, and almost reverently placed in the suitcases. My few things left on their hangers made it look bare.

'Martin,' Auntie Koo said gently, taking my arm and guiding me tactfully towards the lounge, 'why don't you get together Maria's schoolwork. I imagine they'll want that, too.'

No, I hadn't thought of that. Of course they bloody would. They were hyenas, those people. I got Robert to help me sort out her stuff. 'This won't be of much used to them, mate,' he said, his top lip quivering.

'I know. It doesn't matter. They just want to hurt and humiliate me as much they can.'

THEY RETURNED at 2 o'clock, on the dot, and with their customary, peremptory knock on the door. The bags, and two more of Maria's that she brought with her when she moved in with me, were packed and waiting by the door. Auntie Kura opened the door for them and invited them in.

Then the trouble started.

Object war

While Tessa scanned Mihi's typed list Rosemary, the historian, said suddenly: 'We're taking that, too.'

We all spun about. She was pointing at the statue of Mary still on my chest of drawers.

About 12 inches high, plaster of Paris, a statue. An object. I dug my heels in twice that day. Mary, whom Maria always called 'Our Lady', was important to her. She prayed before it, and to the one in the cathedral, too.

'Yes, that's coming, too,' Gemma said briskly, and she started for my bedroom.

Mihi blocked her – 'You don't have permission to go in there, lady' – giving me time to grab it. Another couple of paces and I was by the open window. 'This was an important part of her that you're *not* going to have.'

That startled them. 'I'm not a Catholic. I don't care. I will drop this three storeys to the footpath so that it smashes rather than give it to you.'

'You can't do that! It was blessed by the Pope himself in Rome many years ago,' Elizabeth shouted, her eyes wild with horror.

I didn't give a rat's arse about that. This was a part of Maria they weren't going to have.

Tessa tried to be placatory. 'All right, Martin, I think we can make this concession. We're not unreasonable.' She smiled fakely. All teeth, hard eyes.

'But the rosary beads there,' she said, pointing at them curled on my bed beside their velvet-lined box, 'we should have those, though. You're not a Catholic, so they're of no use to you.'

'Strictly speaking they weren't Maria's, either,' Rosemary said. 'They were blessed by a cardinal at Lourdes and given to one of our uncles there. Brian. She sort of took them over when she was about 9 or 10.'

Elizabeth put out her hand for them. So they had been Brian's. Or given to him. It seemed to me that he might want me to have them more than he wanted these awful people to.

'May I have them?' Elizabeth demanded.

'No.'

'You are in breach of the law,' Gemma shouted.

'We'll see. Shall I phone Uncle Brian and ask him what he wants done with them?'

They faltered.

'I would rather rip them apart than let you get your hands on them,' I snarled. 'I'll go to jail rather than let you have these.'

Destruction of rosary beads – and a statue of Mary – was evidently too much to contemplate for these four Catholic women and their many degrees.

I'd had enough. 'I want you to leave now. Take the suitcases and just fucking go. You people make me sick. Your youngest sister was so unlike you.'

So, they struggled out the door with the heavy bags, and down the stairs, to their cars. Neither Robert, Mihi, Auntie Kura nor I lifted a finger to help them.

A laid egg crushed

Maria was pregnant.

'I was able to get hold of this,' Trevor Clifton said, passing me a yellow envelope. It was a copy of the report from the autopsy on Maria.

In New Zealand an autopsy is an examination by a pathologist on a corpse to determine cause of death.

Precise medical language described Maria's fatal injuries in painstaking, excruciating, detached detail. Too detached, too dry for me.

In plain words then: in one swift, brutally violent moment an accelerating, speeding car had hurled Maria 20 metres against a brick wall.

Her skull broke open like an egg. Extensive brain damage. An eye popped from its socket. Her jaw shattered. Teeth broken and dislodged. Her neck snapped. Broken ribs and spine. Crushed pelvis. Multiple leg-breaks. A broken arm. 'Massive organ trauma.' Ruptures. Extensive blood loss.

'Miss FitzGarratt could not have survived these injuries,' the pathologist wrote. 'In my opinion death was instantaneous.'

Dear God, I hoped so. The detail left me numb. I could not cope with what I had just read and processed.

He'd picked and probed through the mangled wreckage of her remains, which was his job. He had recorded 'a residue of semen' in her body.

I felt sick. *What did that have to do with her cause of death?*

Maria would have hated that being held up for public view, as it would be in a Coroner's Court hearing. It invaded her intimacy and modesty and our privacy. Our last time that morning and she hadn't wanted me to go to work. I thought the pathologist had made it sound sordid. It wasn't. We loved each other. It was the last time I would hold her. I would have done anything for a Head Girl Stare right now.

Anyway, the big news …

The pathologist noted an 'embryo of perhaps seven weeks' gestation'. In her words, her body had 'laid an egg'; I suppose it had to happen eventually. Had she known?

I sat staring vacantly across the newsroom. Happy and sad in a tired kind of way. For a few weeks I was a father of an embryo. Now … When had it happened? Was it when her mother fled our flat after Maria went at her and I calmed her down and we tumbled into bed leaving the dishes undone?

Trevor had smoked another cigarette as I read the report.

'How did you get hold of this?'

He smiled, his eyes squinting craftily, and he tapped the side of his nose. 'It's not what you know, boy, but who you know.'

He fished out another Pall Mall, and lit it. 'I've spared you the photos, Martin.'

He had seen her then? He ignored the question in my eyes.

'Mate, this will be produced at the Coroner's Court. You won't get a copy of this because you're not deemed family.'

Christ.

'She was pregnant, Trevor.'

His eyebrows lifted, and he dragged on the smoke.

'Perhaps seven weeks along.'

'I'm sorry to hear that, Martin.'

He crunched out the cigarette. 'I've gotta run, Martin. The bit about Maria being pregnant will be a headline from the Coroner's Court. Best you're prepared for that.'

He clapped his hand on my shoulder, gave it a squeeze, and was gone.

Years later I would find out via Google that the 'embryo' – our child – would have been the size of a bean.

And yes, he was right about the headline. The tabloid weekly *Truth*'s story – not front page, that was reserved for a politician caught out by a private investigator and photographer with his trousers off in the bedroom of a woman not his wife but someone else's – was on an inside page and headlined:

REBEL CATHOLIC SCHOOL HEAD GIRL, 17, DIED KNOCKED-UP!

It was from evidence given at the Coroner's Court hearing, which essentially was held to inquire into how Maria and Catharine had died, and report it.

Truth unfolded a breathlessly colourful story of Maria and me. It emphasised the prominence and social respectability of the FitzGarratts – Peirse 'OBE, a respected Catholic doctor involved in causes such as abortion and contraception, of which he has been an outspoken opponent'; Órla, 'OBE, a brilliant academic also deeply involved in Catholic and conservative social causes. Mother of 14. Maria was youngest.'

It went on to enumerate them and their achievements, and their Catholic-ness.

Which set the scene for what came next. Maria had been 'head prefect at Our Lady of The Immaculate Conception College – a leading Catholic girls' school – until she had to hand in her badge and leave the school in disgrace' because she had moved in with me.

I was '24, six years older than 17 year-old Maria and a sub-editor on the *Evening Herald* newspaper. Sources say she was infatuated with him and the family was very concerned about her.'

There was a photo of her and me, taken at a work barbecue we'd gone to … when? I think after we'd come back from Hawai'i. Media people from all over the city had been there. She and I were talking to someone, and smiling. She looked so grown-up.

Postscript

I had to move on, as the cliché goes.

I'd come to hate the flat. Maria had been everywhere but nowhere. In the days and weeks afterwards the smell of her lingered in the bedclothes, but that had faded.

One day as I was vacuuming under the cushions of the couch I found one of her hair ties with strands of her hair in it. I stopped what I was doing, held it in my hand.

I wondered how it had got there; she had controlled such things. She was fussy. And I burst into tears and wound my finger through it. I could smell her still. It was part of her with me that wasn't in a cold, polished, wooden box buried in six feet of earth. But in the end it had to go, and I let the vacuum-cleaner swallow it in a roar of air. Another part of her gone forever.

Maria was always in my dreams. In those dreams she was smiling at me, chiding me, her eyes alight with love. Then the disturbing ones: she was in bed with me, kissing me awake along my shoulders; her lips soft and hard against mine and her tongue probing my mouth, she was taking my hand and resting it on her breast.

Those dreams were heart-breaking because I woke up and she wasn't there after all. It was like torture.

At the table in the lounge Maria was hammering out an assignment on the Hermes 3000. Out of the corner of my eye – always just out the corner of my eye – she was emerging from the shower pink, glistening droplets and tangled hair slick, steam curling off her. Or she was telling Dante what a beautiful boy he was; he, of course, with his eyes closed and a pleased grin, agreed. But he wouldn't come back into the flat now.

In the end it was the items often most personal and necessary to a woman that did it. I had forgotten about the contents of her bottom drawer in the bathroom. Or perhaps I just hadn't wanted to think about them. Pretended they weren't there. Anyway, I was rummaging through the drawers because I thought I had another packet of razor blades somewhere. Her tampons and pads were still there, never to be used by her. I sank to the floor, holding them to my cheeks, and once again I was a river of tears. It and the *Truth* story – 'knocked up', for fuck's sake – tipped me over the edge. I handed in my notice next day.

Barnfield didn't hesitate. 'You're doing the right thing, Martin. You need to get out of here for a while.' Then he fished into a drawer in his desk, and tossed an envelope across to me. 'Martin, for many years – close to a century, I suppose – this company has always had a funeral fund. It helps company employees with their funeral costs or those of their families.'

I fingered the envelope carefully.

'Mate, strictly speaking, you don't qualify because Maria wasn't your actual family nor were you on staff long enough.'

He picked up a Parker pen, and twiddled it between his fingers. 'But I have to tell you I and some others around here – including the paper's owners who've known the FitzGarratts for years – were sickened by how her family treated you after she died.'

I swallowed. *Please don't let me cry again ...*

'Yeah, they paid for her funeral, and that of her niece. So what's in there isn't for that. You've been a good bloke, a good sub, and many of us here liked how you cared about Maria. You deserved better from them.'

He sat back in his chair; a long sigh. 'I've known this day would come, mate. So I've had it sitting in the drawer, waiting for the day when you'd come and tell me you were moving on.'

He stood, and leaned forward to shake hands with me. 'It'll help you get to wherever you want to go.'

I opened the envelope back at my desk. There was a cheque for $1200.

I had a month to work out my notice. One day, walking home from work, I sighted Gabrielle among a group of girls from Our Lady of The Immaculate Conception College on the other side of the street. She saw me, smiled brightly, offered a fluttering little wave, and hurried on in her crisp, brand-new uniform.

The day before I finished up Wilson Barker waddled over to my desk, cigarette smoke swirling after him. 'You got anything in mind jobwise, sport? Know where you're going?'

I told him I hadn't. He pulled a sheet of paper from an ink-stained pocket of his shirt and handed it to me.

'The wife's brother-in-law is editor of a small country newspaper in S'thafrica.' He waddled away: 'If yah ever head over that way you could look him up,' he said over his shoulder.

I hadn't expected that from him. The baiting of me had long stopped, replaced by a bluff kindness and respect. I spent the weekend cleaning out the flat. Robert and Alice helped. Dante worried Robert. 'His heart's broken, Martin,' he said.

Two large Samoan men from the church mission shop I was donating the furniture back to came up and cheerfully hefted it all away: the table, the chairs, the armchairs, the couch, the chest of drawers, the bed. Robert took the bookshelf. He needed another one.

There was a discussion over the statue of Mary. I didn't know what do with the statue now. I didn't want to carry it around with me. I didn't want it to go off to the shop, either. I thought of Uncle Brian. Alice said she'd like to have it.

'I didn't know you were a Catholic, Alice.'

'I'm not, love, although I have relations who are.'

She picked up the statue, hefting it in her hands. 'I was very fond of that girl, Martin, as you know. One of the things I liked about her was that she still prayed, and had someone to pray to.' Her voice had caught, and so she paused. 'I'd like her because she will remind me of Maria and you and because I will look after her for you should you ever want her back.'

I gave her a long, close hug. It was settled. And with that I took one last look around the flat. I thought I sensed Maria's spirit.

But no. She was irrevocably gone.

Magdalena and Peter were putting me up for a couple of nights. Magdalena and I went to Mass at Brian's church. It was our last Mass there for Brian and me. The archbishop had sent him off to a remote but well-off rural parish 200 miles away. The congregation all wept with him at the end.

'It's an exile, Martin,' he said later amid his belongings in his presbytery. 'I've been a bit too progressive and down-to-earth for His Grace's liking, and not laying down the Law like a good priest should. My replacement is coming in to straighten them out.'

I told him about his nieces' demanding Maria's rosary beads back.

'I gave them to her at her confirmation,' he said. 'You keep them, Martin. You're not a Catholic, I know, but you believe, and you never tried to stop Maria from believing.'

I slowed as I drove past the cemetery where Maria was buried. It would have been the first time I'd been to her grave since the funeral. *No. Not now.*

THAT AFTERNOON Magdalena and Peter put up a 'Private Function Only' sign, and Alice and Robert and Sue Devonshire came around.

It was a long-delayed wake by people who had become friends. Magdalena brought out bottles of *Żytnia* vodka, and we knocked back toast after toast after toast – to Maria, to her memory, to her and me, to love, to friendship, to each other.

I noticed that the more he drank the more cut-glass English Robert became. Magdalena tearfully embraced him when he said: 'Magda, my dear, I flew with Poles during the war. Wonderful pilots and men.'

Something special among us all was ending.

I'D DECIDED that I would go to South Africa and look up Wilson Barker's wife's brother-in-law. Before that, though, I'd spend a week or so with Mum and Dad. I hadn't gone home to them for Christmas. Dad had understood. The meaning of Maria's death – the meaning of her life to me – had gone right past Mum.

I told him over the phone that Maria was pregnant when she died.

'I'm very, very sorry, son.' He had told Mum, he later told me, but he wouldn't say what her reaction was. She never made a comment. I never heard Mum mention Maria at all.

So, I drove 'home'. Mum wasn't well. The malady was undiagnosed, but its onset had coincided with Dad's retirement from the power board. He saw it as his duty to look after her. And he did. It was as if she had him on a chain.

After that I stayed a few days with Uncle Syd and Auntie Koo. He got me trolleyed, and she and I cried again over Maria.

I ARRIVED in Johannesburg from London the day after the 1976 All Blacks and took a bus to a pretty town in the province of Natal. Barker's brother-in-law Jeff James – 'I am Wilson's brother-in-law but I bet he told you I was his wife's' (it seemed to be a running family in-joke) – was an expat Kiwi.

'I never went back to New Zealand after the war.'

Yes, he could do with a sub, as it just so happened. He ignored Barnfield's reference. 'Wilson might be a bit of a blowharding Noddy, Martin, but he wouldn't have recommended you if you hadn't impressed him. That's good enough for me.'

I STAYED three years, the last as acting chief sub – 'acting' because the chief sub had been despatched to a sanatorium for alcoholics near Cape Town.

BOSS – the South African state secret police – took an excessive interest in a story the paper ran about 'subversives'. I'd thought the story was pretty harmless when I first read the copy, but Official South Africa didn't much like newspapers editors who showed too much independence.

Jeff seemed remarkably unperturbed. 'It seems we've broken a few of the 400-odd laws that restrict our free speech,' he said cheerfully.

A 2am visit to my rented cottage by three jug-eared Afrikaners whose necks were nearly as wide as their ox-like shoulders was disconcerting. They lacked a sense of humour except when they were inflicting pain on a black or 'a sickly *whaate* liberal' such to cause them to scream – the higher, the louder, the longer, the better.

They found me in bed with Tove, a raven-haired, well-developed Swede who had followed her man – son of a wealthy local farmer – back to South Africa. Only his father had liked her more than the son did. And the father was married.

It was all a bit complicated, and with Tove and me. My heart hadn't been in it, even despite her free-minded athleticism in the sexual act. 'Marty, I'm sorry, but I feel as if I'm competing with the ghost of your One Great Love. *Hej då.*' Which, apparently, means '*Adios*'. She was going back to Sweden anyway.

MUM WAS ill. Cancer in her spine. It had spread into her bowel, her womb, her ovaries, her liver, her bones. 'Marty, I think, if you can, come home. Mum would love to see you again,' Dad said on the line from New Zealand.

I didn't recognise Mum when I walked into their bedroom. She had wasted, reminding me of those dreadful photos of the emaciated dead and dying the Allies found in German concentration camps at the end of the war.

She kissed me warmly – if fraily – enough. Poor Mum. It did distress me to see her like this. She'd inflicted intense pain on me over her attitude to Maria. But she was my Mum, and so I loved her. I told myself, as Dad had told me, that she was a product of her time. She hadn't intended to be cruel. *So, I forgive you, Mum.*

Her voice had nearly gone, her eyes were large – and she was frightened. She needed, I suppose, someone like Monsignor Uncle Brian to bring her comfort and reassurance.

Instead she got The Venerable Peter Goldfinch, a portly, man's-man, ex-Australian Army padre who said and did all the right things with professional tact and efficiency.

I didn't like how he spoke to Dad as if he was a dumb Other Ranker. Dad pretended to ignore it, and he winked at me.

Mum and Dad wanted her to die in her own bed in her own home.

Dad and I had to do everything for Mum, changing and cleaning up after her because she had become incontinent. Dad treated her with a tender love, and I'm not sure she appreciated it because she hated not being in control. It brought to my mind again Maria. But for her I would never have got to know my father as I had three years ago.

Auntie Koo arrived to help. I wondered if it galled my mother that *that Maori* was speaking to her gently, lovingly, kissing her on the forehead or the cheek, wiping her bottom, putting on her nappy, and cleaning up her vomit – and then every morning gently brushing what remained of her hair and applying a little make-up to her sunken cheeks so that she looked nice.

'You're that beautiful girl again that caught Ralphie's eye, June,' she said. Mum did permit herself a smile.

Mum died at dawn. I held one hand, Dad her other. He kissed her on the forehead as she stepped out of her life with a last, long sigh. He was tearful and he patted her hand. Since I'd come back from South Africa I'd seen a side of Dad – thoughtful, gentle, considerate and sensitive – that I'd glimpsed only from when I picked up the phone that Friday night to hear him tell me he understood about Maria and me.

Archdeacon Goldfinch – I wanted to call him Goldfish because his mouth moved like one – presided over her funeral. He recited Mum's life from the typed notes I had written for him on the Hermes 3000.

I wanted to hit him because the bastard sounded so indifferent. My Mum was just another number to be done before lunch.

Dad wept, as he had done at Maria's funeral Mass.

Mum had wanted hymns that were 'uplifting' – *Jerusalem*, *Abide With Me*, *The 23rd Psalm*.

New ghosts, old faces

I entered the old block of flats, now tarted up with paints of red, yellow, and green, blue, white. Very fresh. I stopped at Alice's flat on the first floor. A haggard woman in her 20s with a baby staring grumpily at me from her arms answered the door. She didn't know Alice, and had no idea where she'd gone, and, 'If you'll excuse me I've got to get this little one down for her nap'. I could tell by the expression on its face that the 'little one' had no intention of napping.

Oh, dear. I followed the familiar stairs up to the top level. No-one answered my knock on Robert's door. But a woman in a dressing gown and dishevelled hair opened the door to what had been my old flat. She'd just woken up and had heard me knocking. She was a nurse, she said, and went on to tell me that Robert was in hospital, dying. She was chatty, and introduced herself as Gael. I said she was in my old flat, and she invited me in. I nearly did. But – I apologised. 'Too many ghosts and memories, I think.'

She smiled: 'You must be the guy Rob sometimes talked about, with the girl.' Anyway, she told me where to find Robert at the hospital.

He was napping in a small, sunny room he shared with three other men. All they had for privacy were the curtains that could be drawn around each bed. The room reeked of chemicals, disinfectant, decay, and the stench of creeping death.

Like my mother Robert, too, had shrunk. But his eyes were bright and lively in what was nearly the skeleton of his face. His brain was sharp. 'It's the chop for me, Martin. The Hun has caught up with me after all this time.' His voice was frail, almost misty.

Dante had lived only a few months after I left the flat. 'He had an animal's instinct for death. One night he crawled into bed with me – which he'd never done – and sometime in the night his broken little heart just stopped.'

And so that night did Robert's.

I CALLED in at the paper the next day. Clyde Barnfield had gone on to be foundation managing editor of a new Sunday paper. Malcolm Ogle had, apparently, been a surprise choice to succeed him. Despite the pressures on him he was warm and chatty. Barker had retired only a year earlier, but was writing for several racing publications. A practice known in the trade as 'ratting'.

'So many fecund and fertile daughters, so many grandchildren,' Ogle said, tamping his pipe. The truth was that Thelma Barker had told him he needn't think he was going to sit around all day doing nothing but getting under her feet. She understood her man: he had to be kept busy.

Trevor Clifton had died nine months after retiring. 'Poor bugger. He just didn't know what to do with himself. His daughter had gone to England. There was no-one else. He had nothing to do except drink and smoke and hang about here. Clyde tried to get him to write a book about his life as a police reporter, and at first he was up for it.' Ogle shook his head sadly. 'He wrote three or four chapters. Really good stuff. Then he stopped. One night he stepped out in front of a goods train.'

Sue Devonshire had set off on her Big OE. In London she had met a Canadian who worked for a news agency. They had married. Crikey. How things, times, people can change in a little over three years.

I called into Our Lady of The Immaculate Conception College. The awful Mrs MacClatchie still presided over her desk and an electric typewriter. She didn't recognise me, and chattily told me that Sister Hélène had been gone 'a long time'. She consulted another woman in the office. Yes, Hélène had been appointed to a university in Belgium. Margarethe had gone to America.

I'd lost touch with Magdalena and Peter. They'd sold the theatre and café only in the last 18 months, Robert said. They had returned to Europe, to France. Magdalena had written a brief note to say she was pregnant. Alice had shifted to Queensland. 'A bloke, Martin.'

His Honour Mr Justice FitzGarratt, QC, had only weeks earlier been appointed to the Supreme Court, soon to be known as the High Court. Matt had aged since I last saw him, at Maria and Catharine's funeral. His thinning hair had turned chalky.

'Just as well I wear that,' he said, indicating a full, shoulder-length wig on a mannequin's stand in his cluttered office. He had sunk into a plump middle age, and wasn't yet 50. He knew he was destined for the Court of Appeal in time, and a knighthood. You had to be a particularly bad judge not to get a knighthood. Judges loved their titles.

Matt had an hour to spare at his new chambers. He had forced himself 'to move on'. Kay hadn't, and suffered frequent bouts of depression. She was on tranquillisers.

Grannie Annie had suffered 'massive' strokes a year ago, and was a vegetable in a geriatric hospital. Órla and Peirse continued to live under the same roof, 'but Mum took over Maria's bedroom again'. So they lived separate lives, but keeping up appearances.

Removal men had turned up at her flat two days after her daughters had taken away Maria's things from me.

Luke had been posted to the Vatican and made a bishop. He had caught the eye of the new pope, the Polish-born Karol Wojtyla. 'There's a long Latin expression for it, I suppose, Martin, but basically he's a papal message-boy.'

Over the next few years, if you looked at TV footage of the Travelling Pope, Bishop Luke FitzGarratt would be if not at his shoulder then in the entourage. I saw him in the flesh in a cathedral a few years later when I was covering a papal visit. He was portly, bloated, which his sense of self-importance only emphasised, his face as hard as any politician's or tycoon's. Ugly little blue eyes behind rimless glasses watching and noting everything. Tight, mean little mouth. Then I remembered looking at the rest of the papal team: they were the same. Hard-looking men, men used to wheeling and dealing in power. *Does Jesus look like them?*

I asked about Gabrielle. He contemplated a pigeon strutting across the outside sill of his window. 'Biding her time, if you ask me, Martin. Mark and Margaret dealt to her pretty savagely for going up and standing with you on the altar. She's 16 now, and in the seventh form.'

Only a year earlier Mrs Kathleen Agnes O'Daly had nodded off to sleep in the office one warm afternoon. Only for an hour, as had become her wont. No-one would even consider objecting and she was never to be disturbed. She didn't wake up. She was 81. 'Been with the firm for 65 years, starting as an office junior. You know, Martin, we all called her Mrs O'Daly. We couldn't bring ourselves to do otherwise.'

ROBERT'S FUNERAL was a distraction that I welcomed. I attended it in a small, suburban Anglican church. Uncle Syd came, too.

Robert's coffin was open briefly before the service. He had been dressed in RAF uniform, and it looked very much part of him. His medals and crosses were pinned to his chest under his pilot's 'wings'. They had put in his hands a small, coloured photograph of him with Dante curled up on his lap.

Uncle Syd patted Robert on the cheek. 'Rest well, old man,' he murmured. Then he straightened to attention, and his right arm swung up a rigid, quivering salute.

'Not supposed to do that, indoors and out of uniform, but bugger it,' he muttered as we found a pew.

About two dozen people turned up to see Robert off. Gael, the nurse, sat with us. I recognised a couple of senior RNZAF officers. Uncle Syd knew them and chatted with them afterwards.

Two men spoke; Robert had flown with them during the war. He was, each said in his own way, 'a damned fine pilot and commander, a courageous man, and gentleman'.

Yes, he was. I wondered again: what had happened to Gerald? Where was he? Robert had never said what happened to him.

Where were Robert's family? No-one there. The vicar running the service had known the boy Robert – they'd been at boarding school together and he told gentle, funny stories. He was nothing like Goldfish. The sound system played the *Battle of Britain March*. It seemed the funeral perhaps harked back to when Robert felt valued for his deeds and heroism in the air and when he was not an outsider having to hide a secret. In the crisis of war his being a 'poof' – his word – hadn't mattered or a blind eye was turned to it.

An RNZAF air commodore read out messages and telegrams from all around the world: Oxford dons; presidents or deans of American Ivy League universities; professors in Europe; old comrades including a brace of air marshals of the Royal and Royal Australian air forces; a South African general Uncle Syd had also flown with; and an old foe, an ace of Hitler's *Luftwaffe*.

Soon his coffin was heading for the crematorium accompanied by the rousing *Aces High* march, which opened the movie *Battle of Britain*.

I said before that his funeral had been a distraction for me. Part of me wanted to follow the paths amid the headstones down to where Maria lay, 100 metres away. I couldn't do it. And now I had a distraction. Robert had given me some notes he'd made years ago for an obituary. 'I want you to write it, Martin.'

I did. Ogle thanked me, and ran it, and he paid me $50 for it. I rewrote it and sent the obit by airmail to a London daily. I knew that the war, Oxford scholar, yet another New Zealand squadron leader in the RAF, and the DSO and DFCs would guarantee it a run. They paid me £50 for it.

And beyond

I resumed life. For the next 15 years I worked different jobs – an aviation periodical in the UK, an international wire service, newspapers. There were women. As Uncle Syd would say, I ploughed many furrows. I don't mean that in the sense of boasting, man-of-the-world triumphalism. Often it was nothing more than self-serving I used them, they used me. Some of it was unedifying.

In hindsight I could not find someone who filled the hole Maria had left.

Except Jock, and I blew it.

She was baptised Johanna Odette Katrin, the daughter of a German mother who died early and a British Army officer-turned-tweed-suited, knotted tie and waistcoated gentleman farmer. I could never imagine a brawny, hairy-armed Kiwi farmer going to work with a tie around his neck. She took me to meet him. 'Dads' – his name was Hilary – was a caricature of a British officer: upright, chin up, shoulders back, ramrod for a spine, pencil-thin moustache, barking, clipped manner of speaking.

He liked me straight away. 'Ah. Kiwi. Eh? Hmm. Veddy good. New Zealanders excellent soldiers. *Finest* chaps in the world. Could have done with more of them.'

Father and daughter adored each other.

I liked him because the caricature was blatant self-parody. It had to be. When Hilary was widowed Jock was 4. Instead of farming her out to carers and boarding schools he had resigned his commission in an aristocratic regiment nicknamed 'the Armoured Farmers' and went home to the family farm and brought up his daughter himself.

Jock was raised as an almost-boy taught to do anything, and long before the slogan 'girls can do anything' became trendy. Perhaps that's why she was able to get on so well with males – she understood them, could think like them and could talk like them when she had to.

I met her in a newsroom of a southern England newspaper when the Royal Navy returned in triumph from the Falklands war. The Old Empire had shown it still had teeth that could bite hard. The 'Argies' had been taught a lesson for their impudence. Jock was a photographer and stood out because she was the only woman in a crowd of men. Jock's photos were of mothers embracing sons – some still teenagers – and wives and girlfriends kissing their men, children being clutched by tearful dads who only weeks before had been forced to make other men's children fatherless.

She recognised my Kiwi accent and remarked that she'd been in New Zealand in 1981 for the protest-laden tour of the country by South Africa's Springboks rugby side. Newspapers, magazines, and books had carried some of her photos. Our eyes liked each other. My heartbeat quickened, my mouth went dry again, and I remembered an electric thrill similar to that of seeing another girl on a street corner a few years earlier.

I asked her out for a drink, and after that we were together for three years. Perhaps 'together' is the wrong word. She worked for a Paris-based photographic agency – 'Martin, I can talk only for a minute because I'm flying to Beirut this morning' – and I was with a small wire service. Sometimes we were weeks apart and in different parts of the world. But we were together when we were together, if that makes sense. There was no-one else. Jock had a heart and a compassion that echoed Maria. You could see it in the photos she took. But …

In time 'settling down', 'getting married' – 'New Zealand would be nice, wouldn't it, Martin, you've always said it's the best place for children?' – and other such thoughts filtered into our conversations. I just as quickly filtered them out. I wasn't picking up the hints because Jock wasn't usually a hinter. I didn't think what she was saying important enough.

It all came to an end in Moscow, of all places, in May 1985. Our separate employers had sent us to cover the Soviet Union's fortieth anniversary parade marking Nazi Germany's defeat. The parade in Red Square was huge and impressively theatrical – soldiers by the thousand goose-stepping and arm-swinging as one to strident martial music; proud old men and women veterans weighted down with their medals clutching flowers borne on war-era trucks; and the roll-past of tanks and rockets, which was why I was there.

It was a staunch and emotional time for all Russians. An ancient Marshal of the Soviet Union made a speech saying so. Beside him a youthful Mikhail Gorbachev, Russia's newest Red Czar, smiled and waved indulgently down at the assembled masses from Lenin's Tomb and he no doubt was plotting *Glasnost* and *Perestroika. Urra!*

The next afternoon in our hotel Jock woke me and we loved intensely and passionately. She held me wordlessly in her arms for a long time afterwards before showering, dressing, and packing up her kit. I still had no idea what was coming until she kissed me gently and whispered goodbye. 'The trouble is, Martin,' she said sadly, 'You don't want to go through the pain of loss again.' She blew me a kiss and walked out of my life. In a perverse way I felt relieved.

Johanna Odette Katrin Coverdale died hideously several years later in a small African republic waist-deep in the blood and guts and hacked-off arms and legs of yet another black, inter-tribal genocide. She had photographed wicked men and women doing unspeakable things to innocents while UN peace-keepers stood by. They killed her with their sticks and their long, razor-sharp knives. The peace-keepers watched on, merely following orders 'to observe but not intervene'. And, so far as I know, her killers remain free. At least two might have washed up in New Zealand as 'refugees'.

And, you know, that's when I felt guilty about having let her go. How easily we can do it to ourselves. A 17 year-old misfit trying to impress everyone took Maria from me. I let Jock go because I couldn't – or wouldn't – commit.

If I had committed, I reasoned to myself, we would have married. Jock would have been mother of our children. I think Maria would have approved of Jock.

I CAME home in early 1986 for the most unexpected of reasons – Dad was marrying again. At 76.

'You old bugger, you,' I said over the phone when he rang and told me. I'd always thought that Dad would be like a lot of men of his generation – when the wife went first they often followed within a year or two because they couldn't manage without her. Unlike the wives, who managed quite well, thank you, sometimes for decades after being widowed.

Mum's death had given Dad a kind of life extension. He grew a huge spring in his step. He joined the bowls club, and the indoor bowls, and the garden club. Aches and pains disappeared. Old age went on hold. For the first time in his life, I realised, my father had friends. I could never recall Dad having mates, not even from the war. The men who were his friends were Mum and Dad friends. Friends of the family.

He joined a social organisation that provided men to be mentors for children without dads. He was a hit, partly because of his war service, life experience, he was practical, and Maria had given him a kind of confidence to be able to talk to a young person.

Eventually he crossed paths with Elsie Tarrant, a widow of a local farmer. I'd known her son and her three daughters at high school.

Mrs Tarrant was lovely. Like Mum, she was a lady. Unlike Mum, she had a lively generosity of spirit, was welcoming, forgiving, and non-judgmental. Mrs Tarrant was a Catholic. I couldn't help thinking: she and Maria would have got on well.

So, I became my father's best man. He scrubbed up well, as Uncle Syd said admiringly and Auntie Koo fussed about him.

Sue caught up with me. Would I like to work in Canada? Well, why not? Her husband's family didn't just own a chain of country newspapers, but several chains totalling more than 100 tabloid, broadsheet, and magazine titles across Canada and in the United States. More than in New Zealand. Plus more than 100 radio stations and 30 TV stations.

I was sent to a prairie town of about 5000 people that was surrounded by endless grain farms. I stayed for five winters and five summers. Communism ended in the Soviet Union and Europe. The mighty fell, some hard and bloodily. The Berlin Wall was chipped and hacked and pushed over, to the cheers of the world who watched it live on TV. On Christmas day the Romanian dictator Ceausescu and his wife were stood up against a wall and three army sergeants shot them bloodily and messily dead with their AK47s.

Saddam Hussein invaded Kuwait. The poor man believed the Americans had given him the nod and wink to do so. George Herbert Bush and Margaret Hilda Thatcher formed a coalition of convenience and booted him out again, but left him in power. Oil, you see.

White South Africa freed Nelson Mandela from decades in an island jail. The world hailed him. He forgave his jailers. South Africans of all colours elected him president.

The peoples of the old Yugoslavia, freed from the chains of tyranny that had bound them unwillingly together for so long, turned on their friends and neighbours and massacred them. A former squadron commander told me how he'd had to flee with his family because he'd refused 'to bomb any more of my people'. People were after him, he said.

In the middle of endless and endlessly polite Canada it was all so far away. The owners sold the paper chain to a bigger paper chain, which decided that 'transformation of the business' could be achieved only by 're-focusing operations to enable positive outcomes' – in other words they closed newspapers including mine – and 'let go' staff elsewhere to enable them to 'transition to new career opportunities'.

I'd been granted an attractive exit package – in other words, a nice sum of money to help me go away and never come back. Sue might have had something to do with that.

I decided to come home permanently. Uncle Syd was dying. Cancer was clawing his life away, but he was stiff-upper-lipped about it to the end. I wrote his obituaries, too.

Dad and Elsie had shifted to a nice sunny cottage on her family's 1000-hectare farm. She was nearer her grandchildren. Dad had become their 'favourit-est Grandpa'. He was happy.

'You can have the old house now, Martin. Your inheritance.'

I moved back into the home I had left nearly 30 years before, and back into my old bedroom, my old bed even. Somehow I couldn't bring myself to move into what had been my parents' bedroom, so I made it my 'office'. I had an idea of writing a book about my time working internationally as a journalist. Maybe a novel or two, as well. 'Every journalist has a novel inside them,' is a saying. The rejoinder often is, 'yes, and that's where it should stay …'

Maria had been dead nearly 20 years.

Dad's old mate Wally Walton – still editing his local bi-weekly at age 90 – limped up the path one afternoon on his walking sticks to my front door.

'I'm retiring, Martin,' he said. 'The eyesight's starting to go, the ticker's getting dickier, and it's just so blasted hard now to do things. Technology's changing everything.'

He frowned, an old man's irritated frown – bristling, ferocious bushy eyebrows, too. 'I don't mind that. But it's the young reporters. They just don't want to be told anything and they demand respect before they've earned it yet don't give it … You tell them the intro needs rewriting and they stand there and argue. They tell me I should be offering "positive reinforcement and not be negative".'

He'd shaken his old, bushy head, and his tobacco-stained moustache drooped. He couldn't even smoke in his own office any more. The anti-tobacco zealots had won that one in their long war to expunge cigarette smoking from the land by 2025.

He wanted me to take over. 'I still remember you all those years ago excitedly running in to my office to show me the letter that you'd got your first job.'

So, coming full circle, I became editor of my home town's newspaper – circulation 7500. As in Canada a big media company came along and bought us out from Wally's family about two years after he died. He would have hated that, but the family could see the future so they were getting out while the company still had value.

I remained as editor, but my new boss, younger than me, was in a big city elsewhere, and his boss – younger than both of us, apparently – was in another, bigger city in another country. I became not much more than a glorified office boy. Young women in corporate 'HR' whose vocabulary seemed to extend to no more than 'fantastic' (or 'fentestic') and 'awesome' had more control over hiring than I did.

Times had got tougher as we progressed through the 2000s. Advertising dropped away and 'migrated' to the internet, where it was free or cheaper. As well, the government departments had retreated to anonymous, remote call centres. Some of the chain stores pulled out, leaving the main street like a gap-toothed grin. The GFC – the global financial crisis that flowered in 2008 – didn't help.

There had to be cuts – meaning I had to call people into my office, shut the door, and refusing to use the deeply insulting weasel words I despised and laid out in the HR manual tell them in plain English they were being sacked even though they'd done nothing wrong.

The media company closed us down to enable the big boys and girls in the distant boardroom to 'achieve positive sustainable outcomes in a negative global fiscal environment'. My farewell handshake, first negotiated with Wally and carried over by the new owners at his family's insistence, wasn't too bad. Now pushing 60 I could afford to retire.

The final chapter – 2012

The original idea was to sell the house – the town had become a useful bolthole for people fleeing the cities for 'rural living', and so they were willing to pay good money for a house that could be turned into a restoration job villa. The house was in very good nick and had a big section with garden and fruit trees. Dad used to see to that. I would take the proceeds and go somewhere warmer and cheaper to live out my days.

I had nothing to keep me here. Dad had died at 96. Death was kind to him. It stole up one afternoon as he rested after he and Elsie had been tidying up in the garden. His heart just stopped. No fuss, no pain. It just called time. Elsie followed him less than a year later. They'd had 20 happy years together.

One day an e-mail dropped with a 'bing' into my in-box.

I didn't recognise the name, or the e-mail address, only that it was from a university in California.

The subject line said: **Maria**

Hi Martin

'You probably won't remember me after all this time. But I was Charlotte MacBride, Maria's niece. You might recall me as 'Charley'. I met with you a few times, mostly at your apartment with her.

Yes, I remembered Charley. Stubborn blue eyes.

I've been wanting for nearly 40 years to tell you what happened that awful night.

We – Catharine, Rach (Rachael Stephens, who you also might remember) – and a couple of friends were right there when Maria was killed.

She had my full attention.

We were standing in the middle of the street, laughing and talking.

The party had been lively and great fun.

The hosts had welcomed Maria, which was incredibly good of them considering the attitudes of the time. Most of the girls were pleased to see her.

She'd had a good time. She hadn't been drinking any alcohol.

Maria was the first to grasp what was happening.

In my mind's eye I still see her turning, register the approaching car, which was hurtling at us like a fired bullet.

She shouted a warning and then she stepped forward and shoved us aside.

Catharine was slightly drunk, and she was slower. Maria took the brunt of the impact.

It would all have been less than two seconds.

It's been not too many years since I last heard in my dreams that awful, hard *Bang!!!* – like an explosion – of the impact.

I watched her strike the brick fence. I always remember that it was like a slow-motion cartwheel. But blink and you missed it.

It was so violent! The sound of her striking the wall can still make me shudder and feel sick. She crumpled to the footpath like a broken puppet. I just knew then she was dead.

Tears welled in my eyes.

I don't know if anyone has ever told you, Martin, but this is what I have long wanted to tell you. If Maria had just stood where she was he wouldn't have struck her. She wasn't even in his path. **She died in the act of saving us.** [sic]

I got out of my chair and went and lay down on the couch, drew my knees up, and wept. After 37 years the red raw stump of pain had resurfaced barely diminished by time. *How could that be?* She wouldn't have flinched. Her instinct would have been to protect, to shield, to save.

Oh, my God ...

Tears and tears ... how many tears can a man cry? I poured a large rum, downed it, and then poured several more. I went to sleep.

Hours later I stumbled back to the computer and read on.

I said before that I've been waiting nearly 40 years to tell you what happened. We were sworn to silence about you. As my uncle Mark was showing you and your friend Robert the gate the morning after, our parents, our grandfather, and his mother were instructing a group of distraught and shocked teenage girls that we were not to have anything to do with you. We could not talk to you, to come to you with our story.

We had to swear it.

Jesus ...

I've decided – and so have the others – that it was something we should never have had to swear to, or be bound by, which is partly why I am writing to you now.

I have another reason. Did you know that Maria never got a headstone? Catharine did, but Maria's grave is marked only by a nameplate on the ground. It's almost anonymous. The adults – except Uncle Matt, and probably Gran – never forgave her for her relationship with you.

They certainly never forgave her for being pregnant and the Family Name being dragged through the newspapers.

Our grandfather and the lawyers in our family tried to use their considerable social and legal sway to make the Coroner continue the suppression on Maria's pregnancy.

'This injustice has always rankled with Rach, some of the cousins, and me.'

It would have bloody rankled with me, too. Some understatement!

So, we've decided to do something about it. The matter is to be rectified.

We're having a headstone made, and it will be unveiled in a ceremony at the cemetery on 19 January, 2013.

You will remember that 19 January was her birthday. We want to commemorate her on that date rather than remember the date on which she died. We very much want you to be there.'

I replied immediately, thanking her for getting in touch and for her invitation, 'which I accept'.

Mid-January 2013

The day of the unveiling was less than a week away. Something was unsettling me about it, and for weeks I hadn't been able to figure why. Until I woke from broken sleep at 2am and I knew what it was.

Before breakfast I started searching through the house. After turning the place upside-down I went out to the garage, and found them in a crumbling, mouldy carton that I hadn't noticed or looked at since I left for South Africa 36 years ago. The carton was home to spiders, silverfish, and other forms of life. I pulled them out of the small wooden box Maria used to keep them in when they weren't strung over the Mary statue's arms: her amber rosary beads with the golden Jesus on the cross, which had been blessed by an archbishop or cardinal at Lourdes. They had kept well; very well, considering the decay and population of the carton. I kissed the cross, and held the beads to my heart. It seemed as if I was meant to find them and to take them with me.

THE UNVEILING was to be held before sunset, in the cool and shade of the evening – only it wasn't cool even at 7pm as New Zealand roasted under a summer that would turn out to be prolonged, hot, and dry. I didn't need my smartphone to navigate me. I could have, but I wanted to feel the triumph of remembering where to go.

Cars were already there as I pulled up at the cemetery carpark. Mixed feelings. Knot in the stomach. Heart pumping harder than I would have liked. Palms of hands too damp.

Mihi and Auntie Koo were going to be here. But the day before yesterday Mihi had phoned from Western Australia, their home of 20 years. My favourite aunt had had another little stroke. The whanau feared the seven-hour flight from Perth might be too much for her. She was 83.

'She's bloody angry about us not letting her fly, Martin, I can tell you.'

I can imagine. I told them it was all right, and that she wasn't to worry. I knew her spirit would be there.

I was looking forward to what was to come, and also to meeting those of Maria's family who'd be there. What I didn't want – desperately didn't want – was that I would find it meaningless or ordinary. After all this time.

Even after 37 years I knew where to go along the gravelled paths between the valleys of tombs and headstones. I stopped briefly at Trevor Clifton's sad, neglected last resting place. There was a stone, and fungus was already obscuring his name. I looked around. Families were gathered around graves on blankets and rugs, picnicking quietly.

After nearly four decades I recognised the people grouped in the shade of a pohutukawa tree that had been a sapling in 1975. There were middle-aged women, most thickened, lined, bespectacled, and greyed by babies and life, and men who must have been husbands, brothers, partners.

The elderly man carefully trod along an intersecting path. 'You're looking well, Sir Matthew,' I said as he drew closer, 'for an old bugger.'

Recognition was instant. 'Martin!' He thrust out a spotted, bony hand, '*wun*-derful to see you again after all this time. *Great* that you could come.'

He'd lost weight, and despite his 80-or-so years he looked trim, fit, and well-kept. Somehow I knew the grey-haired, brown-eyed, slim woman at his elbow. 'Ariel, this is Martin. He was Maria's partner.'

She put out her hand, which I took gently. I offered a courtly nod. 'Pleased to meet you, Lady FitzGarratt.'

Mum would have loved that. It would have confirmed her view that I'd been taught my manners and how to behave in front of my betters.

She smiled, replied with an English-sounding 'Hel-lo,' before going on to add: 'Ariel will be just fine, thanks, Martin.'

Matthew filled in the obvious gap. 'Kay never got over Catharine, nor really a lot of the business concerning Maria. She could just never overcome the repeated depressions she suffered.'

An old man's sigh. 'I think she just wanted to die, Martin, but couldn't bring herself to do it. And 25 or so years ago she just gave up the will to live and left us.'

He glanced at Ariel. 'A year or so later I was at a judges' conference in Geneva, and guess who came and stood in front of me?'

He put a hand on her shoulder and they smiled fondly.

'We were single and unattached. We married six months later.'

'There was no-one to stop us this time,' she said in her English-Kiwi accent.

Heads turned towards us as we approached the group.

Matthew did the introductions. Charlotte, stout, blue eyes vivid and still stubborn, her Kiwi accent sounding American. 'Heeey, Martin, it's so totally great you can be here for this ceremoanee. Thank you so much for *Coming!*'

She'd gone to the US in her 20s and stayed, now working in the University of California system, lecturing in English literature. Her husband, Steve, was a college football coach, a battered nose and a scarred face. He liked bone-crushing handshakes. She pointed out their two sons, who looked to be in their late teens. They were polite in that courteous American way.

Rachael was a lawyer working for a multinational in China after 20 years in Ireland. Her partner was Serge, a Frenchman, also a lawyer, and far too charming for my liking. Their daughter was 'JoJo', a tall, gawky redhead of perhaps 14 whose attention was welded to her iPhone. Or was it a Samsung?

Jacqueline and Anne, Matt's twin daughters, who'd been at the flat the night the exams finished. Fond hugs by us three there.

Other, younger, nieces of Maria. Some cousins. Some girls who'd been at Our Lady of The Immaculate Conception with Maria – all now middle-aged, mothers and grandmothers.

'Hello, Martin,' a voice behind me murmured. I stopped. I knew who it was before I even turned around, and she was the one I was most pleased about meeting.

'Gabrielle.' And we hugged with great warmth. She was no longer pencil-slim, but attractively trim; I estimated 50. Her face had lines. Her hair had been cut stylishly short and showed some discreet grey.

But her eyes. I remembered Gabrielle's as cautious, hesitant, except at the requiem Mass. The mature Gabrielle's eyes were intelligent and fearless; steady. The set of her jaw was just like Maria's, and my voice caught on a lump in my throat.

She, too, had become a lawyer, then an economist, after leaving home the same day she finished as dux at Our Lady of The Immaculate Conception and going and flatting with her older cousins. 'I never bothered even going home after school finished.'

She'd won a scholarship to Trinity College, Dublin. 'I got a bit careless with an Italian then in my life, and if you look over there, Martin, you'll see the result of that.' She pointed across the slanting sunlight and the shadows to a rugged man in his early 20s.

'He's Frank – or Francisco. After his father, who retreated most rapidly back to *Mam-Ma* – especially *Mam-Ma* – and *Papa* and *Italia* when I confronted him with the fact of my pregnancy.'

'It's an old story, Gabrielle. Told too many times. Unfortunately.'

She smiled again towards her son. 'Unlike his father he has a mind of his own, and unlike his father, a backbone. Against his adoring *Mama*'s wishes he went and joined the British Army. Now he flies helicopters in such exotic locations as Iraq and Afghanistan. He knows Harry.'

Frank had attracted a cluster of young females who were showing their interest in a dark-haired, bronzed, green-eyed man who lived a dangerous life. The evening light suited his looks.

Gabrielle shook her head resignedly. 'Listen and you'll probably hear the siren wail of agitated hormones and the hysterical polka of adolescent ovaries.'

I laughed, and so did she. 'It's always the same, Martin, since he was a little boy. Girls have always adored him.'

Gabrielle was a partner in a legal and economics consultancy, 'living these days in Prague'.

Beyond the veil

The unveiling was brief and straight-forward, and without a priest or bishop in sight, which I think is how they wanted it. The modern FitzGarratts were not as churchy as their elders had been. No priests and nuns from this generation.

Matthew told me later that if Uncle Brian was 'still with us' he would have been there. His exile outlasted two archbishops before he was 'rehabilitated' in his 80s and sent into the diocese's poorest parish. He had refused to retire. 'He died only six years ago, Martin. At nearly 100 – still baptising kids, visiting the sick, performing marriages, doing their funerals, going to the jails, going to the rugby. Then one night he went to sleep and never woke up.'

Then he laughed. 'At his funeral were crims he'd tried to help. They sat next to the judges who'd sent them away. A nice picture it would have made.'

Matthew had been given the task of directing proceedings. I noticed then that none of Maria's other siblings were present. For that I was relieved. Stella – whom I never had got to meet, and those awful other sisters …

We gathered around Maria's grave. At the head of it was the stone, cloaked in a cloth hood.

'We all know why we're here,' Matt said, his voice carrying in the still evening. 'So I won't waste time. We're here to right a wrong that was done to Maria when our family – and I am ashamed that I allowed it to happen – treated Maria differently from my daughter Catharine.'

He turned to the grave next to Maria's, which was Catharine's. 'My daughter got a nice headstone. My sister didn't. That was manifestly unjust.'

Murmurs of agreement around me.

'I had no say in that. I hope she can forgive me for it now.' He glanced at Ariel, and she smiled encouragingly and squeezed his shoulder.

His eyes sought me out, and he cleared his throat. 'Martin, would you mind coming over here, please?'

Eh?

'I don't think you've been told this, but it has been unanimously decided that the honour of unveiling Maria's headstone should be yours.'

No, I hadn't expected that. I went to the end of the grave. The headstone was not big, perhaps a metre and a half high – the same as Catharine's.

Everyone's eyes were on me. I decided against a speech, so I lifted away the hood, revealing the headstone.

The sight took my breath away. The gravestone was near-black granite. They'd used a photo-etching technique to inscribe in white, bold type:

MARIA GORETTI FitzGARRATT
1958 - 1975
Cherished Loved
And Loving Partner
of Martin Blake
AGED 17
NOW RESTING IN PEACE

A head-and-shoulders photo of her – I don't remember having seen it – had been etched into the stone. She was laughing, her eyes wide and alive, and it was as if they were directed at me. They drew me in; once again we were together.

Sobs wrenched out of me. I became a waterfall of tears, sinking to my knees and hugging the cold stone, my wet cheek against her image.

A film reel of memories flickered. Maria standing on the corner waiting for the lights to change; her Head Girl Stare; her eyes changing as I eased into her that first time, carefully so I wouldn't hurt her; Maria briskly enforcing order in my flat … 'Maria … Maria …'

Someone rubbed my shoulders slowly as I remembered: Maria, brave, principled and decent. Intelligent and loyal Maria, who loved me and whom I'd loved like no other.

Yes, she was prone to impetuosity and bossiness. Things were black and white. But we're like that, aren't we, when we're young? She wanted to right an injustice with her sister. Annette's postscript had hurt. Being all but cut off from Gabrielle had wounded her. She had begun to make peace with her mother.

She never threw spears back at those who hurled them at her.

Maria was unselfish. It had got her killed. Is there no greater love? The God she loved would approve, wouldn't he?

Despite that, some still preferred to judge her against the external, rule-keeping standards of her Church.

Here I disappeared into myself. It was like shutting a door on everything and everybody around me. A trance, I suppose. I hadn't thought of her in decades: Saint Maria Goretti. The Catholic Church keeps her wax-covered bones in a glass display case. Minus the right arm, which is stored at another cathedral for public display, the bones are toured to different parts of the world. An entourage of modern-day, berobed witch-doctors goes with them. The bones are venerated. That is, the faithful pray to them and are urged to do so. The witch-doctors recite their Masses and mumble mumbo-jumbo incantations to the bones in the glass case. Praying to a dead girl's bones seems like a ghastly joke on believers because those bones are neither heavenly nor Lovely. They're old calcium. God has no use for dead men's – or a young girl's – bones.

One day back in the 80s I walked into a Catholic church in inner-city Chicago. It was the anniversary of Maria's death, which I sometimes observed by attending Mass and going up for holy communion, too.

Nobody knew I wasn't a Catholic. Besides, it was winter. The church was warm, in a Polish neighbourhood, and the streets were thick with snow.

A poster depicting Saint Maria Goretti had been fixed to the foyer wall. It is idealised and unreal, like much religious art. She is angelic and halo'd. Her pre-teen piety is radiantly evident. Her eyes are directed heavenward. She looks older than 11. Her crossed arms clutch lily palms – the symbols, it is often emphasised, of her virginity.

She had a pure heart. Why would she not? Maria was 11. She was far too young to worry about whether she committed mortal sin if she didn't fight back hard enough. He was 18. Would God really have sent her to Hell if she had succumbed?

Yet as her young life's blood seeped from her wounds Maria Goretti had the fortitude to forgive Alessandro Serenelli, her killer and would-be rapist.

That was God-like. But *that* wasn't what she was canonised for in 1950: it was for 'her heroic virtue in preferring to sacrifice her life rather than commit a sin against the holy virtue of purity'.

In latter years, though, her forgiving him has become more significant in the propaganda. But the rest is like the religious art – unreal, bloviated, religious bullshit.

I returned to the present thinking of my Maria. Luke, the morning he visited, had urged Maria to pray to the 'little saint whose name you honour and bear.'

I didn't ask then, but I did now. Why? What was her 'sin', exactly? Didn't she, too, have a pure heart?

ONE LAST thing to do. Maria – or more likely her family – could have them back. I fumbled in my pocket for her rosary beads, and there were 'aaaahs, oh, yes …' as I draped them over the top of the stone. Other hands caressed my shoulders.

More words of comfort. 'The photo was taken at the party, Martin,' I heard Rachael say. 'Only minutes before it happened.'

In a nearby tree a tui called mournfully; another, in another tree, replied in kind.

A guitar twanged and a drum thudded. Someone had brought along a boombox.

May God bless and keep you always
May your wishes all come true ...

Bob Dylan, *Forever Young*, and I hadn't heard it for decades. I shivered in the heat of the evening. These people had done this for me as much as for Maria and them. We joined hands. The words and music slipped away across the cemetery and faded out into the lengthening evening. Then:

The weirdest sensation – the voice was not so much in my head and ears as in my chest. *I've been waiting a long time to see you again, Martin.*

I blurted: 'You were the love of my life!'

I know.

She was here. I knew it and could feel it. A sudden, warming joy flooded through me. It *was* her voice.

I was aware of people looking at me, but not as if I had two heads. In 2013 someone talking to a gravestone was not considered unusual. Not like in 1975 …

No more tears, little man. Remember the last verse you read at the requiem Mass?

Yes: no more tears.

You were right, you know. I was there behind you, between your Dad and Uncle Brian. It was just my body that was in the box.

I wiped away tears. 'You left a hole in my life that I've never been able to fill. I never got to say goodbye.' Broken-hearted again. How could that be, after nearly four decades? The stump red, raw, and painful again.

Hmmm, I know, sweetie. I'd never heard such gentleness in a voice. It wasn't earthly. She sounded … well, ancient and eternal.

Her mischievous giggle. *You could do worse than my favourite niece, you know. She's had a hankering at the back of her mind for you. Seeing you again after all these years hasn't dimmed her hankering.*

'Did you know you were pregnant?' I was crying again.

A drawn-out silence ensued. Had she gone?

No, sweetie, I didn't. That was a surprise to me, too.

Another giggle. *I slipped up a bit there, didn't I?*

'I didn't mind. It didn't matter,' I blubbed.

You were so sweet to me, Martin.

She was silent again, and the silence dragged, and I thought she'd gone. In Head Girl Tones Maria added sternly, *'But no more tears, sweetie. You've cried enough for me.*

Then I 'saw' her again as she was: Maria Goretti FitzGarratt, forever 17, forever young, forever beautiful, forever not broken and mutilated … She blew me a two-handed kiss, waved, blew another kiss – and faded away smiling behind a gently billowing veil.

THAT WAS in January. For months afterwards I brooded about Maria and me, her effect on me, and the unveiling, which was a restoration, I felt. They were right, these FitzGarratts. A wrong had been righted at long last. The hatred and religious bigotry of Anne, Peirse, and most of his children had been buried with them.

I would wake in the night sometimes wondering if she would come back in a vision. I'd forgotten to ask her two questions: was it true that she wouldn't have known what'd hit her and felt no pain; why did she not want me to go to work that last Saturday morning we had together.

She had woken me with insistent kisses and touches, and it became clear to me I wasn't going to work until she'd got her way. Afterwards she had only reluctantly released me from her clasp. 'Couldn't you ring in sick, Martin?' It was so out of character. Had she known something?

On May 17, 2013, after two days of trying to write something else for somebody else, I realised I had to act. There was a pressure inside me. It was afternoon, and all I could see was her on the corner.

I wrote that first sentence of this account, not knowing what would come next. Then there was the second sentence, and so on. So many memories, so much had been forgotten, and it all tumbled back. And that's how it was for a week short of six months. Writing, day after day, often night after night, of Maria Goretti FitzGarratt and me.

THANKS …

Maria Goretti and Me is a product of my sometimes over-fevered imagination. Having written the story over six months I needed to know what others thought of it.

BRENDA MCHUGO: the first person I gave it to. My older sister – a midwife for 40-or-so years but now a farmer – had expressed dutiful interest. Reading the story on a computer screen was hard for her. But she did it for me, barking out spelling mistakes and observations.

HER FARM ANIMALS: the chooks and ducks clucked and quacked and pecked each other crossly at the farm gate. Kermit and PiggySue grunted worriedly. Brenda had forgotten to go out and feed them all. So I did instead. Briefly they worshipped the hand that fed them. The hawks patrolled watchfully overhead.

COSTAS FLEVAS: a Greek exile in Britain. Costas offered many encouraging and sensitive comments. You helped keep me going.

HELEN CORRIGAN: a cousin who was brave enough to be brutally honest, which I respect. Some changes from the original manuscript reflect her comments.

STEFAN and **JOLA JURCZENKO**: my good friends who read it, got it, and were encouraging. They helped keep me going, too.

VICTORIA JURCZENKO: for her painstaking cover design. **HARRY HEATH**, her friend, helped with the typeface on the cover.

ARIELLE KAUAEROA MONK: who put me right on a couple of details.

REGAN LILY, **CARTER PHILIP**, and **HADLEIGH HOPE CORRIGAN** (Melbourne); **ETHAN MAX** and **ELLA SIOBHÁN CORRIGAN PERMAIN** (Brisbane): my grandchildren. This is for them; love, *Dziadziu*.

Thanks, everybody.

- Paul

Paul Corrigan is a New Zealander.

He is a grandson of Catholic immigrants from Roscommon, Ireland. They were farmers. Relatives include priests and nuns.

His mother's people were English. In his orchard of family trees one features Church of England vicars and deans.

Other, perhaps luckier forebears were Yeoman Grooms of the Wine-Cellar to Kings James I, Charles I, Charles II, and James II.

Another fruit of that particular tree – Landon of Monnington and Credenhill, County Hereford – was the 19th century English poet and novelist Letitia Elizabeth Landon, better known by her initials L. E. L.

She died in Accra, in what is now Ghana, in 1838. She was 36.

Maria Goretti and Me is Paul's debut published novel.

Paul has been a journalist and full-time solo parent of his two daughters and son.

Photo:
Yvonne Tunnicliffe

www.ingramcontent.com/pod-product-compliance
Lightning Source LLC
Chambersburg PA
CBHW070356260626
47161CB00001B/162